Ferret Run: Secrets of Arcadia

G. Scott Freeman

Dedication

For Diane,

who believed in this story before it had a shape.

For Nick and Alex,

who keep my heart young.

For my mother,

whose love made everything possible.

And for anyone who has ever felt out of place in their own world.

You are not lost.

You are between stories.

Contents

Prelude 1

1. Dreams 6
2. Meeting of Minds 12
3. Not the Cubs 16
4. Always There for You 20
5. The Price of Incorruptibility 24
6. Chamber of Knowledge 27
7. The Drop of a Hair 32
8. Unknown Watcher 34
9. Intruders 38
10. Other Impressions 43
11. Interrogation 47
12. Spider Chase 53
13. Planning Ahead 59
14. Cause for Concern 63
15. The Gathering Storm 67
16. Seeing Eye-to-Eye 71
17. Holding the Cards Close 74
18. Arcadian Whispers 78
19. The Weight of Knowledge 81
20. Strategic Alignments 84

21. The Eve of the Revelations 86
22. Legacy of the Torka 89
23. Revelations 92
24. Crossroads of Identity 95
25. The Firing 98
26. The Argument 102
27. She's Here 105
28. The Walk 110
29. Locked Out 117
30. A New Asset 123
31. Denied 130
32. Cohesion 137
33. Impact Chamber Analysis 144
34. The Awakening 153
35. Whispers of Artemis 158
36. The Lies You Tell 160
37. Unspoken Words 165
38. No Questions 167
39. Am I Dead 169
40. First Contact 172
41. Show me your Beans 174
42. Have To Get Out 180
43. The Blocked Door 183
44. Something's Down There 187
45. Regulation 7-A 191
46. Enter Jarvis Pellick 195
47. Quick Thinking 199
48. Just a Little Stuck 204

49. A Flicker of Hope 207
50. Diane 213
51. The Predator's Shadow 217
52. Transcending 220
53. Signals Across the Void 225
54. The Adhesive Truth 229
55. Hidden Corridors 232
56. Echoes at Home 236
57. The Map and the Mark 239
58. The Key 243
59. The Wanderers War 246
60. The Living Key 249
61. Purple Armor 251
62. The Same Mark 258
63. Going Dark 265
64. The Escape 270
65. Already Gone 273
66. Rage 276
67. Demonstration 278
68. Rubber and Reckonings 282
Epilogue Spoken in Silence 285
Chapter 286
About the Author 287
Connect with the Author 288

Prelude

Thirteen years ago.

In the lower levels of the research facility, there were no footsteps and no clatter. Nothing but the faint electric hum of aging panels and the slow exhale of the vents. Dust motes danced in the stale air, settling on abandoned workbenches where cobwebs stretched between outdated monitors. The space had emptied when the newer, more advanced labs opened on the upper floors.

Intricate instruments filled every inch of the room screens, computers, and strange devices that bore little resemblance to the test tubes and basic electronics once used there. Cable clusters snaked between stations, like arteries feeding a mechanical heart.

Professor Lupus Hare and his associate Myles Moleman hunched over their workstations. Myles tapped his hands against the console in a jittery rhythm. Hare's ears twitched as his eyes flitted across a readout.

Myles checked the readings again, but there were no errors or fluctuations. The numbers were impossible yet perfect.

Stacks of printouts and numerous empty coffee mugs testified to the countless nights spent rerunning models. Now the time for theory was over. The vibration from beneath the chamber wasn't simply a proof of concept; it was the first breath of something alive.

No one stepping into this ancient, forgotten sublevel would have guessed that history was about to blink.

Hare looked at the sensor reading and turned to his comrade. "The quantum membrane in the target area is point two gigajoules. Just as Trinn predicted, the membrane is thinner here compared with the other locations. Excellent."

Myles looked up from his screen. "Amazing. That serves as an enormous boost to this experiment." The mole ran a finger along the screen display in front of him, tracing the digital representation of the membrane. This is how they referred to the gossamer-thin barrier that separated their dimension from countless others. At that moment, it was depicted on the screen as a shimmering, translucent layer. He furrowed his brow. "Why here? This place is thinner than anywhere else we've scanned. It doesn't make sense."

Hare shrugged and scratched between his ears. "Myles, my friend, I do not know."

He turned toward the apparatus nestled in the far corner. A transparent orb pulsed at its center, cradling a quivering mass of ridged cerebral tissue Slime webbed veins ran along its surface, dimly glowing with green light. The folds expanded and contracted with a slow, wet rhythm.

Around the sphere, eight tentacles slid out from evenly spaced ports, each one snaking toward a separate keyboard. The tips tapped keys and twisted dials with expert control.

The entire structure crouched on a small platform supported by four jointed metal legs. It shifted slightly, as if listening. Hare addressed it. "Trinn, do you know why the membrane is weaker in Badger Springs?"

A computerized voice responded from a modulator attached to the bubble. "I am uncertain why, and it's really irrelevant to the point. This weakness has created the perfect environment for our experiment, and if it works as we have predicted, I will finally have a way to get home after all these years." Trinn then swiveled to face Myles. "Are we ready to send the drone with the acoustic wave modifier to the location and start the experiment?"

"Say the word, and we can launch," Myles said. "However, I noticed from one of the hidden cameras at Badger Springs that there is a group of about fourteen civilians, a few of them children, residing at that location? Will that impede the experiment?"

Trinn flicked a tentacle dismissively. "The energy frequency we will be transmitting should be low enough that they won't even know it's being emitted."

"I'm sure it will be fine," Hare said. "Besides, think of everything we've done over the past months to ensure Project Sound Bloom can take place. If we miss this opportunity, it will be a long time before we can try again. For the sake of the project, we need to make it happen."

Myles nodded. "Understood, sir. The drone is ready to launch."

A tentacle rose from the small mech and curled at the tip in the closest approximation of a thumbs up that a creature without thumbs could manage. "All good. Let's go for launch."

"Launching," Myles confirmed, pressing the activation button.

"It will take a few minutes for the drone to reach the target area," Hare said. "I'll inform you when it arrives."

After a minute or two of silence, Myles blinked and leaned closer to his screen. "Professor, I'm noticing some unusual fluctuations in the readings. The membrane seems to be pulsing on its own."

"Normal variance," Trinn said. "We've factored this into our calculations."

Hare frowned at his own monitor. "Perhaps, but I've never seen amplitude *this* irregular." He glanced at the security feed showing the families at Badger Springs. For a brief moment he seemed to hesitate, then his expression hardened, and he sat up straighter.

"Sir," Myles ventured, "with these irregularities, we have no way of knowing what will happen to those families down there if something goes wrong. Should we abort and wait for another opportunity?"

Hare's jaw twitched, and his voice took on a tight, clipped cadence. "We've spent months preparing for these exact conditions. The membrane is at its thinnest; the alignment is perfect." He turned from the screen, adjusting his glasses. "If we hesitate now, it could be years before we see this convergence again. This is too important to delay."

"The civilians enjoying a pleasant day at the springs might disagree."

"The probability of any significant effect reaching them is minimal. We proceed."

Myles opened his mouth, then closed it with a snap. He nibbled on the tip of a claw as he watched the monitor.

"The drone is hovering at the target location," Hare said, his voice steady once more. "We are ready to begin."

Trinn's synthesized voice crackled through the air. "The acoustic coupler is keyed up and targeted on the weakest point of the membrane."

Despite the nervous energy coursing through him, Myle's hands were steady on the controls. "Power levels are optimal. We're ready to execute."

Hare's nostrils flared and his breathing quickened. "Then I execute in three... two... one."

The lights dimmed as the Coherent Sound Amplification Device discharged. The device a curved wall of overlapping metal disks embedded with pulsing crystals emitted a low, vibrating hum that made their teeth ache. In the center of the chamber, acoustic energies swirled and merged into a single point of concentrated sound that grew more intense with each passing second. Then there was a sudden surge, and the focused energies discharged upward, racing through a specially designed conduit. Within seconds, the on-site drone received and redirected the signal toward the weakened area of the membrane.

They watched the display, expecting to see a localized distortion, a gentle rippling of reality that would allow them to peer through to another dimension. Instead, the readings spiked wildly. Myles blanched under his fur as a red warning light started flashing.

"Sir, the resonance amplifier has wavered in power, and I can't adjust it. We're pushing well beyond safety parameters!"

"Adjust the power flow through the photonic transducer, and it should level out," Trinn said.

Myles's hands were a blur on the controls as he scrambled to make the adjustments.

Meanwhile, the monitor displayed the disturbing scene unfolding at Badger Springs. The surface of the springs rippled as the sound waves hit them. All around, people hunched over and covered their ears, faces contorted with pain.

The ground beneath them rippled. Water merged with the soil, transforming it into a churning, sucking morass. The air filled with desperate cries as feet and hands clawed at the sinking ground and bodies were slowly pulled under. One after another, each figure vanished beneath the mud until only frantic splashes remained.

Near the edge of the chaos, a small girl lay on a rock, curled tight. Her eyes were squeezed shut, and she was clamping her hands over her ears, trying to shut out the horror. Her body trembled with each pulse of sonic energy.

Myles sat frozen, his hands still poised over the power controls. When he spoke, his voice shook. "Sir, they all just disappeared."

"Myles, what are you talking about?" Professor Hare turned to the mole.

Myles opened his mouth to respond, but Trinn's voice cut across him. "Membrane integrity is down. We are on the verge of penetration."

A klaxon blared. "POWER OVERFLOW IS IMMINENT. VACATE THE AREA."

The room was plunged into darkness, broken only by strobing emergency lights. The warning repeated.

Myles abandoned his station. "Sir, we need to leave the lab! The power bank is overcharged; it's going to blow!"

"Stay at your station, Myles. We're so close!" Trinn insisted.

Hare looked at Trinn, then he stared around his lab as smoke filled the room. Months of work about to go up in flames. The klaxon continued wailing. With the threat of electrical discharge looming, he made his decision. "No, Trinn. We have to evacuate. *Now.*"

Between them, Myles and Hare picked up Trinn's apparatus and sprinted for the door. They had barely cleared the threshold when an explosion erupted behind them. The blast hurled Hare forward, Trinn's device still clutched in his grip. They flew across the hallway and slammed into the opposite wall.

The klaxons' deafening chorus continued as the two scientists and the alien lay sprawled on the floor.

"Trinn, we need to get up and hide you before everyone arrives," Hare groaned.

He staggered up, steadying himself with a hand against the wall. Once he was upright, he stood the apparatus up and checked on Trinn.

The Drowa lay motionless in the container. One tentacle twitched against the glass. So many years away from home. I will get back there, no matter what.

Myles surveyed the smoking ruins of the lab through the doorway. His gaze landed on the monitor, still flickering with its grim feed from Badger Springs. The ground lay smooth and undisturbed, as if nothing had ever happened. He raised a trembling hand to his mouth. "What... what have we done?"

Chapter One

Dreams

There are places where memory clings to the stones, where the soil hums with stories too old for names. Badger Springs is such a place. Once, it echoed with the breath of those who first saw us cross between stars. They built a marker here, not to worship but to remember. Now, the city draws near. Most who visit will hear only birdsong. But one will hear the silence beneath it... and begin to remember.

And though few who visit truly understand its song, the place endures. Let us now speak plainly of what the eyes see, regardless of whether the soul hears more.

Badger Springs is a mysterious oasis located just rootward of the bustling city of Rith. It's a place where the city almost disappears, giving way to the untouched beauty of nature. This enchanting area features shimmering ponds cradled by two lively springs, creating a slice of wilderness hidden within the city's walls.

Yet, amidst this serenity, an unusual rock outcropping stands sentinel. The ivy-draped monolith contrasts sharply with the surrounding environment. Tales of its origin are often whispered by locals. These stories of ancient times contribute to its mystique, making it a source of fascination for many.

For the city's inhabitants, Badger Springs offers more than just visual delight; it's a balm for the soul. Families and lone wanderers alike are drawn to its charm, seeking a reprieve from urban confines. The spring season only heightens its allure, as the very air seems to hum with life. Budding leaves and fragrant blooms blanket the area, painting a canvas of red, pink, yellow, and violet against the emerald backdrop of the springs.

Even amidst the chorus of chirping birds and the rustle of leaves, there's a profound tranquility here. The gentle winds whisper tales of old and carry one beyond the mundane stresses of daily life. In these moments of reflection, one realizes the treasure Rith holds within its walls.

***

Lanell's tail twitched as she tugged on her shirt. Her mind was already skipping ahead to the springs. Laughter echoed from an old memory the splash of cold water, her dad's mock yelp. After their meal, the family usually ventured to the ancient monolith. They climbed to the top of the peculiarly shaped rock, then they would sit and admire the springs.

As Lanell finished getting dressed, her mother entered the room, carrying a bright purple bandana. "Lanell," she began softly, "before we go, I have something for you."

"What's this, Mom?" The young ferret's attention jumped to the vibrant cloth.

Her mother knelt so they were at eye-level. "It's a special bandana. Your grandmother gave this to me when I was your age."

Lanell ran her fingers over the fabric, feeling the embroidered edges. "Why is it so special?"

Her mother smiled gently and tied the bandana around her daughter's tail. "Because it's a symbol of love, dear. Your daddy and I want you to know that no matter where you go, no matter what you do, we will always be with you. This bandana is a little reminder of our love."

"Really, Mom?"

Her mother nodded and pulled her into a tight embrace. "Truly. Your daddy and I love you so much more than words can say. Always remember that."

Lanell buried her face in her mother's fur. "Thank you, Mom. I love you too."

Her mother kissed the top of her head. "Now, go see Dad while I finish getting dressed."

A blur of purple swished down the hall as Lanell skipped to the kitchen.

"Daddy! Daddy, look!" she swished her furry tail around to the front, showing off her new adornment.

"Well, would you look at that." Her father bent down to inspect it more closely. "Isn't that the same bandana your mother wore when she was a young ferret?"

Lanell nodded vigorously. "Yes, Daddy! And now it's mine! Mom said it's a symbol of love and that it'll remind me of you both wherever I go."

Lost in thought for a moment, her father reached out and delicately traced the embroidered pattern on the fabric before pulling his daughter into a hug. "I'm so proud of you, my little purple-footed ferret," he whispered. Lanell giggled, hugging him back just as tightly.

After a brief pause, he said, "We need to get these sandwiches ready, or we'll go hungry. Please sit over there while I wrap things up."

"Of course, Pop."

The young ferret settled at the kitchen table and rested her chin on her hand. "Dad? Why does everyone at Badger Springs refer to that big rock as a monolith? What is it?"

As her mother entered the kitchen, she and Lanell's father exchanged a knowing glance.

"That, Lanell," her father said, "is an ancient marker to help those who are lost find their way."

"Dad, it's just a rock with nothing on it!" Lanell scoffed.

Her father chuckled. "You're right, sweetie. But one day, I'll show you its secret, so you'll never lose your way."

Lanell's eyes sparkled. "Really? That sounds amazing!"

Her mother smiled indulgently. "And if Dad doesn't hurry with the sandwiches, our picnic plans will go astray."

Mist crept beneath the table legs. Lanell blinked as the kitchen lights dissolved, and her parents' voices echoed somewhere beyond the fog. As the mist lifted, it revealed the serene beauty of Badger Springs. She and her family now strolled beside a tranquil pond. Now and then, Lanell cast eager, restless glances toward her mother.

"Mom, can I climb the monolith now?" she pleaded.

Her mother ruffled the fur behind her ears. "Honey, your dad and I treasure our rockhounding moments as a family together. Just the same, if you're itching for a solo adventure, go ahead."

Lanell's face lit up. Her father added, "Remember to stay safe."

"I promise," she called, already dashing off toward the looming rock.

As Lanell ran, she heard a strange, mechanical whirr overhead. She stopped for a second to look up, but her impending climb eclipsed any interest she had in whatever was soaring above.

Up close, the monolith towered over her like an immense tomb. Eagerly, she peeled back the layers of vines, revealing the rich, time-worn brass beneath. Her fingers grazed the surface, and the cold, smooth texture sent a shiver through her. She examined the broad base, which gracefully tapered to a pointed apex.

"Well," she mused with a grin, "challenge accepted. Time to climb."

She anchored herself at the rock's base, craning her neck to absorb its grandeur. Memories of previous climbs flickered through her mind as she attempted to devise a new route to the top. Grasping the sturdy vines with one hand and securing her feet among the ivy, she began her ascent.

With a nimbleness reminiscent of a seasoned mountaineer, Lanell scaled the rock effortlessly. Once at the top, she paused, letting the view engulf her senses. Despite its imposing stature, the rock's surface felt gentle, thanks to the thick blanket of ivy. Almost like nature's mattress, she thought, reclining onto the lush green bed. The ivy cradled her as sunbeams danced upon her fur. The rhythmic flow of the park's life washed over her in a soothing wave. She sat up, crossed her legs, and observed the lively spectacle of families rejoicing beneath her. A contented sigh escaped her lips.

Perfection.

Suddenly, her ears twitched sharply. What began as a soft whine soon rose to an overwhelming noise that consumed the surroundings. The jarring frequency made her fur stand on end, compelling her to press her ears flat against her head. Lanell grimaced.

This is more than just annoying; it's painful.

The shrill sound echoed throughout the park. Lanell buried her head in the ivy and cupped her ears. This meant she was mercifully unaware when the powerful sound waves began to drastically alter the terrain of the park.

Vibrations turned the solid ground into a loose, grainy substance. Water from the springs bled into the soil, transforming it into a sludge that bore a terrifying resemblance to quicksand.

At the sound of screams, Lanell lifted her head. The world below writhed. A panicked victim flailed as mud swallowed their arms. A young child vanished mid-shriek. Her breath caught. This was beyond violence. This was erasure.

The piercing cries of pain soon shifted into desperate pleas for help. Above the chaos, Lanell lay down on the monolith, shielding her ears from the painful sounds.

As time passed, the hellish noise from the sky stopped, and the pitiful cries grew fainter. Finally, chilling silence enveloped the springs, broken only by the occasional gurgle of air bubbles surfacing from the mud pits.

Lanell lowered her trembling hands from her ears and looked up. Her eyes widened as she took in the scene before her. No trace of life remained. Her eyes caught subtle shifts beneath the mud, a heartbreaking sign that some had stopped resisting their swampy tomb.

The little ferret desperately surveyed the surroundings, hoping to spot her parents among the desolation. She called out tentatively "Mom? Dad?" The eerie silence met her pleas, punctuated only by the soft pop of bubbles from the mud below. Tears welled in her eyes, grief overtaking her.

However, as she cried, a startling metamorphosis began. Her once childlike ferret hands transformed, becoming those of a young adult slender and mature like her mother's. Staring in disbelief at her changed form, terror and confusion surged within her. A look of bewildered shock marked her face as she tried to make sense of the surreal events transpiring around her.

Lanell watched the once brilliant blue-sky morph into an oppressive, engulfing darkness. This looming force seemed to swallow everything, erasing the horizon and steadily creeping toward her. Trees, the earth beneath her feet, and even the flowers disappeared, consumed by the encroaching void. Profound sorrow was replaced by stark terror as she found herself alone on the brink of an impenetrable abyss. The darkness stopped ominously close, as if considering its next move.

Lanell hesitantly extended a finger towards it, only to be met by a tentacle that shot out and ensnared her arm. Before she could process this terrifying turn of events, another tentacle snaked out, seizing her other arm. She kicked and twisted, but the tendrils only tightened their cold, slimy grip. Two more tentacles reached and coiled around her legs, rendering her immobile.

The coldness of the void seeped into her, consuming her bit by bit. The chilling sensation crept up her body, numbing everything it touched. She resisted with all her strength, but as moments felt like eternity, her efforts inevitably waned. Only her head remained untouched, and in a final act of desperation, she strained against the tendrils. Despite that, her head, too, was soon swallowed by the consuming darkness.

Victoria Lanell's eyes snapped open. Her heart was racing, and her fur was standing on end. She was drenched in sweat. The clock on her bedside table told her she only had five minutes until it was time to get up. Her chest rose and fell in shallow gasps, the dream still curling around her like a shadow that refused to lift.

For a while, she remained in bed, staring up at the ceiling. The picture of her parents smiled at her from her chest of drawers. She closed her eyes, rolled over, and buried her face in her pillow.

"I can't face it alone anymore," she whispered.

She blinked, willing away the tears that threatened to spill. Then, with a shuddering breath, she pushed herself upright, determined to shake off the cold grip of the dream.

After finally rising from the bed, she made her way to the vanity. She ran her fingers through her golden bob, brushing damp strands from her forehead. The light brown mask under her eyes hadn't faded, but the sparkle had.

The ferret's ears twitched as the faint sounds of the stirring city drifted through the open window. Her long tail swished restlessly from side to side, its furry tip brushing her ankles.

Her morning ritual always started the same way. She opened the top drawer of her vanity, grabbed her purple bandana, and tied it around her tail. Then she began to dress for the day.

She picked a black top with deep burgundy highlights, a black skirt that emphasized her long, slender legs, and burgundy tights to match the top. Her practical yet fashionable ankle boots with just a hint of a heel gave her a small boost in stature. When she was done, a confident, determined young ferret replaced the vulnerable kit from the nightmare. She was ready to take on the world.

Before heading out the door, she looked at the calendar. It was the twentieth. Tomorrow, they would be firing the accelerator at work, and that meant one thing. Professor Hare and his minions would be unbearably annoying.

She grabbed her bag, took a deep breath, and faced the mirror one last time. Her tail flicked behind her as if erasing the traces of the night. "It was just a dream," she whispered, staring down her reflection with a steely glint in her eye.

With that, Victoria Lanell stepped out of her tiny house and dived into the bustling noise of the city.

Chapter Two

Meeting of Minds

Across the span of countless worlds, I have often seen greatness carved from wounds the overlooked, the underestimated, the ones who are told they are too small, too strange, or too late. They rise, not to heal, but to turn their wounds into power.

So it is with Lupus Hare. His mind, exacting. His will sharpened by scorn. Yet brilliance born of spite burns hotter than it should. It does not guide; it consumes. And when it consumes, it leaves only ash where wonder might have taken root.

I watch as the pattern repeats.

Lupus carried the knowledge of his shortness like a stone in his pocket. It weighed him down and nagged at him until he was constantly aware of every missing inch. Each time he stood near his kin, he stretched his back taut, drew his belly in, and thrust his ears skyward like periscopes scanning the horizon. Posture became a protest, a refusal to be dismissed as 'the short one.'

While the other kits wrestled outside, Lupus sat hunched over gears and wires. The family radio became a puzzle to take apart and master. Whenever someone commented on his size, his smile turned cold and precise. For the next week, he would bury himself in formulas with greater ferocity than before, determined that his next discovery would put the mocker in their place.

His older brother, Lucious, fed the fire. Every jibe drove Lupus back to his books. There were so many stacked under his bed that they left an indentation in the mattress. Sleep could be skipped, equations could not. He bore a chip on his shoulder the size of a boulder, and it never fell away.

By adolescence, his room no longer smelled of clean linen. It stank of solder, ozone, and burnt coils. Shelves bowed with the weight of physics texts, and glass tubes crowded the desk. He built a working magnetic levitation engine from kitchen scraps and wire scrounged from the shed. People stopped laughing then. Students gathered outside his door, peering in like supplicants at a shrine, waiting to see what new thing might hum or spark.

Each accolade was a wordless victory over Lucious. But it was the formula that changed everything. What began as scribbles across notebook margins turned into treatments whispered about in clinics. Hospitals demanded it. Journal covers bore his name. The young rabbit, once mocked for his height, now filled auditoriums. His lectures sold out as soon as they were advertised. Halls were crammed with people pressed shoulder to shoulder, desperate to hear him speak. Grants poured in with every new breakthrough.

His first grant became a prototype. The second, a floor-plan. By the third, the locals called it Hare Tower. Lupus called it proof. Under his hand, the place grew into a fortress of research, vibrating with power and ambition.

Politicians hated giving power to scientists too messy, too dangerous. Yet when they needed his discoveries, they bent. One slipped a badge into his palm and he became Minister of Science. Lupus pocketed it with a smirk, as if it had always been waiting for him.

He no longer stretched his spine. Others leaned forward when he entered. Silence obeyed him.

***

The Hare Research Facility stirred awake. White coats flashed past, rapid footsteps struck tile, clipped greetings ricocheted off the walls. Tomorrow, the collider would fire. Three years of sleepless nights and impossible equations all boiled down to this one moment.

Lupus stood beside the android body and ran a over its skin. Seamless. No panel lines betrayed its secrets. A disguise so flawless he almost admired it, even the gray tail and dorsal fins looked natural.

"Such impressive work," he murmured. "If it weren't for me, this masquerade wouldn't exist. Nowhere else on this planet could you pass."

A reply came from the shadows, voice metallic and cool. "Remember who gifted you the foundation. Without me, your kind would be chiseling stone for another century."

"Yes, Trinn, I realize that." He said it lightly, but his fingers stiffened against the synthetic skin.

The oval drone rolled forward on tracked wheels, its three eyestalks rising as its sensors caught the light. Inside its shell, a brain-like body twitched, and tentacles shifted with quiet, deliberate movements.

Hare met the unblinking sensors. "This is what you wanted."

"I am aware." The voice rasped from the speakers. "But when I rule this world, politics will be ash. Until then, I will play the game." The eyestalks telescoped upward until they locked onto his.

The fur at the nape of Hare's neck bristled. "I could stand here all day, but since you never blink, I'm finished," he said, turning sharply away.

The intercom chimed. "Professor Hare, Myles is here. He says he needs to speak with you about the upcoming accelerator firing."

"Send him in."

The door opened to reveal a mole half Hare's size. His thick glasses magnified his squinting eyes until they filled the frames. The lab coat hung loose over a beige shirt with a bulging pen guard at the breast pocket.

"Myles." Hare inclined his head in greeting.

The mole glanced toward the shadows. "Is she here?"

"She is."

Trinn had retreated when the door opened. Now, she rolled back into the light.

Myles drew himself straighter. "Chancellor, I've finished processing the exotic material. When the particles collide, the quantum pressure difference should stabilize the fissure."

"Excellent," Hare said, with a satisfied nod.

Myles' nervous gaze darted to Trinn. "Its antimatter properties should give us a twenty-second bridge. Barely enough time to confirm we've pierced your reality, but enough for readings."

The drone split open. Trinn emerged a brain with tentacles that unfurled like wet ropes. She slithered up the android's spine and slipped inside. The body stirred. Its hammerhead eyes adjusted before focusing on Myles.

"It's been thirteen years since Sound Bloom," she said, the android's modulator giving her the low silken voice of a shark. "Are the safeguards in place?"

Myles's hands clicked against his pen guard. "We've tuned the instruments as best we can. The technology is still raw. My calculations are sound, but certainty is impossible."

Hare's whiskers quivered. "Sound Bloom may have failed, but it gave us what we needed. Now we stand on the brink."

"Sir," Myles murmured, "do not forget the lives lost at Badger Springs."

"You can't make an omelet without cracking a few eggs," Hare replied. "The sacrifice was necessary."

Trinn cut in with a smile that didn't touch her eyes. "My friends, I would love to stay, but I have a meeting in Swan Hill. Tegan Swiftwind waits, and I don't intend to be late."

Hare snorted. "Somehow, I doubt she'll take an interest in your... projects."

Trinn scowled. "Her moral compass is flawless. It just isn't natural." Her frown twisted into an evil grin. "If I had that fusion cannon I mentioned earlier, she'd be the first target."

"Fusion cannon?" Myles blinked behind his glasses.

"Merely an idea," Trinn purred. "But no matter. I'll leave you to your preparations." Her heels clicked against the floor as she swept to the door, purse slung across her shoulder. "Let's do lunch soon." The door whispered shut behind her.

Myles took off his glasses and began polishing them furiously. "Sir, I didn't want to bring this up with her here, but there's been an... incident."

Hare narrowed his eyes. "An incident? The day before our experiment?"

"The specimen from Habitat 2. It escaped. Security's searching the campus now."

Hare tapped his large, flat foot, each strike sharper than the last. "And the collider security?"

"Reassigned spare personnel. I've left instructions for Lanell that she is to assist with recovery."

Hare's shoulders eased a fraction. "Then we'll have it back soon enough." He placed his hand on Myle's shoulder. "You are my number one. Don't forget that. I'll meet you in the collider chamber."

Chapter Three

Not the Cubs

Back then, a path wasn't just a road it was a promise. You could walk from one city to the next without a checkpoint in sight. Or, if you were bold enough, step through a gate and find yourself in another dimension by nightfall. There was a time when paths were sacred. They followed the stars, the rivers, the breath of the wind. They bent to the land, not to the whims of the powerful. The Torkas opened those paths, not for conquest but for discovery. Not for rulers but for seekers.

Now I see cities where the roads are straight, but the souls are bound and twisted. Where movement is permitted not chosen. Where gates no longer open outward, only inward. The lines between cities have not vanished, they've calcified.

I have watched empires collapse under such design. This one will be no different unless something breaks the pattern. And so, let us examine what remains of those sacred paths where they now lead and who controls them.

***

Lanell had never known anything but Epps. In Rith, you walked, or you packed yourself into one of the long white transports that hummed along their rails, doors hissing shut like they were sealing you in. Politicians never touched them. They skimmed overhead in sleek craft, distant and untouchable. Everyone knew the rule: the dome you were born under was the dome you died under. No routes out, not unless your name was etched on a government badge.

On her way to work, Lanell made her usual detour to Starducks. Hare demanded his chica, Myles his nuka. Whatever cup she added for herself was the only perk of the errand.

At least the old rabbit's addiction meant she never paid for her own drinks. Still, three cups were too much to juggle most mornings, so she often left with only theirs.

This morning, she was late. The line spilled out the door, and a constant stream of people flowed from the exit, steam rising from the paper cups in their hands. Lanell sighed and took her place. The temperature was mild under the dome, but waiting still tested her patience. Her gaze drifted to the giant blue and white logo painted across the storefront: a duck reaching for the stars. She'd seen it every morning but never noticed the detail until now.

With all the money they make, you'd think they could hire someone to design a logo that isn't stupid, she thought.

She caught movement on the patio and recognized some of her coworkers clustered at a table, chatting over drinks. A lemur from maintenance lifted a hand in greeting. Lanell nodded politely, but her eyes quickly jumped back to the menu board overhead. She wasn't in the mood to fake interest in their weekend stories.

The line crept forward, and she entered the store. Warm air wrapped her in the scent of roasted beans and syrup. Low lights glowed against wood panels, and soft music hummed under the chatter. Plush chairs sagged with regulars who had no plans to leave. It was cozy, designed to keep people lingering. She'd lingered herself, occasionally, when acquaintances pulled her into conversation, but there was no time for that this morning.

Two tiger cubs stood ahead of her in line, whispering and snickering. They looked no older than eleven, and the mirrored markings on their faces suggested they were twins. One cub's fuzzy, spotted cheeks and tufted ears caught her eye, and she offered him a smile. He stared back, long enough that it became awkward. She shifted forward in line, trying to ignore the burn of his gaze. He kept talking to his brother, but he never looked away.

Lanell slid her tongue across her teeth, checking for anything stuck. Nothing. The stare persisted. Finally, she met his eyes again, and asked, "What's up?"

The cub started, cheeks flushing red. He broke eye contact and turned to his brother. Lanell grinned as she stepped forward with the line.

A few minutes later, when she was third from the counter, the other cub turned. "Hey, lady."

The first cub, still pink, groaned. "Sai, no, don't bother her."

"Calm down, Kai. She can settle this."

Lanell bent to meet his gaze. "Sure, what's up, Sai?"

He puffed up with confidence. "I need you to settle an argument between my brother and me."

Lanell winked at Kai. "There isn't a problem I can't settle. What's the debate?"

Kai's cheeks burned hotter. He ducked his head while Sai launched into his pitch. "I say the most popular drink here is a Venti Ducka Spice Latte with eight shots of Duckaspresso, seven pumps of Duckasauce, and one pump of Maple Ducka Sauce. My brother thinks it's a Venti Salted Ducka Mocha Duckaccino with five pumps of Ducka Roast, four of Caramel Ducka Sauce, four of Caramel Ducka Syrup, three of Mocha Ducka, three of Toffee Nut, double blended with extra Ducked Cream."

Lanell tilted her head, pretending to weigh the question, then she smiled. "Sai, whatever happened to just plain orange juice?"

Both cubs burst into laughter.

"Well, Orange Juice Lady, I guess we have our answer," Sai said, still grinning.

They shuffled forward to the counter. Lanell studied them a moment longer, trying to summon an image of herself at eleven. Nothing surfaced. The smile slipped, replaced by the shadow of last night's dream. The memory of that age was locked away, and maybe it was better left buried.

The cubs collected their drinks. As they left, Sai shouted back, "Hey, Orange Juice Lady! My brother thinks you're beautiful, and he's in love with you!"

"*Sai*!" Kai yelped, and bolted through the door in mortified retreat.

Lanell chuckled under her breath and turned to the barista. "One chica, one nuka, and a cup of orange juice."

Drinks in hand, she walked the short block toward the research facility. The path was second nature by now, her feet took her there without the intervention of her brain. Overhead, the dome arched high, two thousand feet of steel and shimmering glass. They'd started welding it shut when she was still a child, after rocks from the planet's rings had scarred the surface. Smaller ones still streaked across the sky sometimes, burning to nothing before they struck the dome. The committees called it protection. Lanell called it scheduled weather, rain rationed out by vote, sunshine turned on and off like a light.

The research campus rose into view. From the roof, an aircraft lifted into the dome's glow. "That'll be Chancellor Trinn," she muttered. "Which means I'll have a fresh to-do list waiting." She sighed and joined the flow toward security.

Her pace slowed. Usually, one bored guard stood at the scanner. Today, three patrolled the perimeter, hands resting on sidearms. Two more blocked the gate, checking badges like they expected forgeries.

Yeah, that's about right, she thought. With the firing tomorrow, Hare would want the place locked down tight.

At the checkpoint, a familiar face manned the station. Trace Finn herself. That was especially unusual. The chief of security rarely worked the desk.

Trace's glassy black eyes flicked up. "Running late this morning, are you?"

Lanell flashed a thin smile. "No, just a wee bit behind. I'd never be late."

Trace smirked, revealing a mouthful of pointed teeth.

Lanell raised an eyebrow. "You usually stalk the campus. Why are you playing receptionist today?"

"Security is stretched thin. Hare wanted every gate doubled until the collider fires. And an asset slipped its habitat last night. The rest of my team is hunting it."

Lanell frowned. "Can I ask what kind of asset?"

"No," Trace said flatly. "But based on what Myles said, you'll be helping recover it."

Lanell's ears flattened. "You're kidding. I already have last week's results to file, plus prep for tomorrow's test, and now I'm supposed to do your job too?"

Trace's glare hardened. "I've got people working double shifts, ferret. You can take your complaints to Hare, but when we call for support, you show up. That's the job."

The red pupils of Trace's inky eyes fixed on her, unblinking. Lanell felt her pulse spike. Suddenly, she didn't see the chief of security; she saw a predator ready to lunge across the table. She forced a blank expression onto her face, slid her badge across the scanner, and stepped through without another word.

"I hate this place," she grumbled as the door sealed behind her

Chapter Four

Always There for You

Not all temples are built to honor the divine. Some are shrines to the ego, where the faithful trade mystery for measurement and silence wonder in the name of certainty. But when knowledge is pursued at the expense with the aim of control, the cost is always greater than the gain.

Hare believes he commands progress, that nothing lies beyond his grasp if he names, measures, and dissects it, but I have encountered such beings on many other worlds. They do not build the future, they ignite it.

***

The lobby reeked of Hare's ego. His name glowed on plaques, his face filled the intro reel on the wall display, and even the marble floor seemed polished to reflect him. Every breakthrough bore his stamp. Every mishap had his neat, rehearsed explanation. If something sparked in Rith, Hare made sure you knew it was he who had lit the flame.

Lanell stepped in through the gate. Sunlight streamed down from the skylights. Geometric beams splintered across the marble, forcing her to squint and lift a hand against the glare. To her left, a mural displayed Rith's skyline beneath the great dome, captions crowing about progress and declaring Rith to be the world's technological capital. Other cities envied Rith, everyone knew it. But all Lanell saw was a monument to Hare's pride.

Arms folded, she stared at the holographic directory. "Of course he made himself the star of the intro reel."

"Hello, Victoria Lanell. Welcome to Hare Research Facility. Is there something I can assist you with?"

The robotic receptionist's smooth voice jolted her back to the present. Lanell glanced at the screen. The AI's avatar was regarding her with polite interest.

"I'm good," she said curtly. "I'm headed to the collider control room."

"Oh." The AI's voice was tinged with puzzlement. "It seemed like you were standing here unsure of what to do next."

Lanell's ears swiveled with irritation. She shot it a glare and pivoted hard toward Wing B.

The door sighed open at her swipe before shutting behind her. She hesitated, a shiver raising goosebumps under her fur. The dream still clung to her like a damp fog.

The walls of the corridor were bare, except for posters and notices tacked at eye-level. The air was cool and had a faint antiseptic smell. Fluorescent lights buzzed overhead, joined by the drone of vents in a constant mechanical dirge.

She passed closed labs with narrow windows, a scientist bent over a microscope, two more lit ghost blue by their monitors, a tank holding some pale creature suspended in fluid, a bell jar glowing faintly around an object she didn't recognize. The hall felt endless.

Lanell greeted staff as she went. Smiles were returned readily but cautiously. Voices dipped once she passed. Being Hare's assistant meant carrying his shadow, and no one quite forgot it.

Finally, she reached the door she wanted. It bore a plaque marked Chief of Maintenance. She raised her hand to knock, but the door opened before she finished the second rap.

"Hello, my little ferret."

Her papa stood there, weathered but warm, gray fur patchy in places. One horn had been broken long ago, and wrinkles cut deep across his brow. His crooked smile revealed missing teeth, but his eyes twinkled with the same light they always had. The scent of machine oil and old books clung to his coveralls.

"Hello, Papa." Her shoulders loosened, the leftover tension from the night before finally slipping away.

Earl Kidd stepped aside, and she entered. Before he could say another word, she bent to wrap him in a tight hug. Not the usual greeting stronger, needier. After a moment's pause, he hugged her back.

"It's gonna be okay," he murmured.

When she pulled away, she swiped moisture from her eyes. Earl turned to his desk, giving her space.

The office was a world apart from the sterile labs. Tools and parts cluttered every surface, ancient blueprints papered the walls, calendars with crossed out days littered the floor near the desk. An old radio played soft orchestral music. In one corner, candles ringed a carpeted patch of floor, a quiet space carved from the chaos.

"You know," Lanell said with a wry smile, "if you keep answering the door that fast, people will think you camp there waiting."

Earl grinned. "What makes you think I wasn't?"

"Fair enough."

His beige coveralls were worn, and his name was stitched above the pocket. Despite his age, his movements were nimble and deliberate, every step measured with the efficiency of long practice.

"I take it you're on your way to the collider room?" he said, eyeing the cups she'd set on the counter.

"Yes, Papa. I just wanted to see you first."

He studied her face. "Something wrong? That hug felt... different."

"I had one of those dreams again. The kind that felt too real." Her eyes glistened. "Mom and Dad were there. There was that dreadful noise, then silence. And then they were gone."

Earl's rough hand folded around hers, the contrast sharp against her sleek fur.

"Lanell," he said softly. "You lost them in a way no child should. That moment carved itself into you. I can see how heavy you've carried it."

Her eyes filled. "How do I just forget? They were everything."

"I'm not asking you to forget. Their love is still with you. It always will be. Your story isn't just the loss, kid, it's how you've kept walking despite it."

"It's hard to believe in healing when the pain never let's go."

Earls squeezed her hand. "Healing takes time. One day, you'll take down those walls you've built and let people in again. Then you'll see you're stronger than what happened to you."

Silence fell, filled only by the tinny music from the battered radio.

The peace cracked when the desk speaker buzzed to life. "Earl, are you monitoring the radio?"

Earl pressed Lanell's hand one more time before letting go. "Work calls." He grabbed the receiver. "I'm here."

"This is Security Team 2. We think we've located the escaped asset. It's in a duct near Habitat 4. Can you get us into the air unit?"

Lanell knew that was her cue. She gathered the cups and turned back to her father. "Thank you, Papa, for listening."

"You were a strong kid, and you're still strong," Earl said, his eyes fierce with conviction. "It hasn't been an easy road, but you've got this. And never forget that I'm always here for you."

"I know." She opened the door, then paused to look back. "I love you, Papa."

"Love you too, kid." His crooked smile warmed the room.

Lanell brushed the last of her tears away and left, cradling the drinks.

Chapter Five

The Price of Incorruptibility

There are always those who believe the future can be bartered traded like goods across a table. But then there are others. Rare ones. The kind who hold their ground with principle rather than force.

They are never the loudest or the most powerful, but they are the fulcrums around which history pivots. Teagan Swiftwind is one such soul.

Sadly, Trinn, too, cuts a familiar figure. The clever mind convinced that control is wisdom, that strategy can twist destiny. But there is a truth no manipulator ever believes until it is too late: not every soul has a price, and some refusals shape the fates of entire worlds.

***

The blue skies above Swan Hill stretched unbroken, the planetary rings arcing from horizon to horizon. Sunlight glinted off the hull of the aircraft as it banked toward the statehouse.

Inside, Trinn tapped an impatient rhythm on the armrest of her chair. Of all the council leaders, Swiftwind remained an enigma a locked door she had never been able to pick. Every other member of the Council of Seven could be bent to her will with promises or threats, but not Tegan. That stubborn streak gnawed at Trinn, worming its way under her skin like a splinter.

"Everyone has their price," she muttered as the craft dipped toward the pad.

Tegan was already visible through the window. She stood at the end of the red carpet, head unbowed, feathers glowing bright in the morning sun. Trinn's jaw creaked as she tried to flex mandibles that weren't there. "But what is yours, Swiftwind?"

The engines wound down, and the cabin lights brightened. Trinn rose and strode toward the exit. The door slid open. Cameras flashed from the waiting journalists.

As she descended the steps, the crowd bowed. Fear or respect, it was hard to tell. Tegan alone stood tall and unflinching.

"Tegan Swiftwind." Trinn's smile was too tight to be sincere. "A pleasure as always."

"The pleasure is yours, Chancellor," Tegan replied, her tone polished steel.

They walked together through the thinning crowd.

"My chancellor," Tegan said, eyes fixed ahead, "we would've had more of a detail here for your arrival, but the rootward region is flooded. My troops are assisting. If not for this meeting, I would be there myself."

"Always a leader for the people." Trinn's tone dripped honey. "I admire how you care so deeply for their best interests."

"It is my duty. I am here to serve them."

"Of course, which brings me to why I sought you out."

They stopped. Trinn leaned closer and murmured in Tegan's ear. "I have brought you a unique opportunity."

Tegan narrowed her round, black eyes. "And what would that be?"

"A craft crashed," Trinn whispered. "Propulsion beyond our research. Materials unknown to our forges. It's unmistakably alien. I want your help with housing it, studying it, and with any luck, unlocking it."

Tegan drew herself up straighter. "An extraterrestrial craft? And you want to hoard it? A discovery of this magnitude should belong to all cities, to all our people. Kept secret, it tilts the balance of power and invites corruption."

Trinn smiled coldly. "I have told no one. The wreck lies hidden in neutral ground. Imagine what your science and my resources could achieve if we worked together."

They'd reached the memory garden. Tegan paused among the blossoms, admiring the quiet order of the symmetrical arrangements. "Why me, Chancellor?" she asked finally. "Others have larger facilities, more resources."

"Because," Trinn said, "you are the only one I trust to weigh opportunity against risk. Others would chase weapons; you would consider consequences."

Tegan studied her face. The words were right, but something about the offer felt wrong. Her feathers ruffled. She tucked in her wings and faced Trinn head-on. "If you wish my counsel, share this discovery with every leader. Make it a project for all. If not, then destroy it in the lava lake of the ancients before it destroys us."

Trinn's smile thinned. "You have an admirable dedication to fairness, Tegan. One of your... endearing qualities." The sun threw her long shadow over the Avarian leader. "But understand, sometimes progress requires a focusing of resources. By sharing too widely, we risk this process getting bogged down in petty politics. One city must be the beacon. Let the rest see what brilliance without compromise looks like." She paused to let her words sink in. "And if you decline, others will surely seize upon it. Swan Hill could be left behind. Surely you would not let that happen. You *are* an advocate of progress, are you not?"

Tegan stared at her, unmoved. "Progress is not a race, Chancellor. Innovation grows where many voices meet. Nature teaches us that ecosystems flourish by cooperation as much as competition. I cannot support secrecy that breeds imbalance. Not now, not ever."

Silence thickened and curdled between them. Then Trinn inclined her head, every gesture precisely measured. "Very well. I respect your dedication. But think on it, Tegan. The world is changing. Those who refuse to adapt are swept aside."

Tegan merely looked at her impassively. Trinn tamped down her boiling rage and offered a courteous farewell bow. As she walked away, she threw a parting remark over her shoulder. "I hope you do not come to regret this decision."

By the time she reached the aircraft, her jaw was clenched tight, and her smooth, gray hands were curled into fists. Her tail struck the wall with a metallic clang.

"Unyielding. Incorruptible. How inconvenient." The words grated from her throat. "That craft should have been my leverage, but she insists on hiding behind duty. Tiresome."

She lowered herself into the plush passenger seat and let out a long, slow breath. "If the carrot fails, the stick remains. Tegan, you may be incorruptible, but you're not untouchable."

The craft was sealed, and the engines roared. Swan Hill shrank beneath her as the chancellor lifted away.

Chapter Six

Chamber of Knowledge

At the Hare Research Facility, the control room of the supercollider buzzed with activity. The spacious room featured sleek, chrome surfaces and a panoramic view of the sprawling laboratory complex beyond. Various monitors lined the walls, displaying complex diagrams and scrolling data.

The heart of the room was dominated by the massive main console. Its surface was covered in a multitude of buttons, switches, and touchscreens, used to control various aspects of the machine's operation. Each glowing screen displayed a specific aspect of the collider's operation, providing vital information to the scientists crewing their stations.

They watched the energy level displays carefully, ensuring they remained stable and within predetermined parameters. The intermittent blips and beeps from the equipment signaled the continual analysis of the collider's power.

One wall held a large display that presented a comprehensive overview of the facility. It showed live video feeds from different areas, allowing the team to see the workings of the entire research complex. Right now, the screen showed anxious technicians and assistants scurrying around the hulking collider like ants.

As the team worked, the soft click of keyboards and whisper of hushed conversations filled the control room. An urgent notification chimed from one screen, prompting swift responses and adjustments from the attentive staff.

The collider's inner chamber was a marvel of engineering. This massive circular room spanned several stories in height and stretched outwards like an underground cathedral.

Gleaming metallic walls encased the chamber, and a series of concealed light panels bathed the room in an eerie glow.

Hare and Moleman were working in the inner chamber, wearing hair nets and rubber gloves to prevent any contaminants from being exposed to the environment. Lupus adjusted the alignment of a sophisticated array of magnets while Myles inspected the delicate wiring connecting various components and checked the fail safes within the section.

"My friend, this is a pivotal moment for us." Hare said, glancing at digital system clock. "It's a mere matter of hours now. This is it. Are all the particle sources calibrated to the precise energy levels we need?"

Myles nodded without looking up, his eyes still locked on the calibration screen. "We've fine-tuned each particle source, ensuring they emit the desired energy accurately. The calibration process was thorough, and the readings show optimal performance."

Hare stroked his whiskers. "Good, good. And what about the cooling system? We must prevent any unwanted heat buildup during the firing."

The mole pointed to a series of elaborate pipes and coolant channels. "Professor, we engineered the cooling system to dissipate heat. We've implemented redundant mechanisms to ensure the temperature stays within the designated safe range. We regulate the flow rate and pressure."

"And the particle detection system? We need accurate data to analyze the collisions and unlock the secrets they hold."

Myles waved a hand, indicating a trajectory on one screen. "Professor, I assure you there is nothing to worry about. The particle detection system is state-of-the art. We have positioned an array of detectors throughout the chamber, each calibrated to capture and analyze the secondary particles produced by the collisions. These detectors will provide us with valuable data on particle properties, trajectories, and energy levels."

Suddenly, a familiar voice from outside cut across their conversation. "Hey, you two!" Lanell called.

Hare looked at Myles. "Let's take a break."

Lanell was leaning against a machine bank, feet crossed, balancing a tray of drinks on her hand. As the two scientists emerged from the inner chamber, she straightened her posture and flicked her tail playfully. Clearing her throat, she adopted an exaggeratedly formal tone. "Ahem, esteemed scientists, behold! Your well-deserved elixir of brilliance and inspiration has arrived!" She placed the tray on a nearby table with a theatrical flourish.

Then, with a twinkle in her eye, she lifted one of the cups to the light. "These beverages contain the finest concoction of caffeine and humor, guaranteed to stimulate both your minds and your funny bones."

She turned to Professor Hare, offering his drink with a mock bow. "And for you, boss, I had them brew the concoction at triple strength."

Myles's drink was presented with equal ceremony. "Let me warn you" her voice shifted to mimic a pharmaceutical advertisement "you can expect to experience uncontrollable bursts of laughter or sudden epiphanies. Any consequences arising from these events are your responsibility."

She paused for a moment, waiting for their reaction.

Professor Hare set his drink aside and looked at her with one eyebrow raised. "Lanell, I value your contributions to the research facility and our team. Just the same, sometimes your professionalism needs to be refined, especially given this remarkable scientific achievement before us. It's important to show respect and awe for the equipment and the work we're undertaking."

Lanell met Professor Hare's gaze without flinching. "Doc, trust me, I am a professional. You won't find anyone else in this facility with a sharper sense of humor, and nobody else would put up with some of the stuff I've had to do for my paycheck." She shifted her gaze over his shoulder towards the inner chamber, and her tone sobered. "As for our science project here, it's still a work in progress. We have yet to discover what the future holds. It's premature to label it a successful experiment at this point."

Eyes bright and attentive, Hare peered at Lanell over the rim of his cup. His whiskers flicked slightly with each sip, but his expression remained unreadable. He made no move to speak. The only sound was then occasional soft slurp as he continued to drink. Lanell rubbed the back of her neck and averted her eyes, suddenly feeling naked under his scrutiny.

Myles set his cup down. "The collider project is a groundbreaking endeavor in particle physics," he explained. "We've built a machine that accelerates particles to near light speeds and then collides them together. By doing so, we can recreate conditions similar to those found in the early universe."

Lanell furrowed her brow and stared into the inner chamber. "The collider is indeed a remarkable feat of engineering. By recreating early universe conditions, we have the potential to make important discoveries. However, as I mentioned to Professor Hare earlier, we must remain cautious in our approach. We're still in the early stages of this experiment."

"The collisions should generate an enormous amount of energy," Myles continued, as if she hadn't spoken. "It will allow us to study fundamental particles and the forces that govern them. We could uncover new particles, investigate dark matter and energy, and even explore concepts like extra dimensions and the universe's origins." He gestured excitedly, knocking his glasses askew. "This project could revolutionize our understanding of the fundamental building blocks of matter and the laws of physics. It opens doors to new technologies, medical advancements, and deeper insights into cosmic mysteries."

She smiled politely, but her tail gave another swish the kind it only made when something didn't sit right.

Sure, a massive collider is the most efficient way to solve the mysteries of the universe. Why bother with methodical research when we can just throw particles at each other and hope for enlightenment?

"I understand theories provide a foundation, Myles, but there are still significant gaps in our current understanding of physics. We don't have all the pieces of the puzzle yet." Her voice gained strength as she warmed to her theme. "Shouldn't we address those gaps before investing billions in the collider? What if we discover we need to significantly revise our theories? Wouldn't that waste our efforts and resources?" While pursuing knowledge is important, shouldn't we prioritize research with immediate potential for advancements in medicine or renewable energy? There are pressing global challenges that need attention now."

Myles scratched his chin. "You make valid points, Lanell. Addressing gaps in our knowledge is crucial, as is considering practical applications. But the collider project isn't just about confirming existing theories. It's about challenging our fundamental assumptions and exploring uncharted territories. Through these experiments, we might uncover phenomena no one has predicted, revealing dimensions and mysteries that have eluded theoretical work. Even if our current understanding requires revision, the knowledge gained will advance science in ways we can't yet imagine."

Lanell nodded while internally rolling her eyes.

Oh, of course! Let's build a colossal machine to chase theoretical particles instead of focusing on problems we already understand. Who needs a clear roadmap when we can stumble around in the scientific dark?

"Myles," she said, taking care to keep her expression neutral, "while I acknowledge the potential rewards, I believe we must maintain a critical perspective. Science advances best when we balance exploration with addressing immediate needs. Only then can we ensure our efforts truly benefit humanity."

Professor Hare's eyes had been moving between his two colleagues like he was watching a tennis match. Now, he set down his cup. "Lanell," he said, his voice calm and measured, "I appreciate your thoughtful perspective, and I acknowledge your concerns. Scientific progress has always required both caution and boldness. This debate has merit on both sides. But this project has been in development for over a decade. A decade of sacrifices, advances, and setbacks have brought us to this critical point."

He paused, looking at each of them again. "Tomorrow, we will advance to a place no one on this planet has dared to venture. I will lead us into the future, into the darkness of the unknown. The time for debate has passed. Now we must see what our work has wrought."

The ferret and the mole exchanged glances. Over the years, they had become all too familiar with Hare's idiosyncrasies, but they remained eager to hear his thoughts. In that moment, despite their disagreements, a shared feeling of anticipation united them. Each had the sense that they were standing at the precipice of a discovery that would make scientific history.

"Lanell and Myles, my esteemed colleagues, your deliberation has been enlightening, but let me interject with a few insights of my own," Professor Hare said, a self-assured smile playing on his lips. He lifted his mug and drained the last of the liquid before continuing his monologue. All the while, the looming bulk of the collider sat silently in the background, as if it too was listening listening and *waiting*.

Chapter Seven

The Drop of a Hair

The hum of the immense machines cut out without warning. In its absence, even Lanell's breath sounded loud and intrusive. But it didn't last long. A low vibration returned, marking the start of the cooling systems.

"You see, my dear friends," Professor Hare continued. "In this facility, I have achieved feats of brilliance unmatched anywhere on this planet." His voice rose and his posture straightened, as if he were addressing a crowded lecture hall instead of just two colleagues. "As a scientist, I have dedicated years to pushing the boundaries of knowledge."

Myles rolled his eyes. Lanell smirked. The sermon had begun.

"This is not arrogance. It is merely a deep understanding of the magnitude of my own intellect. I am destined to lead our society into a new world order, one shaped by scientific triumph." He locked eyes with Myles. "And you, my dear Myles, have recognized your place beside me, even while acknowledging the vast expanse that separates our capabilities. You have embraced your role as my peer, basking in the glow of my brilliance."

Myles raised a brow. He had always respected Hare's mind, but this soliloquy was tilting toward absurdity.

If Hare noticed, he gave no sign. His grin widened as he turned to Lanell. "And Lanell, you have witnessed the expanse of my intellectual prowess. Though your skills pale in comparison, your efforts shine as a testament to the collaborative nature of scientific exploration."

Lanell let out a low chuckle. Beneath the comedy routine, something real pulsed. His passion wasn't fake, just filtered through ego.

"And so," Hare said, sweeping one arm grandly toward the chamber, "as we step into the unknown tomorrow, remember it is I who leads us. I will unravel the mysteries of the universe and usher in a new era."

"Thank you for your perspective, Professor Hare," Myles said dryly. "We appreciate your... unique insights."

Lanell opened her mouth, then thought better of it. Her father's voice echoed in her mind: *Lanell, my little ferret, there'll be people who won't hear you no matter what you say.* She looked between them both and muttered, "I got nothing." Then she focused her attention on the inner chamber. "So," she asked, "is this the true heart of the collider?"

Hare beamed. "Yes! Our gateway to the unknown."

He launched into an explanation of strange matter, but Lanell's attention had already shifted. She stood on the threshold of the supercollider's inner sanctum. The air tingled against her fur. The chamber stretched before her in a vast ring, vanishing into shadow. Every bolt, every curve it hadn't just been assembled, it had been *crafted.*

She stepped inside. The tunnel curved left and right. In its center, detectors and magnetic coils whirred softly. She weaved around them.

A console blinked to her left, and she tapped it. Menus fluttered open. Then she was looking at a simulation of the event that was to take place the next day. She adjusted a variable. The field responded. Two blips converged, then the screen flared.

Particles collided, light burst, new fragments appeared, then dissolved into rivers of data. She backed away slowly. Her eyes swept the tunnel, left, then right. Matter colliding at near light speed. Forces beyond instinct. She imagined the violence. The birth of particles that lived and died in a whisper.

Her skin felt hot and her stomach fluttered. A disbelieving laugh bubbled up her throat and nearly escaped. She shook her head. This wasn't just a lab. It was sacred ground.

She pushed her hair out of her eyes and tried to slow her ragged breathing. A single golden strand slipped free and drifted, unseen, to the platform below. It landed inches from the injector.

Hare's voice called her back to reality. "The interaction between the strange matter and accelerated atoms will yield the desired reactions."

"The outcomes," she mumbled, "they could rewrite everything."

"Indeed."

They stepped out together.

Myles rejoined them. "Readings are stable. We're ready to seal the chamber and prep for the experiment. Shall we proceed?"

Hare placed a hand on the door. "Not yet. Let's lock it down and inspect the control room."

Chapter Eight

Unknown Watcher

From above, the cities gleam like jewels pressed into the surface of the world. Brilliant. Proud. They pulse with invention, hum with confidence, and believe themselves eternal.

But I have walked among ruins that once shined brighter. I have watched towers fall to moss and domes sink into soil. I have seen what happens when the thread of progress is pulled too tight.

These beings do not fear the wilderness because of its danger. They fear it because it remembers what they chose to forget: the old truths, the deep rhythms of the wild that pulse beneath the grid.

And so they build upward, never outward. They mistake silence for safety. And in their pride, they do not see the ancient world watching them in return, waiting for the inevitable. To understand their blindness, we must first see the world through their eyes. Let us step inside the walls they built and glimpse the pride they call progress.

Earth, the center of this universe, is adorned with seven magnificent cities that stand as testaments to its ingenuity and technological prowess. Each city is a marvel in its own right, a hub of technological advancement and innovation where groundbreaking discoveries shape the world. Among them, the City of Rith shines as the unparalleled epicenter of technology, leading the charge toward a future defined by innovation and progress.

But these cities are more than just large collections of buildings; they are sprawling metropolises with thriving populations. Generations are born, raised, and bid farewell under their protective glass domes. Skyscrapers reach upwards, casting majestic shadows over infrastructure that shapes the daily lives of the inhabitants.

Beyond the cities, the wilderness stretches far and wide. Dense forest canopies provide shelter to a myriad of flora and fauna. Vast deserts span across the landscape, their arid beauty punctuated by resilient life forms adapted to endure the harsh conditions. Jungles pulsate with vibrant colors, all manner of exotic creatures hidden amidst the lush foliage. Complex ecosystems live and die within the marshy waters of swamps and the windy expanse of prairies.

In this untamed world, wild creatures roam, unburdened by the confines of civilization. Here, nature preserves its delicate balance. This world resonates with an all-encompassing harmony that will forever elude those who dwell in bustling cities.

The inhabitants of the cities harbor no desire to venture beyond the safety and familiarity of their urban enclaves. Tales passed down through generations instilled a deep-seated fear of the wilderness within their hearts. Stories of menacing creatures that stalk the forests; citizens getting lost, never to be seen again; enigmatic tribes wandering deserts; unknown dangers lurking in jungle depths. This is what has kept the city dwellers behind the boundary walls.

And still, beyond those walls, things grow. Things live.

***

Across the research campus, clusters of labs and climate-controlled habitats bloomed like terrariums, each tailored to whatever wild experiment the facility's researchers dreamt up. Two modified pulmonated gastropods lived in this one. They'd been tweaked to grow big too big. And to ooze so much slime it could glue a train to the tracks.

In the wild, these snails were small maybe half an inch wide and an inch and a half long. But these? These had been turned into living reservoirs of mucopolysaccharides, thanks to one man's obsession.

Dr. George Crusher chemist, adhesive theorist, sometime philosopher, and full-time oddity had seen potential where no one else had. Where others saw garden pests, he saw walking formulas. The slime these snails produced could be refined, concentrated, and weaponized. Not that he liked thinking of it that way.

Part of him hated what they'd done to the creatures.

They slid across the walls with eerie grace, shells glinting like oil slicked shields, their massive bodies whispering over bark and stone. Seven feet long, two and a half wide, with the ability to lift themselves four feet off the ground. One had tried to body slam a technician last month. Now they were quarantined behind reinforced glass, and there were motion triggered tranquilizers on standby.

Genetic research played a quiet but powerful role in all seven cities. Unlike other scientific branches, this one was handled with care and secrecy. No billboards, no press releases, no bragging. The public didn't want to know what happened in labs like these. And people like Dr. Crusher preferred it that way.

His junior biotech's were usually responsible for harvesting the slime, but today he had come alone. Habitat 4 needed another draw, and frankly, he'd needed a walk.

He stepped into the chamber and stopped cold. Now matter how many times he came here, he was always struck by its strange beauty. It was like stepping onto another planet. Mist curled over neon green moss and flowering vines that looked like they'd been stitched from starlight.

He let the silence settle. Insects chirped softly and light shifted through the dome above. He moved with respectful care. The environment might have been created artificially, but it was their home now. He was a guest here.

"Easy now," he whispered, not sure who was speaking to. Perhaps to himself, or even to the snails if they were capable of listening.

Their iridescent shells gleamed under the artificial light. Trails shimmered. Leaves folded under their weight without protest.

He worked silently and methodically to collect what he needed. His steps were soft. Each sample taken with care.

Above him, in the canopy's shadows, eight legs unfurled. Eight eyes fixed on its target. Each limb twitched like a pianist preparing for a sonata. Crusher didn't notice. He leaned forward, vial in hand, coaxing a curl of mucus into the glass. The spider descended, its body a velvet silhouette drifting down on silken rope.

Its leg brushed his back with the lightness of a tickling breath. Crusher froze. He whipped around and swiped with his left hand. His stomach turned as his fingers grazed something hairy.

The spider latched on. He didn't scream. Not at first.

The next thirty seconds were a confusing mess of flailing arms, jerking limbs, and profanity. He spun. He twisted. The spider clung like a dancer mid routine, matching every move with grace. His arm shot skyward, then down, and then sideways, as if puppeted by invisible threads. His boots scraped moss. His back slammed into a tree. The snails watched in laconic disapproval.

In the midst of his struggle, he felt the judgmental stare of those stalky eyes. "Oh don't start," he snapped, half hysterical. "This is *not* my fault."

The snail's antennae twitched.

Judging intensifies.

He ran. The spider, still clamped to his arm, moved with him, long legs pinwheeling.

He weaved through vines, avoiding the glittering trails that now felt like gooey traps. A steam vent hissed to his left. Without giving himself time to think, he leapt and shoved his arm into the mist.

The spider chittered angrily and released his arm. Wings *wings* unfurled from its sides, and it lifted into the air before vanishing into the foliage.

Crusher stood panting. He stared at his arm. No bite. No blood. No rips. He checked again.

Still no bite. Still breathing.

"Okay," he muttered. "Not venomous or aggressive. Just... rude."

He straightened his coat, ran a hand through his fur, and walked to the door.

A guard strolled by in the hallway, absorbed in a datapad.

Crusher raised his hand. "There is an unauthorized asset," he said, still panting. "It's in Habitat 4. Tell your team. And get it out of my snail's habitat."

Chapter Nine

Intruders

They built their cities as monuments to progress seven pillars of light rising against the horizon, each more daring than the last. Within those domes, the people whisper dreams into wires, and the wires whisper back. Artificial minds shape their thoughts. Nanomachines mend their wounds. Virtual realms cradle their identities. And they call this freedom.

But I have seen other kinds of freedom.

Beyond their glowing skylines dwell those who remember the Earth as it was, not as a system to optimize, but as a living rhythm to honor. The Arcadians walk in the old ways, far from the noise of the cities. Where the wild breathes, they listen. Where machines reach, they withdraw.

To the city dwellers, the Arcadians are primitive relics misguided, even dangerous. But the Arcadians know what was lost. They understand that not all progress is forward, and not all connection comes through wires.

Two civilizations, born of the same world but now walking separate paths.

As the rift between the denizens of the Seven Cities and the Arcadians widens, each group becomes a mirror, reflecting its values and beliefs. In the cities, innovation reigns supreme, and the ceaseless hum of progress echoes through the bustling streets. Meanwhile, in the wilderness, the Arcadians find solace in a life of integrity, simplicity, and reverence for nature.

But even amidst this stark division, there are those who yearn for harmony. Those who strive to forge a future that combines the marvels of science with the wisdom of the Arcadians, seeking a delicate balance between progress and preservation. This emerging movement recognizes the need for a synthesis. They believe that the wonders of technology can coexist with a profound respect for nature and the inherent dignity of life.

***

Trace Finn ran her tongue over her teeth and scanned the bank of monitors in the security control room. The bright glow from the screens cast harsh shadows across her face as she tracked the intruders assembling outside the east perimeter of the Hare Research Facility. The acrid scent of fresh electronics and morning nuka hung in the air while the room's climate control buzzed steadily in the background.

The leather of her holster creaked as she shifted her weight. On screen, figures in earth toned clothing moved with impressive coordination. Unmistakably Arcadians.

"I should have known this would happen today," she muttered, nostrils flaring. She jabbed viciously at the keyboard, magnifying the image to reveal crude wooden weapons and primitive climbing gear.

Instincts honed by years of tactical drills kicked in. She was already reaching for the mic by the time her brain caught up. The particle collider experiment was scheduled for tomorrow. It was precisely the type of technological advancement the Arcadians would attempt to sabotage.

Not today. Not on *her* watch.

The microphone was cool against her palm. "This is Commander Finn. Breach confirmed on the east side. Cobras One and Two, roof and side entrance positions, respectively. Cobra Three on standby. Glue guns only we need prisoners for questioning, not martyrs. Capture and contain. That's your mission."

A chorus of crisp acknowledgments crackled through the speakers. Through the monitors, she watched her teams deploy. Black-clad figures moving as a perfectly synchronized unit.

Trace moved to another console and activated the facility's automated defenses. The system display shifted from peaceful green to alert red. The monitors showed wall mounted immobilization cannons swiveling into position, their barrels tracking movement at the perimeter.

"Teams, maintain radio silence," she said, her voice dropping to just above a whisper. "Let them get closer before engaging."

The Arcadians' approach continued. She traced their path across the screen with one blue finger, mentally counting steps between the fence line and wall mounted cannons. The steady rhythm of her breathing remained unbroken.

A sharp electronic chirp cut through her concentration. She unclipped the handheld radio from her hip. "Shark cage. Report."

"Serpent One here." The voice on the other end sounded tense but controlled. "Asset located in Habitat 4. Awaiting instructions."

Trace's breath hissed through her nose. Habitat 4. Of all the times... The strange matter sample they'd been protecting was critical to tomorrow's experiment, but her best personnel were dealing with the perimeter breach.

"Advise Professor Hare to initiate an alternate recovery protocol for the asset," she replied, keeping her voice level despite the compounding complications. "Tell him we'll assist once this situation is contained. Then report to the shark cage. We have Arcadians on site."

"Understood. Serpent One out."

The security feed showed the Arcadians within fifty meters of the perimeter. Sweat beaded at Trace's temples despite the cool temperature in the room. The muscles between her shoulder blades tightened with anticipation.

"Cobra One, Cobra Two, execute on my mark." She drew a deep breath. The metallic tang of adrenaline coated her tongue. "Mark!"

On screen, Cobra One erupted into action. Six black figures emerged from concealed positions on the rooftop. She could almost hear the soft whir of their weapons as they took aim and the distinctive thwack as the specialized adhesive projectiles launched toward their targets.

Streams of viscous polymer arced through the air, hitting several Arcadians with pinpoint accuracy. The intruders' movements became awkward as their limbs became trapped in the rapidly hardening adhesive. Their shouts of alarm were visible even without audio as they struggled against the binding substance.

Cobra One secured their rappelling equipment and descended the building's façade in perfect formation. They moved efficiently to secure the immobilized targets, methodically removing weapons and communication devices.

But the operation wasn't proceeding as smoothly as Trace had hoped. Three Arcadians had managed to shed layers of clothing and slip free of their adhesive restraints. They darted between the facility's external structures, their movements more frantic now.

"Cobra Two, spread out and establish a containment perimeter," Trace ordered. "They're abandoning gear to escape. Don't let them breach the inner fence."

Through the monitors, she observed Cobra Two's deployment as their formation expanded to cover potential escape routes. But one figure, Sergeant Furfoot, hesitated. His weapon remained pointed downward as an Arcadian stripped down to base layers and prepared to flee.

Trace zoomed in on Furfoot's feed. The escaping Arcadian was clearly visible to him, yet he made no move to engage or capture.

"Cobra Two Six," she called. "You have a target at your four o'clock. Engage immediately."

No response. Furfoot remained frozen while his target edged closer to the perimeter fence.

"Furfoot, acknowledge! Target is escaping your position!"

Still nothing.

The command center fell silent. Trace stared at the screen, waiting for movement that did not come. Furfoot's vital signs showed an elevated heart rate but no signs of injury or distress. His comms were functioning perfectly.

The Arcadian had nearly reached the fence. The rest of Furfoot's squad was occupied with other targets and unaware of the developing situation.

Her finger hesitated over the all-channel button. Was Furfoot frozen in fear? Under duress? Or was this something worse? His family had come from an agricultural community outside the Seven Cities. Not Arcadians, but sympathizers, perhaps?

The Arcadian reached the fence. Furfoot turned his head, watching but not acting.

That was enough.

"All units." Her voice cut through the active channels. "Cobra Two Six is compromised. I repeat, Furfoot is compromised. Detain him and treat as hostile until secured. The priority target is now the escapee at the eastern perimeter fence. Neutralize immediately."

The response was instantaneous. Two members of Cobra Two pivoted toward Furfoot, who dropped to his knees and placed his hands behind his head without resistance. His face, visible on the monitor, showed neither surprise nor defiance, only resignation.

Another team member launched adhesive at the escaping Arcadian, catching them just as they began scaling the fence. The viscous substance expanded rapidly, securing them in place.

Trace set down the microphone. Her heartbeat thundered as the adrenaline peaked. The control room staff avoided her gaze as they monitored the securing of prisoners.

She watched as Furfoot was bound and led away, his steps mechanical and his head bowed. Her eyes stayed on his frozen image. His face showed no panic. No pain. There was just a strange stillness, as if he'd decided something before the fight even began.

"You picked your side, didn't you," she said, barely loud enough for the mic to catch.

The collider project, years of work and billions in resources, could have been compromised by one moment of indecision. The leather like skin around her eyes tightened as she watched the teams secure the last intruders.

A Tularian raised in the technological heart of the Seven Cities, Trace had never understood the Arcadians' rejection of progress. Their backward philosophy threatened everything she had dedicated her life to protecting.

"Compassion is a liability," she said, the words leaving a bitter taste in her mouth. The weight of her decision settled across her shoulders like a heavy cloak, but she wouldn't allow herself to question it.

Not now. Not with tomorrow's experiment hanging in the balance.

Chapter Ten

Other Impressions

There are those marked not by accident but by intention, an echo of purpose whispered through bloodlines and stone. Long before cities rose and silence took root in sacred places, there were the shamans.

They did not seek power. Theirs was the way of obligation, not ambition. Marked at birth by signs older than language, they walked between the seen and unseen, the breath and the beyond.

Where others built machines to conquer the world, the shamans listened to its song. Their gift was not command but communion.

I have watched them on many worlds. They are never many. They are always needed.

In the days before the Great Divide and the burst of technological progress, a sacred calling echoed across the Earth and the shamans were born.

They became guardians of life's turning points: welcoming births, tending the sick, and guiding the dying. Through rituals, sacred herbs, and whispered communion with the Earth, they anchored their people. Their gift wasn't theirs to keep. It was service carried out in silence and shadow.

***

Lanell watched Myles and Hare move among the controls, their forms silhouetted against the illuminated panels like bizarre shadow puppets.

She only half-listened as numbers and readouts filled the room. Her focus kept drifting back to the echo of Hare's words in the impact chamber. *Secrets of the universe unlocked*. The phrase clung to her, repeating with every flicker of screen light. But what did it mean?

Professor Hare's authoritative voice intruded on her thoughts.

"The strange matter is at the desired temperature and stable. The thernatim intake is set at nominal," he announced, adjusting a dial with his nimble fingers.

Myles glanced at a gauge, his glasses reflecting the green indicator lights. "Power reserves and backups are in order." He flipped a switch, and the large central screen came to life, displaying the impact chamber.

Professor Hare smiled. "You've upgraded the monitors."

"Yes," Myles said, a hint of pride in his voice as he gestured toward the vast display. "I thought the twenty-foot screens would give us a clearer view than the fifteen foot ones."

"Always thinking ahead, my friend," Hare said with an appreciative nod.

The pleasant atmosphere evaporated as the communication system chirped to life. Hare straightened his lab coat and positioned himself in front of the console. "Professor Hare speaking."

"Professor, this is Trace." The security chief's voice carried an unusual edge that immediately heightened the tension in the room. "We've had a few incidents in the last few minutes that need your attention."

Hare's foot began to tap. "What's the situation?"

"A squad of Arcadians attempted to breach our facility," Trace said. "We thwarted six but have taken seven into custody. One of them appears to be a spy from our security detail."

Lanell gasped, a cold weight sinking in her chest. "I know almost everyone on our security team," she said, moving closer to the console. "How could one of them be an Arcadian? This is hard to digest."

Hare raised a hand, signaling for calm. "Take the infiltrators to the interrogation room," he said. "We'll decide on our next steps."

Trace's voice crackled through the speaker again. "Sir, there's more. During the confrontation, there was an incident in Habitat 4. We'd have addressed it, but the Arcadians demanded our immediate attention."

Hare ran a hand over his ears as he processed this additional complication. "You've done well, Trace. Oversee the Arcadians; we'll see to the asset in Habitat 4. Thanks for your diligence."

"Understood, sir," Trace acknowledged before the communication line went silent.

Professor Hare stood motionless for a moment, his hands clasped behind his back as he stared at the monitor displaying the impact chamber. His reflection in the screen revealed a calculating expression. After several seconds of contemplation, he turned to Myles. "We might need to expedite our plans." His voice was lower now, almost conspiratorial. "I hadn't expected the Arcadians to be this audacious. We must safeguard our project. Ensure all preparations are thorough every 'I' dotted, every 't' crossed."

Myles nodded and immediately began checking the system diagnostics. Hare then pivoted to face Lanell. "Victoria, I need you to head to Habitat 4 and secure the escaped asset."

Lanell hesitated. Her ears flicked once, then stilled. The fluorescent lights reflected off his eyes, giving them an almost predatory gleam. An uncomfortable pause lingered between them.

Ignoring her hesitation, Hare continued. "First, head to the original lab for any necessary equipment to secure the asset. Once in Habitat 4, I'll ensure those in the know will be available to assist you. Let's resolve this."

"Yes, sir," Lanell said, her voice steadier than she felt.

As she made her way to the control room's exit, she paused with one foot in the hallway. The professor was already deep in conversation with Myles.

"Where will you be, Professor Hare?" she asked.

Hare halted mid-sentence and looked back at his assistant. The harsh overhead lighting cast shadows across his features. "I have to interrogate the Arcadians, find out why they're here and discern their intentions."

A chill ran down Lanell's spine. "And how will you conduct these interrogations?"

Hare's gaze hardened. "Lanell, that's not for you to know."

The cold dismissal hit like a slap. Lanell's throat tightened and her cheeks burned. In the end, she simply nodded and proceeded through the doorway. The control room door slid shut behind her with a final-sounding thud.

Her white lab coat whispered against her legs as she walked. Overhead, the filtered air whooshed steadily, indifferent to her turmoil.

She used to feel pride in her work here. There was a feeling that she was part of something groundbreaking. But now the light panels above her seemed interrogative, exposing doubts she didn't want to name.

The word *interrogation* gnawed at her. Hare's cold eyes, his clipped tone. Those weren't just quirks. Those were shifts. Signals. Even the spider retrieval felt twisted now, not just creepy but symbolic. Something alive, loose, and hiding. A monster skulking in the shadows. The enemy within.

Then, a blessed distraction.

Just ahead, wrestling with one of the facility's vending machines, stood none other than Dr. Crusher. The sight of him, shoulders hunched in goofy frustration, cut through the tension like a warm breeze. She slowed, watching him tap then smack the glass.

"Roughhousing with the machine won't get you your snack," she said, her voice dry and amused.

Dr. Crusher jolted, spun, and nearly lost his balance. He caught himself and flushed beneath his fur. "Oh! Uh, didn't know I had an audience for my defeat."

Lanell chuckled. "I've been watching for a while. How's it working out for you?"

He pointed sheepishly to a bag of crisps wedged between coil and glass. "I may have underestimated its defenses."

She tilted her head impishly. "Maybe you should've gone for the nuts."

"Maybe I should've," he said with a mock-sigh.

She stepped close, gave the machine a knowing glance, then smacked it smartly on the side. The crisps dropped. "You're welcome," she said with a wink.

"Sometimes it really is all about the female touch." He retrieved the snack with a grin.

She smiled. After her recent encounter with Hare, a comfortable silence was a refreshing change of pace.

"How's our mighty overlord and savior?" Crusher asked, as if reading her thoughts.

Lanell hesitated for a breath. "His company is always...enlightening."

"Mm," Crusher said. "The kind of enlightening where you learn things you didn't want to?"

She gave him a sidelong look. "He's brilliant, but brilliance has edges."

He nodded. "It always does."

She let the moment sit, then changed the subject. "I'm off to wrangle a spider."

He lit up. "*You* got the duty? Lucky you."

"Said no one ever."

He laughed. "Watch the ceiling. That's where they like to hang. Last time, I thought I was alone until I felt something crawling down my back. I left my dignity in that room."

Lanell gave her first genuine laugh in days. "Thanks, Crusher."

"Just doing my part."

Chapter Eleven

Interrogation

I have seen many gateways some carved in light, others in agony. But none are so sacred as the Torka.

They were never meant for the masses. Not shrines for worship nor thrones for the proud. They were etched into the fabric of a world already listening, placed where reality softened and sang.

In the beginning, they were only stone markers laid by those who stepped lightly between dimensions. The inhabitants of that world saw the Precursors enter, and they remembered. These ancient beings laid down stone. Stone that hummed. Stone that waited.

Those who bear the mark know this truth in their bones: the Torka is not a door. It is a question. Only a shaman may answer it and only with their whole soul.

The Torka stands enshrouded in layers of myths and tales. As the Arcadian tribe's oral traditions narrate, these monoliths were gifts to Earth, bequeathed millions of years ago by a celestial race dubbed the Precursors. It is said that the boundaries of time, space, or dimensions did not tether these interdimensional voyagers. They could traverse every conceivable plane of existence.

Their journeys were enabled by a distinct conduit called the energy vortex. When these vortexes converged with a planet or realm, the Precursors manifested these towering monoliths as signposts or portals. Ancient societies on Earth christened these structures Torkas.

To the Precursors, Torkas were more than mere symbolic edifices; they were intricate gateways that allowed effortless transition between worlds. But this was not without limitations. Only individuals with the lineage of a Precursor could unlock a Torka's potential. As centuries transformed into millennia, the once frequent visits of the Precursors dwindled until they became mere whispers of the past.

Remnants of their celestial touch lingered on. Descendants on Earth who bore the distinctive genetic markers of the Precursors discovered their innate affinity with the Torkas. Endowed by this rare ability, they became anointed as shamans. These shamans, while holding a place of reverence, bore the hallowed responsibility of guiding departed spirits, ensuring their serene journey to the subsequent plane of existence.

But the legends don't end there. There are tales of audacious shamans harnessing the power of the Torka to venture into alien realms, driven by curiosity or purpose. In their quest to explore these unknown realms, they would sometimes find themselves playing the role of saviors, rescuing entities or creatures entangled in cataclysmic events in their worlds. But at its core, the Torka remains a beacon of hope and guidance, its primary purpose now being to shepherd the souls of the departed to their destined afterlife, wrapping them in the comforting embrace of eternity.

***

Trace pinched the bridge of her pointed nose. The silence of her area was a balm she hadn't realized she needed.

She had nodded once as the last report came in. A rare satisfied grin touched her lips, but only for a second. They'd moved fast, done well. But... Trace's fist clenched around the personnel file. Furfoot's face stared back from the ID photo. One of her handpicked team. She slammed the file shut.

Then there was the matter of the intruders themselves: six individuals with unknown intentions. What were they after? And what other threats lurked in the shadows? Trace pulled up the security footage again. Rewound. Watched the breach point. Rewound again.

Before going to the pool, she stopped by the changing room. Once she'd donned her bathing suit, she flexed her shoulders in the mirror, watching the muscles shift beneath her skin. Her dorsal fin cut a sharp line down her spine. She bared her teeth, revealing rows of perfect, gleaming points. The gills on the sides of her neck contrasted with the dark red muscles visible behind them. At the tip, her dorsal fin elongated and narrowed to a sharp point. As her lustrous black hair fell over her shoulders, it brushed the top of her breasts. Her two-piece suit perfectly complemented the light blue and cream shades that made up her skin. Every inch of her was pure apex predator. She looked in the mirror, adjusted the strap across her chest, and gave her reflection a satisfied nod.

She emerged from the changing room and headed straight for her favorite lounge chair. As always, it had been placed in the optimal position to catch the sun rays filtering through the glass ceiling. The expansive room measured one hundred feet by forty feet and was divided into sections. The lower part housed a deep, wide pool. The water was chilled to Trace's liking and sophisticated pump system created an artificial current. Elevated about thirty feet above it was a platform, with a raised area behind it containing various intriguing devices.

One of the captured intruders was standing on the platform, hands bound. The remaining Arcadians were imprisoned in a large transparent chamber on the opposite side of the pool. Every one of them stood close to the glass, eyes fixed on their comrade.

A door at the far end of the room creaked open to reveal Professor Hare. He approached with deliberate steps. As he neared the edge, he caught sight of Trace and acknowledged her presence with a nod.

She adjusted her posture, bending one leg and stretching out the other. Her mouth was already watering. She knew what was coming.

Professor Hare ascended the stairs to the raised platform. When he reached the top, he circled his captive slowly, his lab coat swishing with each step. "Your fate rests on how you respond to the next few questions."

The bound figure was a wolf, broad-shouldered beneath the restraints, his fur still streaked with dull patches of adhesive the solvent hadn't fully dissolved. Tufts along his shoulders and muzzle stuck together in hardened ridges, giving him a rough, battle-worn look. He held himself with quiet defiance, his amber eyes steady and unbroken.

His gaze was fixed somewhere past Hare's shoulder, toward a point only he could see. After several moments, he closed his eyes and drew in a deep breath. "You'll get no answers from me, Hare. Proceed with whatever you intend."

Professor Hare stopped directly before him and peered at him, head on one side, like he was an interesting specimen in a petri dish. "Why did you break in? What was your aim?"

The wolf's eyes snapped open, meeting Hare's gaze with surprising intensity. "Our aim was to restore balance to a world you've been driving towards ruin."

"Your kind are all the same." Hare's nose wrinkled with disdain. He clasped his hands behind his back and paced along the edge of the platform. "Blind to the enlightenment and progress that knowledge brings. Content in your outdated world, hands buried in the earth, when there's so much more you could achieve."

The wolf curled his lip, revealing the edge of a fang. "That's the narrative you've constructed to justify the harmful advancements you champion."

"Absurd," Hare muttered. His whiskers bristled and his foot began an agitated tap on the platform floor. "I innovate and push technological boundaries to better all, steering us toward a brighter tomorrow."

The wolf leaned forward against his restraints, eyes suddenly ablaze with an almost bloody hue. "Hare, you misuse extraterrestrial technology." His voice dropped to a harsh growl. "You propel us forward with tools and devices beyond your comprehension. You ride the coattails of other scientists, attempting to replicate their achievements."

"Lies!" Hare's voice ricocheted around the room, the sudden volume making even Trace flinch. The detainees in the transparent chamber watched the exchange with bated breath, some pressing against the glass.

Goosebumps broke out on Trace's skin and she rose to her feet, muscles tensing as she sensed the situation escalating toward its inevitable conclusion.

Hare smoothed down his lab coat with trembling hands. When he spoke again, his voice had returned to its measured calm. "This is your last chance. Why the infiltration? What were you hoping to accomplish?"

The wolf straightened his spine. He looked toward the chamber one final time, then he refocused on Hare. "I've said all I wish to. Do your worst."

The room held its breath. Even the hum of the lights seemed to falter. Without another word, Hare reached into his lab coat and produced a small gray remote. At the press of a button, a red indicator illuminated beneath the platform.

There was a mechanical groan as a hinge mechanism released. The floor under the wolf gave way, and he plummeted with a startled cry. He crashed into the rippling water below with a splash that echoed throughout the chamber. As he submerged, the ropes binding his arms dissolved into nothing.

Confusion flickered across the wolf's face as he surfaced, finding himself suddenly unbound. Hope sparked in his eyes, and he began swimming toward the pool's edge with powerful strokes.

Trace slipped into the water without disturbing the surface. The wolf was so focused on his escape that he remained oblivious to her presence beneath him.

Trace's powerful tail propelled her through the water like a torpedo while her quarry swam above her. She held back, toying with him, savoring his impending defeat. He was on the cusp of safety, his fingers almost touching the pool's edge, when she struck. She seized his leg, dragging him back into deeper waters.

The wolf's eyes bulged. He gasped, legs kicking wildly beneath the surface. No longer swimming, just flailing. Reluctant for the fun to end, Trace released him. He made another frantic bid for the edge, swimming with all his remaining strength.

This time, Trace struck in earnest. Darting forward with preternatural speed, she swiped her dorsal fin across the wolf's chest, leaving a deep and bleeding gash in its wake. A cry of pain tore from his throat. He clutched at his wound as blood bloomed around him in a crimson cloud. His strokes gradually became weaker.

Trace circled slowly, savoring the metallic scent in the water. Her strokes were effortless. Deliberate. This was what she was made for. Despite his injuries, the wolf fought on, twisting and turning in a desperate attempt to evade his fate.

Trace watched him with the patience of a seasoned predator. She sliced through the water with smooth, measured turns, each approach closer than the last. The wolf could feel her icy stare as she drew near and prepared for the final strike.

His labored breathing echoed throughout the silent pool, each wet gasp signaling his fading strength.

Trace locked eyes with her prey. A moment of silent connection amid the chaos. In that fleeting instant, the wolf's gaze held a mixture of terror, defiance, while Trace's eyes shimmered with excitement. Time seemed to pause as their fatal ballet reached its climax.

Then it was all over.

The Tularian dove deeper, dragging her struggling prey with her. From his vantage point, Professor Hare observed as the wolf disappeared below the turbulent water, now crimson with blood. A terrible silence enveloped the pool.

Hare jotted down a few observations in his datapad, then shifted his gaze to the captive audience. Some stood with fists clenched, their knuckles white with fury, while others wept openly.

"Let this serve as a lesson." Hare's voice cut through the heavy air like a scalpel. "Resistance is in vain. Opposition to my agenda will be met ruthlessly. Reflect upon the pool's grim shade of red. It foreshadows your potential fate should you withhold the answers I seek."

The door closed behind him with a soft click that echoed like thunder in the silent chamber.

Chapter Twelve

Spider Chase

There is a rhythm to every world. Some honor it. Others try to overwrite it with steel and circuits.

When the Arcadians turned from the cities, it was not out of fear. It was foreknowledge. They knew the shape of collapse long before the first machines began to speak, long before time itself was pulled into equations.

And so they became the planet's memory. Its watchers. Its whisperers.

After the Great Divide, the Arcadians made a choice to detach themselves from the urban sprawl and the relentless march of technology. They believed in the sanctity of Earth and its spirits, emphasizing that life's answers lay in communion with the planet rather than the machines.

For all of that, while they chose a life away from the cities, they could not ignore the growing shadow of progress looming over the horizon. From their natural retreats, they watched with increasing trepidation as the cities expanded and technology advanced at an unprecedented rate. To the Arcadians, these were not milestones of achievement but harbingers of calamity.

And their concerns were not unfounded. The drive for innovation threatened to unearth powers that could jeopardize the planet. The Arcadians remembered the old tales warnings from past civilizations that fell, not because of external adversaries but because of their hubris and unchecked ambitions.

Despite their detachment from city life, the Arcadians felt it was their duty to monitor these developments. They sent emissaries, skilled in the old ways but adept at navigating the modern world, to gather intelligence and assess the potential threats. These envoys would report back at regular intervals, ensuring the Arcadians remained informed and prepared.

Deep down, they hoped for a harmonious coexistence in which the allure of technology and the wisdom of the natural world could intertwine. But until that balance was achieved, they stood vigilant, ready to act as Earth's last line of defense against the unintended consequences of society's creations.

***

The door to the habitat's decompression chamber slid open. Lanell tightened her grip on the folded capture net at her side, uncertain what she might be walking into. She felt a gentle breeze as the pressure equalized between the two rooms. Her shoulders stiffened as the humid air pressed against her fur. The dense foliage from the trees muted the light that tried to pierce through the ceiling window. Small tubes sprouted from some of the trees. Now and then, they released puffs of steam, adding yet more humidity to the environment.

Lanell's furry ears perked up and tilted forward, straining to pick up even the slightest sound. She closed her eyes and focused on the surrounding silence. The faint rustle of leaves, the drip of condensation everything sharpened as she ignored her other senses and honed in on what she could hear.

Nothing. Just the normal ambient sounds of the artificial rainforest.

She cast her gaze to the left and then to the right, but nothing caught her eye. As she advanced forward, she kept watch on ground in front of her. Eventually, her patient search was rewarded. A thick silken dragline stretched between two trees, obstructing her path.

"Goodness," she mused, "this must belong to a colossal spider."

She approached it and saw it ascended the tree before her. Suddenly, she remembered the conversation she'd had with Dr. Crusher. The thought of the spider on her back made her quicken her pace, avoiding any contact with the branches and foliage. She winced and shivered as she brushed imaginary legs off her arms.

"Focus on the positive," she whispered to herself, ignoring the little voice inside her that demanded to know what the positive in this situation was.

Weaving her way through the dense habitat, Lanell continued her search for the elusive arachnid, making sure to scan around *and* above her for any clues.

She emerged from the underbrush and found herself in an area where the foliage was less dense. The light pouring through the glass ceiling was as good as a breath of fresh air. She tilted her face upward and exhaled.

A sharp burst of static from her radio, followed by an impatient voice, interrupted the serene interlude. "Lanell, have you located the asset yet?"

Lanell tightened her grip on the radio. "Professor Hare, I'm in Habitat 4. There are signs of the spider. Please exercise some patience; these things take time. Besides, aren't you supposed to be interrogating someone right now?"

"Lanell, the asset you're after is pivotal to our first-generation project. We're gathering vital data from it. And regarding the interrogation, I wrap up such tasks promptly." His voice sharpened further. "I trust you understand the asset's worth. Ensure its safety and the safety of the habitat's inhabitants. The responsibility is on your shoulders."

Lanell rolled her eyes. "I'm well aware. Let me work."

"Just make sure you complete "

She silenced the device with a firm click. "Lanell out," she muttered, holstering the radio.

Her ears perked as she detected an unfamiliar noise emanating from nearby. The quiet gurgle sounded like something being expelled. Her brow wrinkled. There was a micro-second's pause then, acting on some instinct from deep in her hind brain, she leaped to the side, narrowly avoiding a glob of slime that hurtled through the air and struck the branches of a nearby tree with a wet *sploit*. Viscous residue clung to the bark as it oozed downward and dripped onto the forest floor.

Tracing the trajectory of the goo, Lanell spotted a massive snail, lounging under a tree on the far side of the clearing. "Of course, it would choose to sunbathe in here," she grumbled.

The snail, spanning at least five feet, swiveled its eyestalks toward her, and its colors darkened in agitation.

"Great. They should've moved these creatures. Now, alongside the spider, I have to dodge this snail."

A sudden prickling sensation on her nylon-clad leg made her breath hitch. A chill shot through her limbs as she looked down, The oversized spider was furry, gray and covered in coarse bristles. Eight ink-black marbles stared insolently up at her while its fuzzy legs each about twelve inches long clung to her calf. It began grooming its gleaming black fangs with its pedipalps.

Lanell slowed her breathing and forced her muscles to remain still.

Stay calm.

Just when she thought the situation couldn't get any worse, she heard the whispering scrunch of leaves as the disgruntled snail approached.

"Well, on the bright side, I've found the spider."

As Lanell weighed her options, her gaze settled on a nearby net, the intended tool to capture her quarry. The creature began moving up her calf, the little claws at the tips of its legs pinching through the nylon to grip the fur on her leg.

If it just gets off me, I can grab the net....

Lanell remained motionless, fighting the urge to freak out as a giant spider crawled over her leg. The crunching of leaves grew louder as the snail inched closer and closer.

"Please, please just let me be boring enough for the snail to lose interest," she whispered.

The immense spider had reached her thigh and was now clinging to her hip. She stared down incredulously as it sat there calmly, absorbed in its own little world. Then it extended what looked to be a pair of extra legs. Lanell's eyes widened as the small appendages unfolded and fluttered a few times before gaining momentum. With rapid flapping motions, the massive spider lifted off and hovered at her eye level before zooming off toward the tops of the nearby trees. Lanell watched it settle on a high branch and resume grooming itself.

"Well, I'll be," she marveled. "That's why this asset is so valuable. They've engineered it into some kind of hybrid."

She rose to her feet, retrieved the oversized insect net, and approached the tree where the spider had taken refuge. The branches were slick with residue from the snail's earlier assault. As she walked, she kept an eye out for any sticky goo that might drip from above, anxious to protect her lab coat. Unfortunately, in her single-minded focus on the threat from above, she forgot to keep watch on the ground. A large puddle of goo had accumulated in a shallow depression on the ground. Oblivious to the hazard, she planted her left foot squarely in the center of the slimy quagmire.

"Eww!"

Fortunately, the snail had diverted its attention to a nearby pile of leaf mold and was now grazing happily.

Lanell sighed, "*Whew*. Now to focus on that spider."

As she attempted to move forward, she felt an unexpected tug on her foot. The substance wasn't just slimy, it was sticky and gluey. Lanell struggled to lift her foot, but gooey tendrils, reminiscent of a sticky liquid rubber, yanked her boot back into place.

"Dang it," she muttered, wrestling to free her foot from the tenacious snail mucus. It was becoming more and more apparent that she was stuck.

"Wonderful."

Despite her best efforts to pull her foot free, the secretion clung stubbornly to the sole of her boot. Eventually, she threw her hands up in defeat. "Fine, have it your way."

After a few deft wiggles of her ankle, her burgundy nylon-covered foot emerged, leaving the boot stuck in the goo.

Now painfully conscious of each step and terrified of what she might put her foot in next, Lanell sidled up to the tree's base, keeping herself hidden from the snail while maintaining a watchful eye on the spider. She'd just found the perfect vantage point when a growl and a familiar rustling squelch echoed from behind her. Whipping around, she saw the snail oozing towards her.

"You know," she said, putting her hands on her hips., "I'm really getting tired of this game."

She kicked off her remaining boot. It spun through the air and she snatched it mid-flight. Then she hurled it at the branch where the spider was squatting. The boot struck its target, dislodging the arachnid and sending it tumbling toward the ground.

Wasting no time, Lanell dashed across the clearing, her feet a burgundy blur against the lush grass. With a perfectly timed leap, she thrust her net forward and caught the spider midair. She quickly secured the open end, ensuring it couldn't escape.

"And that's how you do it."

Her grin faded as a deep gurgling sound rolled through the foliage. She turned and there it was, the habitat's oversized snail, its glistening shell reflecting the filtered light. Lanell's ears flattened. Quick glance left, then right no clear path. She scanned the perimeter, searching for the safest way around before it slimed directly across her exit route.

She swiftly made her way to the doors, more than ready to leave the controlled environment. A sharp *whoosh sound* filled the air as the habitat doors opened. To her surprise, her father was waiting for her, along with one of the facility security guards.

"Lanell," the old goat said, looking over her anxiously, "did you get it?"

"Yeah, Pop, I have it," she said. "Though, as you can see, I lost my boots. It appears someone neglected to remove the snails before I entered." She handed the net containing the trapped and wiggling asset to the security guard, "Treat it carefully. Make sure it reaches its destination."

The guard nodded, replying, "Yes, ma'am," before departing with the net held securely.

With him gone, Lanell refocused on her father. "Did you know the asset was a bio-engineered spider?" she asked.

Earl gaped at his daughter. "I wasn't aware. I knew there were discussions about bioengineering, but I didn't think they'd done it."

"It had *wings*." Lanell's voice carried more than a hint of disgust. "Dad, if you don't mind, can you arrange for Dr. Crusher to visit the habitat and collect my boots? One is glued to the floor in one location, and the other should be under a tree someplace."

"Of course. I'll ensure they are recovered and returned to my favorite daughter."

Lanell paused and shot him a teasing wink. "You mean your number one daughter?"

"Why can't it be both?"

Lanell gave him a brief, hard hug, breathing in the comforting smell of his fur. In her mind, she could still feel slow insidious prickle of the spider's feet as it climbed up her leg.

Chapter Thirteen

Planning Ahead

The weave tightens.

Where once I spoke of balance, of echoes and origins, now the strands twist in silence, pulled by hands that do not understand the tapestry they tangle.

Some chapters require no narrator, only the patience of the Watcher.

For now, let their ambition speak louder than my voice.

***

Delicate frost adorned the glass of the expansive meeting room window. Chancellor Trinn looked out over the icy city of Chillborn, her eyes drawn to the frozen plains beyond the gates. To the rootward, she could make out towering peaks. Their sharp edges were obscured by the swirling clouds that seemed to dance around them. As her gaze shifted spineward, the landscape changed: harsh plains gave way to a creeping expanse of permafrost.

The sight reminded her of her home world, where frozen methane covered the ground and sparkled under a blue sun. No breath to fog the glass. No pulse to quicken. But something in her core stuttered for a nanosecond as she stared out at the icy horizon. It wasn't her home, but it echoed it. She tapped a fingertip against the frost-laced pane. Protocols urged stillness; the twitch betrayed something older, hungrier.

Her gaze didn't linger. Internal schematics flickered in her HUD timelines thresholds, energy yields. The collider. The breach. The way home.

A memory intruded: methane mists brushing the undercarriage of her native form, twin moons overhead bathing everything in cold fluorescence. She had abandoned that world. Betrayed it. But she would not return empty-handed. She pictured veins of molten trilineum writhing under this planet's skin, oceans of fire waiting to be cracked open. Her world would drink deep, and she would be the hand holding the cup. This world would be dragged home behind her like a prize. Her eyes hardened as the frosty winds sculpted the endless ice.

The heavy door creaked open, breaking the stillness. Arzul Coldstream entered. Her powerful, white-furred frame filled the doorway, and the soft thud of her padded feet on the stone floor resonated through the chamber. Her deep blue eyes scanned the room with quiet shrewdness as she moved toward Trinn.

The chancellor turned from the window, and the two leaders faced each other, a silent acknowledgment passing between them.

Arzul stopped a few feet away. "Trinn, you don't make it here too often. I trust there's something important you would like to see me about."

Trinn smiled. "Indeed, there is a good reason I am here," she replied smoothly. "Some changes are coming. And with them, opportunity. I wanted to see how you feel about that."

"We both know my answer to that question depends on a lot of factors."

"Oh, I know," Trinn said. "But this is pertaining to the Council of Seven."

Arzul's nostrils flared, and a sharp breath hissed through her teeth an unmistakable Chillborn signal of political exhaustion. "Trinn, you know how I feel about this governance."

Trinn's smile widened. "I am well aware. That's why I'm here. The changes I'm speaking of could shift the balance of power within the council. Think of it as an opportunity. An opportunity for Chillborn to gain more influence, to reshape the council in a way that aligns with your vision."

She let the silence stretch, knowing Arzul was already weighing the losses and gains with meticulous exactitude.

The Ursidi studied her for a while the way a fisherman might contemplate a suspicious crack in the ice. "So, what do you have in mind that you're bringing this proposal to my attention?"

Trinn met Arzul's piercing gaze and weighed her next words carefully. "I can't divulge all the details yet, but I assure you, something monumental is about to happen. This event will shake the Council of Seven to its core." She stepped closer, voice dropping to silken purr. "When it happens, those who stand with me from the outset will be the architects of the new order."

Arzul drummed her hands against the table. Ideas. Risks. Open doors. Too many variables. Not enough time. Her silence was not hesitation but calculation. Let Trinn speak first. Always let the ambitious ones fill the silence.

"And where do I fit into this new vision of yours?" she asked at last, cautious yet curious.

Trinn stood beside her and gestured as if to paint a picture on the empty air in front of them. "Chillborn has thrived under your leadership despite the Council's oversight. Imagine what you could achieve with even less restraint, with a council that supports your vision rather than hinders it. You would expand, innovate, govern without the constant pushback."

Arzul's jaw shifted. "And the risks?" she asked, voice cool but probing.

"The risks are real," Trinn conceded. "But with high risk comes high reward. Our success would not only secure our power but ignite a renaissance for both our worlds. We would lead, not as usurpers but as reformers. As saviors of a system that teeters on collapse."

A hush descended on the room. Arzul's expression thawed slightly. "And what of the specifics?"

Trinn turned away just in time to conceal the triumphant flash in her eyes. "All in due time, Arzul. For now, we lay groundwork. The details will come when the moment is right."

"Very well, Trinn," Arzul growled. "We will proceed as you suggest."

Trinn inclined her head. "Excellent. Now, has there been any news from the council that I should know about?"

Arzul's expression darkened. "The council has been quiet, but discontent simmers. Some are frustrated with resource allocation and worsening shortages." She tapped a control in the table. A hologram flickered up, showing a storage hall with yawning empty spaces. "Our grain stores are thinning. The games our peers play don't feed my people. I am growing tired of it."

"Intriguing," Trinn mused. "Discontent could be an asset. If we channel it, it could quicken our plans."

Arzul scratched her cheek with a steely claw. "Yes, but we must be cautious. The council still holds power. Any misstep could be ruinous."

"Agreed. We proceed carefully."

Arzul hesitated, then added, "There are rumors that Rith is working on new technology. If true, it could be a threat."

Trinn waved her hand in a gesture of feigned nonchalance. "Psh! Rith always trumpets projects that never see daylight."

There was no reason for Arzul to know about her plans for collider. Not yet, anyway.

The holographic map bathed their faces in cold light. Two leaders plotting the course of worlds, unaware that their ambitions would soon collide with a much more powerful force.

Chapter Fourteen

Cause for Concern

Professor Hare marched toward his office, ignoring the nods and greetings of those he passed in the corridor. The wolf's blood-red eyes still burned in his mind.

You misuse extraterrestrial technology. You propel us forward with tools beyond your comprehension.

The echo chased him down the hall. Somehow that insignificant terrorist had seen something in him. He'd seen the truth. Science had long hailed Hare as a pioneer; his 'discoveries' were praised and coveted. But every triumph had come from Trinn. He had taken the knowledge she'd gifted and filtered it through his hands as if it were his own.

No one can know.

The thought burrowed in like a tick. Was it someone on the inside? Someone close who knew Trinn's secret? The idea twisted in his gut. Every nod in the corridor felt too curious. Every sealed door too thin. He wasn't used to feeling exposed, but today, the walls pressed in.

By the time he reached his office, suspicion had tainted everything. He paused at the threshold, eyeing his administrative assistant. "Stacie, I mustn't be disturbed. No exceptions."

The Felivex technician nodded. "Understood, sir."

He shut the door behind him and crossed to his desk. After sinking into his chair, he activated his console and pulled up the secure files. Line after line of access data glowed across the screen. He searched for any hint, any anomaly that might reveal how their work had been compromised. A chill crawled up his spine.

Even the walls might be listening.

Hare keyed into the conference system. For a moment, the screen remained dark, then one of Chancellor Trinn's large, round eyes blinked into view. She adjusted her position so that her gaze locked with his.

"Hare, what a delightful surprise!" she exclaimed. "In case you've forgotten, I was scheduled to meet with Arzul today." The camera shifted, revealing the snowy bulk of the polar bear, who rumbled a deep greeting.

"Hello, Hare. How are you today?"

Hare attempted a polite smile. "I'm well, Arzul. Thank you. But I need a private word with Chancellor Trinn. Would that be possible?"

Arzul studied him a moment, then gave a solemn nod. "Of course, Professor." She tilted her head graciously and stepped out of frame.

Trinn raised a brow. "So, what is so pressing that you'd interrupt my schedule?"

"I think you need to come by here when you are done," Hare said. "This discussion has to be face-to-face."

That gave her pause. He'd never made such a request, not with this much urgency. The playful edge vanished from her tone. "What has transpired?"

He looked around him, then lowered his voice. "During an interrogation this morning, there was mention of my use of extraterrestrial technology."

Trinn blinked rapidly. "That's... unexpected." She nodded once and made a visible effort to gather herself. "I'll rearrange my schedule. Two hours. Prepare for my arrival."

"Good. The walls even virtual ones have ears. I will make sure we have privacy."

Her lipless mouth compressed to a hard line. "Very well. Ensure everything is secure for when I arrive."

The screen went dark.

Hare leaned back, mind racing. Secure meant more than locked doors. Data this volatile demanded vigilance against sabotage. He accessed the directory and pulled up Tabitha Snickers. He could rely on Trace for muscle, but he called on Tabitha when a job required finesse surveillance, diagnostics, security tech.

The call connected. The walls of the research complex blurred past the lens, and then a whiskered face swung into view. Tabitha's bright, piercing eyes glinted with mischief. She was in motion.

"Tabitha," Hare sighed. "Didn't we discuss you skating inside the facility?"

Tabitha smirked. "Professor, I'm more efficient on wheels. This place is massive. Would you rather I walked?" She spun mid-call, and the background became a whirling streak of color.

Despite himself, Hare felt a flicker of amusement. "Just... be careful. We don't need more problems."

"Understood." She tapped her wrist console mid glide. "I'm already patching into the mainframe. Any areas you want prioritized?"

"Physical security first," Hare said. "Scan my office immediately. Then the conference rooms. Finally the Tier 1 labs."

Her expression sobered at his tone. "Alright. Redirecting. Two minutes."

"Thank you." He cut the call. His knuckles whitened as he gripped the edge of the desk.

If this breach ties to the Arcadians, the fallout could paint a target on the facility itself.

A buzz crackled from his intercom. "Professor Hare, Tabitha is here."

"Send her in."

The door swung open. Tabitha rolled in. She tapped her wrist console and the wheels on her shoes retracted, dropping her onto solid footing. A checkered top hugging her frame, a black pleated skirt swaying with each motion, striped socks that reached her knees a mix of chaos and precision that was pure Tabitha.

"I got here fast as I could," she said briskly, pulling a handheld device from her kit. She began scanning. The detector chirped as it caught a signal.

"Look at that," she murmured. "Something's transmitting in a masked frequency." She held up the display for him to see. "They're hiding in a standard wireless band, using a sub-channel to keep it covert."

Hare knitted his brow. "So, they hid in plain sight. Clever, but sloppy."

"Exactly. Classic Arcadian tricks." Following the readout, she moved to his bookshelf and crouched low. With a flick, she dislodged a small circular device from under the base of a globe, then held it up between two fingers. "What do you want done with it?"

"Can you trace it? Block it? Perhaps use it to feed false data?"

"Not sure yet." She slipped it into her kit. "I'll need to analyze it further."

"Take it. After this, sweep the other sites. Then the entire facility. I want every bug out of here."

"No one breaches security on my watch, Professor." She extended her wrist, and the wheels snapped back into place. Then she gave herself a push and glided out of the room, calling out to Stacie as she passed.

Hare blew out a breath and sat back down. Somehow, the office felt heavier now, and the walls pressed in closer. A spy had walked his halls, and he would root them out before the wolf's warning proved true.

Chapter Fifteen

The Gathering Storm

Lanell padded down the quiet hallway toward Wing B, her toes curling against the chill of the tile. She sighed. Her dad's office would be warm, and the calming atmosphere might help clear her head. Normally, her boots echoed with every step, now the soft shuffle of burgundy stockings barely broke the silence.

Wing B had always been more serene than the bustling labs, its hushed corridors reserved for administrative and maintenance offices. Earl's office always smelled faintly of oil and old metal. She used to sit cross-legged on the floor, blueprints spread out like treasure maps while her dad tightened bolts and told stories. She recalled tracing the lines with her finger, pretending she could read them. This pipe feeds coolant to the reactor, Earl would say, tapping his wrench against the plans. No room for error.

The door to the office stood ajar. A soft golden light spilled into the corridor, along with the sound of music from the radio and the familiar tang of machine oil.

She found Earl at his desk, tools and datapads spread out before him. The room was cluttered yet organized, filled with mechanical parts, strange implements no one but Earl knew the use for, and the ever-present cup of black coffee steaming beside him.

He looked up, eyes crinkling. "Ah, Lanell! Glad to see you again, little one. Still haven't gotten your boots back?"

She smiled ruefully. "Not yet. I'm sure they'll bring them to me whenever they find them."

"Good. So does that mean you're going to hang out for a bit?"

"Yeah," she said, perching stiffly on the corner of the desk. "But there's something I need to talk about. Been eating at me since this morning."

Earl set aside his work and gestured toward the couch in the corner. Its faded upholstery was worn shiny, marked by countless conversations just like this one.

Once they were seated, Lanell hesitated, then met his gaze. "Earlier this morning, before the spider retrieval, I was in the collider with Hare and Myles. Hare was being his usual grandiose self, but something about what he said struck me differently this time."

Earl frowned. "Go on."

"It's not the tech that scares me," Lanell said. "It's who's holding the wrench. Hare's not just curious. He's aiming at something, and I don't think it's truth." She drew a breath. "Today, when he spoke, there was this... intensity in his eyes. I don't know how to explain it. It felt like he sees the collider not as a tool for discovery but as a way to reach some other end."

"You think he might be motivated by something other than scientific curiosity?"

"I do," she admitted. "It's just a gut feeling, but it's strong. And between that and the Arcadians apprehended earlier "

Earl leaned forward. "Honey, what Arcadians?"

Lanell raised her eyebrows, taken aback by the sudden urgency in his tone. "Just a small group. They made some kind of assault on the facility walls. We were finishing up the final checks when Trace called in to report a situation. I didn't hear the full context, but it sounded like six Arcadians were caught on campus. And one of the security team was arrested too." She plucked at the material of her tights. "But what shook me most was Hare's response when I asked about the interrogation. He looked right at me and said that it wasn't for me to know. I'm his assistant; I've worked with him for years. Why would he say that unless he's hiding something?"

Earl's knuckles whitened on the cushion. "That *is* odd," he said tightly.

Lanell gave a one-shouldered shrug. "I don't know. I've always felt Hare was a straight shooter. But today, he seemed so prickly and on-edge. Maybe he was protecting someone... or *something*."

"External pressure, maybe? Someone powerful leaning on him?"

Lanell toyed with the end of her tail, tugging at loose tufts of fur. "The collider tech is revolutionary. It's bound to attract attention and not necessarily the good kind."

Their exchange was cut short by a knock.

"Come in," Earl called.

Dr. Crusher stepped in. He was cradling a pair of boots as though they were precious artifacts. There wasn't a scratch on them, not even a smear of slime. "Thought you might be missing these," he said, offering them to Lanell with a crooked smile. "Seems they've had quite the adventure."

Lanell grinned and snatched them back eagerly. "You're a lifesaver." As she slipped them on, she glanced up. "That slime from the snails clings like glue. What exactly is it?"

Crusher leaned against the desk and slipped seamlessly into lecture mode. "Technically, it's a mix of mucus and a specific secretion. In the wild, it cushions movement and doubles as defense. When stressed, the snails release more, and that's when the adhesive properties really kick in. We're researching its potential for high-grade adhesives and sealants. I've even got prototypes planned for military and security applications."

Lanell raised a brow. "You're telling me snail slime could revolutionize the adhesive industry?"

"Absolutely. Though it's... slow to catch on." He flashed her a grin. "See what I did there?"

Lanell laughed, shaking her head. "Always with the jokes, Dr. Crusher."

Earl groaned. "That's enough snail puns for one day."

Crusher chuckled and pushed off the desk. "And as much as I'd love to stay, I need to get back to the lab. Ms. Lanell, thank you for your consideration with the snails. Both of you have a good day."

As soon as he was gone, Earl turned back to his daughter. "What do we do about Hare?"

"We need to watch him. If he's hiding something, I want to know what."

Earl nodded gravely. "I agree. But there's something else we need to discuss, and this isn't the place."

"Your place or mine?"

"Yours. Tonight. This needs privacy."

"Dad? This sounds serious."

His expression softened, and he lowered his voice. "Lanell, there's more to your story. Things I never told you. Things I should've."

A chill ran through her. "About my parents? And me? What do you mean?

Earl's face creased with pain, and he rubbed absentmindedly at his broken horn "It's difficult to put into words, but the story of who you are and how you came to be under my care isn't as simple as you believe."

"Why now?"

"What Hare's digging at, it's not just science anymore. If someone else uncovers it first..." His jaw tightened. "I won't let that happen to you."

Lanell suddenly felt like there was something stuck in her throat. "How can you ask me not to worry after saying that?"

"You're right." Earl placed a hand on her shoulder. "I shouldn't have hinted without telling you more. I'll explain everything, but in the right way. I promise."

She nodded slowly and swallowed. "I'll try not to overthink. But this feels big."

"No matter what, we'll face it together."

Lanell stood, flexing her toes inside her boots. "Well, now that I've got these back, I should head out. I'll see you tonight."

"I'll be there," Earl promised.

She managed a smile. "You be safe, Dad."

"I will, little one."

Chapter Sixteen

Seeing Eye-to-Eye

Late afternoon cast long shadows across the lab floors. One by one, workstations powered down with soft beeps, and their displays faded to black. Conversations dwindled. Chairs scraped back. The day's quiet exodus began tired hands, glassy eyes, a yawn from someone already fantasizing about supper and bed.

From his position on the walkway above, Professor Hare watched them like a general at the end of a battle. Through the glass wall he saw Dr. Hogsweth, who had been buried in genomic research earlier, now chatting with Sarah from robotics. A trio of interns trudged out in a loose huddle, laughing over something dumb, backpacks slung over one shoulder.

He drummed his fingers on the hand rail and eyed the reinforced gate, barely visible through the windows. The Arcadians had not succeeded in their earlier sabotage, but they had already gained access to confidential files through covert means. Who among his staff might already be theirs? Which of these familiar faces had been wearing a mask?

Hare rubbed his temples. Trust, once so routine, now felt like a luxury.

He didn't have time for this now; there was too much at stake. Everything hinged on the collider his crown jewel. Too many years. Too many signatures. Too many ghosts. A machine one breath away from changing everything. Tomorrow, it would fire.

He fished his pad from his pocket and pulled up his schedule. The official time of the firing was mid-morning, but the fear of another attack gnawed at him. A pre-dawn firing fewer personnel, less exposure, a move the Arcadians wouldn't expect. Risky, yes. But safer.

Decision made, he keyed his comm. "Myles, I'm considering moving the collider firing to early tomorrow morning. I know it's a stretch, but it may be necessary. Can we manage it?"

There was a long silence on the other end before the reply came. "That's quite a pivot, Professor, but I understand. Give me a few hours. Calibrations, cooling cycles we'll need to work through the night."

"I know. But if anyone can, it's you."

"We'll make it happen."

"Thank you, Myles."

He'd barely closed the call before the comm chimed again. Stacie's aggressively cheerful voice burst through the speakers. "Professor Hare, Chancellor Trinn is here."

"Send her to my office."

When he got there, the Tularian android was already inside waiting, heel tapping impatiently. The hammerhead profile, with those wide-set eyes, always gave off the eerie sense that she was seeing more than she revealed.

"Hare," she said, voice edged, "explain how after so many years, our plans are suddenly at risk."

He rose. "It won't derail us," he snapped. "But it means we need a strategy for the Arcadians."

Trinn moved to the far side of the room and began the shutdown process on her android shell.

"Stop!" Hare barked. "Not here. What if there are cameras?"

Her response wasn't spoken. It slipped into his head like ice sliding down the back of the neck. *They already know about me, Hare. If they want a show, I'll give them one.*

"I might be able to manage damage control for the espionage," he hissed aloud, "but why hand them more to exploit?"

The Drowa emerged from the android's hatch. Hare suppressed a wave of revulsion as the gray tentacled body skittered across the floor towards him. Then, without warning, one limb lashed out and coiled around his wrist.

Hare's eyes rolled back. Reality peeled away. The office dissolved into smoke and shadows. A flickering bulb. The sharp tang of burning wires. He blinked and he was small again ears too big, glasses slipping.

From the haze came Lucious. "Lupus," he said, "you worry too much. We have this under control."

Hare's voice cracked. "Trinn, you know I hate it when you do this. Stop clothing yourself in my memories."

Lucious's form warped into Jeremiah Hare, their father. "You've always been sensitive, Lupus. Insightful. I read your memories not to invade, but to guide you."

"No," the young Hare whispered. "You don't guide; you manipulate. And you need to accept that the Arcadians know about you. This breach proves it."

The smoke thickened. Jeremiah's face rippled and morphed. A second later, Hare stood face-to-face with himself. She liked to wear his shape, always choosing the one that made him flinch the most.

"Let's work together," his reflection said, "and wipe them from existence."

Hare's cold stare didn't waver. "Get out of my mind."

The vision broke. His office reformed around him as the tentacle snapped away. The Drowa scuttled back and climbed into the android shell. The hatch sealed behind it with a muted *click*.

Trinn's voice was smooth and unperturbed. "Understand, I don't do this to make things awkward. I do it so we see eye-to-eye. We must be aligned."

"Yes," Hare said stiffly. "We are in the same boat, with the same goals."

"Good." She pivoted toward the door, dorsal fin swishing through the air.

Stacie barely looked up from her monitor as the chancellor exited. Lanell sat in the overstuffed chair, arms wrapped tightly around herself, eyes fixed on Trinn. She didn't blink. It was the stare of a student staring down a final exam.

Trinn swept past Stacie with a saccharine smile. "Have a good one, sweetie."

"Thank you, madam," Stacie answered automatically.

The Chancellor turned to Lanell. "Victoria, it's been too long. How have you been?"

Lanell rose from her chair, the picture of composure. "I've been well, Chancellor. Thank you."

"You're a gem," Trinn said lightly. "Always a pleasure. But duty calls. Take care, too-dles!" She swept out without a backward glance.

Chapter Seventeen

Holding the Cards Close

Lanell stopped just shy of the door, pulse beating hard in her throat. She forced her shoulders loose and tried to look casual.

Her fingers hovered on the handle a moment too long. When she finally pushed it open, the tremor in her chest made the motion feel heavier than it was. The shelves were crammed with leather-spined volumes. Lenses and brass caught the late afternoon light. Dust motes drifted in a slow ballet, but the air seemed to be holding its breath, as if the room was waiting for something. Faint murmurs were coming from one corner.

Lanell smoothed the wrinkles from her clothes and stepped inside. Professor Hare's reflection hovered in the window glass. His gaze was fixed on the trickle of staff disappearing into the glow of the parking lamps.

"Professor Hare?" she ventured.

He didn't answer at first. When he did speak, his voice sounded distant and weary. "Everything's changing, Lanell. Faster than we can keep up."

"Sir, is everything alright?"

He sighed and answered without turning. "Some days the weight of our work becomes overwhelming. Do you realize I have maintained this research facility at the highest standards for over thirty years? Nearly all the major breakthroughs on this planet originated here."

"I've always admired the work done here," she said carefully. "Your leadership is a big reason this facility is known. But I can't imagine the pressures you must feel."

Hare chuckled softly. "You see the accolades, the awards, the breakthroughs. But with those come responsibility. Every time we achieve something, the world watches for the next move."

"Professor, there's something specific I need to discuss. The asset I recovered from Habitat 4 was a winged spider. That doesn't happen naturally."

"Yes," Hare replied. "We gave it life. It flew. It spun a web. We did that, Lanell." His brow tightened, lips thinning. He turned from the window slowly, jaw set, ears angling back as if weighing his next words. "We live in times of immense challenge. Cities compete for knowledge and resources. The planet needs solutions." He gestured emphatically. "That spider's silk is stronger than any material we've tested. Its wings give range. That changes everything transport, defense, even medicine."

"But at what cost?" Lanell's voice sharpened. "Where do we draw the line between scientific advancement and ethics?"

"Sometimes advancing science means pushing limits. You need vision to ask the big questions and persistence to follow answers wherever they lead."

Lanell crossed her arms. "Creating a cross-species merely to compete with another city doesn't sit right with me. Enhancing fruit so it grows without soil, maybe. But a living creature? There *is* a difference."

"I understand your reservations," Hare said patiently. "It wasn't a decision taken lightly. With dwindling resources and escalating competition, we cannot ignore unconventional possibilities." He removed his glasses and began polishing the lenses with a corner of his lab coat. "Our competitors are not waiting. I assure you, every experiment undergoes ethical evaluation."

"But we must also be guided by our *moral* compass," Lanell insisted. "And there's one more thing from earlier today I need to ask about." She met his gaze directly. She hadn't planned to say anything, but the words came out before she had time to reconsider them. "'Lanell, that's not for you to know.' Professor Hare, I have issues with that. I'm your assistant. I assist you with everything, from ensuring you have your morning beverage to recovering rogue genetically modified spiders. Now you tell me you're doing something that's not for me to know?"

Hare's expression softened for a moment. "Your commitment is unquestionable, and you deserve transparency. Some projects, given their sensitivity, require exhaustive caution. It is not about trust but protection."

"Protection from what?"

He sighed. "Sometimes knowledge of certain experiments places a person at risk, not just from external threats but from the internal burden of that knowledge."

"But what does that have to do with interrogations of Arcadians?"

For a beat, he looked flummoxed; his mouth stayed half open a second too long. "The Arcadians are complicated. Their interests intersect with ours in ways that are not always apparent. Our dealings often revolve around technology and resources, but sometimes it becomes a matter of information."

"You expect me to accept being kept in the dark for my own good?"

"It's not only about protecting you, it's about maintaining operational integrity. The less you know about certain things, the lower the risk of unintentional leaks or compromises."

She subjected him to a probing stare.

What are you hiding?

"I know it's difficult," he continued. "But every decision I make and every secret I keep is in the best intentions for this facility and those who depend on it."

"Professor, I have always respected you and our mission. But when I'm left out of the loop, it's hard not to feel sidelined, hard not to doubt."

"I'm sorry. I wish it were simpler. All I ask is for your patience."

Lanell sighed. "I'll try. But you ask for loyalty while handing me blindfolds. I can only support you if I'm informed."

"Lanell." He folded his hands behind his back. "You're wrong to think I have abandoned trust." He paced ponderously. "I have trusted you more than anyone. I shielded you from things that could destroy you. That is not a blindfold, it *is* protection. And perhaps it's a kind of loyalty you won't understand until you stand where I stand."

Lanell's face was a mask of stillness. "Maybe," she said quietly. "But loyalty and obedience are not the same."

She let it hang long enough for its weight to settle. "I don't need to stand where you stand to know when something isn't right." She made as if to leave, then paused at the door and turned back to him.

"If shielding me from the truth is your way of protecting me, Professor, maybe it's time you trusted me to survive it. Is the firing still occurring at the time we planned, or has there been a change?"

"It's scheduled for the same time we discussed. Given the complexities, it's crucial we are both onsite early for final checks."

"Understood. I'll ensure everything is in place and the team is prepared."

"Thank you," he said, visibly relieved. "Your efficiency has always been invaluable."

As Lanell exited, Hare leaned back in his chair and rubbed his temples. As she left, Lanell did not see the sly smile that crept over his face.

Once the door clicked shut, he touched his communications screen. "Trace, come up here. We need to have an important discussion about tonight."

The chief of security responded with a nod. "I'm on my way now, sir."

"Excellent." He shut off the screen and sank into contemplative silence.

Chapter Eighteen

Arcadian Whispers

Earl lingered in the doorway of his office, fingers hooked over the frame, scanning the deserted corridor for stragglers. But only the drone of lights and the echoes of departing footsteps remained.

He retreated inside and locked the door behind him, cutting off the outside world. His oak desk reflected the golden glow of a lamp. For once, it was clean and polished instead of buried in papers.

It was time to retreat to his sanctuary. A corner of the workshop had been discretely curtained off and furnished with a plush azure mat, soft cushions, and leafy plants. Three lavender and sandalwood scented candles guttered gently, releasing a warm, fragrant haze that loosened the knot between his shoulders.

He slipped off his boots and sat cross-legged. *Quickly,* he thought. There wasn't much time before his meeting with Lanell. He placed his hands on his knees, thumb touching finger, and closed his eyes.

His breath slowed. The constant grind of the day thinned. Candlelight collapsed into a single thread, twisting into a horizonless void. Time peeled back like paper.

Earl stood in a place where the sky breathed. Colors beyond naming shimmered. Sounds, more felt than heard, moved through him. Luminous wisps drifted close, brushing him with a wisdom older than language.

From the shifting light came two forms elders of the Arcadian High Council. A fox with silver eyes, and a wolf whose voice carried the weight of stone.

"Earl," the fox said warmly. "It's been too long."

"Artemis," he answered, a flicker of relief in his voice. "Good to see you."

"My old friend, I trust you have news?" Her silver eyes roamed over him, absorbing every detail of his appearance.

"Yes. The collider, the infiltration. Tomorrow's firing is still on schedule. The breach caused no delay."

Artemis frowned. "So our efforts were wasted?"

"Not wasted. Lanell noticed something. She pressed Hare, and his response unsettled her."

"What did she sense?" Artemis asked eagerly.

"Hare flinched. Slipped. She saw it. Questioned him directly."

Artemis's fur glowed like a dying ember in the void. "Then this may be the crack. She can see for herself without you revealing your purpose here."

Earl grimaced. "I've kept my role hidden behind wrenches and oil. If she discovers on her own, we gain time. But as her guardian" his voice became thin and strained "I fear the weight of her heritage."

The wolf's deep voice rumbled like distant thunder. "Her lineage carries power that can both embolden and engulf. The question is not just of her readiness. It is how the world will respond when she awakens."

Artemis touched his arm. "Destiny has its timing. Trust your instincts, but when you reveal the truth, ensure she has support. We've seen moments like this define entire eras. For her, understanding her lineage will be such a moment."

Earl lowered his eyes. "What pains me most is watching her search for meaning."

"A guardian's role," the wolf said, "is also knowing when to release and trust."

"You've gone beyond any guardian's duty," Artemis added. "Your guidance will anchor her."

The wolf's eyes hardened. "The team we sent was willing to sacrifice everything to stop the experiment. They failed. Now we must intervene more directly."

Artemis's aura brightened. "Earl, you are our eyes within, and time is short."

"I never envisioned this path," he murmured. "But I'll do what is necessary."

The fox circled him, tail flicking. "We've faced worse. Remember the Uprising of Orion? We were outnumbered, but unity carried us through."

"There were many casualties," Earl reminded her, a sad smile creasing his face.

Her impassive face betrayed nothing.

"I have a plan," he continued. "I'll arrive before dawn tomorrow, before the firing. It's risky after today's breach, but I believe I can prevent it."

"We stand with you," Artemis declared. "Remember, Hare's technology is not of this world. It could trigger another Badger Springs."

The name struck him like a hammer. His hand curled into a fist against his knee, jaw tightening.

"It isn't only the technology," Artemis pressed. "The intent behind it is what matters. Hare tells himself he advances science, but what he really craves is power. The consequences could be catastrophic."

"The balance of this world and many others hangs in the scales," the wolf added solemnly.

Earl lifted his head. "I understand. With your guidance and my knowledge, I'll prevent another tragedy."

"Remember this meeting," the wolf said. "We have faith in you, in Lanell, and in the mission."

"The lessons of the past will guide me," Earl promised.

The fox nudged his arm playfully. "You've got this. You're never alone."

A wan smile broke over his face. "Reassuring words."

Light flared and Earl was back in his meditation room. Candles guttered, shadows stretching across the walls. He sat a moment to steady himself, then he stood, laced his worn boots carefully, and glanced once more around the sanctuary.

"It's time," he said quietly. "Lanell and I need that talk."

With that, he unlocked the door and left.

Chapter Nineteen

The Weight of Knowledge

Myles stood in the control room and gazed at the sprawl of consoles. Machinery whirred beneath the occasional sharp beep of panels. Each flicker of light, each shifting line of data was a thread woven from decades of research and relentless refinement.

This wasn't just equipment. It was a key to places once thought unreachable. He let his fingers trail across the cool, smooth metal of a console. A short sequence of commands could bring the collider to life and pierce the fabric of reality itself. The thought pressed on him like a hand at his back.

For Myles, the collider was more than a machine. It was a question pointed straight at existence. The unmapped void, silent and waiting, seemed to call to him.

Memories rose: nights bent over stolen scraps of tech with Hare, unraveling each piece until they could claim it as their own. Deceit polished into brilliance.

A shadow flickered through him. Every accolade tied back to that lie. Yet standing here, staring at the scale of what they had built, the deceit seemed small compared to the discovery ahead.

We're about to open a doorway into another dimension.

A thought once reserved for fiction now hovered at the edge of reality. He didn't know what waited. They could be on the verge of uncovering truths that could fracture everything they knew. His heart was pounding, and sweat prickled on his upper lip. This wouldn't do. Hare was counting on him.

Myles clasped his trembling hands behind his back and cleared his throat. The operators looked up from their stations.

"My friends," he said. "We have new plans. The collider must fire within the next eight hours."

The room stilled. Bandow, his most trusted technician, contracted his brows. "Sir, the strange matter won't have time to stabilize at the right temperature, and the trilineum may not reach the charge we need."

"Then we start now," Myles answered. "Arcadian activity today forces our hands. We can't wait."

Mara Graven, pushed her glasses up. "Trailing charge takes sixteen hours. Halving that is extraordinarily risky."

"I know the risks, Mara, but the Arcadians have never been this bold. Waiting may be worse."

Dr. Tabin Raskin glanced up from his terminal. "Their patterns suggest they know what we're doing. Every delay gives them space to move against us."

"But rushing could play right into their hands," Mara countered, lips pressed thin. "The trailing's stability isn't something we can fake."

Myles turned toward the large console display of the collider's ring. The blue glow cast his frowning face into sharp relief. "No, Tabin is right. Hesitation works in their favor."

Bandow ran a hand through his tousled fur. "What if we used the auxiliary reactors to accelerate stabilization? Not tested for this, but in theory, it could cut the time in half."

Myles's eyes lit up. He turned to Bandow and beamed. "That's the thinking we need. Tabin, Mara, work with him. Make it happen."

Tabin gave a single stiff nod. "We'll do it. But constant monitoring. First sign of instability, we stop."

"Agreed," Myles said. "Professor Hare will be here in a few hours. Be ready to make history."

"We won't let you down," Bandow said, already keying commands into his console. "Every drill has led to this moment."

Minnie Whiskerfield, silent until now, leaned forward. Her voice trembled. "This isn't just about recognition. We could alter the laws that bind the universe."

Myles studied her. "Your trepidation is understandable, but isn't it our place to ask the questions no one else dares?"

The air in the room tightened. Fingers hovered over keys, and glances darted between stations. Then Minnie broke the silence. "Tabin, prime the auxiliary systems. Mara, monitor trailing levels. Bandow, recalibrate the quantum sensors for the new timeline."

As the shuffle of feet and clatter of keys replaced the hush, Myles drifted toward a secluded terminal.

Through the glass wall, the collider's massive ring stretched into shadow. In a matter of hours, they would try to open a door no one had ever breached.

Should it stay closed?

He brushed the traitorous thought aside.

"For knowledge," he whispered, furry hands shaking as he entered commands. "For progress."

Chapter Twenty

Strategic Alignments

The sun dipped below the horizon, painting the walls in amber light. Earlier, the floors had echoed with chatter and boots. Now each step Trace took landed in silence so complete it pressed against her ears.

In the quiet that followed the end of the working day, machines became the heartbeat of the facility. The lighting system dimmed automatically, casting a ghostly glow over the sterile white halls. Trace preferred it this way. With no distractions, small details stood out a crooked label on a specimen crate, a faint vibration from the reactors three levels down.

She logged every inconsistency. Nothing escaped her eye.

Rounding a corner into Wing C, she spotted the tall, stooped figure of Dr. Crusher locking up his lab. As their paths converged, he glanced up, tired eyes softening into a smile. "Evening, Trace."

"Working late again, Doc?"

"Yeah. A few tests ran long. Worth seeing them through."

Trace nodded. She studied him a moment, then said, "Doc, I've got to give you credit. Earlier today when my forces used your adhesive guns, the Arcadians barely made it three steps before the foam locked them mid-stride."

His eyebrows shot up. "Really? They attempted another incursion?"

"Yeah." Trace's tail flicked irritably. "Six of them tried to breach the west end of the facility. My team was ready. No escapes."

Crusher flushed and rubbed the back of his neck. "I put a lot into the cohesion factor. Consistency had to be perfect for it to hold in the field," he said, unable to conceal the tinge of pride in his voice.

"It paid off." Trace glanced up and down the corridor. "And that's why I wanted to talk." She lowered her voice. "I've got a team that operates outside this facility. With your skill set, you'd be perfect for designing the gear they need."

He arched an eyebrow. "You're leading mercenaries now?"

Her smile was all teeth. "Think of them as a security force for hire. You've got what it takes, Doc. You'd excel."

Crusher chuckled and scratched the back of his head. "That's certainly an unexpected offer. But lab rats like me don't make good bounty hunters. I tinker, I test, I make glue. I stick things together. It's what I like."

"Think it over, at least." Trace said. "Whether you're in the field or behind the bench, your work could be invaluable."

Crusher grinned. "Trace, I appreciate your confidence. The adhesives, the weapons, they're my passion. But I value the peace of running my lab. I like doing the work, then going home. I don't think I could handle the chaos that comes with bounty hunting."

"I understand," Trace said smoothly. "Not everyone is cut out for the field. Everyone shines where they belong."

Crusher glanced back at the sealed lab. "This is where I belong. But if your team ever needs a custom tool, you know where to find me."

Trace's grin widened. "Indeed. Have a good evening, Doc."

Chapter Twenty-One

The Eve of the Revelations

Lanell tapped in her door code on the second try, her fingers hesitating over the keys as the day's conversations looped uninvited in her head. Work should have stayed at the facility, locked away with the rest of the day's headaches. But the thoughts slipped in with her anyway. Even inside her own hallway, her shoulders stayed tight, like she'd carried the day's weight home in her bag.

The last time she'd let work follow her home, it'd soured every corner of the night. This one already tasted the same. Then there was her looming conversation with Dad.

She stepped into her den, the one place in Rith where her pulse eased. Warm, earthy tones glowed across the space: the same clay-red throw pillows her mother once used, the same oak lamp that had stood in their living room.

Every detail matched her memory, a living room rebuilt from fragments of the past. The focal point was a recliner draped with a red plush blanket. It was the spot where she could curl up with a book or simply enjoy a moment of quiet reflection.

Between her bedroom and the den stood a bookshelf lined with her odd collection of literature, from classics like *Amelia the Great* to modern debates like *Us and Them: In the Divide of Tech and Beliefs, Who Is Right?* This reading corner offered an escape into other realities when the pressures of her job pressed too close.

She kicked off her boots and flexed her toes against the cool floor, savoring the small freedom. After placing them neatly to one side, she glanced at the clock. If she started supper now, she could have the grogba simmering by the time Earl arrived.

Behind the house, there was a small yard with a few spindly trees. Several leetles crawled in the grass, glossy shells glinting under the porch light, black spots shifting as they moved. Larger and rounder than insects, leetles were a familiar sight in both city alleys and open fields.

Lanell crouched low, muscles coiled, damp blades of grass whispering against her knees. A leetle twitched near a tuft of weeds. Her father's words replayed in her mind. Whatever he needed to tell her, she only hoped it wouldn't change everything.

She lunged and closed her hands around the creature. The others scattered, their high-pitched *meeps* filling the air as they lifted away. She turned the leetle over in her palms, weighing it. Enough for a hearty pot to share. Yet as she rose, the nagging unease about the conversation returned. *At least preparing grogba is straightforward*, she thought.

Inside, she laid the leetle on the board. Bowing her head slightly, she whispered thanks before drawing the knife and bringing the blade down.

That's not for you to know.

The words still prickled cold between her shoulders.

As she pried the leetle from its shell, her thoughts circled between Hare and her father. What could be so crucial that he needed to share it with her tonight? Was it somehow connected to Hare's behavior at the collider?

She cut the meat into even pieces and seasoned them with herbs. The scent of rosemary and citrus-leaf filled the air as she poured oil into the pan.

The soothing rituals of cooking pulled her thoughts toward quieter waters. Soon, the rich aroma of grogba rose around her. While the pot simmered, she wiped the counters down, her resolve solidifying.

Whatever Papa has to say, I'll face it head-on.

With the kitchen clean, she slipped into her bedroom to change. She paused to check her reflection as she passed the mirror. Another day, another mystery. She brushed a stray strand of gold-blonde hair from her eyes. If only doubts cleared so easily.

Her parents smiled from their photo frame, frozen in a sunlit moment before a stone outcropping. What had Papa called it? Trunka? The name hovered just out of reach.

Mom. Dad. What would you make of this?

She pulled on soft gray pants and a long-sleeved lavender shirt, comfort without frills. She barely had time for one final check in the mirror before the smell of simmering grogba tugged her back toward the kitchen.

A knock came at the door. She smiled. She knew before she even answered it that Earl would be there, bottle in hand.

"Papa, you know fermented fruit doesn't go with grogba," she teased.

"You're right, little one. But after a day like today, fermented fruit goes with just about anything."

He set the bottle on the counter and checked the pot. Lanell followed as he rummaged in the drawers.

"It's almost ready. Do you want to wait so we can eat together?" she asked.

"Of course," Earl said, fishing out a spoon. "But you know it's not official until I test it." He lifted the lid and dipped a scoop.

"Papa, you may want to let it cool before "

Earl's eyes went wide as the heat hit, and he flailed for a moment, cheeks puffed like bellows. Rushing to the sink, he filled a glass with water, drained it to the last drop, then thudded it down.

"Daughter," he panted, "the grogba is delightful. Warm but delightful."

Lanell smirked. "You know, the discussion you wanted to have with me has been eating at me all afternoon. Do you want the den or the table?"

Earl's expression sobered. "The table," he said gently. "Let's talk there."

Chapter Twenty-Two

Legacy of the Torka

"Lanell," her father said. "The tale I'm about to share is woven from the threads of our past. Some of it you'll recognize from stories you grew up with. But there are parts you've never heard." His voice caught. He pressed his lips together, staring down at his hands until he steadied. "Every story has its shadows and its light. Understanding both is the only way to understand ourselves and where we're headed."

Lanell folded her arms on the table, ears angled toward him, tail tip flicking once before settling.

"Long ago, on the outskirts of Rith," Earl began, "there was a curious professor named Lupus Hare. Back then, he wasn't famous. He wasn't powerful. He was just... searching. For some reason, he became obsessed with the legend of the Torka."

Lanell thumped the table. "Torka. That's the word. I was trying to remember it earlier. Dad mentioned them sometimes when I was tiny, but never in detail."

Earl nodded. "Most folks treat it as a whisper of a myth. But to the Arcadians, a Torka isn't a legend. It's sacred. A cornerstone of who they are. And it isn't just a strange stone or a marker. It's a bridge between worlds."

Lanell leaned forward. "So Hare wasn't just chasing a story. He was walking straight onto their spiritual ground."

"Exactly," Earl said. "And they noticed long before he knew they existed. Arcadians are masters of concealment. They watched him from the moment he began sniffing around the old ruins and forest paths. He never saw them, not once. But they were always there, guarding what needed to stay hidden."

"What did he find?" Lanell asked.

"Nothing concrete. Just fragments old carvings, patterns, lines in old journals he didn't understand." Earl exhaled slowly. "But then came the night when he and his team drew too close."

He closed his eyes briefly before continuing.

"It was a moonlit night. The forest was quiet, still... almost listening. Hare and his team were close enough that the ground itself felt uneasy. The Arcadians knew something had to be done. They gathered around their council fire. I've heard elders describe that night the fear, the urgency, the firelight on their faces."

Lanell didn't blink.

"The shaman was reluctant," Earl said. "He didn't want to use the ancient rites. They're not meant for conflict. But he had no choice. With the power in the Torka stirring, he called upon it. He pulled on its latent force and summoned a guardian one made of shadow and stone, with eyes burning like embers fresh out of the forge."

Lanell shivered, shoulders folding in.

"The forest shook as it came," Earl said. "Trees trembled, birds scattered into the night, and the beast roared. That sound was older and more primal than anything Hare had ever encountered. His team panicked. Ran. Three of his researchers never made it out. Their screams..." His voice tightened. "The trees still carry them."

Lanell clasped her hands together, fingers digging into her own fur. "It's hard to picture Professor Hare tied to something that violent. All because of a Torka?"

Earl met her gaze solemnly. "The Torka was at the heart of it."

She frowned. "What exactly *are* they? Truly?"

Earl leaned forward. "A Torka is a nexus. A place where the veil between realms grows thin. Shamans can guide lost spirits there, send messages, even glimpse the In-Between. The Arcadians guard them because they understand the danger of what happens when one is disturbed."

Lanell swallowed. "And Professor Hare, what would *he* want with something like that?"

Earl's face darkened. "He is a man of science, driven by curiosity. If he ever learned what a Torka truly is, he would study it. He would measure it, probe it, try to harness it. But without reverence for what it means, without the training of a shaman, meddling with a Torka could tear the balance apart. Not just in our world, Lanell, but between worlds."

The kitchen felt suddenly too small. Too quiet.

"Papa," she whispered. "Why tell me this now?"

Earl hesitated, then his voice softened with something like fear and love tangled together.

"Because the shadows of this story are reaching toward you, my girl. And you deserve to know the shape of them."

Chapter Twenty-Three

Revelations

Lanell shuddered as the weight of her father's words settled over. After everything that had happened, the thought of Professor Hare with that much power at his command made her blood run cold.

Eyes closed once again, Earl continued his story. "The Arcadians didn't know what Hare was really after. That's what cut the deepest. Was it just curiosity? Was someone pulling his strings? Too many questions, not enough truth. So they sent for Artemis.

She isn't someone you call unless the weight's too much for one set of hands. But this was bigger than a patrol, bigger than a fight with outsiders. This was about whether the old ways could be kept safe at all."

He leaned back and stroked his beard. "Artemis heard them out. Didn't shout, didn't rush. Just listened until the fire burned low. Then she told them what had to be done. Fifteen souls, with one shaman to lead them. They'd walk away from the rivers, the hunt, the songs of the wind... and step into the city of Rith."

Lanell listened with her chin in her hands. So far, this talk hadn't been what she'd expected, but she was hanging on every word.

"It had never been done before," Earl said. "Not like this. Living there. Wearing city life like it fit. All the while burying their true selves so deep no one could dig them out."

His thumb traced the worn edge of his belt. "They had to hide everything about themselves. No Arcadian turns of phrase. No scents of home on their clothes. That's the price give up the life you know to protect it from the inside.

"It wasn't just about Hare nosing near the shrines. They had to know why. What drove him? And whether they could stop him.

"The Elders picked the group careful. Those who could change their voice, their stride. Who could smile without showing their teeth. They were given new names, given paper histories that would hold up under a neighbor's questions. The mask had to breathe, work and fit in this world.

"The leader of the group was a shaman. Not just to watch over their mission, but to keep their hearts from drifting. City life changes you faster than you think. One can forget the wind through pine. You stop hearing the old songs. He was there to keep them remembering, even if they couldn't speak it out loud.

"When they finally stepped into Rith, it was like walking into another world. Stone and glass instead of trees. A thousand voices, none speaking the same. They found work in shops, docks, rail yards. Made friends where they could. Kept their eyes on Hare without ever letting him see theirs. Every scrap of what they learned went to the shaman, and then from him to Artemis. It was a chain that couldn't afford a weak link.

"It was a tightrope. Lean too far toward the mission, you drew attention. Lean too far into city life, you forgot why you came."

Earl's words slowed, then stopped. Firelight caught the lines at his eyes, as if age had crept up on him. Lanell leaned in, fur prickling. She knew that look, the one he wore when he was about to share something that couldn't be taken back.

"You see, Lanell" his eyes held hers steady "that mission? It wasn't just history. It was the start of us. Two of those fifteen, they're the reason you're here."

Lanell gasped.

"Your mother and father were a part of that group."

Lanell saw flashes her mother humming at breakfast, her father's cedar scent. Then she imagined them skulking in alleys, watching from shadows, carrying secrets before she was even born.

"They were Arcadian to the bone," Earl said. "But in Rith, they spoke like city folk, ate like them, worked among them. Never slipped. Never showed their true stride in the street. But inside, they carried the old ways like an ember buried deep in the ashes.

"They didn't start out promised to each other," Earl said, a faint smile flickering. "But when you share the same shadow, the same danger, you learn to trust the one beside you. Rith tried to pull them into its pace, but they kept their own rhythm. Somewhere along the line, the mission stopped being the only thing that mattered.

"They chose each other." His eyes softened. "And then you came. Small enough to fit in my hands. A piece of Arcadia born in Rith."

Lanell's eyes burned. She had never thought of herself that way, half belonging to a world she'd never seen, carrying its weight in her own skin.

"There's something else," Earl said, eyeing her with apprehension. "Something the shaman saw the day you were born."

Lanell's tail curled against her side. She gripped the tip and began toying with the purple bandana "What was it?"

Earl took a long breath. "The shaman marked you. Said you were touched by the Precursors."

Lanell's fingers froze on the bandana. There was a rushing in her ears, and her mouth went dry. "What... does that mean?" she managed.

Earl stood. His movements were slow and deliberate as he untucked his shirt. He turned and lifted it, showing her his bare back. Across his fur ran a pattern she knew, the same curling lines, the same faint, impossible geometry as her own.

Her breath hitched.

"These aren't just marks, Lanell," Earl said. "They're a language older than Arcadia itself. The shamans say they're the Precursors' signature, a sign you can stand with one foot in this world and one in another."

Lanell's hand drifted to her shoulder blade, brushing the hidden spiral beneath her shirt. It seemed to pulse under her fingers like something awake.

"When your mother saw it," Earl said, "she cried. Your father didn't speak for a long time. They knew what it meant. That you weren't just theirs. You were part of something older, something waiting." He leaned forward. "And we're not at the end of that story yet, Lanell. Not by a long shot."

Chapter Twenty-Four

Crossroads of Identity

Lanell rose slowly, head tilted, ears angling forward as if straining to hear more than words. "I didn't know," she murmured. "I always thought it was just a birthmark."

"Technically, it is," Earl said. "But it's also a genetic marker. It transcends species, passes through bloodlines. It marks you as kin to the Precursors, and it carries the weight of the Shaman."

A crease formed between her brows. "But wait... neither of my parents had it. At least, not that I remember."

Earl shook his head calmly. "No. Your parents didn't carry the mark. But you inherited it. The mark shows you bear the bloodline and, with it, the abilities of a shaman."

"When were you planning to tell me?"

Earl met her stare without blinking. "When it was safe. When we knew more about Hare's intentions. Until then, this truth was dangerous to hold."

Not for me to know.

Lanell's mouth tightened. "It's been nearly thirty years, Papa. You and the others spying on Hare should have figured it out by now, don't you think?"

He turned toward the window and stared out into the deepening dusk. "You're right to be angry. But listen, on that day at Badger Springs, you weren't the only one who lost a family. Our whole tribe was there. Everyone but me."

He braced against the sill, voice dropping. "I should have been with them. Maybe things would be different. But I wasn't. When I reached the springs, all I found was you, huddled on the Torka. No one else made it." His shoulders sagged, his jaw flexed, and his eyes wouldn't meet hers.

Lanell gripped her chair until her knuckles turned white. She forced herself to hold steady though each word added to the gnawing ache in her chest. "So, I carry the mark of a shaman. What does it mean?"

Earl turned back, some of his composure restored. "In Rith, nothing. Here, no one honors it. But among the Arcadians, it marks you as a leader. One who guides life into the world and souls on their journey beyond."

Lanell bit her lip. "I've lived one life for years, but it doesn't feel real. It feels... fake."

Earl shook his head. "No, Lanell. It *is* real. I raised you. My love is real. Your life here is real. But now you know there's more, a heritage you can choose to embrace.

Lanell's eyes widened. "So, I have the option to step into this? To explore what it means to be a shaman?"

"Yes. Nothing you've lived in Rith is undone by this. It adds to you, it doesn't erase you. It's your choice."

"Then what do I do now?" she asked, hating how small her voice sounded.

Earl took her hand. "Nothing. Not tonight."

Her ears shot back. "Nothing? You tell me all this and then say do nothing?"

He pressed her hand tighter. "Yes. You need time to breathe. To think about all this. I'll be here to answer your questions. We'll take it at your pace. This isn't a path to be rushed down."

Lanell exhaled shakily, then asked, "What about the Arcadians captured today? What about Hare? The collider?"

"All important, but they won't be solved in one night. We'll move carefully. Step by step. First, you come to terms with who you are, then we'll face the rest together."

Lanell studied him, then nodded. "Okay, Papa. One step at a time." She gave him a watery smile and pulled him into a hug, holding tight.

He dropped a kiss on her head. "We've weathered storms before, Lanell. This is another. And we'll come through stronger."

She stepped back, sniffing and wiping her eyes. "Where do we start?"

A twinkle touched his eyes. "With supper. I'm starved."

Lanell let out a tired laugh and followed him toward the kitchen, letting the moment be what it was. The warmth between them felt real, solid, but underneath it, something heavier was settling in. The truth Earl had given her tonight still churned quietly in the back of her mind. The mark. Her parents. Badger Springs. Everything she wasn't told. She pushed the thoughts down for now, choosing to cling to the comfort of his presence a little longer. Supper would come. Answers would follow. But the weight of who she was and what she had just learned sat in her chest like a stone, waiting for the silence of night to give it room to grow.

Chapter Twenty-Five

The Firing

The big board already burned white, displaying T minus ninety seconds. Fans whined. The floor hummed through Myles Moleman's boots.

"Field stabilization?" Hare asked.

"Climbing," Mara Graven said. The graph knifed toward one hundred. Behind the wall, the capacitor bank gave a low animal rumble and settled into a steady thrum.

The guest door whispered open.

"I prefer to witness history from the front row," Trinn said. Her reflection cut across the one-way glass.

"We are almost there," Hare replied, eyes on the readouts.

Myles scanned the camera tiles that showed the impact chamber and the injector throat. A small platform rose into frame beside the matter injector. A single thread of golden hair lay across the steel. It lifted, stood on end, then drifted toward the injector as if the machine were breathing in.

He told himself to ignore it. *Focus*. He cleared his throat. "Minnie, strange matter at target temp?"

"Negative three. Rock steady."

"Rail status?" Hare said.

"Trilineum transferred," Tabin Raskin replied. "Velocity at three quarters. Loop interval tightening."

Hare nodded. "Push to full."

Every pair of eyes was fixed on the countdown board.

"Pressure variance," Mara said. "Point zero seven below set. Trending up. Still inside tolerance."

Trinn leaned toward the glass. "Your capacitors sing when they are afraid."

"They sing when they're working," Myles said. His voice was so tight he barely recognized it.

Trinn's smile showed no teeth. "To think, Professor. You lecture me on caution in a building built on my gifts."

Hare kept his gaze on the board. "You provided tools. We will decide how to use them."

Myles spoke without looking back. "Chancellor, please mind the glass. My team is not cleared for outcomes."

"So serious," Trinn said, almost fondly. "Very well. I will watch."

Myles exhaled, slow and shaky the kind of breath you release when you've almost forgotten how to.

"Mara, hold the field at one hundred. Raskin, confirm coil temps."

"Coils at eighty-four Celsius," Raskin said. "Climbing slowly. Green."

"Minnie, lock injector alignment," Myles said. "Final confirmation."

"Locked."

Hare's hand hovered over the control that would bend the field and send the payload home. His finger tapped once. "Proceed."

"Confirming chamber seal," Myles said. "Confirming magnetic alignment." He watched the hazard band quiver. "T minus ten."

The countdown voice took over. "Nine. Eight."

Mara's numbers crawled. "Variance point one two. Still within."

"Three. Two. One."

Hare flipped the switch.

The rail's pulse snapped into a razor line. The chamber camera washed out, then returned. A corona of light unfurled in the center of the room like fabric turning inside out. Frost webbed across the viewport in a spreading fern. The building released a long, low moan. The capacitor thrum climbed a note and held.

"Pressure dump," Mara said. "Dropping fast. Doors hold. Control atmosphere stable. I can't stabilize because there's nothing left *to* stabilize. Chamber is at hard vacuum."

"Hold your stations," Hare barked. His pupils darted, clinging to each rising digit like they might slip away if he blinked. "Do not move."

The corona tightened into a whirling bowl bright at the rim, black at the throat. Dust motes spun into it. A small glass cylinder flew across the room and shattered against a conduit. Something heavier slammed the far wall with a wet sound and slid to the floor.

Hare spoke, but the words were pinched and shrill, betraying more fragility than command. "Is that the fissure?"

Trinn did not blink. "That is not my sky."

"It is a breach," Myles said. His console ticked. Vacuum at zero. Seal intact. Coil temps at eighty-six. Field jitter point zero three. Every instinct screamed to power down. He waited for Hare.

The whirlpool trembled, then closed like a pupil. The frost on the viewport creaked. Silence rolled in, broken only by the capacitors, still singing.

Hare found the door with his hand. "With me."

At the chamber, ice smoked from the gasket. Myles cleared the interlock. The door groaned and gave. Frost cracked under their shoes as they stepped inside.

The body was small. Female. Bare. Pale skin. Platinum gold hair. Blood beaded where glass had kissed it. The cold had raised a rash of bumps across her arms. The broken cylinder leaked a thin amber line that shivered in the airless cold.

Myles crouched, two fingers to a throat he did not understand. He looked up. "It's breathing."

Trinn's mouth tightened. "Good news and bad news."

Hare did not look away from the figure. "Start with good."

"You opened a door," Trinn said. "Bad news: not to my world."

Hare finally faced her. "And worse?"

"You now have a case of the humans."

Myles glanced at the injector platform. That golden hair still clung to its rim. He couldn't stop staring at it.

Hare's jaw unclenched a fraction, the first hint of release since the switch flipped. He pressed a button on his communicator. "Trace, bring a bio-containment to the collider impact chamber. We have a new subject for Sublevel 1."

"I'm on my way," Trace said.

Hare ended the call and turned to Myles. "Release the crew. Two days. No notes. Nothing leaves this room."

"Yes, sir."

Myles stood and took one last look at the human. He told himself the hair in the chamber meant nothing, but he didn't believe it.

In the control room, Raskin exhaled heavily. "If you collide with something at the speed of light and we can still walk away, I vote success."

Minnie didn't answer. She watched the frost melt in slow veins across the glass and tried not to think about the sound the building had made when the universe bent.

Chapter Twenty-Six

The Argument

Night pressed close around the house. The hallway clock ticked like a heartbeat out of rhythm. The grogba pot sat empty, stew crusted to its sides. An unfinished sweetrise bottle caught the dim kitchen light. She moved to the den and sank into the old sofa. The weight of Earl's truths pressed harder with every silent second.

Lanell studied her father across the room. His gaze skittered from the door to the lamp to the empty pot, never landing for more than a heartbeat.

Her fingers worried the hem of her shirt. She drew a breath. "Papa. You told me so much tonight. I need to understand one thing."

Earl sat up to face her. Her blue eyes did not blink.

"Why did you wait? Why make me carry it for years? Why?"

Earl didn't answer right away. His eyes dropped to his hands resting in his lap. He opened his mouth, then closed it again. The hallway clock grew loud enough to count; even the lamp's filament seemed to buzz. He cleared his throat. When he spoke, the words rasped. "I was afraid... Not for me. For you."

Lanell said nothing, but her body stiffened, her shoulders locked; the fur along her neck bristled.

"I didn't know how to raise you, Lanell. I'm a shaman, not a father. Not really. When I brought you back from Badger Springs, you were broken, and I... I was barely holding myself together."

He leaned forward, elbows on knees, staring into the floor as if the answer were carved into the wood grain.

"Every time I looked at you, I saw them. Your parents. My friends. My failure. He pinched the bridge of his nose and squeezed his eyes shut. "And every time you laughed or smiled, it felt like I didn't deserve to hear it. Because I should've saved them. I should've stopped that experiment. I should've failed less."

He paused, swallowing hard. "I thought I was protecting you by letting you live a normal life. A safe one. But maybe I was protecting myself from the truth."

Lanell's jaw clenched. Her eyes glistened with the kind of pain that runs deeper than anger.

"So you thought silence was better? Even more, leaving me ignorant of the true intentions of my parents and you. Letting me get close to Hare did you ever think about the repercussions of that? What if Hare isn't wrong? What if *you're* wrong? Did you think that leaving me to wonder who I really was would be easier?"

"No," Earl said, his voice breaking. "I thought it would buy me time to become the kind of father you deserved." He finally looked up at her, eyes rimmed red. "But I waited too long, and I know I can't fix that. I can only hope... maybe now, you'll let me try."

Lanell stood in place, fists clenched, her voice rising as years of confusion turned to heat. "You watched me drift into his orbit and said nothing. Not even a hint. You let me work for Hare like it was nothing. Do you know how much of myself I gave to that lab? To the facility?"

Earl's face twitched, but he didn't interrupt.

"I walked the same halls they did, your friends, without a single warning. I asked the same questions, but you let me believe I was just some nobody with a knack for science. You let me think my dreams were mine, not leftovers from a life I didn't even know I came from. You buried the truth, and you buried me with it. That wasn't protection. That was control."

Earl's throat bobbed. "I thought I was sparing you the pain."

A single sharp laugh tried to escape and died in her throat. "Sparing me? You think this hurts *less* now? You think finding out I've been living a lie for thirteen years feels like kindness?"

She turned away, running a hand through her hair, her breathing ragged. "I don't know what to believe anymore. I don't even know who *I* am, and I sure as hell don't know who *you* are."

Her voice leveled out to a flat line. By sheer force of will, she stopped her hands shaking. "I need you to go."

Earl's face broke, just for a moment. His lip quivered. "I never meant "

"Please. Just leave." She didn't raise her voice. Her words were clipped and controlled. "Leave me alone."

That said, the conversation was over.

Earl stood, eyes still fixed on her. She wouldn't meet his gaze. "I'll come back," he said softly, "when you want me to."

Lanell didn't respond.

He lingered at the door for a breath too long, then stepped out into the hallway. The door closed gently behind him, muffling the sound of his retreat.

Lanell's breath hitched, once, then again. She stared at the door. Her mouth opened. Closed. Nothing came out.

She moved deliberately toward the kitchen. Reaching for the bottle of sweetrise, she grasped it firmly, feeling the cool glass against her palm. Tilting it to her lips, she drained the last remnants of the sweet, tangy liquid, the taste of fermented purple fruit lingering on her tongue. Pausing, she stared at the now-empty bottle, a wave of frustration washing over her. With a sudden burst of emotion, she hurled it against the wall. The bottle shattered upon impact, an explosion of glittering glass shards and droplets of deep purple juice splattering across the surface in a chaotic display. A cold mist of sweetrise flecked her cheek. The room smelled like crushed fruit and glass dust.

She stood in the kitchen, her eyes fixed on the slow descent of the purple liquid as it trickled down the wall, leaving a vivid stain in its wake. With a heavy sigh, she turned away from the mess, her shoulders slumped in defeat. She trudged over to the sofa, collapsing into its worn cushions. Her body sank into the familiar fabric as she lay back and raised a trembling hand to shield her eyes. Tears welled up, spilling over and tracing warm paths down her cheeks. A shard pinged on the tile as her shoulders started to shake. She squeezed her eyes shut, unable to hold back the sobs.

As Lanell lay on her couch, exhaustion settled over her like a heavy blanket. Her eyelids fluttered before they finally closed, and her breathing became a slow, soothing rhythm, like the gentle lapping of waves against a shore. The tightness in her shoulders and neck melted away as she surrendered to the quiet embrace of the night, seamlessly slipping into the vibrant world of dreams that awaited beyond the veil of sleep.

Chapter Twenty-Seven

She's Here

Lanell moved down the hallway, the purple tights hugging her legs as her nylon-covered feet glided silently across the cold, polished floor. The fluorescent lights overhead emitted a faint buzzing noise, their sterile, bluish glow illuminating the space with an unsettling precision. White walls threw back the blue light until the corridor felt overexposed, too clean to touch. This was the lab, or at least, a section of it. But not any part she'd ever seen before.

The walls were pristine, devoid of keypads or security checkpoints. There were no signs of any kind, no panels to disrupt the smooth surface. Just endless white walls, creating a corridor that stretched ahead into eternity.

The floor was polished to a gleam, reflecting the harsh lighting overhead. Her heel lifted, set down; lift, set. No memory of the first step. No urge to stop. It was as if the corridor itself whispered her forward into its depths. Then, abruptly, she felt a hand grip hers. Her breath hitched violently in her chest. She glanced down, startled to see her fingers intertwined with a hand like her own but larger. She was younger, transported back to childhood. Her gaze shot upward. Beside her, her mother walked with an eerie calmness. A soft smile played on her lips, a smile Lanell had almost lost to time. On her other side, her father materialized, towering and silent, their strides perfectly in sync. "Mom?" Lanell's voice wavered with a mix of hope and disbelief. Her mother's smile deepened, but she remained gazing ahead, her eyes fixed on some unseen horizon. "Dad?" He nodded, a silent acknowledgement, his eyes gentle yet unfocused, as though they were locked onto something distant and unreachable behind her.

Lanell's steps faltered for just a moment. "Wait."

Her pace stuttered. Instinct said let go; her mother's gentle squeeze said keep walking. Her parents had been dead for years. She'd watched them disappear beneath the mud at Badger Springs. The memory was seared into her mind: their reaching hands, the screams, the way the ground had swallowed them whole.

So why did their presence feel so... normal? So expected.

She tried to slow her pace, to pull her hand free and demand answers, but her mother's grip tightened inexorably, and somehow, her feet kept moving forward of their own accord. The corridor stretched ahead, and the part of her mind that should have been screaming questions felt muffled, distant, like it was wrapped in cotton.

Her parents didn't respond and didn't even seem to hear her.

Lanell's voice trembled, cracking under the weight of emotion. "I don't remember this."

Still, they remained silent. They just walked, each grasping one of her hands, guiding her down the immaculate corridor lined with gleaming white tiles. The overhead lights began to dim behind them, casting long shadows that crept forward. One by one, the bulbs winked out, leaving the hallway behind them in darkness. Only the small circle of light around their feet persisted, like a spotlight on an otherwise dark stage.

Her father was the first to stop. He turned toward her with a deliberate slowness, his face an unreadable mask. When he spoke, his voice was low and unfamiliar, as if it belonged to someone else. "She's here," he said. "She just arrived."

Her mother's fingers clamped down around Lanell's hand with sudden urgency, squeezing her skin against bone. The grip was so tight it shot a sharp jolt of pain up her arm.

Lanell twisted to face her mother, confusion and a hint of fear in her eyes. "Who's here now?"

Her mother leaned close, breath warm at Lanell's ear. "You need to run," she whispered. "Don't let them catch either of you."

Lanell's panic finally broke loose. "What are you talking about? Why do I need to run?Who's going to catch me? Who's here?"

The questions tumbled out in a raw, breathless rush too fast, too messy, too terrified to line up into anything neat. But her mother didn't slow. Her father didn't react. It was as if they didn't even hear her.

They continued down the corridor, their footsteps echoing against the cold, polished floor. As they reached a gentle curve, a door emerged at the far end. It was a stark contrast to the corridor's sterile white walls a smooth, dark metal surface that bore no marks or handles, only a solitary vertical seam running down its center. Her mother halted in front of the door. Her father stepped up beside her, letting go of Lanell's small, clammy hand.

They both pivoted to face her. "We can go in here," her mother said, her voice warm and soothing, like she was reading a bedtime story. "We'll be safe."

Lanell hesitated. A shiver of unease prickled at her skin. Something about the door felt wrong. It was too clean, too polished, and somehow too... final. All her instincts told her that stepping through that door would mean the end of something and, perhaps, the beginning of something else.

Her parents showed no trace of fear or hesitation. Lanell watched open-mouthed as her father stretched out a hand towards the door. It opened with a hiss, as if responding to his mere presence. Soft amber light spilled across the hallway floor like liquid gold. Lanell felt an inexplicable pull towards it. Her steps were tentative, but the comforting presence of her mother and father urged her forward.

The first thing she noticed when she crossed the threshold into the chamber beyond was a strange sensation beneath her feet. The floor wasn't cold and hard like the floor in the corridor. It yielded slightly under each step not sticky but not firm either. It was like walking across dense gel.

The door slid closed behind them, sealing them inside the tranquil chamber. Lanell turned to speak to her parents, but no one there. The room echoed with emptiness.

"Mom?" she whispered, barely penetrating the oppressive silence.

No answer.

The smooth, featureless walls loomed around her. There was no furniture. No exit. No shadows to hide in. Just silence the suffocating kind that presses down on you and tries to swallow you whole.

Lanell took a step forward, her heart pounding in her ears.

In the far corner of the chamber, a figure crouched with its back turned toward her. Shoulders hunched, arms locked tightly around its knees. The creature's body shuddered with shallow, panicked breaths. As Lanell got closer, she could hear it mumbling to itself.

"Where am I?" it murmured. "What am I doing here?"

Lanell moved closer.

Sensing her presence, the figure trembled more violently. "Please... don't let them take me back. I don't want to go back. I didn't mean to be here. I didn't mean..."

The figure wore red tights. They had a couple of runs and numerous stains. Golden hair hung over her face, tangled and damp with sweat.

Who was this? Something about this creature tugged at the edges of her mind. "Are you alright?" she asked gently.

It flinched. The head lifted slightly, but the hair still hid the face. "I don't want to be here," it sobbed. "I didn't ask for this. I want to go home."

Lanell froze. That voice.

It didn't make sense, but it didn't have to. The moment wrapped around her like a fog. She lowered herself to the floor and knelt beside the creature. That's when she felt it. The floor gave a little more. A quiet shift.

"It's okay," she said. "You're not alone."

The trembling lessened. Lanell reached out. "Come on. We'll get out of here. Just come with me."

The figure raised its head. Her face for it was her was streaked with tears. Her wide eyes were shining with something unfamiliar and yet unmistakably known.

The being wasn't Arcadian. Lanell was reasonably sure she wasn't even from this world. But her eyes those eyes held something. A spark. A thread.

For a moment, they just stared at one another, caught in a state of quiet, indefinable recognition. Then the being gave a weak, tremulous smile. Lanell felt something shift inside her.

She took her hand. "Let's go," she whispered. They rose up and turned toward where they had entered. But the door was gone. In its place, just a wall.

Lanell took a step forward and stopped. Her foot refused to lift. She glanced down. Her foot had disappeared into the soft, yielding floor. She tugged again, harder this time.

Nothing.

Beside her, the creature whispered, "I can't move."

Lanell crouched. The gel-like floor had changed. What had once felt merely strange now revealed its true nature. It was a strong adhesive. Her fingertips brushed the floor and stuck fast. When she pulled, milky threads stretched and snapped back with a rubbery twang..

This wasn't just sticky; it was industrial. It had a slight give to it, just enough to taunt its victims with the possibility of freedom before it snapped back.

She shifted her weight and tried to lift her right foot. It barely moved an inch. The glue gripped the sole of her foot. It had made its position clear, and it wasn't interested in negotiating. She jerked harder. There was a sharp, wet pop sound, like suction breaking under pressure. Still, her foot wouldn't come loose.

Lanell looked over at her companion. She was struggling too, both feet stuck fast to the floor. The glue held like strong rubber cement. The more they moved, the more it clung.

Lanell gritted her teeth. "Don't panic."

She pulled with every ounce of strength she had, but it was like being chained to the ground by invisible bands. The glue didn't need to sink them. It didn't need to pull them under. It just needed them stuck. And they were.

Then the lights went out. They didn't flicker; they pulsed and then faded. Slow and measured.

The chamber descended into utter darkness. There was a rustle of movement, then a shape emerged from the oppressive gloom. This was followed by another and another, indistinct yet undeniably present. She tilted her head back, her eyes straining against the black. Above her, the darkness thickened, then became populated with eyes. Dozens. Bright, unblinking, close enough to count if she dared. They hovered in the blackness above, stars in a night sky. Each pair pierced through the shadows, focused and alert. They were watching her.

Then a voice broke the silence. A hissing whisper that seemed to brush against her skin, sending a shiver down her spine.

"Gotcha."

Chapter Twenty-Eight

The Walk

Lanell shot upright from her couch, gasping. Her heart hammered against her ribs like it was trying to escape her chest.

Still dark, still here, still alone.

The small blanket draped over her sofa now clung to her fur with sweat. The material was twisted and damp, like vines pulling her down into the dream she'd barely escaped. The silence in her den felt too deep, too artificial.

She rubbed her arms and stared at the small timepiece on the table and saw that the night was still early.

That dream, she thought to herself. It wasn't like the ones she'd had before. It wasn't a memory like Badger Springs. It was something else. Something that wrapped snare-tight around her ribs. The voice, that other being...

Lanell whispered into the dark, "What the hell is happening to me?"

She sat still for a moment, chest rising and falling. The urge to cry clung to the back of her throat, but nothing came.

Don't sleep again, she told herself. You know what's waiting.

She got up and slid on her boots, lacing them with trembling fingers. Then she reached for a hanging jacket.

"Walk it out. Breathe it out. Keep moving."

She stepped quietly to the door, the motion sensor clicking as it slid open. The front walkway beyond was dark, empty, and humming faintly with the artificial heartbeat of the dome's systems. The air was scrubbed thin.

She didn't know where her feet were taking her. All the while, she kept circling back to the same thought.

If I stay here, I'll drown in my own mind.

The air carried no breeze, no scent of earth, just the recycled sterility of life support systems and over filtered moisture. The city around her slept beneath a wash of quiet blue lights. Homes were dimmed or dark. Somewhere in the distance, a low-pitched rumble buzzed, maybe a drone sweeping the outer perimeter. Maybe just the dome itself breathing.

Lanell walked, looking at the ground.

My parents were Arcadians, not even from here.

She kept walking.

What does that mean, how am I supposed to reconcile this, what do I do?

Her path took her past silent plazas and looping transit lines that hadn't moved in hours. A tiny drone whirred overhead, but she didn't look up.

My parents were Arcadians. I'm a shaman. And I've spent my whole life thinking I was just... normal.

The words tasted foreign in her head. None of this made sense. Arcadian blood. A spiral birthmark, she'd thought was meaningless. And now dreams that felt like messages, or warnings.

What does that make me now?

Why didn't Earl tell me sooner?

Her steps slowed in front of a gated maintenance corridor, a place she'd never cared about before. Tonight, she stopped. A keypad glowed faintly beside the gate. Her thumb hovered over the 7, then pressed.

The last time she was here was during the final installation of some systems by the facility, She felt pretty confident her access code still worked.

After she entered the sequence, the light above the panel blinked red, then shifted to green as an arrow pointed down. The elevator confirmed its call with a soft mechanical chime.

Lanell stepped aside and leaned next to the doors. She lifted one foot, planting it against the wall behind her, knee bent. Her head tilted back, eyes closing.

I don't want to do anything. I just want a normal life.

But even as she thought it, the words rang hollow.

What even is a normal life? Just... being allowed to exist? To work, to breathe, and not to feel like everything is some kind of test? I just want to do what I do and be happy. Whatever that's supposed to look like.

The elevator doors opened with a slow hiss, and she stepped inside. It was dimly lit by a single overhead panel that flickered for a moment before stabilizing. The walls were smooth metal, lined with scratched panels and forgotten smudges. This was an old lift. Probably hadn't been used in months.

She tapped the button for the observational deck, then leaned back against the cool wall, arms folded across her chest.

The elevator began its ascent with a low hum. Lanell watched the floor counter tick upward, and for the first time all night, her mind stopped spinning. Just a little.

She exhaled slowly, letting her shoulders drop.

Maybe I don't need to figure it all out tonight.

The motion of the lift was soothing, like being rocked gently from beneath.

I don't have to do anything yet. I just have to keep going.

She didn't feel better, exactly, but the tight knot in her stomach loosened a notch.

The floor counter blinked once, then stopped. Top level. The doors slid open, and a cool blue glow spilled in.

Lanell stepped out. Something was drawing her toward the glass and the night beyond.

She looked to one side and leaned on one of the rails, gazing out over the city of Rith, where most of its citizens were already asleep.

Did I overreact? Papa revealed to me a lot of things that I can't believe he told me. He has that mark on his back as well. What does this mean for him? What does that mean for me? I know he wouldn't let me live a lie. I know he wants the best for me.

She stopped, then realized how much guilt he must have been carrying all these years.

And even after all that, he stayed here to watch over the facility, and watch over Hare.

She stared out across the city, but her eyes weren't seeing Rith. They were seeing mud. Screams. Her parents are reaching for her, then vanishing beneath the sludge.

That dream was familiar. Horrible but known. A scar her mind often reopened.

I was just a kid. I couldn't save them. I couldn't even scream.

She blinked, trying to will it away. Another image pressed forward, the one from tonight. The other dream. The corridor of white. The trap. The voice. And that being. The one who held her hand.

That wasn't a memory.

She shivered despite the dome's steady warmth.

That was something else. Something watching me.

A dozen eyes blinking from the dark. A voice whispering, gotcha.

What the hell was that? A dream or a warning?

She touched the rail, grounding herself in the feel of the cold metal under her palm.

I've had the Badger Springs dream all my life. That's trauma. That's a pain. But this...

She looked up toward the glass above, beyond the shimmer of the dome lights.

This was a trap. Not in the past. Not in my head. This was... outside.

And suddenly she wasn't sure which was worse: the nightmare born from loss or the one that felt like it came from something watching her through the dark.

Lanell stood up and walked onward to the left, toward the far curve of the dome where the glass panels stretched floor to ceiling. This was the closest anyone in Rith could get to the stars. Not real ones, of course. Their light was filtered through layers of containment glass and atmospheric shielding, but it was close enough to pretend.

Up here there were no guards, no cameras, no voices. Just her and the distant hum of life support systems gently thrumming like a second heartbeat.

She reached the glass and pressed her fingertips to its surface. Outside the dome was pure wilderness: dense forests, jagged peaks, twisting rivers all swallowed by shadow. But above that darkness, arcing across the night sky like a frozen ripple in time, stretched the ring. Rith's planetary halo, ancient, massive, and impossibly wide, caught stray light from the distant sun and scattered it in shimmering bands across the world below.

The glow it cast wasn't bright, not really. It was silvery and soft, like moonlight from a world that had never known a moon. It painted the trees in pale outlines. Gave the clouds a ghostly sheen. Turned the glass under her hands to something otherworldly.

Lanell stared into that alien twilight.

That's where I'm from.

The wild. The unknown.

I belong to something I can't explain. And I've spent my life pretending to be normal.

The ring light shimmered in her eyes, and in it she saw no answers, just a vast question wrapped in silence. She watched the trees ripple under the dim glow, their shapes shifting like old memories trying to resurface. Her breath fogged against the glass, and she didn't bother to wipe it away.

How much of me is real?

The question came sharply and suddenly.

Who would I be if Earl had told me everything sooner? If my parents had lived? Would I be out there running through trees, barefoot and wild? Would I have learned to use the mark on my back instead of hiding it like a scar?

Her fingers curled against the glass.

I'm not one of them. I was raised here, under lights and rules and lies.

She closed her eyes for a second, breathing in the sterile, recycled air of the dome.

But I'm not one of them either, the ones in here. They don't dream of voices in white corridors. They don't wake up screaming someone else's name.

She turned and looked over at the city again. Neat blocks and ordered lines. Everything in Rith was arranged to stamp out chaos.

But chaos finds a way in.

Her hand drifted down to her hip, brushing against her jacket. She could still feel the heat of the dream, those ghostly eyes, that girl reaching for her hand.

Was she calling for help or warning me?

I don't want to be part of something ancient and broken. I don't want to carry the past.

But maybe I already am.

She stood, arms folded against her chest, forehead gently pressed to the glass. The dome felt like it wrapped around her, not as a shield but a cage. One she hadn't noticed until now.

All this time, I thought I understood who I was. Lab assistant. Research tech. The good one. Hare's golden pupil.

Her mouth set in a hard line.

But he never truly saw me. I was just someone useful. Malleable. Contained.

A faint gust from the air vents stirred her hair. It almost felt like wind, almost. But, like so many things here, it wasn't real. Her eyes drifted to the reflection of the city behind her.

They call this safety. I call it survival dressed in soft lumen.

She thought of Earl.

You lied to protect me, but maybe it wasn't just for me. Maybe you couldn't face it either. The guilt. The tribe. Everything you lost when Badger Springs went quiet. And now I'm standing here afraid of the same grief. Afraid if I open that door and let it in, I'll fall apart too.

Her hand strayed to her chest, feeling the steady beat beneath her fur.

There's power in me. I feel it. When I touch the stone. When I dream. When I see her.

She blinked as the name bloomed uninvited in her mind.

She was in the dream. The newest one. Not the nightmare from my childhood. That was mine. But this latest one...

Her lips parted, her voice low. "That was someone else's memory. And somehow, I was her." A shiver traced her spine. "She wasn't like anyone I've ever seen. But I knew she didn't belong here. And she was scared. Alone. Just like I was."

Lanell stepped back from the glass but not away. Her fingers hovered, then slowly traced a circle on the surface, absentmindedly at first. But then she stopped, staring at the mark she'd made.

A spiral. Like the one on her back.

There are too many coincidences. Too many signs. But if this is fate, then why does it feel like I'm being watched instead of guided?

The silence around her didn't answer. The dome just stood there quiet, protective, and utterly indifferent. She stayed there, eyes fixed on the shadowed wilderness beyond. The trees out there didn't belong to the city. They grew wild and unchecked. Free.

She wasn't.

"Badger Springs," she murmured, the name bitter on her tongue. "It always comes back to there."

The old dream, the one that returned like a broken record, was different from the one she'd just had. The Badger Springs dream was soaked in pain and memory. It was real, or it had been. She had lived it. Seen the earth turn to liquid, heard the screams, watched the sky collapse. But this new dream?

"It wasn't mine," she whispered, frowning.

That was the terrifying part. It felt inserted. Like something had been placed behind her eyes while she slept. Sterile corridors. A trap of white walls. A presence, watching. Not threatening. Not comforting.

Observing.

A chill snaked down her back. "What are you?" she asked the darkness. "What do you want from me?"

Her reflection stared back at her in the glass, dim and indistinct, but the eyes... They looked wrong somehow. Like someone else was staring through her face. She screwed them shut, willing it all to stop.

I'm just tired. That's all. Between Earl and what he told me...

She couldn't even finish the thought. Her father's words were still fresh. Still echoing in the hollow of her ribs. He had told her the truth, or a version of it. That he wasn't from here. That she wasn't from here. That the mark on her back wasn't just a birthmark it was a sign.

A sign of what?

Destiny? Doom?

"I didn't ask for any of this," she muttered, wiping at her eyes. "I just wanted to be good at my job. Just wanted to live a life with meaning."

She thought of how carefully she'd shaped herself to be useful to be essential to Hare, to the lab, to the city. Every part of her was molded for approval.

But now it all feels fake. A play I didn't even audition for. Her stomach twisted. How long have they known? How long have they been watching me, shaping me, waiting for something?

She stepped back from the glass, the weight of it all pressing down again.

I don't want to be special. I just want to be free.

And as she stood beneath the great skeletal curve of the dome, the wilderness stretching out beyond the glass, a quiet whisper stirred somewhere deep in her chest. It wasn't a voice or a message. She could only describe it as a feeling.

The dome hummed once, too long, too low. Her pulse answered. Something was coming.

Something that would not wait.

Chapter Twenty-Nine

Locked Out

It was early morning at the facility. Much earlier than Earl Kidd usually arrived. The night before had been restless, his thoughts running in circles too tangled to escape.

As he walked the corridor toward the main hall, the building was still and quiet, but as he stepped in farther, something caught his eye. The lights were still on in Professor Hare's and Myles's offices on the upper floors.

He had hoped to get there before them to intercept, but he was already too late. Still, he didn't dwell on the lights. Not yet. His mind was consumed with something else. Something far more personal.

Lanell.

He couldn't scrub the picture of her face the way she wouldn't blink, wouldn't give him a soft landing. And the worst part? She was right.

She had every reason to feel what she did. He'd tried to protect her, yes. But maybe he'd also hidden from his own grief. And now that truth had cost them both. He rubbed his tired eyes and sighed, then he turned toward the control center.

The elevator was slow this morning. Earl stared at his reflection in the brushed metal panel opposite him. He looked tired. And older.

His eyelids sandpapered when he blinked. Every time he closed his eyes, he saw Lanell's face.

Not fury. Disappointment, quiet and exacting. She'd trusted him not just as a guardian, but as someone who understood. And he'd failed her. Again. Tried to control what she learned. Tried to steer her away from the truth.

"You did it to protect her," he whispered to his reflection. "But maybe you did it to protect yourself too."

The elevator dinged softly. Doors opened. No turning back now.

Rolling chairs sitting ajar, screens breathing in standby, an abandoned cup of nuka. At some point the drink had overspilled, surrounding the mug in a brown halo.

This was odd, he thought. The place should have been active, alive with anticipation. The collider was scheduled to fire this morning. By now, there should've been staff running final diagnostics, techs coordinating from terminals, at least someone checking readouts.

He moved to the nearest console, swiped his access card, and brought up the system logs.

His breath stalled.

[COLLIDER FIRING LOG: 3:17 A.M. EVENT COMPLETE]

"Three seventeen?" he muttered aloud. "Why would they run it at that hour?" He pulled up the diagnostic feed, scanning for anomalies. At first glance, the system reported a clean sequence. But further down, buried in a secondary log, was a brief note. "Localized pressure loss recorded post-firing. Contained."

His brow furrowed. He mouthed the word contained? tapping a knuckle against the console.

He dug deeper into the event logs, jumping between sensor data and environmental feedback. A faint heat signature had lingered in the chamber longer than expected. Residual electromagnetic fluctuation. Or perhaps... spatial instability? He squinted at the waveform.

Then the door hissed open behind him.

Myles Moleman stepped inside, moving like a creature made of static. His shirt was half-untucked, his coat wrinkled. It looked like he hadn't changed his clothes since the day before. His eyes looked bloodshot and damp, but alert too alert.

"Myles," Earl said in what he hoped was a mild tone of voice.

"Didn't expect to see you up with the ghosts," Myles said, dragging a hand through his messy fur. His voice had that too-cheerful edge Earl didn't trust, like someone trying to pretend they hadn't buried a body an hour ago.

Earl turned back toward the console. "Didn't expect to see the firing completed already."

Myles gave a slow, theatrical shrug and ambled into the room, hands in his pockets like he owned every wire and panel. "Hare wanted to run it during off-hours. Cleaner telemetry. Fewer distractions."

"No one notified me," Earl said. His voice was flat, but his heart had picked up speed.

Myles scratched his neck, deliberately not meeting Earl's gaze. "Must've been a last-minute decision. You know how the Professor gets when inspiration strikes. Can't slow him down once he's locked in."

Earl studied him. "I've been going through the logs. Pressure spike. System flicker. Then... nothing."

Myles leaned against the edge of the console, eyes scanning the monitor a little too casually. "Yeah. Minor instability. The shielding caught it. No breach."

"But something happened," Earl pressed. "Didn't it?"

Myles smiled coolly. "Define 'something.'"

Earl's jaw tensed. He felt it in his gut the same feeling he'd had the night before. It was the feeling of standing on the edge of truth, only now there was no storm, just carefully manufactured silence.

Myles stepped forward, his movements slow and deliberate. He stopped just short of Earl, eyes flicking to the console. "Excuse me," he said in a light, almost sing-song voice. "I still need to review some of the data sets from the firing."

Earl didn't move.

Myles tilted his head. "Is there something I can help you with, Mr. Kidd?"

Earl didn't answer. He stayed planted where he stood, shoulders squared.

Myles glanced at the console, then back to Earl. His smile sharpened to a scalpel's edge. "Let me ask you something," he said. "As of this moment, does anything in this control room have an open work order with your name on it? Any maintenance request. Any official directive."

Earl said nothing.

Myles' smug grin widened. "That's what I thought." He took a step closer, invading Earl's space."So, if I may offer a professional suggestion. You may want to relocate to a department where your presence is, let's say... authorized." He motioned toward the door with a flick of his fingers. "Because right now, Mister Kidd, your presence in my control room? It is neither required nor welcome."

Earl didn't flinch. He just stared at Myles for a long moment. "You've always been this territorial, Moleman?" he asked quietly. "Or just when there's something worth hiding?"

Myles' smirk twitched, but he kept his tone breezy. "I just respect boundaries, Earl. You should try it sometime."

For a second, neither moved, then Earl stepped back slowly. "Fine," he said. "Wouldn't want to get in the way of whatever this *is.*" He turned to leave, but not before letting his eyes sweep across the monitors. One feed flickered just for a blink. Static, then nothing. He paused.

"Problem?" Myles asked.

"No. Just making sure the telemetry's nice and clean. Like you said."

And with that, he walked out. He kept his pace steady. He even managed a nonchalant whistle, but as he rounded the corner and vanished from Myles's view, the tension didn't leave with him. Frowning, he thumbed the note field open on his tablet and left it blank. His pulse was thudding harder than he liked to admit. It'd been a long time since he'd felt this furious.

That smug little toad.

Same clothes. Same stink of burnt ozone clinging to his fur. He hadn't left the facility last night. Which meant the firing had already happened without authorization, without oversight, and sure as hell without him.

They ran it behind my back. But why?

He rubbed his temple. Cleaner telemetry was what you said when you'd already pulled the trigger and needed a label. That was the kind of language people used when they were covering their tracks.

Earl could feel it like a storm in his bones. The air inside the facility had changed. He didn't know what they were hiding, but he was damn sure going to find out. And when he did, Myles Moleman wouldn't be smirking anymore.

Pressure loss. That's what the logs had said. Recorded at 03:17:25 local time. That was no simple system burp. The collider chamber was vacuum sealed, insulated with triple redundant magnetic containment.

He pictured the sequence in his head. The rail system firing. Magnetic containment spooling up. Then, just after the collision, a sudden pressure drop. Not a rupture. Not a slow leak.

An instantaneous change. There was only one thing that could cause a reading like that in an otherwise sealed vacuum: a spatial event. Something opened... and something came through.

Earl slowed his pace, brow furrowing. The way Myles had deflected the twitch in his eyelid, the way he'd guarded that terminal like a nest of his own young. This wasn't just a deviation from protocol. This had all the hallmarks of a cover-up. Hare had run the collider outside the scheduled window, without notifying him, and Myles had been involved. Probably the one who pushed the button. But why hide it?

His gut churned. Something had gone wrong, and no one was talking. Earl stopped at a maintenance alcove and leaned against the console, staring at his reflection in the polished metal.

"Something came through," he whispered to himself.

And if his instincts were right, it was still here.

Earl straightened, his reflection warping slightly across the metal surface. "If they won't show me what happened," he muttered, "then I'll find out myself." He pushed off the wall and began walking with more purpose, his boots striking the floor in a firmer rhythm.

The collider room. That's where the truth would be. Not in the polished lies Myles tried to fob him off with, but in the walls, the equipment, the readings. He tapped into his maintenance tablet, fingers moving quickly.

Request: Diagnostic sweep of chamber seals. Environmental sensors. Magnetostat field integrity.

He glanced down the hallway toward the elevator banks. No alarms. No lockdowns yet. If they hadn't restricted access already, he might still have a window.

"I need to get into the collider room," he said aloud. "I need real data. Sensor readouts. I need to see it with my own eyes."

Whatever they were hiding, whatever came through that rift, it would have left a footprint. And Earl Kidd was going to find it.

The impact chamber was located on the far side of the facility's main floor. Isolated by thick blast doors and protective shielding, it had always been a place of controlled danger. Earl had been there countless times, but this time was different.

Myles was lying. That much was clear. He'd claimed a simple overnight firing. Off-hours telemetry. Cleaner results. But Earl knew the protocols. A chamber like that didn't just fire without redundant oversight, and definitely not without him being called in for a safety review.

Pressure loss. That term in the log still scratched at him. Pressure loss meant violent decompression, an anomaly in the chamber's containment. And anomalies left residue.

As he reached the central junction, he turned left down the industrial-grade corridor that led to the collider's observation vestibule. The walls here were thicker. Reinforced. The air colder, like the room itself remembered the forces it had once held at bay.

A set of double security doors stood ahead, locked with a biometric panel. Earl stepped forward and pressed his palm against the reader. It scanned him with a quiet chirp, followed by a pulse of red light.

ACCESS DENIED.

Earl frowned. That had never happened before. Not once in all the years he'd worked here. His clearance had always granted him access to this room. Second scan. Another red pulse. A camera iris tightened above the door. His blood chilled.

They locked me out.

Chapter Thirty

A New Asset

Across every world ever spun, there is a line that must not be crossed. A line between curiosity and violation. Between wonder and desecration.

Professor Hare crossed it willingly.

He does not see a child stolen from her world. He sees variables. Equations. Anomalies to be cataloged and controlled. But the girl is not what he believes her to be. She is not just flesh and data. She is consequences. And consequences have a way of echoing.

Even now, beneath the soil of this campus, in the cold belly of his machines, the girl stirs. The air around her remembers where she came from, and it will not forget. The breach was not a moment. It was a door. And doors can open both ways.

There are places in the world that sleep even when the lights stay on. Where memory itself has settled into the walls like dust, and those who built them no longer speak of why they did.

The lower laboratories of the Hare Research Facility were once the apex of ambition, constructed in secret, retrofitted in haste, upgraded with technology the world was never meant to touch.

After the Badger Springs incident, experiments were moved out of sight. Conducted in the shadows, behind doors no longer listed on any schematic.

Time passed. Equipment was shut down. The projects reassigned. The lights dimmed but never turned off. The world above moved forward. And this place held its breath.

Until now.

Now the lights glow brighter. Sensors flicker with renewed purpose. The dust has stirred. The old machines have been summoned back to life. In one of these sealed rooms, a stranger now lies beneath sterile bulbs. A question wrapped in flesh and fear.

The girl sleeps, but the laboratory does not. It breathes again.

***

The reflection of the overhead lights gleamed off the glass partition as Professor Lupus Hare stood with his arms folded behind his back, staring the figure on the table. For all the thousands of hours he had spent in these lower levels, this moment was unlike any he had experienced.

She was human. And utterly, unmistakably alive.

She lay motionless on the exam platform. Her skin had lost its reactive color in the chill of the containment cell, taking on a soft pallor under the clinical lighting. Medical monitors hummed softly nearby, displaying pulse, respiration, thermal fluctuation. All within acceptable range. More than acceptable, actually, remarkable.

Hare's ears twitched. He hadn't expected stability this soon after transit. The dimensional shift should have compromised tissue cohesion. Internal systems should have shown trauma, if not complete failure. And yet, here she was. Breathing. Unbroken. Naked truth, in every sense of the word.

She had been carefully placed face down for the current scans, her golden blonde hair brushed aside and secured to expose the upper spine. He'd clipped her hair to the tray with two sterile clamps, never once averting his eyes, only adjusting the angle for the camera, for clarity.

Between her shoulder blades, slightly lower and off-center, was a mark. Not a scar. Not pigmentation. He increased the magnification.

Hare had seen thousands of skin anomalies in his time freckles, birthmarks, deformities. But not this. Not even close. It resembled a kind of spiral, interconnected nodes etched into her flesh like nature had drawn them with intent. He leaned in, activating the imaging overlay.

No raised tissue. No reactive protein. No ink or burn residue. Just... present. In the epidermal layer. Subtle but fixed. A signature, perhaps. Or a mutation. He made a note on his tablet.

Subject: External Marking

Location: Dorsal T3–T6 range

Visual: Geometric spiral pattern

Theory: Unknown origin. Not synthetic. Not tattoo. Biological anomaly. Further tissue mapping required.

Then, after a long pause, he typed possibly genetic before immediately backspacing so hard the stylus taps echoed. Something so clearly formed should have been cataloged, traceable. And yet it wasn't.

"You brought secrets with you," he murmured. "And I intend to pry out every last one."

He adjusted the overhead lamp, tilting the beam until it lit her form cleanly. His eyes narrowed behind the lens of the scanner, not with disgust or pity, but with wonder.

He dragged anatomy overlays on split-screen: her humerus length fell inside his model's variance band, ulna/radius ratios nearly overlaid too. When the curves almost matched, he stopped and tilted his head, ears flicking. He paced slowly around the table, muttering. "Structure. Limb-to-torso ratio. Bilateral design. Even the cranial volume isn't outside theoretical range. Not entirely."

He stopped by her outstretched arm and ran a scanner just above the surface of her skin, watching the readout dance. "Muscle density... comparable. Skeletal structure denser than a hare's, lighter than a mole's. And look at these digits. Opposable. Refined motor capability."

The scanner pulsed as it passed her feet, then her hips. Hare didn't falter. This was data. This was progress. "What evolutionary pressure," he mused aloud, "drives this level of parallel development across dimensions?"

She wasn't just another species. She was an echo. A ripple from a different pond that had landed in his. "How can something from outside look like something from here," he whispered, stepping closer, "unless... the rules are the same everywhere?"

He looked again to the scanner's readout. A near-match on several organ placements. Brain activity dormant but stable. Respiration shallow. Heart rate slow.

He drew two river-lines on the glass different courses, same mouth then circled the convergent node and underlined it twice. A mirror, distorted but recognizable.

He stopped near her head, studying the lines of her cheekbones. A twitch. Was that a spasm? No, just the tremble of breath.

There was intelligence there. Hare could feel it pressing through her unconsciousness. Waiting.

"But who are you?" he asked quietly. "What are you?"

He circled back to the monitor and saved the data logs with a swipe. No one else had examined her yet. Myles was due later, and that gave Hare time. Time to prepare. Time to poke deeper into the unknown. Time to claim the discovery as his alone.

He glanced from the vitals to the collider timestamp. The digits blinked 03:17. His mind churned. "What force, what chain of events, what invitation brought you across the breach?"

His eyes drifted back to the panel displaying the collider data. Time stamps. Particle drift. Energy spike. Then the anomaly. The singularity.

He wrote strange matter and trilineum, then printed PERCUSSIVE DIMENSIONAL EVENT in block letters. He circled it so hard the cursor flickered in protest.

His scribbling gradually escalated to a feverish pace, symbols and equations stacking like bricks of a theoretical temple. When strange matter is fired into trilineum at full resonance, you get more than just energy exchange. You get dimensional percussion. He paused, tapping the stylus to his chin. "Yes... that's it. A percussive dimensional event." He wrote PDE and underlined it.

"A concussive reaction that rings the local dimensional membrane like a bell. And this," he gestured toward the unconscious girl, "was the resonance." His voice dropped to a hush. "You were caught in the wave. Or maybe you answered it." He studied her closed eyes. "Why you?" What about you was... attuned?

"Some aspect of you... your biology, your patterning, something encoded in your makeup resonated with the PDE." He drew two sine waves on the glass, phase-shifted them until the peaks kissed, then mouthed synchronized.

"And if that's true," he whispered, eyes widening, "then there might be others who could resonate too."

The door seal hissed. Myles slipped in. "I've locked the wing," he said. "Oh, and I've restricted access to the collider wing. Full lockdown. No one's getting in or out without my clearance."

Hare raised an eyebrow. "Not even Earl?"

"Especially not Earl. Biometric clearance scrubbed. Even maintenance override won't work now. If he wants in, he'll have to knock. Loudly."

"Good." Hare tapped the comm closed without looking up, already turning back to the scan.

He turned his attention back to the still form on the table this impossibly alien girl who shouldn't exist and yet did. Every detail of her anatomy puzzled him. Fascinated him. Conflicted him. But one question kept circling in his mind like a hawk over prey.

Something had triggered the rift. The collision had followed all projected vectors. The strange matter had aligned, but instead of opening a doorway to Trinn's world, it had ripped a hole somewhere else. Somewhere unintended. He spoke ponderously, half to himself, half to Myles. "Tell me, do we have an internal scan of the impact chamber prior to the firing?"

Myles blinked. "You mean... pre-ignition?"

"Yes," Hare said. "Not the environmental sweep after the fact. Not the post-collision readouts. I want the chamber's condition before the firing. Every micron of it. Every particle in that room."

Myles frowned. "You think there was a contaminant?"

"I think something interacted with the strange matter mid-sequence," Hare said. "Something unexpected, perhaps insignificant. But in quantum systems, the tiniest anomaly can redirect an entire waveform."

Myles shifted uncomfortably. "I mean, the pre-firing scans are archived, but they're buried. System only does full-spectrum internals once every twelve hours unless you request it."

"Then pull it," Hare said. "Now."

Myles sighed. "Right. I'll queue it up. It could take a few minutes."

Hare's mind was already racing. If something had been in that chamber, even the smallest foreign object, it might have disrupted the strange matter's entanglement pattern. Redirected the collision. Altered its dimensional targeting. His attention wandered back to the girl on the table. "You didn't arrive by chance," he whispered. "Something pulled you here. Or someone."

Hare and Myles stood beside the metal observation table. The being, still unconscious, lay on the table beneath a translucent bioscreen, her skin marked only by the faint bruises of dimensional transfer and a strange spiral-like mark along her upper back.

Myles leaned in, adjusting his glasses as he scrutinized the contours of her leg. He reached forward and prodded the calf muscle with professional detachment. "Structure's sound. Musculature's almost identical to our own. Joints, tendons, flex points it's like someone played evolution's same melody in a different key."

Hare's eyes didn't leave the girl's face. "You know," he began, his voice distant and reflective, "there was a time when I would've argued loudly and publicly that we were the only intelligent life in the universe. That consciousness was some rare, improbable accident unique to us."

Brow furrowed, he folded his arms as he watched her chest rise and fall.

"And now?" Myles asked.

"Now I'm wondering if the universe is threaded with a pattern we never saw. A similarity in biology. A kind of echo between dimensions."

Myles straightened. "You think this is convergent evolution? That our kind and hers arose independently but came out... similar?"

"No. I think there's something older at work. Something that bridges biology and physics. Something in the architecture of existence itself. Look at her. She's alien but not foreign."

He took a step closer. "What if dimensional physics doesn't just transport matter, but favors certain patterns? What if there's a design at the core of reality that selects for this kind of form?"

Myles let out a low whistle. "That's not science; that's metaphysics."

Hare's eyes twinkled with the thrill of forbidden thought. "Perhaps. Or perhaps we're standing in a moment that rewrites everything." He rotated the skull overlay until orbital widths aligned. "Pattern," he said, tapping the glass. "Architecture." Not just that life exists beyond our world, but that it wants to connect. That there are echoes. Rhymes.

Myles smirked. "You sound like a poet, Hare. That's dangerous."

"No," Hare replied, eyes blazing. "What's dangerous is pretending we understand this already."

Hare's eyes lingered on the girl's face, still and unknowing beneath the soft shimmer of the bioscreen. His voice, when it came, had lost its usual clinical sharpness. "You remember when I met Trinn?"

Myles gave him a sidelong look. "Of course. Hard to forget the day you dragged that thing back from the desert with half its skin missing and a language no one could translate."

Hare chuckled darkly. "That was the moment everything changed for me. Before Trinn, I was like every other academic scrambling for peer review, polishing old theories, pretending we'd already figured out most of the universe and were just tidying up the corners." He shook his head slowly. "Trinn was more than simply proof of extraterrestrial life. Trinn was impossible. She broke rules we didn't even know we had. Materials. Language. Cognition. Physics. Just being near her made you feel like a toddler pretending to read a map."

Myles nodded, half-listening, still inspecting the human specimen's form with fascination.

"That encounter shattered the illusion," Hare continued. "Of control. Of certainty. After Trinn, I realized just how blind we've been. This world... our dimension... It's a box. And we've been decorating the inside of it, convinced it's the whole house. And now this human falls through the ceiling. From where? Why her? How? It's another crack in the box, and I can't help but look through it."

Myles tapped a console absentmindedly. "You think Trinn and this girl are connected somehow?"

"I don't know," Hare admitted. "But the universe doesn't just drop impossible beings into your lap twice unless it's trying to say something." He armed the long-duration monitor, set the mic to sub-threshold capture, and pulled a stool close enough that his knees touched the gurney's steel. "And I intend to listen."

Chapter Thirty-One

Denied

Lanell's eyes burned from a night without sleep. She hadn't gone home, hadn't even tried to rest. After the nightmare, if that's what it even was, she'd walked to the observation dome and stayed there, watching the stars fade into the morning. The dream still clung to her, souring every breath with the phantom sting of ozone. The strange being. The trap. That voice. Gotcha.

As she stepped through the facility's quiet entrance hall, her only goal was to get to her office, change into the spare clothes she always kept there, and pull herself together before the collider test began. Hare and Myles would probably already be in their offices, gearing up for the final diagnostics.

She glanced down the hallway as she passed. Sure enough, the lights were on in both their offices. Good. That meant she still had time to clean up before heading to the collider wing.

The corridor lights held steady, but nothing moved behind the glass. Her eyes skipped past it, the way they do when you've run out of questions and nuka.

She made it to her office and shut the door behind her with a quiet thud. Her legs ached, her shoulders were tight, and her fur still carried the faint prickle of static, like her dream had left an invisible charge humming beneath her skin.

She sighed and crossed the room, heading straight for the narrow cabinet tucked behind her desk. Inside, a backup outfit waited. She rifled through it with stiff fingers and pulled out a pair of black tights, light blue hoodie, and some jean shorts. "Little casual," she muttered under her breath, holding the shorts up to the light, "but maybe no one will notice."

She changed quickly, grateful to be out of the rumpled clothes from the night before. The tights hugged her legs snugly, and the denim felt cool against her fur. Yeah, this is better, she thought. If I'd kept those stretched-out pants on, I'd be turning more heads than I want today.

She looked in the mirror and gave herself a once-over. Not perfect, but passable. Her blue eyes were rimmed red and there was a hard set to her mouth she didn't recognize, but she mostly looked like her again.

She turned toward the door, then hesitated. For a moment, she considered stopping by Earl's office. Maybe he could ground her thoughts, make sense of that dream. But the thought passed as quickly as it came.

No. Her hand tightened on the knob. Collider first. Hare and Myles are probably already gearing up for the review. I need to be in that room when it happens.

The light under Hare's door glowed, but the dust along the threshold lay undisturbed.

No movement behind the frosted glass. No voices. No rustling papers. Dead silence.

Okay... maybe they're already in the control room. Yeah, that makes sense. Big day. Early prep.

Still, her insides felt cold.

The HVAC's steady wash seemed to thin, as if the vents were listening. She took a steadying inhale, but even the air felt wrong ionized and dry, with a faint metallic bite on the back of her tongue. The kind of charge that made fur stand up before a lightning strike.

Quit it, she scolded herself. You didn't sleep. You're spiraling. Just get to the collider, check in, act normal. This is what professionals do.

She turned toward the corridor that led to the collider wing, her boots clicking softly on the floor. The hallway stretched ahead, unnaturally quiet. Fluorescent lights buzzed above, but there was a strange rhythm to it like a beat missing from a song.

Don't do this. Don't let the dream mess with your head. Glue traps and strange beings. It wasn't real.

But the memory refused to be silenced. She could almost feel that rubbery substance around her ankles, tugging. The walls felt tighter here. Longer. Too long.

You've walked this hallway a hundred times. Why does it feel different today?

Her pace quickened, even as she told herself to slow down. She resisted the urge to check over her shoulder.

"Let's just get this over with," she muttered under her breath.

But the air still whispered at her, a low sizzle that crawled across her skin like a warning. Like the building knew something she didn't.

Lanell reached the end of the corridor and stopped in front of the heavy security door that led to the collider control room. The hallway behind her fell away into silence.

She glanced at the control room window. The lights inside were on but dim, like an old photograph that had faded with time. The glow was sickly, tinted yellow, and cast long shadows across the room's interior. She stepped closer. The glass was cool enough to fog her breath.

Through the thick reinforced pane, she could see the central console. One of the monitors was still active, glowing pale green, the phosphor hum just audible through the frame. A half-full cup of something sat next to the console. Steam no longer rose from it, but the liquid hadn't settled into that forgotten, opaque ring of old coffee yet.

They'd been here recently. Very recently. But now? The chairs were empty. No one was in sight. Lanell tilted her head.

Where the hell are they?

She reached toward the keypad and punched in her access code, confident in the routine. The keys were greasy-smooth under her fingertips, and the panel answered with a dull beep. She had been in and out of this room countless times. This was her domain, her schedule, her experiment. The panel blinked red.

ACCESS DENIED.

The words flared on the small screen like a slap. Lanell stared at them.

That's not right.

She tried again, slower this time. Key by key. Her heart tapped against her ribs, just a little faster now.

ACCESS DENIED.

She double-checked the panel. Her credentials were still valid. She hadn't heard anything about a lockdown. And why would they lock her out? She was scheduled to be here. She was part of this project. She leaned closer to the window, peering in. No signs of damage. No alarms. Just that cup. That one stupid, lingering cup, like a ghost from the last moment someone sat there.

She knocked gently on the glass. The sound thudded once and died. Professor Hare?" she called. Her voice barely echoed, muffled by the reinforced frame.

No response.

A shiver unfurled down her back, and fur along her arms roughened, then settled. She took a step back. The silence pressed in. She rechecked the security panel, looking for override options, alternate access, or anything else. Nothing but red.

Her hand hovered over her comm, tempted to call someone Earl or security. But she hesitated.

What if this is some kind of test? Was I not briefed on some protocol? No... No one said anything. This is off-book.

She bit her lip.

So where are they?

And then, unbidden, the dream slid back into her mind like a shadow slipping under a door.

The strange creature. The silence. The feeling of being trapped, restrained, and observed.

Lanell stepped back from the sealed collider door, her fingertips tingling. She took one last look through the glass at that abandoned console. That forgotten half-cup. That flickering green glow.

Okay. Fine. If they're not in there, maybe they're back in their offices.

She turned on her heel. The air still felt weird and charged, like something had just happened. Or was still happening. She passed a few early staffers in the hallway research interns, some admin aides but they barely glanced up from their tablets. Even the chirp of the badge scanners on the security panels sounded bored.

So maybe it's just me. Perhaps I'm overreacting. Maybe I just need sleep. Or a damn reality check.

She rounded the corner toward Professor Hare's office and came to a halt.

Inside the adjacent admin cubicle, Stacie Pinecone was tucking her satchel under her desk and booting up her terminal. Citrus cleaner hung faintly over the cubicle fabric. The striped lemur adjusted her headset with practiced ease, the foam pads squeaking as her long tail curled idly around the leg of her chair. "Oh, hey, Lanell!" she chirped brightly, glancing up. "You're in early. Or... late?"

Lanell offered a polite smile. "Early, technically."

Stacie tilted her head, then gave Lanell an appraising look. "Huh," she said. "Didn't expect to see you in shorts and tights. Bold combo for a collider firing day."

Lanell glanced down at herself reflexively. "It's all I had in my office," she said with a shrug. "Long night."

Stacie raised an eyebrow. "Trouble sleeping, or just avoiding it?"

Lanell didn't answer right away. She was already looking past Stacie toward Hare's office. The lights were on. "I'm looking for Hare and Myles," she said. "Are they in already?"

Stacie blinked. "I mean, I saw lights on when I walked in, but no one's come through here. Not since I sat down. Thought they were already down in the collider wing."

Lanell's brows pulled together. "They're not."

Stacie leaned back in her chair. "Weird. I figured you'd all be buzzing down there. Didn't they have that firing scheduled this morning?"

Lanell didn't know what to say. She gave a quiet, "Thanks," and moved toward Hare's door.

Behind her, Stacie called out casually, "Oh! One more thing there was a weird smell in the air this morning when I walked in. Kinda harsh and burnt. Maybe like... old electronics? Thought it was just the dehumidifier acting up again."

Lanell stopped for half a second. That static buzz she'd felt in the corridor. The dry charge in the air. She turned slightly, giving Stacie a sidelong glance. "What time did you get in?"

Stacie tapped her screen. "Ten minutes ago? Around 6:40? Why?"

Lanell didn't answer. She just kept walking, the hallway suddenly feeling tighter around her.

Down the corridor, past the row of closed doors and darkened labs. The collider was locked. Hare and Myles were nowhere to be found. Something wasn't right.

She turned the corner and stopped at Myles Moleman's office. The door was slightly ajar. She knocked once, out of habit, then eased it open.

Empty. Of course.

She glanced back down the hall. No one was watching. No one cared. Lanell stepped inside. The scent of graphite lubricant and synth-ink lingered faintly. The overhead lights buzzed above the cluttered desk, where Myles's terminal was still active, screen aglow with telemetry data. The desk fan ticked once each rotation, a tired bearing announcing itself.

She closed the door behind her. The latch clicked softly. The chair gave a low squeak as she sat, and the cushion exhaled trapped dust.

Sensor Telemetry Collider Firing Event 0317 HRS.

Her brow furrowed. "Wait... that's this morning."

She tapped the trackpad. Up came graphs radiation spikes, magnetic field disruptions, a burst in strange matter compression followed by a rapid dip in trilineum cohesion.

Residual waveform echo: persistent.

Unknown spatial signature: recorded.

Impact chamber anomaly: confirmed.

She leaned in. Warm plastic breathed from the terminal vents. The collider already fired? She scrolled to a frame-capture from the impact chamber's internal sensor log. Not a live feed, just data. Still, it was enough to reveal something strange: a momentary spatial fracture. A sharp pressure drop. And then, flatline silence.

This was getting weirder and weirder.

She opened the security log. Access to the collider wing had been locked down from the control hub remotely at 0520 hours. About ninety minutes after the firing. And someone had entered the control room after that.

E. Kidd.

Her fingers hovered above the desk. They fired it without telling her. Locked it down. And Earl saw it before anyone else even knew it happened.

She exhaled slowly through her nose. "What are you hiding, Hare?"

Lanell quickly scanned the room again. She was still alone. She reached beneath the desk, opened the lower drawer, and grabbed a small unused data disk from the stack of blanks Myles kept for transferring field samples. The thing was dusty. That felt appropriate.

She slid it into the terminal's side port. A tiny static nip kissed her knuckle. She dragged the event logs over sensor telemetry, timestamps, waveform anomalies, and the access records showing Earl's presence.

TRANSFER COMPLETE.

She ejected the disk and slipped it into the inner pocket of her shorts.

Outside, the halls were still deserted. She made her way toward the break area. The lights there were dimmer, more forgiving. A coffee machine clicked quietly in the corner; the compressor under the counter kicked on with a tired rattle. One of the admin assistants had left a half-eaten protein bar on the table, the wrapper curled like a wilted flag.

Lanell slid into the booth near the window and let herself sag. The vinyl was cool and a little tacky through her tights. The data disk burned in her pocket like it wanted out.

She rested her elbows on the table and stared at her own hands. Placing them flat on the tabletop was the only way to stop the shaking.

"I should go to Papa," she murmured. "He'd know what to do."

But she didn't move. How was she supposed to explain all this? That she hadn't slept. That she'd seen something no one else had. That she'd gone snooping. That she was scared, confused, and unsure if she was even supposed to be involved.

He'd look at her with those steady, worried eyes. He'd ask gentle questions. He'd try to fix it. And somehow, that made her feel small.

No. Not yet.

She sat back in the booth and stared at the ceiling.

I need more facts first. Then I'll go to him.

She glanced toward the hallway beyond the breakroom where the spineward wing curved off toward the equipment annex and the materials lab.

Dr. Crusher.

He had a reputation for showing up early, especially on days with scheduled events. Said the air tasted less stupid before the rest of the facility woke up.

Lanell had crossed paths with him a few times during early shifts. The badger mainly kept to himself, but he'd always been sharp. Eccentric, yeah, but sharp. And he wasn't part of Hare's inner circle. He hadn't been fed the same half-truths, so maybe, just maybe, he'd noticed something too.

It was worth a shot.

She headed for the spineward wing, already bracing herself for whatever strange project Crusher might be knee-deep in this time.

Chapter Thirty-Two

Cohesion

This wing ran cooler and cleaner brighter LEDs, harder echoes, doors that opened with a stingier hiss. She rarely came over here, no reason to really. It was mostly home to the molecular binding teams, the robotics bay, and the drone tech labs. Each doorway glowed with its own color-temp, like islands with different weather systems. Whiteboards argued with code printouts; a calibration arm clicked to itself like it didn't need an audience. Work here continued whether anyone watched or not.

She passed the final HAB-4 stencil. "Where molecular bonding meets drone warfare," she mumbled. "Great. Real casual stuff."

She eyed the door tags as she walked. Robotics. Drone Tech. Materials Integration. Each one more specialized and less inviting than the last. A flaking K. FOXX DO NOT POWER CYCLE sticker clung to a junction box. This was his domain, all right. That little flash of fur and arrogance. For weeks, he'd tried everything short of serenading her in the atrium to get her attention. Smart. Talented. And absolutely insufferable. He finally backed off after she told him very plainly that her interest in robotics didn't extend to dating one.

She smirked at the memory. At least he'd taken the hint. Crusher though, he was different.

Dr. George Crusher. Lead researcher in adhesives. Keeper of the weirdest lab in the entire facility. And, against her better judgment, someone she'd always found... kinda cute.

She wasn't sure if it was the streak of white in his otherwise dirt brown hair, or the way his mullet somehow always looked perfectly intentional instead of tragic. Maybe it was the eyes sharp but curious. Or the way he always looked like he was thinking three layers deeper than everyone else in the room and just hadn't decided whether to share yet.

Her ears had the nerve to tilt forward. "Focus. You're here for intel, not eye candy." Still, she smoothed her shorts a little before reaching for the lab door panel.

Her breath fogged as she stepped into the transition corridor leading into Habitat 4. The temperature shift was subtle but noticeable, like entering a greenhouse that hadn't quite woken up yet. The soft hum of overhead lights buzzed against her senses, and the air carried a faint tang of synthetic chlorophyll, cleaning solvents, and... something else. Something earthy and warm, like soil and rubber melted together.

She passed by a sealed window looking into the hydroponics test chamber. The lights were low, and nothing moved inside except the slow trickle of nutrient fluid cycling through clear tubes. This early, before the shift-change chatter and comms traffic flooded the halls, she could hear her own footsteps echoing back at her.

She glanced down the long hallway. No movement. Just closed doors, quiet labs, and faint glows from motion sensors catching her approach. Her shoulders tensed as she neared the corner where the adhesive lab's door came into view. The glowing panel beside the door was green. Occupied.

"Well, at least someone's awake," she muttered.

She took a breath, her hand hovering just inches from the sensor. A strange tension coiled in her stomach. Not fear exactly. More like déjà vu. Like she'd been here before, in a place where things stuck to you, and the air felt too still. She shook it off.

A dream. Just a dream.

"It's just glue," she said, forcing a smirk. "Not a trapdoor to the void."

And with that, she tapped the panel. The door whooshed open with a soft hiss of pressure.

Lanell stepped through the door and paused. She hadn't known what to expect, but this? This was something else.

The lab wasn't a lab so much as a biomechanical jungle. The open space was divided into zones, each weirder than the last. Just ahead, a large observation window framed a twenty-by-twenty-foot garden enclosure, clearly a subsection of Habitat 4. It buzzed under full-spectrum lamps, casting simulated daylight over coiled vines, dense foliage, and a scaffolding structure overtaken by crawling greenery. Leaves mirrored leaves at perfect intervals, veins ran ruler-straight under lamp glare. And in the center of it all, two oversized snails, the size of small dogs, slid languidly across the garden floor, leaving behind thick, iridescent trails that shimmered like oil in water.

Her whiskers twitched. "Gross," she said. "That cannot be regulation."

She looked away from the snails and stepped deeper into the lab. To the right, massive cylindrical vats loomed like industrial silos, each at least twelve feet tall and six wide, veined with tangled tubing that disappeared into the floor, ceiling, and probably the fabric of reality. They hissed softly, exhaling intermittent puffs of vapor that tasted like warm batteries and orange rind.

But it was the center of the lab that truly stole the show. There, like some sort of industrial baptismal font, sat a massive, round, one thousand gallon glass tank about six feet high filled to the brim with a thick mustard-yellow fluid. The surface burbled occasionally, releasing lazy bubbles, like the thing was dreaming.

Lanell squinted. Were those... eyes? Two of them. Suspended in the goo. Watching her.

She stopped cold. Her fur prickled along her arms. The eyes blinked. Then one winked.

"Okay, absolutely not," she muttered.

Cautiously, she stepped forward. Her boots made a soft squish on the resin floor. She raised a knuckle and gave the tank a firm tap.

The fluid rippled. The eyes blinked at her again.

"You better be part of a classified experiment," she said under her breath, "and not the reason I end up as a screaming victim on grainy security footage in some cheesy documentary." She took one more look, just to be sure the thing wasn't going to sprout a mouth, and backed away, wiping her fingers on her shorts. "Dr. Crusher, if this goo has a name and you forgot to mention it, we're having words."

"Come here. You've gotta try this."

Lanell stepped forward warily. "This isn't going to melt my skin off or bond me to a containment barrel, right?" She flexed her hands against the bench. It was clean but faintly tacky.

Dr. Crusher pushed his goggles to his forehead. "Perish the thought. I only bring out the volatile stuff for interns and full moons." He gestured to the small tray of amber goo on the bench beside him. "This is Goo-8147S. Still in early testing. Perfectly harmless. Completely inert until I tell it otherwise."

Lanell peered at the shimmering surface. "It looks like someone harvested the purest honey, but then she looked at the badger and said I know this isn't honey."

"Flattering," he said. "Now, go on. Stick your finger in."

She shot him a flat look. "This feels like a trap."

"It's science," he replied. "Also possibly a trap. But mostly science."

Lanell sighed and dipped her finger into the goo. Warm. Silky. Like sliding through heated satin. She gave it a little swirl, then pulled her finger out clean. No stick. No mess.

"Huh. That was "

"Try again," Crusher said, flipping a nearby switch with a smirk. "Now it's awake."

"Awake?"

"Go on. Same motion."

Against her better judgment and every instinct that had evolved to avoid sticky substances, she put her finger back in.

At first, nothing happened. Then she tried to lift it. A tendril snapped upward with her finger. It stretched, viscous and shimmering, refusing to let go. She tugged. It pulled back.

Lanell's ears betrayed her by angling forward. "It's flirting with me."

Crusher grinned. "Low-current phase shift. The molecular bonds become permanently fused, but in a state of flex. Clingy but not judgmental."

She used her other hand to pry herself free, only for that hand to get caught too. Her breath hitched. The elastic pull was unpleasantly familiar. She tried a twist, but the bond tightened. "Crusher, release. Now, please."

"Technically," he said, leaning on the bench, "you're experiencing about 38 PSI of adaptive resistance. See, once it recognizes motion "

"Crusher!"

"Hmm?"

"Release me or I will take this tray and introduce it to your face."

He pretended to think. "Counteroffer: dinner Friday. And then I release you."

Lanell smiled sweetly. "Or I skip dinner and go straight to kicking you in the glue globes."

He chuckled, then hit the release toggle. The goo slackened and slid away like obedient molasses. Her hands dropped free with a soft plop, no residue in sight.

She flexed her fingers. "You're a menace."

He grinned. "You're the one who touched it twice."

Lanell crossed her arms. "Okay, Dr. Crusher, show-and-stick appreciated. I'm actually here for a serious reason."

He raised an eyebrow. "You mean this wasn't a social call?"

She gave him a look. "Not unless your goop takes dinner reservations now."

He snorted, then gestured for her to continue. "All right. What's eating at you?"

Lanell leaned against the workbench, arms still crossed. "I came in early today because I was under the impression the collider was scheduled for its next test firing."

Crusher nodded. "Yeah, I'd heard the same. Big push on the data-gathering schedule or whatever. So?"

"So, by the time I got in, that entire section of the facility was already locked down. No access. No warning. No usual crew around. Just sealed doors and a blinking panel telling me I didn't have clearance."

He frowned, the playfulness draining from his face. "That's not protocol."

"Exactly." Lanell reached into her pocket and pulled out the small data disk. She didn't hand it over, just let him see it. " For sake of protecting the innocent, all I am going to tell you is I found this sitting naked in a relay room. Telemetry logs. I haven't cracked them yet, but the timestamps are... off."

Crusher scratched the back of his head, his goggles tilting slightly. "Hare and Mole-man?"

"Nowhere to be found. Not in their offices, not answering comms. I even asked Stacie and She said they were on campus someplace, and that was it."

Crusher's brow wrinkled. "That doesn't sound like Hare. He lives to monologue."

Lanell nodded. "Something happened. I don't know what. But I think these logs of the collider, it has already been fired."

"And you want me to help dig."

"I want your opinion first. You're one of the only ones around here who still tells the truth without running it through five layers of politics and budget approvals."

"You just like me for my glue." He drummed two fingers; they made a tiny unsticking sound.

She rolled her eyes. "Right now, I like you for your clearance level. Can you get into the collider logs? The real ones, not the ones they send to PR."

Crusher tapped his fingers against the bench thoughtfully. "Depends on how much noise you want to make. If they locked that room down before the shift started, it wasn't random. Someone's covering something."

Lanell gave him a steady look. "I know."

Crusher hesitated for a fraction of a second, then motioned toward the far workstation. "Come on. Let's pull it up over there."

Lanell followed, stepping around a stack of coiled tubing and labeled trays. As they walked, Crusher cast a glance at her outfit. "Didn't realize today was casual adhesion awareness day," he said deadpan.

Lanell smirked. "Well, if we're triggering chemical reactions, might as well dress to cause one."

That earned the tiniest upward twitch of Crusher's lips. "Fair point. Just warn me if the boots are explosive."

Lanell slid the small data disk into the port beside Crusher's terminal. "It's from the collider room. Picked it up about thirty minutes ago."

Crusher leaned in, already tapping at the control panel. Lines of telemetry and system diagnostics began to scroll across the screen waveform spikes, containment readings, timestamps. He squinted "This is from today?"

"Yeah. That's the thing. I was under the impression the collider hadn't been fired yet. Everything was supposed to be prepped for later today, but..." She folded her arms, watching the screen with a deepening frown. "Myles and Professor Hare are nowhere to be found, and the whole collider wing's locked down."

Crusher muttered something under his breath and punched a key to isolate the readout timestamps. "These numbers, this isn't idle data. These are post-activation readings. Thermal spikes, magnetic disruption, particle return signatures..." He looked at her. "Lanell, they already fired it."

She blinked. "But there was no announcement. No staff in the chamber. No posted safety clearance. Nothing went over internal comms."

"This wasn't a scheduled run," Crusher said. He scrolled further. "Power draw matches full activation. And this" he tapped one spot on the graph where a sharp dip broke the line "this isn't standard. There was a containment breach window. Brief but measurable."

Lanell's voice dropped. "So either they jumped the schedule, or someone didn't want anyone to know it happened."

Crusher straightened up, the glow of the screen flickering in his goggles. "You're not wrong to be worried." He exhaled through his nose and leaned back from the screen. "I'll pull a copy of this for you. No problem there."

He reached for a portable drive, inserted it into the console, and began the transfer. Then his voice shifted. It was warmer now, less analytical. "But, Lanell... Look, I don't mind helping you. You know that." But whatever this is?" He tapped the screen gently. "It was done for a reason. Quietly. Deliberately."

The whir of the terminal filled the space for a beat before Crusher continued.

"If Hare wanted you looped in, you'd have been standing in that chamber beside him. Myles too. But they didn't tell you. Didn't even tell the system to notify staff. That's not a glitch. That's intent."

Lanell's shoulders tightened. But Crusher's tone wasn't patronizing, just matter-of-fact.

"I stay in my lab," he said. "I do my work. I make my glue. I don't ask questions when the answers come wrapped in red tape and disappear into Level Two." He handed her the drive. "My advice? Do your thing the job Hare hired you for. He had his reasons, whether you like 'em or not."

As Crusher leaned back from the console, Lanell stayed still, eyes fixed on the scrolling data. The screen glowed cold blue, but it was everything behind it that weighed on her: the confrontation with Earl, the restless sleep, the locked collider doors, and now this evidence of something big... and hidden. She didn't speak for a moment. Just stared.

Then slowly, she rose. "Maybe you're right," she said quietly. "Maybe I should stay in my lane." She looked down at her hands, flexed them once, then looked up. "Or maybe not. Maybe I need to do more." Her gaze turned to him now. She looked more focused, more certain. "Either way, it feels like there's a choice to make. One I can't walk around anymore." She tilted her head, gauging his reaction. "Wouldn't you say so, Dr. Crusher?"

He didn't answer right away. Lanell watched him, expecting something anything but the badger just stood there, unusually still. No quip. No grin. It wasn't indifference. It felt more like a restraint. Like whatever he was thinking didn't quite make it out of the gate.

"Thanks for the assist," she said. "I really do appreciate it."

And with that, she turned toward the exit. She'd made it three steps before his voice followed her.

"Bizlok."

She paused and glanced back over her shoulder. "Bizlok? What's that, the name of a solvent or something?"

Crusher gave a half-smile, hands still in his coat pockets. "No. My friends call me Bizlok."

Lanell turned fully toward the door, that knowing smirk returning. "I'll remember that, Dr. Crusher."

The door slid shut behind her, leaving a breath of citrus-ozone and trouble in her wake.

Chapter Thirty-Three

Impact Chamber Analysis

Trinn seethed. Another failure. Another wasted cycle. For all his posturing and promises, Hare still couldn't crack the dimensional barrier. The collider test had fizzled. No breakthrough. No signal home. Nothing but static, excuses, and a rift that dropped a human in the impact chamber.

The drone pulsed with a dark crimson glow. The vessel, a spherical biomechanical construct, lacked the comforts of humanoid design. No chairs. No console. No atmosphere. Only the living walls and the pilot's will.

Filament lines, thin as nerves, threaded the hull. Through a neural interlink directly jacked into her cranial array, the drone's ambient light adjusted in real-time, a reactive synesthetic system called Mood-Color Phase Feedback. In theory, it helped regulate stress. In practice, it turned the interior into a roiling mood ring powered by rage. Right now, that meant crimson.

The craft veered flowward, hugging the low clouds like a shark beneath ice. Its outer hull, a lattice of photoreactive plates, masked it from most passive scans.

Trinn sat in silence. The neural tether fed her information on terrain, air composition, and minor fluctuations in gravitational resonance. All irrelevant. All noise. She wasn't flying to sightsee. She was en route to the crash site.

The battle platform remained embedded in a chasm beyond the city's reach: an entire fortress entombed beneath the surface, shielded by quantum camouflage and cloaked from planetary scans. It was there, within its sensor core and impact chamber, that she might finally extract something useful from last night's failure.

Professor Hare had promised her a gateway. Instead, he'd delivered an unspecified rift and a naked alien. A brute with wires. He lacked the nuance, the discipline. He didn't understand the layered intricacies of near-dimensional convergence. And worst of all, he pretended he did.

Inside the drone's neural pod, her biomass pulsed in an uneven rhythm. The red light bathing the spherical cockpit darkened, flickering with each spasm of frustration. She flexed her mandibles.

As the drone neared the crash zone, a sharp blip on the navigation array snapped Trinn from her brooding. The forward display revealed a jagged rupture splitting the terrain wide open. A chasm. Visible. Exposed.

That was impossible. If the systems were functioning correctly, the site should have been concealed by the platform's holographic camouflage, just another stretch of scorched, desolate wasteland. But instead of blank terrain, there was an open wound in the earth.

The cloaking matrix had failed. Trinn gave a tight, subvocal growl. Her drone halted midair, stabilizers flaring in silence. Sensor probes fanned outward, scanning for power signatures, electromagnetic distortions, and nearby movement.

She didn't wait for diagnostic confirmation. She already knew what this meant. Something had interfered with the field since her last visit. Something or someone.

She eased the drone downward, hovering just above the mouth of the crevasse. Dust spiraled beneath the craft, caught in its silent grav-thrust as she initiated a full-spectrum scan. The readings came back fast and infuriating. Six figures inside the breach, clambering across the collapsed support structures and exposed hull of her battle platform. Her mandibles clicked sharply.

The drone's visual filters zoomed in and locked onto their insignias. Blue bands. Crest of the wave. Umbrahaven. Of course.

Before the thought could fully form, a shrill metallic ping echoed through the cabin. Then another and another.

Impacts. She blinked her primary eye. The Umbrahaven scouts had spotted her and opened fire.

Idiots.

The drone lurched upward, veering hard into an evasive arc. Crimson lighting strobed in sync with her rising fury as she dove toward the platform's hidden docking port. She didn't return fire. Not yet. She had standing orders not to engage. But if they followed her inside...

The drone dropped into the chasm with surgical precision, slipping through the fractured ceiling of the buried battle platform. As it entered the dock tunnel, proximity signals pinged familiar ones. The vessel acknowledged her return. Docking clamps engaged with a low metallic thrum, and the craft settled into its berth with finality.

Trinn didn't move right away. She extended her tendrils across the neural interface, routing directly into the platform's dormant systems. A silent pulse issued from her core, an encrypted command string designed for one purpose: security activation.

She felt the ship respond. Deep beneath the central deck, hatches hissed open. Atmospheric stabilizers engaged for the first time in years. Hydraulic actuators flexed. Across the barracks holds, charging coils surged to life. One hundred and fifty autonomous battle droids standard frontline loadout rebooted in sequence.

They had been offline since the crash, perfectly preserved and waiting for instruction. Each unit, roughly humanoid in form but unmistakably alien in motion, snapped through startup protocols with mechanical grace. Optic lenses ignited with cold blue fire. Servo limbs rotated. Gauntlet-mounted plasma arrays initialized.

As one, they turned toward the command signal. Her signal. Back in the drone, Trinn's mouthparts twitched with satisfaction. "Let them try," she muttered.

Then she disengaged the neural tether, and the cockpit light faded from red to neutral blue. She slid into her transport pod, tentacled form uncoiling, and moved toward the hatch ready to reclaim her fortress. The command pulsed through the platform like a thunderclap.

DESTROY ATTACKERS. NO SURVIVORS. NO PRISONERS.

Deep within the sublevels, the last of the droids snapped online. Target directives poured into their cores like scripture from a war-god. Every unit synchronized, locking into formation as hatches groaned open along the lower hull of the buried platform.

The scouts never stood a chance.

The first warning was the sound. A low, mechanical rumble that didn't echo, it vibrated the marrow. The second was the hiss of steam and the sudden flash of harsh blue light pouring from the seams in the rock face. Then came the metal.

The droids poured out in waves, each one a seven-foot instrument of war, carapace in carbide-iron alloy. Their frames gleamed dully in the ambient light like insect husks forged in a furnace. The first volley from the scouts hit hard, primitive rifles slinging metal slugs and ignition-propelled darts.

The slugs sparked, pinged, and ricocheted harmlessly off the droid chassis. Not one dent.

The Umbrahaven soldiers shouted. Adjusted. Fired again. Still nothing. Undeterred, the droids continued their relentless, methodical advance. The plasma cannons came next.

Bolts of superheated matter screamed through the chasm, cutting trails of light that seared across stone and flesh alike. One scout vanished mid-sprint, reduced to a vaporized outline against the rock wall behind him. Another was caught center mass. His comrades watched in horror as his torso liquefied under the heat, and the rest of his body folded in on itself.

Panic broke the line. The remaining scouts scattered, diving behind broken outcroppings, scrambling for cover that didn't exist. The droids advanced.

Two broke formation, flanking wide around the perimeter to collapse the ambush. One opened its chest cavity, releasing a concussive shockwave that sent the last scout tumbling end over end across the gravel. Before he could crawl away, a metal foot came down.

From her place inside the platform, Trinn watched the feed with cold detachment. Tactical overlays scrolled across the interface. Enemy vitals: null. Signal sources: terminated. Terrain scans: secure.

The droids were clean, swift, and efficient, exactly as she'd programmed them.

The inner hatch spiraled open with a wet hiss, and Trinn's pod eased into the main docking bay.

The air was thick with charged ions and the faint smell of scorched metal, remnants of the platform's awakening. The lighting adjusted automatically, bathing her path in cool white strips that pulsed to her bio-signature.

Beside the docking chamber, a transit tube waited. Its design was sleek and efficient, designed to compensate for the platform's artificial gravity misalignments. Trinn slid in; the pod sealed around her like hardened skin. With a silent jolt, it launched down the magrail tunnel, zipping her through the veins of the dormant titan. The bridge awaited.

Moments later, the doors irised open to reveal the command chamber in all its dormant glory. Towering consoles lined the perimeter. Holo screens flickered to life. The air here was colder, more sterile. She liked it that way.

Her voice echoed across the neural network. "Summon core units. I require Sentinels VEX-9 and OLLO-2 at the bridge."

A discrete chime acknowledged her request. Thirty seconds later, the sound of mechanical footfalls approached. The two droids entered in tandem, their distinct shapes cutting twin silhouettes in the cool glow of the command deck.

VEX-9, tall and gaunt, moved like a watchful sentinel carved from bone and brass. Its head was narrow, snake-like, and constantly tilting as though evaluating invisible threats. VEX-9 served as the platform's primary tactical overseer in Trinn's absence. It processed battle scenarios, even in idle mode. Default behavior: anticipate war.

By contrast, OLLO-2 was stout, with multiple arms folded neatly behind its cylindrical torso. It emitted a soft hum and blinked with blue diagnostic lights. OLLO-2 managed science operations, AI uplink security, and environmental systems the tech-priest of the platform. Ever humming. Ever precise.

The command chamber flickered to full power as Trinn's pod rolled through, the metal deck beneath her trembling slightly from the activation surge. Panels awakened in a cascading wave of cold illumination. VEX-9 and OLLO-2 arrived as ordered, silent, dutiful too damned serene for her current mood.

"Why is the holographic shielding down?" she demanded.

Her voice hit the deck speakers and the cooling fans spooled a notch higher. VEX-9 tilted its serpentine head. "External cloaking array registered a systemic voltage drop during the last seismic cycle. No structural failure was detected. Shielding remained at "

"It was supposed to be invisible!" she barked.

OLLO-2 shifted. Its diagnostic lights blinked in a syncopated pattern she'd learned to hate.

"The projection grid is operational," it offered. "However, power cycles were diverted to maintain internal cryo-stabilizers in Sector Seventeen. Standard automated protocols deemed camouflage a lower priority."

Trinn's eye ridges contracted. "So, because some coolant line needed babysitting, the platform decided, hey, let's broadcast our existence to every mud-worshipping backwater tribe with a telescope?"

Neither droid answered. She swung the pod toward the main viewport. "There were Umbrahaven scouts crawling around the hull like termites. Six of them. Armed. Shooting at me. If I hadn't triggered the security forces, we'd be down another battle platform, and my patience would be buried right next to it."

VEX-9's voice hissed from behind her. "Hostiles eliminated with 100 percent efficiency. Orders were executed without deviation."

"Not the point," Trinn snapped. "You're keepers of a battle platform, not some glorified maintenance closet. I shouldn't have to remind either of you that stealth is not optional on a planet full of imbeciles who barely understand combustion but definitely understand how to lay claim to shiny things that don't belong to them!"

OLLO-2 rotated slightly, making a soft, placatory beep. "Recommend diagnostic sweep of environmental shielding and recalibration of priority stacks for next planetary cycle."

"Oh, now you recommend it." She interfaced with a console and glared at the shimmering overlay of the outer shell. "I swear, the next one of you that downgrades active cloaking for a leaky air duct is getting retrofitted into a janitor-drone on a garbage scow."

The bridge fell silent. Even the cooling fans hesitated.

Trinn inhaled slowly, clamping down on the rising bile of irritation. "Reinstate the holographic field. I want that chasm erased from every sensor that doesn't belong to me. And then we're relocating the platform. We can't risk another leak."

She turned toward the sensor bay. "After that, we'll deal with the real mess." She pivoted and jabbed a claw toward VEX-9. "Since our location has now been spectacularly compromised," she said, voice clipped and venomous, "I want options. Can we relocate? Are thrusters operational? Can anti-gravity fields sustain lift in this hemisphere's density profile?"

VEX-9's processing lights cycled quickly, its long arms folding behind its back in what passed for readiness. "Primary thruster systems are intact but have not been cycled since atmospheric entry. Internal heat sinks require purge prior to ignition. Anti-gravity nodes remain at 82 percent efficiency. Relocation is feasible within a 4,000-km radius, assuming terrain allows for vertical clearance and temporary de-camouflage."

Trinn narrowed her eyes. "Four thousand kilometers. That gives us some room to vanish. Find me a site uninhabited, geologically stable, and with natural magnetic interference. I want us off every scope that doesn't speak my language."

"Understood," VEX-9 replied. "Initiating geospatial analysis now."

"Good. And reassign a portion of the droids to perimeter sweep until we're airborne again. No more surprises." She guided the pod to the command dais, exhaling hard. "I left this world a child's puzzle to solve. Somehow, the pieces have begun rearranging themselves. That is not acceptable."

OLLO-2 moved closer, careful with its tone. "Shall I ready the impact chamber for analysis?"

Trinn nodded once. "Yes. It's time we reviewed exactly what that test did and why a human showed up in the results."

OLLO-2's scanning array ticked down its final sequence. The chamber image stabilized, overlaid with spectral energy trails and biometric data fields rendered in Drowa script. "The scan is complete," the drone intoned. "Sensor feedback identifies anomalous energy resonance consistent with Precursor imprinting. Probability of artifact interference: 2.4 percent. Probability of latent genetic contamination: 91.7 percent."

Trinn froze mid-type. "Repeat that," she ordered.

"An active Precursor signature was recorded within the impact chamber during the firing sequence. Cross-referenced against all historical energy matrices stored in the library, the signature is consistent with known Precursor residuals. Suggest further analysis."

For a long moment, the only sound was the ever-present drone of the platform's systems. Then Trinn spoke in a tone of forced calm. "OLLO-2, do you know what you are saying?"

"Affirmative. Readings are within the threshold for a confirmed contact event. Cross-indexed against Precursor energy decay models and historical telemetry from Sector Vathoris, the match is precise. You may confirm the results at Terminal Three."

She didn't move to the terminal because she didn't need to. Deep inside, she already suspected something had gone wrong with the firing. But this, this was not supposed to be possible. The technology she had seeded into this world wasn't capable of summoning them. Unless...

Her tentacles furled pensively. Unless the signal had been corrupted by something local. Not artifact interference. Not random noise. A variable she hadn't accounted for.

"Cross-check that signature with any residual biological material still logged in the chamber," she instructed. "Trace organics. Follicular cells. Keratin filaments. Anything with a root-bonded genome."

OLLO-2 chirped as it processed. "Match located. Single filament. Genetic origin: unknown. Proximity to firing center: less than 0.3 meters. Integrity: 82 percent. Requesting permission to sequence the full strand."

"Do it," she growled.

OLLO-2's optics narrowed to slits as matrices unfolded. "Sequencing," it said. "Locking to root."

Spectral lattices bloomed across the main display braided helices overlaid with pulsing glyph-clusters. Two traces separated, one faint, one bright. "Result set ready," OLLO-2 reported. "The chamber retained two distinct biological profiles: Alpha: local keratin filament recovered pre-firing nonhuman. Beta: the impact subject human." Numerics crawled along the margins. "Alpha expresses Precursor neural-glyph motifs at 41 percent congruence across twelve loci. Beta expresses the same motif family at 67 percent congruence across nineteen loci, including three chiral inversions and a stabilized phase-key repeat in the epi-helix."

"Meaning?" Trinn prompted.

"The resonance firing did not behave as a blind passage," OLLO-2 said. "During convergence, the field indexed for a lowest-work completion of the active pattern already present inside the chamber. The local filament, Alpha, provided a seed vector for Precursor glyphing. The convergence field then scanned across the adjacent membrane for a higher-fidelity homolog of that same motif." It highlighted the brighter trace. "Beta matched the seed with greater density. The field phase-locked to Beta's genome and minimized membrane cost by importing the best-fit carrier, rather than amplifying the incomplete local signal."

Trinn leaned closer. "So, the hair in the room "

"Served as the phase-key," OLLO-2 finished. "Its partial Precursor imprint attracted a near-template from the other side. The event acted as a mirror, not a projector. In other words, it completed what it was given." A final overlay showed shared clusters pulsing in tandem. "Conclusion: we have two carriers of Precursor code, one local and one imported human. Likelihood both derive from a common ancestral seeding line: 94.2 percent. If either carrier re-enters a strong resonance field, recurrence or signal amplification is probable."

Trinn's pupils thinned to needles. "Locations?"

"Alpha was present before ignition within 0.3 meters of the focal core," OLLO-2 replied. "Beta is the subject removed post-event. With authorization, I can initiate a phase-hum sweep to track both carriers within short range."

Trinn stared at the screen. A single hair. A contaminant. Someone who was never meant to be there. A genetic echo of something ancient. Her voice dropped to a whisper. "It wasn't a gateway; it was a mirror."

If we can't force the portal, we pull a line. Not through, back.

"Option two," she murmured. "We don't push through; we reach home." She straightened, voice crisp over the net. "VEX-9, bring the long-band comms spine out of hibernation. Cold-boot the array, cycle the phase-key ramps, and tune for home-band. I want a channel to Command as soon as the carrier stabilizes.

"OLLO-2, compile and encrypt a science packet: chamber telemetry, resonance maps, and both genome traces. Flag the Precursor imprint and mirror-event hypothesis. Priority seal."

She glanced once more at the twin traces pulsing in tandem. "VEX-9 lock down the deck and harden the antennae. No leaks. Confirm when we have handshake."

Chapter Thirty-Four

The Awakening

Cold fluorescent lights shone above the chamber. On the center table, the human lay strapped to a diagnostic gurney. Monitors blinked; disinfectant and metal clung to the air.

Professor Hare rubbed his temples with shaking fingers, dark circles carved deep beneath his eyes.

"She's stable," Myles said from where he was hunched over a display panel. "Neural activity's spiked twice in the last hour, but there've been no seizure patterns. Just... dream cycling."

"Fascinating," Hare muttered. "Every scan confirms baseline mammalian structure, yet the brainwave harmonics are oscillating in both hemispheres. It's like she's thinking on two channels at once."

Myles leaned back and sighed. "She's thinking, all right. I wonder what she's thinking about."

Hare moved to the head of the bed and studied her in silence. "If she's waking, I wonder how she'll respond to external stimuli."

A soft alarm beeped. Myles glanced down. "Theta wave spike. She is waking."

Hare straightened, the fatigue melting from his posture like he'd been plugged back into a wall socket. He tapped a sequence into the control panel, activating the biometric restraints. Thin bands of flexible alloy glowed faintly across her wrists and ankles.

On the table, the human stirred. Her eyelids fluttered, then snapped open. The eyes darted across the ceiling, taking in the sterile lighting, the wires, the straps. Her chest began to rise and fall in rapid pulses.

"Vitals escalating," Myles said quietly. "Heart one-sixty, respirations thirty panic response."

Hare took a cautious step closer. "Subject is exhibiting heightened distress. Administer sedative if she crosses protocol redline."

But the human didn't wait. She screamed, a full-throated, feral sound that tore through the lab like a warning siren. The ceiling tiles threw it back in jagged shards. She thrashed against the restraints. Her back arched, legs kicking, wrists yanking against the glowing bands now biting into her skin. The diagnostic monitors spiked into the red.

"Restraints holding," Myles called out. "Margin five percent."

Hare didn't move from his post above her. She snapped her head toward him.

Her eyes, wide, wet, and unblinking, locked onto his face. Pure panic poured out of her, not just in the scream but in the words that came tumbling after. "Let me go! Get off me! What the hell is this?!"

Hare blinked slowly. He didn't understand the language, not a single syllable. But the meaning? That was universal. "She's vocalizing," he muttered. "Complex phonetic structure. Rapid cadence. That's not animal distress that's language."

The human thrashed again, harder this time, screaming louder. "Get away from me. I swear to god, Get away!"

"Neuromuscular response climbing," Myles said. "She'll tear something."

"She's aware," Hare replied, stepping slightly to the side. "And very, very unhappy."

The human's gaze followed him like a hawk tracking prey. Her voice cracked under the pressure, but she didn't stop yelling. "Where am I?! What did you do?! I swear, if you touch me again..."

"She's focusing on me," Hare said, intrigued. "Associating me with authority. Possibly perceives me as a captor."

Myles looked up, wide-eyed. "I don't know, sir she seems a little too excited, and not in a good way."

She bucked again, her entire body trembling from the effort. The monitors screamed their protests. Hare tapped a control on the side panel to increase the bed's inertial dampening field. The gurney's hum deepened, and her kicks weakened. Still she fought. Still she screamed.

A wild, untamed energy throbbed from her chest with every breath. And through all of it, her eyes never left him. Wide. Furious. Terrified. "You don't get to do this!" she cried. "I'm not a lab rat! I'm not "

Another scream erased the rest of her words. It didn't stop; it worsened. Her raw, animalistic screams cut through the sterile air like shrapnel. She twisted, kicked, and thrashed until her voice began to crack, red-faced and frantic, her eyes wild with panic.

"She's going to hurt herself," Myles muttered, backing away from the display. "This is no good."

Without asking, he darted across the lab, opened a drawer beneath the console, and grabbed a small metal canister with a trigger nozzle. He didn't hesitate, just moved to the table, pulled back slightly from her face, and sprayed.

A fine mist hissed across the human's mouth and nose, a pepper-sweet tang cutting through the antiseptic air.

She coughed once. Twice. Her scream broke into a sputter, then a groggy, strangled whimper. Her limbs twitched once more, then fell slack. Her breathing slowed. Within seconds, her eyelids fluttered closed. The monitors stabilized. Silence fell again.

Hare raised a brow. "Quick thinking."

Myles exhaled. "Tranquilizer gas. Short half-life, clean metabolite."

"She'll be out for hours," Hare said, stepping back to the console. "Which gives us time to reassign containment." He tapped a control, dismissing the restraint interface. "We've logged every biological metric we can get in this state blood panels, neural signatures, structural mapping. No sense keeping her strapped down like livestock."

"I think she's scared," Myles said quietly.

Hare didn't respond. He was already paging through schematics.

"Observation chamber?" Myles asked.

"Exactly." Hare nodded. "We isolate variables. Control the environment and monitor her behavior. No more panic-induced interference."

Myles sighed. "So... a terrarium. For a human."

Hare's eyes didn't leave the screen. "Call it whatever you like. Make sure it's sterile," he added. "And quiet. I want to see how she handles silence."

Myles hovered near the console, eyes darting toward the door. "We've got a problem."

Hare didn't even look up. "Let me guess: Lanell."

"She was scheduled to be here for the firing, and she knows it didn't happen while she was in the room. She's going to start asking why."

Hare finally looked over, eyes sharp and calculating. "Then we tell her the truth."

Myles's eyebrows shot up. "We do?"

"About the firing? Yes." He rose from the console, rubbing his palms together slowly. "The Arcadian breach forced our hand. We couldn't risk the window closing, not with those variables active, so we moved the timeline up."

"That won't go over well."

"She'll be angry, but she'll understand.

Myles shifted uncomfortably. "And when she asks about the results?"

"Then we lie. Tell her it misfired. No breach. The targeting vectors didn't hold. Chalk it up to corrupted trilineum or misaligned injectors, something she can't verify on her own."

"We're going to gaslight your assistant?"

Hare gave a thin smile. "We're going to protect the integrity of this facility. If she finds out what really came through that rift" he gestured toward the unconscious human "we lose control of the narrative. We cannot afford that. Not now."

"Earl's already sniffing around," Myles muttered. "He's suspicious."

"Then let him sniff. So long as we stay ahead of them both, we dictate the terms. Keep Lanell looped in just enough to think she's a step away from the truth. That'll keep her off-balance."

"And when she realizes we're stonewalling her?"

"By then," Hare said, turning back to the monitor, "it won't matter." His eyes lingered on the unconscious human for a long moment, then he turned to Myles. "As a matter of fact, let's address something else now."

Myles looked up, puzzled. "What are you talking about?"

Hare didn't answer. He pulled a sleek communicator from his coat and tapped it twice.

"Lanell, this is Professor Hare. Are you out there?"

There was a short burst of static before her tense, impatient voice crackled through. "Yes, I'm here, Professor. Where are you? Why is the collider locked down? What have I missed?"

Hare cut in before she could build momentum. "Listen, Myles and I need to speak with you. Privately. Head to my office. We'll meet you there and explain everything."

He clicked the communicator off and slipped it back into his coat. Myles gave him a cautious glance, but Hare was already turning for the door, his coat billowing behind him. "Before you move her, apply the LinguaGel to her ear canals and install the Voxseed at the carotid mount. If she's intelligent, those modifications will permit two-way comms on waking."

Myles nodded. "Yes, sir."

Chapter Thirty-Five

Whispers of Artemis

The room dissolved. The floor beneath Earl vanished into starlight. The sound of machines was gone. All that remained was wind, dry, ancient wind whipping across a silver desert beneath a sky carved with spirals.

Earl opened his eyes. He knelt at The Spiral Grounds, where the world thinned. And across from him, rising from the shimmering sand like smoke from a sacred flame, came her.

Artemis. Tall, faceless, cloaked in a twisting veil of feathers and arc-light. Her presence carried gravity. The air bent around her like heat on stone.

"You return," she said, not aloud but inside him. Her voice moved through his ribs like a breath he hadn't taken.

"There's been a shift," Earl said into the stillness. "Something's taken place."

"Yes." a leaf-rush in his inner ear. Her voice was layered like a thousand leaves turning at once, soft but undeniable. "A threshold opened something came across."

Earl's brow furrowed. "Who, or what?"

There was silence. A pause wide enough to cross lifetimes.

"A mirror made flesh. A spark born of paradox. The world blinks... and sees itself."

His pulse climbed into his throat. "I don't..." The air pressed at his temples.

"You will."

The silver sand beneath him rippled. A shimmer of heat and light rose into a vision brief, fractured. He saw her. A human. Strapped down. Screaming. Eyes wide with terror, voice torn raw. Then gone. Like smoke through fingers.

"The mirror cried out. Far off, answering panes trembled."

He reached out, hands shaking. "What am I supposed to do?"

"Do as you were shaped to do watch, wait, then choose."

The light dimmed again. The candles guttered once, then steadied. The Spiral grew quiet, but nothing felt calm. Earl opened his eyes slowly, already knowing the next phase had begun.

The Spiral finished speaking, leaving a copper tang on his tongue and a tremor in his hands

He remained kneeling in the center of the Spiral, but the vision pressed against the edge of his senses like a storm building behind glass.

He felt her. Not a name, a hairline crack running through the day. Somewhere, the arc of the world had bent. Artemis was gone. But the words lingered.

Watch. Wait. Choose.

Earl staggered as the vision left him, one hand bracing against the cold tile floor. The room returned slowly walls reassembling in his awareness, the hum of electronics creeping back into his ears like gnats. But something inside him stayed there, back in The Spiral. Back with her. He exhaled, long and low, then stood, brushing sand from knees. The message was clear. The storm had arrived, and he had just been warned.

Chapter Thirty-Six

The Lies You Tell

Lanell sat in the plush waiting chair outside Professor Hare's office, positioned neatly across from Stacie's reception desk. The vents whispered without moving the sticky note on Stacie's desk; disinfectant clung to her tongue. It was too quiet, the silence punctuated only by the soft clicks of the secretaries' hands on the keys of her console.

Her heel kept a metronome under the chair She could still hear Dr. Crusher's voice.

Lanell, they already fired it.

She folded her arms tight across her chest and stared at the frosted glass door ahead. Her foot tapped against the floor in a rhythm that betrayed her growing agitation. The silence. The locked doors and controlled access. Lies upon lies. But the telemetry hadn't lied. Neither had the goo-covered scientist, who barely looked up from his chaotic lab when he dropped the truth into her lap like it was nothing.

And now she was waiting like a polite student outside the headmaster's office. She sat in the 'guest' chair, legs boxed by the coffee table, exactly where people were parked to cool off.

Stacie gave a polite smile from behind her desk. "He'll be just another moment."

Lanell nodded. "Of course he will."

She glanced casually toward the corridor camera feed above the reception desk. A figure approached. Her ears tipped forward, then flattened. It was Hare.

He wasn't coming from his usual route the wing that led from the admin and lab corridor. No, he was entering from the far end of the hallway. From the service corridor. The one that led to the lower levels.

Lanell straightened in her seat, masking her curiosity with a neutral expression. But her mind worked like a steel trap, snatching up the information and filing it away.

Hare's coat was ruffled slightly. His gait was brisk, just short of hurried. He adjusted his collar and cleared his throat as he approached. "Victoria," he said smoothly. "Thank you for being patient. Come in."

"Well," he said, adjusting his glasses and stifling a yawn. "Didn't realize today was casual."

Lanell gave a bland half-smile. "Last night was long. Casual happens." She tilted her head and let her eyes travel down his coat. "But look at you. Are you not still wearing what you had on yesterday? Or have you even been home yet?"

Hare's smile was thin and tight, like stretched plastic. "Science doesn't sleep, Miss Lanell."

"No," she said, folding her arms, "but even science eventually needs a shower."

He gave a soft exhale that might have been a chuckle or a sigh and gestured toward his office door. "Well then, let's talk. I imagine you've got questions."

"Oh, you have no idea," Lanell muttered as she followed him inside.

The door clicked shut behind them. The overhead lights cast a sterile glow across the room, but it didn't feel clean; it felt clinical Hare moved to his desk like it was just another morning, like nothing had happened, like Lanell wasn't burning up inside.

She didn't sit. "You lied to me," she said simply.

Hare blinked, halfway into pulling up his chair. "Excuse me?"

"Don't do that," Lanell snapped. "Don't give me the owl-eyes and pretend you don't know what I'm talking about."

Hare stayed standing now, posture stiffening. "Lanell, if this is about "

"The collider," she said. "You fired it yesterday. You and Myles."

He held her gaze without speaking.

"I saw the telemetry myself," she pressed. "Magnetic field spikes. Thermal surges. Return signatures. You launched the sequence hours before I even got here, and you locked me out."

"Your access was temporarily suspended for safety reasons," Hare replied evenly.

"You mean I was excluded."

You were exhausted. Unstable. You pulled an unsecured disk from Relay-2 at 0554."

"I didn't tell you that."

"The system did. Asset 7YQ left its cradle and pinged my console. Did you think this facility runs on trust?"

Lanell laughed. It wasn't a nice sound. "And what about you, Professor? Running secret firings in the middle of the night like some bargain-bin mad scientist?"

Hare's jaw twitched.

"You violated protocol," she continued. "You hid it from me, from Earl, from everyone, so don't act like this was all part of some grand plan."

"You're overreacting."

"Then tell me what came through."

That landed. Hare flushed. Lanell stepped closer. "You moved that breach vector on purpose, didn't you? You adjusted the injection timing, you fired it early, and you didn't tell me because something came through."

"You're making assumptions."

"I'm connecting the dots," she shot back. "And the picture looks a hell of a lot like a cover-up."

Hare turned, walking slowly behind his desk now, retreating to higher ground. "Lanell, I know you're upset "

"No. Upset was yesterday. This" she stepped in closer and planted her hands on his desk "this is me done being kept in the dark."

He looked at her, and for just a second, just a flicker, she saw it. Sweat at his temple. The ghost of panic beneath the stoic veneer. "You don't understand the implications," he said finally.

"Then enlighten me."

"You need to let this go," he said quietly. Not a suggestion, an order.

Lanell stared at him incredulously and shook her head. "Oh, we're way past that."

The door glided open behind her. Myles Moleman stepped in, balancing a datapad on his hand and chewing the edge of a stylus like it owed him rent. He looked between the two of them, sensing the tension immediately. "Oh," he said, awkwardly. "Is this a bad time?"

Hare didn't look at him and continued to stare Lanell down. "Just in time, actually."

Lanell crossed her arms again. "Perfect. Maybe you can help your boss explain why you two fired the collider behind everyone's back."

Myles froze mid-step. "We didn't fire it behind anyone's back."

"You expect me to believe it was a scheduled adjustment? That's what this is?"

"No," Myles said quickly. "It was more of a... recalibration. A pre-ignition diagnostic sweep that triggered a soft-mass ignition spike. Happens sometimes. Phantom thermal loops in the trilineum phase react to lingering harmonics from previous firings. It's rare but not unheard of."

Lanell stared at him like he'd just coughed up a bag of wet socks. "You seriously practiced that in the mirror, didn't you?"

"It's a known phenomenon," Myles protested, running a claw under his collar.

"You both said nothing," Lanell shot back. "Nothing about the breach. Nothing about the telemetry. Nothing about the goddamn spatial echo. And now you're trying to float the idea that it was just phantom harmonics?"

She turned back to Hare. "That's what you're going with?"

Hare smoothed his tie, eyebrows lifting a fraction. "I beg your pardon?"

"Don't," she snapped. "Don't do that wide-eyed routine with me. I know the collider was fired early. "I saw the telemetry the energy spikes, the waveform echo, the trilineum dip." You ran the test hours before schedule."

Hare's brow furrowed, just slightly. "And where did you come across this telemetry?"

Lanell held his gaze, then flicked her eyes toward Myles. "Your golden mole has some leaky files."

"With all the signals and anomalies," she pressed, turning back to Hare, "you expect me to believe that? You weren't even in the control room."

"No," Hare said calmly. "I wasn't. I was handling unrelated work on the lower levels."

"You never go to the lower levels."

"And you never wear jeans shorts to meetings. Shall we chalk both up to an unusual morning?"

She didn't laugh. Her arms stayed crossed, gaze boring into him like a drill.

"Lanell, you're tired," Hare said with a sigh. "You're under a tremendous amount of pressure. The collider is a complex system. It's easy to misread diagnostics when you're chasing phantoms."

Her mouth opened, ready to fire back, but he raised a hand. "I'm not accusing you of anything malicious," he said. "I'm saying that perhaps your instincts, however sharp, are leading you toward conclusions faster than the data supports."

"You're gaslighting me."

"I'm offering perspective," Hare replied smoothly. "And I'd encourage you to rest before jumping to further conclusions. This facility relies on clear minds." He gave her that same clinical smile, the one that never touched his eyes.

Myles shifted awkwardly by the wall, not meeting her gaze.

Lanell exhaled through her nose, slow and controlled. "Right. Clear minds." She stepped forward, eyes flashing. "You keep brushing me off like some overworked intern, but let's be clear. I've earned my place here. I've studied the collider more than half the panel you've got on payroll. And if I say something's off, then something's damn well off."

Myles opened his mouth, but Hare raised a hand without looking at him. He turned to Lanell slowly, deliberately. When he spoke, his voice dropped into that chilling, precise register he reserved for moments when his authority was challenged. "You are not here to decide what is and isn't 'off.' You are here to observe, to record, and to report to me. I decide what matters. If you continue to challenge that chain of command, you may soon find yourself on the outside looking in, and I would hate," he added, voice soft and venomous, "to see a promising mind waste itself chasing shadows."

The silence that followed landed like a punch. Lanell stood frozen, fury bubbling just under her skin. But she said nothing. She turned, walked past Myles without a glance, and left.

Chapter Thirty-Seven

Unspoken Words

Lanell didn't slow down.

She walked fast, furiously fast, each step sounding like a gunshot in the deserted corridor. Her fists were clenched, knuckles pale beneath her fur, jaw set like stone. Her heart pounded like it was trying to shake something loose. Something buried. Something rotten.

They were lying to her. All of them. Hare. Myles. Trace. And the worst part? She had let them.

She rounded the next corner too quickly. Her heel slipped on the smooth floor, and before she could correct her balance, she collided with someone solid. Lanell staggered. A hand caught her arm.

Earl.

His eyes widened. His grip loosened the instant he saw it was her. She pulled her arm back, not violently but with enough force to make it clear she didn't want to be steadied. Not right now.

He froze. She froze. In that moment, the hallway might as well have vanished.

Concerned eyes searched hers, and she stared back accusatory, defensive. So many questions bloomed in the air between them.

Are you okay? Do you know what they did? Did you help them?

But none were asked. Neither dared go first.

Lanell broke the silence, her voice clipped. "Earl."

"Lanell," he replied, stiff as a board.

They stood there, surrounded by the hum of lights and the roar of what neither of them was saying. She crossed her arms, casting a glance past his shoulder as if to gather herself. "You're up early."

He shrugged. "Maintenance backlog. Wanted to stay ahead of it."

A blatant lie. The worst kind, the kind they both instantly recognized. Lanell gave a tight nod. "Right."

They stood like statues for a beat too long, then she added, "Have you seen Tabitha this morning?"

Earl blinked, thrown. "Snickers? Not since yesterday. Why?"

Lanell hesitated not because she didn't have a reason, but because she wasn't sure she wanted him to know it. "Need to ask her about something," she said finally. "Access permissions."

"To the lower levels?"

She snorted mirthlessly. "That obvious?"

"You're not exactly subtle when you're storming out of Hare's office."

The edge of a smirk formed on Lanell's face, there and gone in an instant. "Didn't come here to be subtle."

Another awkward pause stretched between them.

"You find anything?" Earl asked.

Lanell looked at him, then looked away. "Shouldn't you be fixing a pipe or something?"

He gave a humorless chuckle. "Guess I should."

She started to turn away.

He added, quieter now, "Lanell."

She paused but didn't turn back.

"If you find something... be careful."

She didn't respond immediately. Then she said, over her shoulder, "You too."

Earl stood in the hallway, watching her walk away.

She knows.

He could see it in her eyes. But she didn't trust him. Not yet. And the hell of it was... he couldn't blame her.

Chapter Thirty-Eight

No Questions

Tabitha Snickers crouched beside an inventory crate, sorting a tangle of portable consoles. Her tail flicking with every annoyed sigh. Earbuds dangled from her collar, looping idle sy̆nth beats that didn't match her expression.

Someone was coming. She could hear the thud of their boots. It wasn't long before she recognized the distinctive clipped rhythm. Lanell always walked that way when something was bothering her and she wasn't ready to admit it.

Tabitha looked up and grinned. "Well, damn, Lanell. Jean shorts and black tights? Are we doing fashion statements with a hint of emotional repression now?"

Lanell offered a half-hearted smirk. "It's called field-ready sarcasm. Keeps people guessing."

"Guessing what? If you're about to bust someone or start a punk band?"

"Can't it be both?"

Tabitha stood, dusting off her knees. "You bring chaos to my hallway, I'll bill you in paperwork. What's up?"

"I need a favor. Hare wants me to check old logs from Sublevel 1. Something about historical resonance data. But access is locked down, and you know how slow clearance requests are right now."

Tabitha inspected her hands. "Let me guess: you want me to hand over a keycard, no questions asked, while pretending this conversation never happened?"

"Not no questions. Just fewer."

Tabitha gave a theatrical groan. "You really know how to make a girl feel like an accessory to a breach of protocol."

Lanell tilted her head. "You're good at accessories."

Tabitha rolled her eyes, fishing out the access fob from her vest. "You know, if I didn't like you, I wouldn't do this."

Lanell took the fob with a wry smile. "Yeah, but we both know that's your problem, don't we?" She winked.

Tabitha barked a laugh. "One of many, apparently."

That got a genuine smile.

"Flattery is a war crime if it's not backed up with snacks," Tabitha warned.

"No snacks," Lanell said. "But I'll owe you."

Tabitha held the fob a moment longer before handing it over. "This one logs under my ID. So if you disappear down there and get eaten by a wall anomaly, I'm ghosting your memorial."

"Appreciated," Lanell said, slipping the fob into her coat.

As she turned to leave, Tabitha wrinkled her nose and sniffed the air. "You smell that?"

Lanell paused. "What?"

"That weird ozone tang. Like something ionized the hallway and forgot to apologize."

"I don't smell anything," Lanell lied.

Tabitha raised an eyebrow. "Okay, but if this is my new hairspray reacting to your aura of suspicion, I'm suing."

Lanell's mouth twitched. "Pretty sure I signed a waiver when I got here. Not responsible for psychic side effects."

They shared a glance lighter, almost playful but Lanell's shoulders were still tense under it.

Tabitha's voice softened. "You okay?"

"Peachy," Lanell said too quickly. "Just... checking boxes."

"You check boxes like a rogue packet scanning an unsecured subnet. With precision, and zero regard for protocol."

"Sounds like projection."

"Sounds like deflection."

They both smiled, but the pause afterward said more than either of them wanted.

Lanell nodded once and turned to go. "Thanks, Tabs."

"Be careful, Lan. Don't do anything I'd do."

"That's a long list," Lanell called over her shoulder.

Tabitha grinned. "And every damn thing on it starts with trouble."

Chapter Thirty-Nine

Am I Dead

The lights were too bright.

Diane stirred on the padded gurney, arms rising tremulously, unbound but sluggish. Her breath caught in her throat as her eyes opened fully. White. Not off-white or hospital beige. Blinding white. The kind that erased shadows and made it impossible to tell where the walls ended and the ceiling began.

She sat up slowly, blinking. The room was small. Ten feet by ten, give or take, and built for function over comfort. There was no furniture, no equipment, no sink, and no mirror. Nothing but a gurney and a featureless panel in the far wall that might've been a door.

To her right, a thick pane of glass broke the illusion of privacy. A window but not one she could see through. There was a subtle shimmer to the polarized surface, like it knew she was looking.

Her throat was dry. Reaching up, she brushed her neck with her fingertips. She froze. There, tucked just beneath the skin, was something small. A hard nodule, maybe the size of a grain of rice. It didn't hurt, and if she hadn't touched it, she wouldn't have known it was there.

Her heart thudded harder.

Where am I?

Last thing she remembered was...

Panic. A lab. That thing with the metal table. Cold fingers. Needles. A voice.

Now she was alone. Not restrained or monitored, but alone.

She stood shakily. As she rose, a strange feeling of thick fullness in both ears tugged at her attention. She reached up and found a wet, viscous film clinging to the skin.

She wiped it away, blinking slow.

It felt like the time Uncle Eddie ambushed her with double wet willies at Grandma's Fourth of July barbecue. She'd screamed and dumped orange soda on his new fishing vest. He called it revenge for the water balloons she'd stuffed in his tackle box.

Her lips twitched, half a laugh, half disbelief.

What the hell did they stick in my ears?

Bare feet pressed against smooth, cold floor. It wasn't freezing, but it was cold enough to send goosebumps lacing up her legs. She padded toward the glass, lifted a hand, and knocked once.

Thud.

No response. No sound, except the hush of filtered air and the faint hum of facility infrastructure echoing somewhere beyond the walls.

She paced slowly. The floor offered no clues. Like the walls, it was an endless expanse of sterile white. The corners were rounded. The walls too smooth. Too perfect.

It wasn't a hospital room. It was a holding cell built by someone afraid of what the patient might do.

Where am I?

Her head throbbed from the sheer absence. Like someone had scooped her thoughts out with a spoon.

She squeezed her eyes shut, reaching, groping through her memories.

Grass, wet against her legs. Her body curled in a ditch. The sky above boiling with motion. A tornado. Sirens.

Lightning.

Then light. Blinding, engulfing, pulling her into something... wrong.

After that, nothing. She touched her chest. Still warm. Still breathing. But...

"Am I dead?"

The thought slithered in uninvited.

Is this the afterlife? Is this what it's like to be on the other side? A padded room with no doors and lighting that never shuts off?

She turned, slowly this time, and froze. Beyond the window stood a figure watching her. A man in a white coat.

No, not a man. A rabbit. Standing upright on two legs. Piercing eyes, and ears that curved like devil's horns over the back of his skull.

Her breath hitched. Her stomach went cold.

I thought that was a dream.

But it wasn't. He was real. Motionless as a statue and regarding her with detached interest.

She took a step back. Then another. Still, he watched. Then she noticed he wasn't alone. Another creature stood next to him. Smaller. Rounder. Its head all but swallowed behind thick glasses like coke bottles. It peered at something glowing in its stubby hands. A tablet? A datapad? It looked like a leftover prop from a rejected episode of Star Trek.

The smaller one gestured, tapping its screen. The rabbit nodded once. Their mouths moved, but Diane heard nothing. It was like watching ghosts argue about how best to haunt you.

She backed up another step. Her heel brushed the gurney she'd woken up on. The rabbit's stare hadn't budged, and now the other one was watching too. Her throat tightened. She pressed a hand to her chest. Her pulse was a jackhammer in her ribs.

If this is the afterlife, she thought, it has terrible taste in interior design.

She lowered herself into a crouch, spine to the cold wall, then looked down. She was wearing white. A loose, soft robe clean, shapeless, and unfamiliar. Where had it come from? She didn't remember changing. She didn't remember anything past...

The ditch. The wind. The light.

Her fingers gripped the fabric tighter. She looked up again. The rabbit was still watching. Its ears twitched like antennae tuned to some diabolical frequency. The smaller one tapped its screen again. Light flickered across its lenses. Neither blinked. Neither left. She pressed harder into the wall, wishing she could melt into it.

What is this place, and what are they?

Chapter Forty

First Contact

Beyond the one-way glass, Professor Lupus Hare stood as still as marble, arms folded beneath the crisp lines of his lab coat. His reflection ghosted back at him faint, warped by the polarization, lending him the eerie presence of someone both inside and outside the moment. Behind him, Myles Moleman tapped at a control pad with careful, sausage-thick fingers, adjusting the data feed.

"She's responding to stimulus," Hare murmured, mostly to himself. "No vocalizations. No overt aggression. Posture's cautious, not defensive. That puts us in quadrant two of the skittish-reactive spectrum."

Myles grunted, squinting at the panel. "Quadrant two assumes baseline cognitive stability, sir. Which we haven't exactly confirmed."

Hare tilted his head. "No," he admitted. "But she's self-regulating. Look at the pacing pattern. She's back-tracking along her own footprints. Confirming terrain. That's not panic. That's processing."

Myles blinked. "Processing or pattern repetition. I've seen raccoons do the same thing in confinement."

"Exactly," Hare said, with a flicker of satisfaction. "It's not who the subject is, it's how the subject copes. Behavior's the bridge. Always has been."

They stood there, two sentient mammals in clean white coats, dissecting the reactions of a creature more advanced than either of them would openly admit.

"Did the implant take?" Hare asked.

"Confirmed. No inflammation at the site. Neural responses are within acceptable margins. And the gel's started assimilation."

"So she can hear us?"

"She will once the nanos finish mapping phonemic structure. Give it twenty minutes, maybe less. Then we can test comprehension."

Hare nodded thoughtfully. "Then we observe. See how she handles isolation. You learn more from what an animal does without instructions than you ever do with a prompt."

"She's not an animal," Myles muttered, eyes still locked to the display.

"She is to us," Hare said flatly. "And we are to her. Symmetry's just perspective, Mole-man. What matters is who's holding the clipboard."

Behind the glass, Diane turned. Her gaze found them, not with fear, exactly. With awareness. The weight of realization. A line crossing from observation to confrontation.

"She's watching us now," Hare said.

"I think," Myles said wryly, "she's starting to figure out she's not the scientist in this equation."

Hare didn't look away. "You know," he murmured, "when we studied wild assets preda-tors, scavengers, anything outside the curve we always assumed they didn't understand. That they couldn't." He finally turned toward Myles. "But look at her. The way her eyes track. The way she's backed into that corner not panicking, just minimizing exposure. That's not instinct. That's inference."

Myles gave a noncommittal hum. "So the question becomes: how do we initiate con-tact?"

Hare nodded. "We've never really had to ask that. So how do you approach something that might be intelligent but doesn't know you are?"

Myles didn't hesitate. "I don't think it's that hard."

Hare raised an eyebrow. "Oh?"

The mole tapped the side of his head. "I think all we need to do is talk."

"To a creature who doesn't speak our language?"

"To a mind that does. Words are just packaging. Thought is the payload." He stepped to the window and slid open a small access panel, revealing a mic jack inside the frame, then he glanced back at Hare. "This is a first-contact moment. I think you should have the honors."

Hare gave him a sideways glance. "Well. Thank you."

He stepped up, adjusted his coat, leaned slightly toward the mic. A soft beep. The line opened.

"Hello," he said, calm as glass. "Can you understand me?"

Chapter Forty-One

Show me your Beans

Diane pressed her palms to her ears.

The vibration had crept in slowly at first, a muffled hum, like distant machinery buried deep beneath concrete. Now it buzzed like a live wire threaded through her skull. She winced, pressing harder as if pressure might smother the sensation. It didn't. If anything, it got worse. It wasn't painful; it was irritating. Like a mosquito with a megaphone had taken up residence inside her head.

She staggered a step sideways, palms still locked over her ears. Behind the glass, the two white coats moved. Their lips were moving too.

She couldn't hear them, not clearly, but fragments pushed through the fog like static-tuned voices on an old car radio.

"...see? Bots are setting in... always some mild irritation."

"...handling it surprisingly well..."

They were monitoring while her brain was being rewired. Commenting on her reaction like she was a pet at a vet exam. A muscle ticked in her jaw.

The vibration in her ears began to fade, softening into a tingling itch before fading to nothing. The sudden silence hit harder than the noise.

She lowered her hands. The creatures were still watching. One of them gestured toward her ear, lips moving again.

No more static. This time, she heard it. Faint, distorted, but real.

"...audio channel should stabilize now. Cognitive sync in progress..."

Diane took a breath and backed further into the corner, eyes locked on the glass. Her heart thundered in her chest. Whatever they were doing to her, it was working. Her hands trembled at her sides.

"...channel stabilizing..."

Her brows pulled together. What. The. Hell? The words didn't just pass through her ears, they landed in her brain like they'd been pre-processed. Converted. Squeezed into shape and stuffed through a funnel straight into her mind.

What did they do to me?

She pivoted, paced half a step to the side, then stopped. Her bare feet left slight prints on the smooth floor. She traced them with her eyes. She hadn't noticed them before. How long had she been walking in circles? Was that... part of the test?

What kind of lab is this?

It didn't look human. Even beyond the people-animals in lab coats, the architecture seemed alien. The proportions. The way the room sloped and swept. It felt like it had been designed for someone else. Something else.

Icy terror flooded her stomach.

Was I abducted? Is this Earth? Am I still in my own universe?

The memory of light. Of pain. The sensation of being sucked out of her own skin that was still too raw to unwrap. Whatever had brought her here, it hadn't been voluntary. She looked down at her arm. No chains. No cuffs. But freedom? That felt like a joke.

She turned back toward the glass. The taller one rabbit ears, lanky frame, white coat stepped closer. Then he said it.

"Hello. Can you understand me?"

The words came through her, not just at her. There was no accent, and the audio fuzz had completely gone. His voice hit her like someone dropping a stone in a perfectly still lake.

She opened her mouth. Her lips parted. She moved her jaw experimentally. "Yes," she said, or at least, she thought she did. It was a whisper. It had to be. She couldn't even hear her own voice.

On the other side of the glass, the mole Myles, she remembered the name from earlier perked up slightly. His fingers froze on the panel.

The rabbit's ears twitched. "She said yes," he murmured, a flicker of amusement in his tone. "Good. The implant's reading active. We have bidirectional interface."

Diane blinked.

Wait, what?

She tried again. "Where am I?"

Again, nothing. No sound. No feedback. Her mouth moved, but the world didn't respond the way it should have.

"She's forming structured questions," Myles said, nodding at something on the console. "Semantic clarity confirmed. Translation relay is stable."

Once again, the words didn't translate. They just were.

No one told her how surreal it would feel to speak without sound. To express thoughts that weren't heard but were understood, anyway.

Is this how they hear me now? Directly? Like I'm thinking through them?

She glanced back at the mirror-glass, her reflection ghostly and pale. She swayed a little, catching herself with a hand against the wall. That surface was cool, too. Smooth, and wrong somehow.

What else did they change?

Diane winced as the strange pressure in her ears finally released. The older one had just said something about irritation. About gel. About observation.

Her brain scrambled for meaning, desperately trying to build context from scraps. This had to be a prank, right? A really elaborate one. She peered at the glass. "Okay, guys," she said aloud, a tired smirk tugging at the corner of her mouth. "You got me." She gave three slow claps. "Very funny. Jack, Chris, whichever one of you came up with the sci-fi theme? Gold star. Whole Westworld meets Rick and Morty vibe? Love it."

She took a breath and barked a laugh. It bounced off the walls, sounding more hollow than she'd hoped.

"Yeah, no, I'm impressed. You got the animatronics down real smooth. And that dream thing? That was a nice touch. I mean, the whole thing with the light and the vacuum and the falling and" her voice cracked "and the girl..."

Her smile faltered. No response came through the glass. Diane's fingers curled at her sides.

"...Right?" she added, hopefully.

She turned, glancing up toward the corners of the room as if a camera crew might lower from the ceiling tiles.

"Alright, where's the host? Ashton? That you back there?" She gave a weak chuckle. "Chris and Jack, you absolute nerds. You went all in on this escape room setup, huh? The whole lab has a creepy biohazard theme. Seriously, who did the costumes? You even got the lighting right. That weird backlight haze chef's kiss. And the language implant thing? Real Black Mirror. I'm not even mad. I'm impressed."

Silence answered.

Her smile began to slide. No crew stepped out. No friends came forward to break the illusion. Only the rabbit. Watching. Recording. The mole muttered something while adjusting controls. They weren't actors; they were real. The specimen was her. She crossed her arms and looked away, blinking hard. "I want to go home."

The rabbit's face twitched not quite a smile. Not sympathy either. His head tilted with the slow precision of a predator contemplating prey. "As do we all," he said. "But no. There is no simulation. No prank. No staged environment. My name is Professor Lupus Hare. You are in a controlled research facility, following a high-energy event involving a dimensional breach." He said it like he was reading off a menu. Diane's mouth gaped open. The mole murmured something behind him, and he gave a small wave of his hand, silencing him without looking away from her. "I understand this reaction," he continued, voice flat but oddly gentle. "You are experiencing what we term a perceptual collapse. The mind's attempt to preserve itself through reinterpretation of stimuli humor, deflection, rejection of empirical context. It's common in early-phase interdimensional displacees." He took a slow breath and folded his hands behind his back. “If it helps,” he continued, “your reaction aligns with predictive models. Most matter introduced through a breach arrives... unstructured. Unclothed. Inert. You, however, are articulate.”

He bent towards the glass, as if inspecting a specimen that had just moved unexpectedly. "You are unique, my new asset. The only human known to exist in this universe. That fact alone makes you of immeasurable interest. But you're also conscious, responsive... even witty." His lips pulled revealing too many teeth. "So I'd appreciate it," he said, "if you continued to speak. Humor, distress, denial it's all useful data."

Diane gave a tight laugh. The kind that starts in the throat but never quite reaches the lungs. "You're not real," she said, pointing at them like it settled something. "This is like Disney World. Or maybe Chris and Jack decided to prank me with one of those immersive VR things."

Neither the rabbit nor the mole moved.

She crossed her arms. "Fine. If you're real... then show me your hands."

Myles blinked.

"I'm serious," she snapped. "Put them up, palms out."

There was a beat of silence, then Hare glanced at Myles with a shrug. He raised both hands slowly, palms forward. Myles followed suit, though he looked thoroughly baffled.

Diane stepped closer to the glass. Her eyes dropped. And there they were. The pads. Not quite like cat hands. Not cartoonishly cute. But the flesh was darker, textured four oval nubs arranged in a familiar, instinct-satisfying pattern on the underside of each digit. Animalistic. Real. Alien.

"Beans," she muttered, voice thin.

"See?" she added. "You've even got..."

She stopped. The words died in her throat. Professor Hare turned one hand, inspecting it himself. "Beans?" he repeated. "Do you mean palmar pads? Tactile nodules?"

"It's a colloquialism," Myles said, tapping a note on the control pad. "Refers to the appearance of metacarpal epidermal nodes. Common in feline species, though ours are evolutionary holdovers."

Hare gave a wry look. "You expect me to believe everyone calls them that?"

"But you have them," Diane whispered.

"Yes," Hare said calmly. "I do." Professor Hare turned one hand, inspecting it himself.

She stared. Like maybe the beans could still be fake. Like perhaps the universe would let her rewrite the rules if she just stared hard enough. Then quietly, almost to herself: "What are you?"

She didn't know what answer she expected. Maybe a we-come-in-peace. Perhaps a Disney sidekick quip. But not what came next.

Hare dropped his hands and took a small step forward, his voice low and smooth. "No, no," he said, with the patience of a man correcting a child. "You need to understand something. We ask the questions here."

Diane gasped.

"You," Hare continued, "you just need to be a very good little element of study. That means cooperative, quiet, and ideally conscious." The smile that followed made her skin crawl. "You have so much to teach us."

Behind him, Myles made another note on his pad. Diane's back hit the wall. She hadn't realized she'd been backing up. She wasn't a guest. She wasn't a visitor. She was a subject.

And the beans didn't mean jack.

The small comm port in the wall clicked shut, cutting off all sound. She blinked at the sudden silence. Behind the glass, the two figures stepped back into the shadows and out of sight.

Professor Hare let out a long breath and turned to Myles. "Well, I'd call that a successful test. Not perfect, but promising. I think we've got an unexpected new opportunity ahead of us." He rubbed his temple with one hand. "It's been a long night. And morning. I think we both need to go home, rest, and come back fresh. Tomorrow we study the subject hard."

Myles nodded, tapping one claw thoughtfully against his clipboard. "Before we go... have you noticed anything particular about it?"

Hare frowned. "What do you mean?"

Myles chewed his lip, gesturing vaguely toward the glass. "The being. The subject. It appears a lot like us. Bipedal, symmetrical, expressive. And based on basic observation alone, we may be looking at a being with dietary needs."

Hare's nose twitched. "You're suggesting we... feed it?"

"I'm suggesting," Myles said patiently, "that we not let our groundbreaking specimen expire from dehydration or starvation while we're off getting coffee and naps."

Hare rolled his eyes. "So what? Put a leash on it? Take it outside for a nice stroll before bedtime?"

Myles snorted. "Hardly. Just go to the breakroom and grab a few snacks. Something sealed. Something... palatable. Maybe some hydration packs. And maybe" he motioned toward the far corner of the observation room "we give it a place to, you know, go. If it needs to."

Hare sighed, rubbing the bridge of his snout.

"Fine. But make sure whatever you give it won't turn into a diplomatic incident."

Myles was already turning for the hallway.

"I'll get the neutral stuff. Dry fruit cubes, maybe a protein bar, filtered water. Nothing spicy. And I'll requisition a waste station. We've got an old specimen pan in storage."

Hare waved him off. "Good. Then go home. I want to be here early tomorrow. This asset might be the most valuable thing we've ever dragged through that collider."

Chapter Forty-Two

Have To Get Out

Hare stood at the console, the blood sample spinning slowly beneath a layer of clear gel, backlit by a pale violet diagnostic glow. Genetic sequences flooded across the monitor like a language written in static. He narrowed his eyes. "Common frameworks... but not native," he muttered, adjusting a slider. "This doesn't drift like anything local. It bends. Oscillates. Like it's resisting classification."

Behind him, Diane sat in the holding cell's corner, arms folded, face slack, unreadable. Her eyes followed him, but she said nothing. He didn't expect her to.

He zoomed in on the highlighted data strand. "Selective pressure in noncoding regions... who gave you this blueprint, I wonder? Or did it evolve all on its own?"

No reply. Not even a twitch.

He jotted something on a physical clipboard. Sometimes he preferred the tactile certainty of ink and paper to the digital record. "Subject remains uncommunicative. Previously verbal, now silent. Volition assumed. Behavioral instability pending."

The door let out a muted chirp. Myles entered with a tray in hand, overloaded with what looked like vending machine rejects: a rectangle of processed nutrition, a foil-sealed bottle sweating purple condensation, a pack of something calling itself 'crisps' in eight languages. He didn't look at Diane.

"Dropping this off," Myles said. "She's either going to eat it or throw it."

"Leave it," Hare replied, eyes still on the monitor. "No contact unless she initiates."

Myles set the tray down beside the wall panel without ceremony. "She been like this long?"

"She's conserving information," Hare said. "Like a damaged terminal that knows it's under audit."

Myles didn't laugh, but the corner of his lip ticked. "Trace is sealing the level. No access unless it's you or me," he added, dusting his hands off.

"Good. No variables."

Hare looked at Diane with the cold detachment of someone trying to reverse-engineer a puzzle box. "We resume diagnostics tomorrow. If she speaks before then, log it. If she doesn't, log that too."

Myles gave a short nod. "And if she screams?"

"Still data."

Myles lingered, arms folded. "So, what's the plan for tomorrow?" he asked.

Hare didn't look away from the monitor. "Bloodwork continues. I want to isolate protein-binding characteristics in her hemoglobin, see if it reacts to quantum flux the way her hair did."

Myles raised a brow. "Hair reacted because it was caught mid-phase during the breach."

"Exactly, which makes it ideal. But her blood is alive. Present. If we stimulate it properly, we might trigger another echo event."

Myles glanced toward Diane. "What kind of stimulus?"

"Localized pulse harmonics. Low amplitude. Possibly a microdose of trilineum, but isolated. I also want the cranial scan suite ready. We'll be looking for resonant feedback in the midbrain and the upper temporal lobes." He paused, eyes narrowing at the monitor again. "Her neurostructure isn't just unfamiliar it's optimized. She's not like anything on this planet. A prime specimen. Do you understand what that means, Myles?"

Myles didn't answer, and Hare didn't wait for a reply.

"There is no analog for this in any known genome. Not in our population. Not in controlled fauna. Nothing." His voiced dropped to a whisper. "The brain structure alone... It's not more evolved. It's not less. It's parallel. Like someone built a different version of the same operating system and let it run on separate hardware." He stepped away from the console, clipboard clutched loosely in his hand, and slowly approached the observation glass. "She's a mirror," he murmured. "Of what we might have been if shaped by a different hand."

Diane didn't react. Her eyes didn't rise. She stared at the floor, as though his words belonged to another room, another universe.

Hare's gaze sharpened. "And now she's here. Not theorized. Not postulated. Here." His reflection stared back at him in the glass, hovering beside Diane's still form. "We have the asset. We're going to learn everything we can." He finally turned away. "Run pre-checks on the neuroband tuner," he instructed. "She'll be useful tomorrow, even if she doesn't know it yet."

Myles gave a short nod and followed him out.

The door hissed shut.

Diane stayed perfectly still. The only sign she was still thinking at all was the slow way her fingers curled tighter around the edge of the blanket.

Her silence wasn't submission. It was strategy. But strategy couldn't cage panic forever. A beat passed. Then another. And then she moved.

She tore the blanket off, casting it aside like it burned. Every muscle screamed to act, to do something. She scanned the room, eyes flicking over seams, corners, panels. Looking for a flaw. A hinge. A weakness. Anything.

Her hands hit the walls. She pressed her palm to the seam where the door had closed, then ran her fingers along its edge, praying for something to catch, something mechanical, something stupid and forgotten.

Nothing.

She circled again, pacing now. The floor. The ceiling. The vents that offered air but no hope. Even the light panel above was just out of reach unless she dragged the tray table and stood on it. She considered it.

She looked to the corners. To the shadow beneath the table. Under the slab they'd given her to sit on. Just a bench. Fixed. Sterile. She dropped to her knees and pressed her ear to the wall.

Still nothing.

Her chest was tight. Head swimming. A dozen TV shows and spy thrillers had sold her lies. There was no hidden panel, no magic code, no trick with a spoon and a loose bolt. Just four walls, a sealed door, and her.

She was not getting out. Not tonight.

She sank back against the wall, breathing ragged. Her hands shook, fists clenching into the fabric of her thin gown.

Her eyes burned. Her throat closed. But she pressed her palms hard against her face, forcing the heat back down. She would not give them that.

Not yet.

Chapter Forty-Three

The Blocked Door

Lanell moved softly down the hallway, her pace slow, almost reluctant, as though her body moved forward while her thoughts hung back, clawing at doubt.

What if there's nothing down there? What if Hare was telling the truth? What if the collider mishap, the telemetry, even Trace's icy deflections were all just routine complications, blown out of proportion by a ferret too angry to think clearly? Her stomach turned at the thought. What if this isn't about secrets or lies?

What if this wasn't about truth at all? What if it was just the echo of Dad's imploring voice, the memory of slamming that door behind him shoving her down this path, one bitter step at a time?

She breathed out sharply through her nose and stopped walking. Her eyes drifted toward the tall window lining the east wall, and she stepped closer, drawn by the motionless world outside.

Beyond the glass, the horizon split between forest edge and industrial gray. The rubber factory loomed in the near distance drab, blocky, perpetually sweating steam. She squinted at a processing silo, its upper catwalks caked in old polymer crust, like layers of skin the building hadn't bothered to shed. Just beneath it, a cluster of insulated transport pipes curved out from the base of the facility and into the factory grounds. One of them thick, sun-faded orange ran directly overhead, visible even from here, tracing a diagonal route along the ceiling before disappearing through the outer wall. It carried harvested snail slime waste, the sticky by-product of Crusher's little ecosystem, and funneled it out to be reprocessed into the compound's stock of rubber. Boots, belts, grips, mats, maybe even the soles of the guards' own shoes, it all came from snail slime.

What if I'm wrong about everything? What if all I've done is get myself fired... and the only job left is scrubbing half-cured rubber off mixing vats at the plant next door?

She pictured it wading through puddles of tacky goo in industrial boots, scraping polymer off stainless steel with a dull spatula while some greasy supervisor barked, Put your back into it, purple-feet!

A bitter snort escaped before she could stop it. She shook her head.

Real cute, Lanell. You unravel your life and then laugh at the ruins. Good strategy.

But the sarcasm was just armor. Beneath it, something raw kept pulsing. Guilt. Grief. Ghosts. Maybe it didn't matter what she was chasing only that movement hurt less than stillness.

What if this is self-destruction disguised as heroism?

She pressed her forehead lightly to the cool windowpane, breathing, watching steam rise from the rubber plant like an omen. Her eyes wandered back to the corridor. Back to the sealed levels below. Whether this was justice or just the hangover from one hell of a night she had to know. And if it cost her?

Well, at least I'd go down swinging.

She pushed off the glass and turned down the corridor, steps quickening. Hesitation melted off her like steam on cold metal. She didn't have a plan. She didn't need one. Not yet. Conviction was enough for now.

I know I'm not wrong.

Something had happened, she felt it. In the telemetry. In the evasive answers. In the way Hare's eyes had darted skittishly when she pressed too hard. Something didn't line up the data, the timing, the way Trace suddenly seemed one step ahead. She didn't have proof, but her gut was still screaming, and it hadn't been wrong yet.

She rounded the final corner toward the lift to Sublevel 1, breath tight in her chest. She reached for her keycard and froze. Trace Finn stood squarely in front of the elevator doors. Arms crossed. Stance casual. Eyes anything but. No clipboard. No datapad. Just that unsettling stillness.

"Going somewhere?"

Lanell kept her expression neutral, leaning her shoulder against the wall beside the elevator. "Well," she said lightly, "I might have been."

"Yeah? If it involves the lower levels, that's a no."

Lanell took a long breath and squared her shoulders, forcing herself to look Trace in the eye. "You know, we've both been around here long enough to know things. The rhythms. The routines. What's usual, and what's not."

Trace didn't blink.

"And usually," Lanell continued, her voice tightening just a notch, "you're everywhere else on this campus. Doing what you do best. Keeping things locked down. Keeping us safe from... what was it you called it last time? 'Emergent chaos?"

"Mm," Trace hummed, noncommittal.

"So imagine my surprise," Lanell said, "that on the exact day I come down to pull some old test records, you're suddenly here. No squad. No alert. Just you. Right where I'm going. Funny timing, isn't it?"

Trace's mouth twitched not a smile, something harder. "Funny, yeah. Just like how every time someone's about to make a stupid mistake, they start talking in riddles like they're the only one holding the map."

"I'm just saying your presence here raises questions."

"And I'm saying," Trace snapped, stepping in close, "you don't want the answers."

Lanell's back pressed firmer against the wall, but she held her ground.

"You want to chase ghosts?" Trace hissed. "Fine. Go write a memoir. But the lower levels? That's not curiosity turf. That's containment. That's classified. That's touch-it-and-lose-your-clearance territory."

"I just want the truth," Lanell said, voice steady.

Trace's voice dropped to a growl. "No, you want closure. And that's always the first lie people tell themselves before they blow their lives up."

Lanell cocked her head. "I would walk away. But the wall behind me's not nearly as interesting as the secrets you're guarding."

Trace's thin nostrils flared. "You always were the curious type. Cute in a classroom. Gets people killed in real life."

"And you always were the stoic shadow. Just standing there. Letting the fire burn, long as it wasn't your corridor."

Trace stepped closer until they were almost nose to nose. "Keep going. Maybe if you say enough clever things, the vault door will just open for you."

"I'm not here to be clever," Lanell said. "I'm here because something's wrong, and you know it."

"The only thing wrong is a junior analyst with no clearance sniffing around sealed corridors like a nosy raccoon."

Lanell smirked, trying to ignore the faint metallic smell as the Tularian's cool, moist breath fanned her face. "Guess that makes you the trash can."

Trace didn't laugh.

Lanell's own smile vanished. "You know I'm right. About the firing. About something being moved down there. You're not posted here by accident."

"And you're not being subtle. Hare's always had compartments you weren't cleared for. So has Myles. So do I."

"And I've always let it slide. But this time it's different."

"Different how?"

"Because this time it feels like I'm the only one not in on the lie."

Trace held her gaze. "Sometimes you're not in the circle because the circle is keeping you safe."

"And sometimes that circle's just a noose that gets drawn tighter every time you ask a question."

That hit home. Trace blinked once, her gills rippled.

Lanell pressed. "Tell me I'm wrong."

Trace's lip curled. "You're not stupid."

"But I am disposable. Right? That's what this is about. Keep the idealist out of the loop. Keep the questions quiet. Lock the doors and put the quiet dog at the gate."

Trace stepped in closer. "I don't like you calling me a dog," she snarled.

"Then stop growling at ghosts."

They stood there for a breath, silence heavy, tension thrumming. Finally, Trace pulled back. "I could detain you. Right now."

"And that'd confirm everything I suspect," Lanell said. "So go ahead. Make my day."

Trace didn't move. Didn't reach for cuffs. Didn't radio anyone. She stood rigid, like steel locked into the floor. "You've always been the thorn in everyone's protocol," she muttered.

"And you've always been lonely. But let's not psychoanalyze each other today."

Trace looked away.

Lanell took the moment not a victory, but a draw. She stepped back and nodded. "You know, I appreciate what you do. And seeing now that there's clearly something down there you're protecting us from, I'm just going to walk away and appreciate that you're there keeping us safe."

"Uh-huh," Trace grunted.

Lanell turned and walked away without another word. Her nerves buzzed, but her face stayed composed. Breath even. Gait controlled. Trace let her go, but Lanell could still feel her stare. And somewhere behind her, she swore she heard a holster creak.

Chapter Forty-Four

Something's Down There

Earl sat in the dim quiet of his office. The only light spilled from the cracked screen on his desk terminal. He hadn't touched it in hours. Not since the logs showed a firing sequence he hadn't authorized. Not since the system told him, in its blunt, indifferent way, that access had been granted to someone else.

The whirr of the ventilation system filled the silence, a mechanical lullaby that failed to soothe. His fingers rested on the arm of his chair, absently tracing the deep, time-worn grooves in the wood. He'd carved one of them himself, back when he first took this post Back when he still believed his presence here mattered. That oversight, pressure, and quiet resistance could keep the worst impulses in check.

But this? Being locked out of the collider. Finding out after the fact. The moment he saw that activation timestamp, something old and cold had coiled in his gut. Something he hadn't felt since Arcadia. Since the day he learned what Hare was really capable of. He leaned forward, elbows on knees.

Three seventeen a.m. It hadn't been an error or a glitch. Someone made a choice without him. Without oversight. And worse, they'd gone to some lengths to hide it. The sensor logs had been truncated. The power readouts smoothed. A mask, layered over the truth.

He grunted, low in his throat. This was more than a breach of protocol. This was a breach of trust. A betrayal of every uneasy alliance he'd forged to keep things stable. To keep Lanell safe. To keep the Arcadian Council off his back. And now Lanell was asking questions good ones. The kind he should've been asking himself. The kind that made Hare squirm. Which meant she was getting close. Maybe too close.

He exhaled sharply through his nose, pushed up from the chair, and began to pace.

They're cutting me out.

He'd seen it before. Hare did it to anyone who stopped being convenient. The only difference now? Earl hadn't stopped being useful. Which meant whatever they were hiding, it was big enough that not even loyalty could buy access.

He turned toward the window. Outside, the compound lights flickered in the dark like distant stars. Somewhere below, beneath feet of concrete and decades of secrets, something had come through that collider. Something Hare didn't want to talk about.

And he was running out of time. Soon, silence would no longer be an option. The door behind him creaked. "It's open," he said, without looking around.

Lanell stepped into the office, looking like someone who hadn't slept in two days and hadn't decided yet if she ever would again. She paused near the threshold, arms hanging limp at her sides.

Earl turned to face her. One half of his face remained in shadow, the other lit by the blue spill from the desk monitor. He didn't say anything. He didn't have to. She looked at him, and for a breath, he saw his daughter. Not the shaman. Not the investigator. Just his kid.

Her voice was steady, but it cracked around the edges. "Something is down there."

Earl tugged at his beard. "What do you mean?"

"I ran into Trace Finn. She was guarding the elevator to Sublevel 1 like her life depended on it. And she knew I was coming."

His eyes widened. "Did you get down there?"

Lanell shook her head once. "No. She blocked me. Didn't threaten me or anything. Just stood there like a damn mountain in boots."

Earl regarded her cautiously. "And you're sure that's not just Trace being... Trace?"

"I was sure it was paranoia," Lanell said, pacing now. "I thought maybe it was just fallout from the fight with you. Maybe I was pushing too hard to prove something, to punish you for " She stopped, sucked in a breath, reined it in.

"But she was there, Dad. Waiting for me."

Earl stepped around the desk but didn't move closer. "Lanell, what are you saying?"

She met his eyes now. "I think they fired the collider. I think something came through. And I think they're hiding it below us. And before you ask, no," she added. "I don't have proof. Just locked doors, evasive answers, strange telemetry, and a head of security who suddenly isn't everywhere else on the compound." She crossed her arms. "I'm not chasing ghosts, Dad. I know when I'm being handled, and I'm done with it."

Earl didn't respond right away. He leaned back in his chair, the old wood creaking beneath him, eyes fixed on some invisible point on the far wall. One hand rubbed slowly across his chin, thumb digging into the edge of his jawline like he could scrub the disbelief out of his skin. "Damn it," he muttered.

Lanell's gaze took everything in, catching the twitch in his jaw, the pause in his breath.

"You're right," he said. "Something is down there." He turned to face her fully now, eyes burning with conviction. "And if what came through that collider is what I think it is, then we're in deeper than anyone up top's willing to admit. And if they're hiding it this hard, it means they're scared of it."

He moved to her side and placed a hand gently on her shoulder. "You were never disposable," he said. "But I think you just became dangerous."

Lanell looked at him, unblinking. "I need to get down there."

"You want Trace off the access door?"

"Yeah. I don't need her gone long. Just long enough to get into that elevator."

Earl tapped his knuckle against his lower lip. "I might have an idea that'll work."

Lanell raised a brow.

Earl gave her a crooked smile. "Regulation 7-A. When a high-value biological asset escapes containment, the facility is required to conduct an internal audit within eighteen hours. That audit must include a senior-level tech lead... and a senior-level security officer."

"So if you file the audit..."

"Trace has to accompany me. Personally. No delegating."

A matching grin broke over Lanell's face. "And while she's chasing security leaks down in Habitat 4..."

"I'm buying you a window to slip in through the basement," Earl finished.

They shared a look. Trust layered over tension like old scars over muscle.

"I'll need to make it convincing," Earl added. "Give me twenty minutes. I'll file it, walk it in myself."

Lanell nodded. "I'll be ready."

"And Lanell..." His steady tone wavered. "Whatever they're hiding, don't face it alone."

Lanell hesitated at the door, looking back at her father. "Dad, you know she's not gonna leave that door unattended."

Earl gave a half-shrug. "Maybe she will. Maybe she won't. But if she does?" He looked her dead in the eye. "You're my daughter. I raised you. I know damn well you'll come up with something."

Lanell's lips twitched, almost a smirk. "That's what worries me."

Chapter Forty-Five

Regulation 7-A

Earl leaned back in his chair and thumbed the desk radio, the click of the transmitter oddly satisfying. He watched the second hand on the wall clock creep past twelve.

"It's almost lunchtime, Trace," he said, voice casual but edged with iron. "Thought I'd get this little mess wrapped up before it's over."

Silence stretched. He could practically hear her rolling her eyes. Then her hoarse, strained reply crackled through. "So... we're doing this, huh?"

Another pause.

"What exactly are you referring to?" she snapped. "I'm occupied. Go away. Leave me alone."

Earl chuckled, swiveled in his chair. "I've been sitting at this desk all morning, waiting on you to do your job. Regulation says we've got a deadline. And since I haven't heard a peep from your end, I figured I'd give you a nudge."

Static.

"What are you talking about, you old goat?"

"Oh, come on. Trace Finn. Head of security. Professor Hare's top enforcer. Steel spine. Acid tongue. Did you really forget?"

"I didn't forget anything," she growled. "I've been knee deep in guarding a restricted asset for six hours. I don't have time for petty bureaucracy."

"Petty?" Earl repeated, his tone climbing a notch. "You call this petty? Because to me, it sounds a lot like you're dodging accountability."

"You want a fight, Earl? Because I promise, I will end it before you finish your sentence."

"Tough talk from someone who's slipping."

The radio hissed. "Watch it," she said, voice colder and flatter. "I don't care how long you've been hanging around this place. I will bury you in paperwork so deep you'll need a mole to dig you out."

Earl leaned forward, elbows on the desk. He was beginning to enjoy himself. "Well then, since you clearly forgot, let me remind you." He cleared his throat, theatrically. "Regulation 7-A: If a high-value biological asset escapes containment, a mandatory high-level investigation must be initiated within eighteen hours of recovery. This review must include both a senior-level research officer and the head of facility security, conducted onsite at the location of the breach."

This time the pause was so long that Earl began to wonder if she'd hung up on him. Then there was a quiet, "Shit."

Earl let that hang. He wanted it to sting. "Yeah," he said. "That asset. The one we all danced around yesterday. The one that caused half the compound to get locked down. Time's up, Trace. Clock's ticking, and Hare isn't going to stick his neck out when Regulation 7-A gets ignored."

"You think I don't know that?" she hissed.

"Honestly?" Earl said, rising to his feet. "I think you got so wrapped up in playing bodyguard that you forgot the job you were actually assigned to do."

Once again, Trace didn't respond. He gave it five seconds. Then ten. Still nothing but the faint hum of background chatter on the line.

He raised the radio again. "Trace. This is happening whether you like it or not. So you can stomp your boots and puff your gills later, but right now? You're gonna meet me at Habitat 4. We're going to do this by the book."

A long sigh finally broke through. When her reply came, it was clipped. All steel. All business.

"I'm on my way."

Earl clicked off the radio and grinned to himself. "Thought so."

That stubborn, slippery eel had finally bit. Trace Finn was on her way, which meant the game was now entirely in motion. He rose from the chair, stepped around the desk, and opened the narrow storage cabinet near the back wall. His datapad was precisely where he'd left it, screen still blinking with the time-stamped alert from this morning. He tucked it under one arm, then grabbed his badge lanyard from the hook above. No sense walking into a hornet's nest without armor.

The audit protocol binder was thicker than it had any right to be, but protocol was protocol, and when it came to regulation 7-A, skipping steps wasn't just frowned upon; it was grounds for permanent suspension. Or worse. Earl wasn't worried for himself. He had tenure, gray hairs, and enough blackmail material on Hare to start a bonfire. But Lanell? Lanell was different.

Smart. Too smart. Brave too. Braver than she realized. And clearly caught in the crossfire of something above her paygrade. Earl didn't know what she was doing down in those tunnels late last night, but he had his suspicions, and those suspicions were wearing boots and a tangled tail.

He sighed and double-checked the datapad for the habitat's current clearance logs. Her name didn't show. Of course it didn't. She'd probably found a back route. Probably borrowed a keycard. Hell, probably learned how to shapeshift into a janitor by now, with the week she'd been having.

"Please let this work," he said softly. Not a prayer. Just a hope. Maybe the last one.

He slung the binder into his bag, hoisted it over one shoulder, and headed toward the office door. As he passed under the low arch into the corridor, his eyes shifted to the ceiling and caught the glint of the orange conduit pipe running overhead.

That pipe.

It ran the length of the hallway like a glowing arterial vein, pulsing faintly with coolant from the upper reactor rooms. If he followed it far enough, it eventually fed straight into the ventilation systems around the old rubber fabrication wing. Habitat 4.

"Great," he muttered. "Spiders."

They loved it in there. Warm ducts. Old polymers. That sweet recycled humidity from the curing chambers. Every time he'd done an inspection in that wing, they'd skittered across the walls like the place belonged to them.

Earl hated spiders. Not in a squealing, jump-on-the-chair sort of way. No. His hate was patient. Deep-seated. The kind you develop after getting bit twice on the same ankle during a security sweep and nearly losing your balance on a ten-foot scaffold. There were grudge levels of hate. Earl was on tier five.

He rubbed his wrist absentmindedly, as if the memory alone was enough to make his skin crawl.

Still, Habitat 4 was where the escaped asset had been found, and if Trace didn't show, he'd have to go in alone. With the cameras down for maintenance and the sensors on intermittent ping, that whole sector was practically a blind spot. Exactly where you'd hide something... or someone.

The thought made his stomach turn. Protocol wasn't about convenience. It was about the process. And sometimes that process led you into webs you'd rather avoid.

He rounded the last corner and swiped his badge at the junction gate. He was so deep in thought that the mechanical hiss of the security door barely registered. He paused just before stepping through. "This better not be for nothing."

Whatever was waiting for him in there, it would all be worth it if it bought Lanell time. With one last glance at the flickering hallway monitor, Earl stepped through the gate, datapad in hand.

Habitat 4 awaited.

Chapter Forty-Six

Enter Jarvis Pellick

Trace Finn muttered curses as she stomped back down the corridor, hand still twitching from slapping the radio button too hard.

"Damn goat and his clipboard gospel," she growled. "Of course he pulled 7-A. Hasn't used that one in six years, but suddenly it's time to be by-the-book?" She tapped her comm. "Teyla, come in."

"Go ahead, boss," came the crisp reply.

"Where are you?"

"West wing. Escorting the transport team. Moleman's specimens just came up from Sublevel 3. We're headed for Quarantine."

Trace swore under her breath. "That's today?"

"Was on the docket. You signed off on it."

Right. She had. Dammit. "Carry on, then. Eyes sharp."

Click.

She tapped the radio again. "Silas, report."

"Silas here. I'm with the Chancellor's entourage. Perimeter sweep and shielding verification. You said no interruptions unless "

"Unless I needed you. Which I do."

"Understood, but we're mid-pattern. Disengaging now would leave a hole."

Trace gritted her teeth. "Stay on it. Don't let them out of visual."

Click.

Two down.

She tapped again, already annoyed at the next person on her list. "Mika, what's your status?"

Static. Then: "East tower. Evac drill. I've got forty researchers pretending not to panic. Want me to yell audit and see what happens?"

Trace gave a noise between a laugh and a growl. "No. Hold your post."

Click.

She stared at the comm. Three of her sharpest agents, all doing what she told them. Damn her for training them well. She looked at the roster and scrolled down past the hotshots, the elite, the ones she wanted.

And there he was. Jarvis Pellick.

She didn't even sigh. It was too late for that. She just hit the button and braced for impact.

"Jarvis here!" came the far too eager reply. "I'm on backup patrol near Hydraulics. Just finished logging a coolant line check that wasn't even on my list! You need something, Chief?"

Trace stared at the radio like it had just called her Mom. "Yeah," she said. "I need you to get down to Sublevel 1. I've got a... situation that needs watching while I deal with an audit."

"Audit? As in, regulation-level? You want me to "

"Yes, you," she snapped. "Hold the post until relieved. Full protocols. Helmet on. No ad-libbing."

"Copy that! I won't let you down! You can count on Jarvis!"

"I swear," she muttered under her breath as she clicked off, "if he salutes me when he arrives, I'm walking into a spider nest with my arms wide."

She turned, already heading for the lift that would take her toward Habitat 4. Of all the damn days for protocol to rear its head. Of all the backup to get... Jarvis.

Trace crossed her arms and leaned against the access elevator's reinforced door, boot tapping impatiently. The seconds dragged. She checked her wristband. Five minutes late. Jarvis was probably 'double-confirming' some imaginary checklist or chasing a loose bolt down a corridor.

She closed her eyes and took a breath. The scent down here was dry metal and old air filters. This whole level was dull and dim, nothing but pale strip lighting and rust-tinged ventilation covers. Perfect place for a nobody to sneak through. Exactly why she hated leaving it unguarded.

A shuffle of footsteps echoed from around the far corner. Trace snapped her head up, ready to deliver a lecture. Then came the voice.

"Chief! Over here! Look what I found!"

Jarvis came trotting into view, pointing dramatically at something offscreen like a bad stage actor entering his moment. He skidded to a stop beside a recessed alcove in the wall.

Trace blinked. "What?"

"There!" he said, now wheeling out a rust-flecked utility cart from the shadows. "Someone left this unsecured in a storage nook! Just sitting here, tucked out of sight. Tools, maintenance forms this could've been stolen or tampered with! You want me to take it to the tool shop?"

He stood proudly, both hands on the cart like he'd just discovered a bomb. Trace stared at him in disbelief.

"Pellick," she said slowly. "Put. That. Back."

"But "

"Now."

"Okay, okay."

With visible reluctance, Jarvis shoved the cart back into the nook, aligning it with unnecessary precision. Then jogged back, looking eager for more orders.

Trace met him halfway, hand on her hip. "Here's what you're going to do," she said, voice hard as sheet metal. "You are going to stand right here. This elevator, this exact one, goes to Sublevel 1. It's off-limits. No one no researchers, no engineers, not even a janitor gets on that lift unless I say so."

Jarvis nodded. "Got it. I'll log every interaction."

"No." She took a deep breath and mentally counted to ten. "Don't log anything. Don't chat with them. You're not here to make friends, Pellick. If someone walks up to this door, you ask for clearance. If they don't have it, you deny access and call it in. Immediately."

"Even if it's Professor Hare?"

Trace's eye twitched. "Especially if it's Professor Hare."

"Whoa," Jarvis breathed, standing a bit straighter.

She rubbed at the back of her neck, where the stress knot had been building all morning. Jarvis made it worse. Regulations made it worse. This whole damn week...

"You are not to leave this post," Trace continued. "Not even for a bio break. If your bladder becomes a problem, you will suffer silently like the rest of us. And if anything goes sideways, anything, you don't improvise. You comm me, and you wait."

Jarvis saluted.

Trace slapped his hand down midair. "Don't ever do that again."

He cleared his throat. "Understood."

"Good." She gave him a long stare. "You're not first string, Pellick. You're the sub. The bench. You're in because there's no one else. That doesn't mean you get to showboat. This post is serious. Treat it that way."

Jarvis's face turned a deep shade of red. "Y-yes, Chief. I'll handle it."

Trace stepped back, gave one last long look at the access door, then turned on her heel and stalked away.

"If he leaves his post to organize tool carts, I swear I'm feeding him to the spiders."

Chapter Forty-Seven

Quick Thinking

Lanell paused at the edge of the corridor. She didn't peer around it. Not yet. That wasn't the play.

Instead, her eyes tracked upward, past the cold glow of the hallway lights to the orange pipe running vertically along the wall. It rose from the floor, then curved overhead, snaking its way toward the access elevator.

She followed its arc with her eyes. The pipe exited just above the corner where the wall curved sharply out of view. That's where the elevator doors would be, along with whoever, or whatever, was guarding them.

Her gaze traveled lower. A tool cart sat pressed into a shallow alcove near the edge of the hallway, like someone had stashed it and forgotten about it.

I don't remember seeing that last time.

The cart was ordinary enough tall handle, two stacked trays, a folded cloth tossed over the top. It didn't seem threatening, but its presence bothered her. Everything down here was supposed to be sterile, ordered. If a cart was abandoned, it meant someone had been interrupted, or someone had left it intentionally.

She dropped her weight slightly and bent her knees, letting her stance go loose, ready.

This was it. There wasn't going to be another opportunity. If someone was posted at the elevator, she'd have to improvise fast. If not, she'd slip by and get down to the restricted sublevel before anyone knew. But either way, she had to get through that door.

No turning back.

She didn't check the window this time. That glass had become her crutch. Every time she passed through here before, she'd let herself glance out, let the view distract her, lull her into thinking she still had time to figure something else out.

She was done waiting.

Her hand hovered near the satchel at her side, brushing the clasp. She stepped back from the wall, just enough to give herself clearance if she needed to pivot or bolt.

She bit her lip. What if they moved the cart to draw her attention? What if they knew she might try this route again?

Can't second guess now.

The orange pipe above gave no answers. The cart didn't move. And she still couldn't hear anyone. But that didn't mean no one was there. She gave herself three more seconds.

Three...

Two...

One...

Lanell stepped around the corner.

And there he was.

Jarvis. Standing like a statue in front of the elevator doors, feet square, chest puffed, hands clasped neatly behind his back. Not a twitch. Not a fidget. Full ceremonial posture, like someone had wound him up, pointed him at the door, and said, stand guard like your job depends on it.

Which it probably did.

She stopped and gave an internal groan. Of course it was Jarvis.

She didn't need to look at his face to confirm it. That stance, so earnest and over-the-top it almost squeaked, was unmistakable. No one else on the entire campus stood like that. Maybe the chancellor. Maybe a wax figure of the chancellor.

Lanell's breath hitched in a tiny, ironic laugh.

Of all the people Trace could've posted here, it had to be the one who still said things like roger that in casual conversation. And just like that, a memory bubbled up.

The first time she met Jarvis, she'd been elbow-deep in a busted telemetry pod when he walked in, wide-eyed and practically saluting. He told her she was the smartest systems analyst he'd ever seen, then nervously asked if she needed any tools. And backup tools. And backup tools for her backup tools.

He'd meant well. Still did.

I'm gonna hate doing this to him.

There was no way around it. If she wanted to get down to Sublevel 1, Jarvis was the last obstacle standing in her way, and for all his awkwardness, he was doing his job. She tightened the strap on her satchel and let out a long breath.

Let's hope he hasn't recognized me yet. Let's hope this goes quietly.

She was close enough now to see the little twitch in his ear, the subtle sway of someone who'd been holding a pose too long. He hadn't noticed her. Or if he had, he was pretending like hell not to.

Which made her next step even harder.

Lanell inched closer, eyes scanning the space still no movement behind the glass doors. No alarms and no sign of Trace.

One chance. One move. One poor guy in the wrong place at the wrong time.

Jarvis whipped his head around when she stepped into view, eyes bright with a weird kind of eagerness.

"Miss Lanell," he said with a nod. "State the purpose of your approach to this access point."

She blinked at him. Is he... serious?

Then again, it was Jarvis. Of course he was serious. She crossed her arms, letting her hip shift slightly as she tilted her head. "Wow. Starting to think you practiced that in the mirror."

Jarvis didn't waiver. "Regulation requires verification of clearance prior to "

"Yeah, yeah, save the brochure." Lanell paused, letting her eyes sweep slowly over the sealed elevator behind him. Her expression flattened. "Let me ask you something," she said, tone dipping into that dry, sardonic place she usually saved for bureaucrats and sour juice. "Why exactly are you guarding a door that leads to a sublevel where, officially, nothing exists? Just felt like standing in front of the most boring part of the building today?"

Jarvis opened his mouth. Closed it. Blinked twice. "Because I was ordered to," he said, a little less certain now.

She gave an exaggerated yawn. "Right. Real inspiring."

Poor guy. Wish I had time to dance around this, but I don't.

Jarvis's eyes dipped downward, lingering a moment. "I didn't realize today was casual," he said. "I like those boots, by the way. Practical. Stylish. Good grip."

Lanell stifled a snort and offered a small, polite smile. "Thanks, Jarvis."

Seriously? We're talking boots now? You sweet, awkward goof.

"Sorry, I must've made a wrong turn somewhere," she said lightly, even putting a bit of sheepishness in her tone. "I'll just circle around."

Jarvis gave a stiff, dutiful nod, still holding his formal pose. "Understood. Be safe, Miss Lanell."

She pivoted on her heel and started toward the corner. As she rounded the corner, her face shifted, soft smile fading.

A faded stencil flaked across the pipe just beside the spigot.

LIQUID RUBBER PROCESSING FEED SAMPLE SPIGOT | DO NOT ADJUST

The grin that bloomed across her face wasn't wide. It wasn't playful. It was sharp and confident, the kind of smile a saboteur makes before cutting the right wire.

Now she had a plan, and Earl was going to hate it.

Lanell approached the spigot, reached for the pressure knob, and gave it a slow twist.

At first, nothing.

Then, with a soft glook, a thick, clear fluid began to snake its way out of the nozzle. It oozed out in one long, uninterrupted rope. Viscous. Slippery. It had the consistency of sweet cake syrup after it had sat too long in the bottle.

She crouched, cautiously extended one finger, and dipped it into the stream. Her eyes widened the moment contact was made.

Yep. That's Crusher's goo, alright.

Sticky didn't begin to cover it. It clung to her skin with a sudden biting grip, elastic and stubborn. Unlike her earlier experience in the lab, she could pull away from it, but she had to mean it.

She flexed her hand. Freed her finger. Took a breath. "Yeah. That'll do," she muttered.

The stuff just kept coming. Within seconds, it was pooling across the floor, spreading outward like a lazy flood. Thick tendrils began to stretch, forming adhesive puddles that gleamed under the low hallway lights. The air took on a chemical sweetness, a now familiar tang of citrus.

Lanell stayed to the right side of the corridor, out of the path of the flow. The pipe's angle and floor gradient worked in her favor, funneling most of it across the hallway.

She didn't need to be a genius to know how this stuff worked. The more that came out, the more surface area it covered and the more dangerous it became to touch. By the time someone stepped into it, there would be no casual retreat. One foot in and you'd have to leave a boot behind. Two feet in and... well, you'd better have a team with ropes.

She folded her arms and leaned against the wall again, watching the translucent flood creep along the tile.

Anyone else, I'd have serious doubts this would work.

But this wasn't anyone else. This was Jarvis.

She could already picture it. That eager salute. The dopey confusion. A sudden slip. Flailing. Shouting. Attempting to remain professional while completely glued to the floor like a fly on a sugar trap.

She grimaced. "Sorry, Jarvis."

Chapter Forty-Eight

Just a Little Stuck

Lanell, now positioned out of sight from the access door, grabbed the unattended tool cart with both hands. She braced herself, then gave the cart a hard shove.

The crash echoed like thunder down the quiet corridor, metal clanging against concrete in a jagged symphony. A wrench skittered across the floor, spinning to a stop just beyond the reach of the growing pool.

Moving quickly, Lanell positioned herself next to the over-turned cart, half-crumpled, one hand on her side, an exaggerated wince on her face, finally letting out a sharp yelp for good measure.

"Miss Lanell?!"

Jarvis's panicked voice shot through the hallway like a flare. Heavy boots pounded toward her, fast. Too fast.

Then came the moment. Jarvis barreled into view at a dead sprint, all puffed chest, wide eyes, and noble concern. He locked on her like a homing beacon, body angling to intercept and assist. "Don't move, I got you!" he called.

The instant his boot hit the edge of the goo, it betrayed him. First his foot slid. Then his balance broke. His arms windmilled. The second boot tried to correct but only carried him further in. It was like he'd dived into quicksand made of corn syrup. His knees slammed down with a sickening squelch, palms flung forward to break the fall, but only succeeded in slapping full-speed into the slick, adhesive mess.

Jarvis fell face-first with a whap that would've been funny if it weren't so... tragic. He hadn't even had time to curse. Just goo, floor, and shame.

"Unnghh... I'm okay!" he croaked.

He pushed with one hand. Nothing moved. The goo pulled at him like warm bubblegum, stretching and snapping with every desperate motion. Sticky strands clung to his arms, his uniform, even his eyelashes. It was everywhere, and it wasn't letting go.

He tried to raise a knee, and there was a wet pop as the goo stretched with it, then yanked it back.

"Oh, come on," he grunted.

Jarvis gave one last noble heave. The goo laughed in return, slurping him deeper into its embrace. He attempted to straighten his shoulders, as if proper posture could somehow restore his authority. A strand of goo stretched between his chin and the floor like a stubborn spider web. His bravado dimmed, swallowed by frustration and the slow, humiliating realization that he wasn't going anywhere.

Lanell blinked, eyes wide in feigned shock as she carefully skirted the edge of the mess. The smell of the goo was sugary and chemical, like antiseptic mixed with molasses, and it hissed softly where it spread under the warm hallway lights. It seemed to pulse slightly, growing tackier as his body heat warmed it.

"Are you... OK?" she asked, crouching just outside the goo's reach.

For a split second, Lanell's hand twitched toward her comm. She could call this off. Say she'd slipped too. But the elevator access card practically burned in her pocket.

She bit her lip. She hadn't meant for it to go this far, not the chest-first belly flop. She just needed a few minutes of clearance, not a full takedown. Still, it was working.

Jarvis, still trying to prop himself up like this was totally fine, gritted his teeth. "Nah. Just... uh, just a little stuck," he said, tugging one hand and making zero progress. The floor slurped in response.

"Because it looks like you're stuck," she observed.

His uniform was soaked across the chest now, pressed to the floor in gooey defeat. His elbows trembled. His neck flushed. Still, he clung to dignity.

"Okay," he muttered, eyes closing briefly. "Maybe a little more than a little."

Lanell gave him the kindest, most understanding nod she could muster under the circumstances. "I'll go get help," she said. Then, in a softer voice, added, "But do me a favor?"

Jarvis looked up, eyebrows furrowed.

"You didn't see me, okay?" she said, lowering her voice to a conspiratorial whisper. "They might think I caused this mess. And honestly, I don't even know what happened."

Jarvis blinked goo out of one eye and managed a weak nod, not fully grasping the betrayal, but too occupied with his slow descent into adhesive misery to argue. "I won't say anything," he mumbled into the floor. "Promise."

As she stepped quietly away, Lanell gave him one last glance. She hated that it worked this well. She hated that it needed to. But most of all, she really hoped he didn't have to pee anytime soon.

Chapter Forty-Nine

A Flicker of Hope

Sublevel 1.

She'd heard it mentioned in passing once between two junior techs trading gossip, and another time while sifting through archived telemetry. Nothing official. Whispers and loose ends. Years ago, curious and aimless, she'd wandered these halls.

That day, she had turned back before reaching the cell blocks. No alarms sounded. No guards stopped her. It wasn't a sign or voice that made her retreat, it was the stillness. A feeling like she was walking through a place that used to breathe.

This level had once housed the beating heart of the original facility, long before the upper labs expanded. Before the funding, before the spotlight, before the rot set in. You could still see the bones if you looked hard enough worn grooves in the floor where carts once rolled, faded outlines of department labels etched in the wall plates.

Now it felt like a mausoleum. No warmth. No motion. No stray datapads or coffee mugs left behind. Emptiness, sterile and intentional.

She passed a bench bolted to the wall, old and scuffed, the kind techs used to wait on before shift rotations. Nearby, a row of lockers stood open and empty, doors yawning like mouths long deprived of speech. She remembered pulling old test results from one of them once. Early genetic studies, partially redacted, misfiled where no one would think to look. The files had mentioned Category X anomalies and Subject Class: Divergent. But no names.

She hadn't stayed long that day.

Her skin prickled as she passed through the threshold into the outer access corridor. The air felt heavier here. Warmer. Like breath gone stale.

"Why does no one come down here anymore?" she whispered, testing the silence.

It didn't answer.

She stepped back from the door, retreating into shadow. The holding cell wasn't the only thing alive down here.

Beyond the next bend, another room was lit a lab chamber. It wasn't fully illuminated, but the low murmur of powered equipment pulsed like a heartbeat. She crept closer, ears tuned for movement. There was none. The electric thrum continued, punctuated by occasional flicks of data cycling on untouched displays.

The door had been left open.

Inside, monitors lined the far wall, each running loops of diagnostic data in real-time. Scanning equipment stood active, aimed toward the adjacent observation cell. On one station, gene sequences scrolled past in neat green columns. Another showed a biological panel: hormone levels, white cell counts, neurological responses.

And right there, at the edge of the console, a fresh nutrition bar. Sealed and still cool to the touch. Next to it, an opened drink bottle, condensation beading down the side. Someone had been here. Recently.

Lanell picked up the bar, turned it over, then glanced toward the data still updating on-screen. The readings looked oddly familiar. Not in a way she could explain, but there was something off. The markers weren't from a local subject. Too much variation. Too many unidentified alleles.

One of the gene pads caught her eye. She was closer now, so she could make out the spiraling double helix in high resolution. At the base was a small spiral symbol stamped digitally into the footer.

The spiral. The same symbol Earl had called a shamanic mark.

What the hell?

No one outside the Arcadians should have access to that biometric signature. The fact that it was showing up on a datapad tied to this room made no sense.

She tapped the edge of the pad, bringing up the next screen. Still spiral-stamped. Still active. Another panel showed a thermal scan of a body. Bipedal, probably primate. Entirely hairless. Not shaved in preparation for surgery, but absent of it. As if the subject had never grown fur to begin with. She stepped back, unease writhing in her chest.

How could the shamanic mark be connected to that? This wasn't Arcadian. It wasn't even anthropoid. If it wasn't native to their world, then...

There was a quiet part of her that wanted to take it. Slip it into her coat, disappear, analyze it later where no one could interrupt. It was proof that something was being kept down here.

"No. I'm not here for that."

She dropped her arm, jaw tightening as she turned away from the console. Whatever they were doing down here, this wasn't a defunct wing of the old lab. Someone had been keeping secrets. Dangerous ones. And she wasn't here to collect trophies. She was here for answers.

Lanell turned toward the wall, where the tinted glass of the observation window loomed like a blank slate. She approached, then slid her fingertips across the lighting control beneath the glass. The dial was already partially turned up. Someone had been observing recently.

Her pulse jumped as she adjusted it further, drawing the veil back. The room beyond materialized like a memory surfacing from murky water.

And there folded, into the far corner, knees pulled tight to chest, head buried, was a figure. Lanell stepped closer to the glass, her heart drumming in her ears. She didn't know why, but a creeping feeling unfurled in her gut. Not fear exactly. Heavier. Like déjà vu wrapped in static.

Then it hit her. The dream.

Her fingers hovered over the glass. This room. This corner. That dim light. The sloped shape huddled with its back turned and knees pulled tight. Every fragment aligned with the nightmare, the one that had clawed into her sleep and left her waking drenched in sweat and full of dread.

She's here now.

That voice wasn't her own. It didn't feel like a thought. More like a message delivered from somewhere else. She swallowed hard and looked again.

The being in the corner hadn't moved. Its limbs were slender and pale, unmarked by fur or scales or feathers. Smoothness. Naked, exposed. Vulnerable. It looked cold even without shivering.

The body from the scan.

Lanell's brain struggled to make sense of it.

It didn't fit any known classification or resemble any species she recognized. All the same, it felt familiar. Not in the way you'd recognize a species but in the way you recognize your own reflection in a funhouse mirror.

The being didn't stir. Lanell raised her hand and tapped gently on the glass.

Nothing.

She tapped again, louder.

A pause. Then, the shape shifted. Its head lifted a fraction, and a pair of wide, haunted eyes peeked up over bent knees.

Lanell stared into those eyes, and deep inside her chest, something felt like it was being drawn out. Like those eyes weren't looking at her but through her. As if somewhere on the other side of that pain-glazed stare, there was a quiet question hanging in the dark.

She didn't move. The silence pressed in like fog, heavy and hard to breathe through. She couldn't tell how long they stared at one another only, that time felt skewed.

What was this thing? Why did it feel like she already knew?

Lanell stood in front of the door. It wasn't locked. The panel glowed green. All it would take would be the touch of a button.

She'd already tapped twice. Whoever, or whatever was inside had barely acknowledged her. She told herself that was a reason not to go in. It didn't work.

This wasn't mere curiosity. It was primal. An ache behind her ribs that said, You've been here before. You don't remember.

She looked at the door. "This could be the dumbest mistake I ever make," she said aloud, voice dry and half-laughing. "Maybe I get fired. Maybe I disappear."

Her fingers stretched towards the button.

There was a beep and the door slid open Air moved past her skin. It tasted stale, like it had been recycled too many times without the presence of life to justify the effort.

She stepped through. One foot, then the other. The door eased shut behind her with a whisper. Inside, the room was stark white and painfully empty. Lanell took a step forward. Then another. Each footfall sounded too loud.

She was halfway across the room when she noticed how still the figure was. Frozen. Like the body had curled inward to escape something it couldn't fight.

Lanell slowed. She didn't know what to say. Didn't know what she was seeing. Her brain scrambled for a name, any classification or medical tag or species profile that could explain what she was walking toward.

Smooth pale skin, bruised in spots, the shape too small to be anything but a child, but not a child of this world. The being didn't react to her presence. Not even a twitch.

Lanell crouched and whispered, "Hey... are you alright?"

No response.

She tried again. A little louder. "Can you hear me?"

Still nothing. Her gaze flicked up to the observation camera in the corner of the room. On and watching. Probably recording. The weight of surveillance pressed against her shoulders.

"I don't know what happened to you," she said softly. "But you're not alone anymore."

Stillness.

The head lifted again. Enough for one wide, exhausted eye to peek out between the arms. No evidence of emotion or understanding, but it was contact.

Lanell's breath caught.

She's here now.

That voice again. Her eyes moved over the figure fragile limbs, frail shoulders, strange proportions. Yet...

That mark. The spiral. Not drawn. Not scarred. Born. Etched into skin like hers but not hers. That symbol felt ancient. Heavy. Like something sacred she didn't have words for yet and seeing it here made her skin crawl.

She licked her dry lips. Then, almost without thought, she raised her hand. Her fingertips trembled as they hovered above the bowed head. She paused for a moment.

What are you doing?

But the question was already too late. Her hand descended. She touched her.

Her fingers met warm skin that vibrated faintly like the hum of a power line. The scent of burnt ozone lingered where their flesh connected.

For a suspended second, the world faded. The lights, the equipment, the room all gone.

Lanell felt like her soul had drifted out of her body and found its mirror. As if light from one star had traveled across the black to find another. Two signals resonating. Not understanding, aligning.

"I'm here," Lanell whispered, barely knowing why.

The girl didn't speak, but her hand moved.

Lanell saw the thin, trembling fingers start to lift from the knees. They rose slowly, like it hurt. Like every inch of motion was borrowed strength. And Lanell responded without thinking. Her hand extended down.

The hand rose up. They met. Palm to palm. Warm to warm. The fingers curled. They held. Not tight. Not desperate. Delicate. Like both were afraid the moment would break if they squeezed too hard. But also like it was the only thing in the room that wasn't broken.

Lanell looked into those eyes again. No tears, and she still hadn't spoken a word. But there was a flicker now. A flicker of hope, fragile but real.

Lanell's throat tightened. Her own eyes burned. She wasn't ready for this. She hadn't come here expecting... her. And yet, here she was.

In the quietest voice she could manage, she said, "It's okay. I don't know what you are. But I see you."

The hand in hers gave the tiniest squeeze.

The creature didn't know what this touch meant, but it didn't hurt. For now, that was enough.

Lanell closed her eyes. That was enough. For now.

Chapter Fifty

Diane

The girl's lips parted. At first, Lanell thought it was nothing. But then, soft as dust falling through moonlight, a whisper emerged.

"You came."

The words were brittle, as if they'd been stitched together from the last scraps of hope.

Lanell froze. The floor beneath her seemed to shift. You came. Not who are you? Not what is this? Like she'd been waiting.

Her hand tightened around the creature's trembling hand. "Yeah. I guess I did."

Nothing moved. Just two heartbeats, trying to align across the great unknown.

"I " Lanell started, but the words tangled. What could she even say? I had a dream about you? I saw your mark? It all sounded insane, even to her. She tried again. "I don't know who you are. I don't know why you're down here. But you're not alone, not anymore."

She reached up with her other hand and gently brushed a matted strand of golden hair away from its forehead.

"You're hurt." Lanell kept her voice soft.

It didn't answer with words, but the posture shifted. Her knees dropped a little. Her arms no longer shielded her head.

"What's your name? Can you talk?"

A long pause. Then, the creature opened her mouth again. Her voice cracked against itself, dry and broken, like it hadn't been used in days. "Diane."

Lanell's breath caught, not because of the name but because of the way she said it. Like she was trying to remember it as she spoke it aloud.

"Okay, Diane." Lanell said the name back, tasting it. Letting it settle between them. "That's a pretty name."

Diane's lip trembled. She blinked again, and this time, a tear slipped down her cheek.

"I don't know what they've done to you," Lanell said, "but I'm going to find out. And if I can help, I will." She meant it. Not as a promise. As a truth.

Diane's hand squeezed hers tighter this time.

Lanell shifted so she was kneeling beside her, shoulder to shoulder. "I think you were brought here by mistake. Or maybe on purpose. I don't know which. But I do know this, if I leave you here, I won't sleep again."

A shaky breath from Diane. She leaned her head against Lanell's shoulder. Not a full collapse, just contact.

And Lanell didn't move. She hardly dared to breathe.

"There was a tornado," Diane said quietly. "I was in a gulley, trying to find cover. Everything was shaking. Trees were sideways. I thought they were going to rip out of the ground." She shut her eyes tight.

Lanell didn't say anything. She just held her hand, letting the silence hold space around the story.

Diane's grip suddenly tightened, like the memory itself had just grabbed her and dragged her backward. "I remember the wind. It sounded like it was screaming."

Lanell's throat tightened, but she stayed still. Listened.

"I curled up in the mud. I remember the smell of wet dirt. Lightning hit a tree not far from me and everything went white. I thought that was it." She opened her eyes. They glistened under the low light, hollow with exhaustion.

"And then the light came. Not from the sky. From below, I think. Or everywhere. Like it swallowed me. I didn't feel my body anymore."

Something in her words made Lanell's gut twist. "You didn't choose this. You didn't want to be here."

Diane shook her head. "I just wanted to survive the storm." Her breath hitched. "I never asked for this."

Diane hesitated. Her fingers curled tighter in Lanell's hand. "They kept asking questions," she said finally. "Over and over. Like if they said them enough times, I'd start making sense."

"What kind of questions?"

"About my body. My blood. My skin." Her voice thinned. "They took samples. Watched how I reacted to things. Lights. Sounds. Needles." She flinched at the last word. "Sometimes they talked like I wasn't there."

Lanell felt something cold settle behind her ribs.

“They said I was important,” Diane whispered. “But they never said why.”

Lanell’s voice dropped to a whisper. “I’m going to help you. I’m going to find a way to get you out of here.”

Diane’s lips quivered. “You believe me?”

Lanell nodded solemnly. "I don't know what I believe about a lot of things anymore, but I believe you. That's enough for me."

The two of them stayed there, locked in a moment neither fully understood. Diane's hand clutched Lanell's like it was it was her only tether to reality. And Lanell, her whole body humming with the gravity of what she had just promised, knew there was no turning back.

Whatever this was, it had already begun.

Lanell gently loosened her fingers from Diane's. The contact lingered like heat after lightning, alive in the space between them even after it broke.

She stood slowly, careful not to make a sound, ears perked for any change in the general background noise of the lab. "I have to go. I shouldn't even be here."

Diane's lip trembled and tears swam in her eyes. Panic didn't surface, but the fear was there, silent and deep like water pressed behind glass.

Lanell knelt one last time and put a hand on each of Diane's shoulders. "Listen to me. If anyone comes in here, you haven't seen me. Understand?"

Diane blinked. A small nod followed.

"No one's been here. Not a soul. They can't know I saw you. They might think I... “They might think I... that I let you out. Or interfered.” Her throat tightened, but she pushed through. "I will come back. As soon as I can. I don't know how long, but I will."

Diane's hand, now resting in her lap, gave the barest twitch. She was clearly trying not to cry.

Lanell brushed a hand lightly against Diane's arm. "I'm going to get you out of here. And when I do, we'll figure out what happens next. Together."

Then Lanell rose, backing toward the door. She gave the room one last glance. The scan displays were still active, quietly glowing with data that didn't add up. The air still smelled like antiseptic and filtered air, but something had shifted. The silence wasn't sterile anymore, it was sacred. Like a place where something real had finally happened.

Lanell stepped through the doorway and pressed the button to close it behind her.

After taking one last look at the holding cell, she vanished into the shadows of the lower hall. Her footsteps were nearly silent against the cold floor, but in her head, they echoed like thunder.

What have I just done?

The ghost of Diane's touch still pulsed in her skin.

What I had to do. What no one else would.

Her pace quickened, eyes scanning corners, ceiling panels, shadows. Her presence here had to vanish like a shadow at sunrise. Unseen, unspoken, erased.

I can't let Hare do this. It's not right. It's not the order of things.

The order of things. That last phrase hung on her like a weight. She stopped, hand against the wall, steadying herself.

The term natural order rang differently now. It was no longer a bland phrase from textbooks or lectures. It felt personal. Raw. Lanell closed her eyes. For so long, she had taken that phrase to mean balance. Stability. Systems playing their roles. Life on its proper track.

But now?

Her eyes snapped open. "This place has removed that."

The words fell from her lips with cold finality. It wasn't spoken with rage. It wasn't even said with judgment. It was simply the observation of a fact. The same way one might say the forest is on fire or the stars are going out.

This place had carved nature open with surgical tools and force-fed it their own version of truth. They didn't preserve the natural order. They replaced it.

And now, whatever had come through that collider wasn't part of their order. But it might be part of hers.

Lanell pushed off the wall, steadied her breath, and slipped deeper into the passageway, her heart carrying a promise and her mind echoing with the truth she could no longer unsee.

Chapter Fifty-One

The Predator's Shadow

Lanell's thoughts tangled as the elevator hummed upward.

An alien. Not just strange, but something utterly other. What do I even...

The bell chimed. Doors parted with a mechanical sigh. Her gaze was still downward when she saw them: a pair of scuffed combat boots planted firm on the tile. Her stomach lurched. She raised her eyes slowly.

Trace Finn.

Red irises glared like embers under a storm-dark brow. Beside her, Jarvis stood stiff, one arm bandaged crudely, blood soaking through. His ears drooped.

Trace's low, silky voice cut through the air. "Did you do this to my troop?"

Lanell's pulse spiked. She shook her head fast, words tumbling. "No. I-I was looking for some solvent down in the lower levels."

Trace tilted her head slowly. "Solvent. That's cute." She took another step closer. "You just can't help yourself, can you? Always down where you don't belong. Always scratching at locked doors. I've got half a mind to drag you to Hare myself tell him you can't follow orders. You know what he'd do then? He wouldn't just gut you. He'd gut me. He'd gut my whole unit." She closed the last bit of space between them. "You're not curious, Lanell. You're reckless. And when reckless people tangle with Hare, they get people like Jarvis here carved up and left bleeding in the hall."

Lanell instinctively retreated, heel hitting the back of the elevator.

"Chief, she didn't " Jarvis's protest wavered.

"Shut up," Trace snapped, never looking away from Lanell. The single command hit like a gunshot.

Their eyes locked. Trace leaned in, face so close Lanell could feel her hot breath. Then, without breaking eye contact, Trace's arm slid sideways. The door button clicked beneath her finger.

The elevator doors slid shut. Now it was just the two of them.

The doors sealed with a heavy thunk. Lanell's throat tightened. She pressed herself back against the paneling, the air suddenly close, thick with Trace's scent of steel and saltwater. She said nothing. Not a word.

Trace didn't leave the silence to linger long before she started in. "You realize what this looks like, don't you?" Her voice was a slowly drawn blade. "My troop comes back gummed up, and disgraced and you just happen to be creeping around where you don't belong. If Hare knew" Trace leaned closer, lips curling into a humorless grin "it wouldn't just be you in the hot seat. It would be me. My command. My troops. And do you know what happens to a chief when she looks weak in front of Hare?"

Cold sweat prickled on Lanell's back, but she held steady, eyes fixed just above Trace's shoulder.

Trace's grin vanished, replaced by a snarl. "He doesn't fire us; he replaces us. And when he replaces us" her fingers flexed at her side "we disappear."

Lanell kept her lips firmly pressed together.

Trace's voice came again, softer now but sharper for it. "You think silence makes you invisible? That Hare won't notice? He notices everything. A chief with a wounded man. A ferret who can't stay in her lane. Do you understand what he sees? Weakness. And weakness doesn't last long around here."

Her hand hovered near Lanell's shoulder. "You want to know why I'm still alive? Why my unit's still standing? Because I don't let anyone make me look weak. Not Hare. Not Jarvis. Not you."

The silence between them thickened until it buzzed in Lanell's ears. Trace's red eyes bored into her, searching, testing, daring her to crack.

Finally, Trace exhaled through the gills along the sides of her neck. A wet hiss of air, a predator reining itself in. She straightened, rolling her shoulders back. "You'd better pray Hare doesn't hear a whisper of this. Because if he does" she tapped the elevator panel with unnecessary force "I'll know where to find you."

The elevator jolted as it climbed. The numbers above the door ticked upward, agonizingly slow.

Then, quick as a striking eel, Trace's hand shot out. Fingers clamped around Lanell's jaw, forcing her chin up until her eyes met the burning red above. The pressure bit into her cheekbones, rough hands grazing skin but not breaking it.

Lanell's breath hitched, but she didn't fight back. Trace leaned in close, voice soft, almost intimate. "Don't mistake silence for safety. You keep stepping where you don't belong, and next time, I won't stop at a warning." She squeezed once, hard, then released.

Lanell staggered back against the panel, her face throbbing where Trace's grip had been. She knew it would bruise visibly, a dark brand she'd have to carry for days.

The elevator chimed. Doors parted. Trace stepped out first, shoulders squared, never once glancing back. For her, the moment was over. The predator had toyed with its prey and walked away.

Lanell remained inside, pulse racing. Her reflection in the polished panel showed the faint red imprint already rising along her jaw. She lifted a trembling hand to it. Trace's mark. Proof she was serious.

Jarvis lingered at the threshold, ears twitching. He looked from Trace's back to Lanell's face, guilt in his eyes.

"Sorry." His voice was low to the point of being almost inaudible.

Lanell didn't answer. The warning pressed deeper than the bruise. It told her that next time, she might not walk away at all.

Chapter Fifty-Two

Transcending

After the confrontation with Trace, the walk to Earl's office had been a blur of hallway lights and clenched fists. Lanell stepped into the office and let the door hiss closed behind her.

Her shoulders sagged the moment she was inside, like the strength she'd worn in front of Trace had been a borrowed costume.

Earl looked up from where he sat hunched over his desk. His eyes searched her face immediately finding the red mark on her jaw. "She hurt you."

"Yeah," Lanell said, not looking at him. "She made her point."

He stood, slowly and cautiously like he was afraid she might bolt. "About last night Lanell, I "

She crossed the room, reached up, and wrapped her arms around him tightly. He froze. Then held her back.

For a long while, neither of them said anything. There was just the sound of their breathing. The quiet whirr of the air recycler overhead.

Finally, she pulled back slightly, still holding on. "I love you, Dad."

His breath caught, just a little. "I love you too, little root."

He pressed his fingers gently to the side of her face, brushing the reddened skin where Trace had struck. His expression hardened. "Just know, Trace will have her reckoning for this. One way or another."

Lanell closed her eyes, leaning into the touch for a beat. Then stepped back and wiped at her face. "I don't know what I'm doing anymore."

"You need clarity," Earl said. "And I think it's time you saw something."

He motioned for her to follow him through his office, into the small meditation area beyond. The air shifted the moment they entered. It was fresh and clean, filled with the smell of pine resin and old stone.

"You've never transcended before," Earl said, "not properly. And you shouldn't do it alone the first time."

Lanell raised an eyebrow. "I'm not exactly in the mood for spiritual tourism, Dad."

Earl gave a warm chuckle. "It's not that. It's... centering. It's remembering how to listen."

He stepped over to a low table and opened a small wooden case. Inside, two tiny colorless gummies nestled in cloth. He picked one up. "As shamans, this is how we communicate. How we get guidance. I've done this for years. And now I want to show you how to do it too." He glanced at her seriously. "Now I'll be honest, you've never done this before, and that makes it hard to get into that frame of mind naturally. So I'm going to share this chewy with you. It'll help you get there."

She eyed it suspiciously. "Is this one of those kinds of snacks?"

Earl smirked. "No. Not that kind. It doesn't make you see stuff that's not there, it just helps quiet the noise."

She looked at the mat, the incense, the carved symbols in the stone. This all felt like a story that belonged to someone else, a script she hadn't memorized. But Earl was watching her with those patient eyes, and she was tired of being afraid of everything.

She chewed it cautiously and winced. "Tastes like bark and moon dust."

"That means it's working."

He gestured to the floor mat. "Shoes off. Sit cross-legged, hands open."

She obeyed, half-reluctant, half-intrigued.

"Close your eyes," he said, kneeling across from her. "Breathe. Deeper than you're used to. Let the thoughts come, but don't chase them. Let them pass."

Outside, the world spun in its chaos. Inside, the stillness began to bloom.

Lanell exhaled, long and slow, and let herself sink.

At first, all she could hear was the unrelenting buzz of her own thoughts. Trace's hand on her face. The heat of shame. The sting of doubt. The echo of Earl's voice from the night before.

She shifted.

"Don't fight it," Earl urged. "Let the noise come. Don't try to chase it away. Just... let it pass."

She exhaled steadily through her nose. The gummy had started to kick in a little. She felt... looser. Like her bones weren't set so tight anymore. Her breathing fell into a rhythm. The warm, earthy scent of incense wrapped around her. Earl was whispering now, not to her but around her. The words were half in Arcadian, half in something older. She didn't understand it, not exactly, but it curled around her spine like a lullaby.

Something shifted. It was like her weight dropped through the floor, but she didn't fall. More like the floor gave permission to release her.

Her eyes flickered open, but the room was gone. In its place, forest. Silver light filtered through thick branches. Snow that didn't chill. And a stillness so profound it felt sacred.

Lanell stood barefoot. Her usual clothes gone, replaced by a simple robe tied at the waist. The air tasted clean. Time moved differently here, if it moved at all.

Something stirred from the tree line. She turned. A figure stepped forward. It was tall and lupine, draped in flowing cloth marked with ancient spiral glyphs. Fur black as obsidian, tipped with silver. Eyes like moons.

Lanell's breath stuttered. A name. From forgotten chants and half-remembered stories. From somewhere deeper than memory. "Artemis," she whispered.

The wolf bowed its head in acknowledgment. "Welcome, Shaman."

Lanell shifted uncomfortably. "I'm not sure that's what I am."

"You are what you've always been," Artemis replied. "Even when you forgot."

Lanell crossed her arms. "Okay, sure. Riddle-talk. Got it."

The wolf chuckled. "You saw her in the lower lab."

Lanell nodded. "Yeah. I've never seen anything like her. She wasn't from here. I don't know what she was."

"What did you see?"

Lanell hesitated. "She was scared. Alone. She didn't even know where she was. But she... she asked me what was happening. Like I was supposed to have answers."

Artemis stepped forward, closer now. “You will rescue her.”

Lanell’s breath caught not in surprise, but in recognition. She had already said the words. Already crossed that line.

“You will take her from that place,” Artemis continued. “And, together, we will get her home.”

Lanell swallowed. “How? I don’t even know who she is. What she is. Why she’s here.”

Another voice, this one deeper, worn by centuries, rumbled from behind. "You do not need to be told that which you already know."

Lanell turned. An older wolf stood just at the forest's edge. It was grizzled and scarred, and ancient spirals marked his fur like battle honors.

"The Memory Keeper," she breathed, the title rising from somewhere she couldn't name. "But what does that even mean?" she snapped at them both. "You're all talking in riddles and fog. I'm tired of it."

Artemis placed a hand on her shoulder. "You know what to do, my shaman," she said. "Even when the path is hidden. You do not walk it alone."

Lanell opened her mouth to protest, but the world began to dissolve.

Lanell blinked.

The forest was gone. So were Artemis and The Memory Keeper. In their place dim light, incense, and the soft flicker of Earl's lantern. Her robe was gone. She was back in her clothes. Her boots were set neatly by the wall, and there was a blanket tucked around her shoulders.

She sat up slowly, brushing her hair back. "Did that really happen?" she asked. "Or was that just the gummy?"

Earl gave her a soft smile as he stirred the coals in the fire bowl beside them. "I told you, it's not one of those kind of snacks."

Lanell stared at him.

"Yes," he said. "It happened."

She looked down at her hands. They didn't feel different. But something inside her was buzzing. "I don't know what to do with that," she said. "I mean I saw her. Artemis. And the Memory Keeper. They talked like I already knew all of this. Like I've been walking some path I didn't even realize I was on." She rubbed her arms. "How do I even do this? What happens next?"

Earl stood up, stretching his back with a grunt. He crossed over to her and crouched, his weathered hand brushing her cheek. "I don't know," he admitted.

Her eyes widened.

"But I know what needs to be done," he added hastily. "And I know you saw her. That poor creature down there. You were right, Lanell. She doesn't belong in that place."

Lanell sniffed and blinked fiercely. "She looked at me like I was supposed to help. Like I was the only one who could."

Earl nodded. "Maybe you are."

Lanell laughed, but it came out more like a sob. "I'm not some hero, Dad. I'm just a lab assistant who screws things up. I got in a fight with you. I broke security protocol. I don't even know how to be a shaman, much less rescue someone."

Earl gave her shoulder a squeeze. "You don't need to know it all today."

She looked at him, unsure. "Then how do I even start?"

"Same way the rest of us do," he said. "One foot in front of the other. We listen. We watch. And we don't stop moving just because we're scared."

Lanell blew out a breath. "I don't want to screw this up."

"You won't," he said. "Because I'll be with you. Every step I can take, I'll take beside you. And the ones I can't, you'll take for both of us."

She nodded slowly, but the fear didn't vanish. It just had company now.

Earl stood and offered his hand. "Come on. Let's go see what happens when a lab assistant and an old goat try to take on a fortress."

Lanell snorted. "You're not that old."

"Don't ruin my dramatic exit line," he muttered.

Lanell rubbed the back of her neck, her fingers brushing the edge of her spiral mark without thinking. "Well, with Hare off wherever he's slithered to and Finn itching to pin my pelt to a wall, I'm thinking all that's left for me tonight is to crawl home and try to get some sleep. If you get off rotation, swing by. Maybe we can put our heads together. Try to figure out how the hell we're going to get Diane out of his hands."

Earl said, "I appreciate your determination, Lanell. I really do. But let's say we get her out. Then what?"

Lanell stopped mid-step.

"Where would you go?"

There was a beat of awkward silence. She let out a breath through her nose. "Yeah," she muttered, eyes dropping to the floor. "We need to talk. Come up with a real plan."

Chapter Fifty-Three

Signals Across the Void

The stabilized carrier wave pulsed through the cracked interior of the cruiser. The air throbbed with tension. OLLO-2 chirped. "Subspace aperture holding. Lock phase delta confirmed. Channel open on Command Node Sela'rhakt."

Trinn loomed over the interface, tendrils coiled. She hesitated for a moment, then she sent the request. "Access historical archives. Priority alpha-one. All known encounters with Precursor entities, anomalies, or technology. Send the full data stream."

Seconds passed, then a voice crackled through. It sounded sharp, unimpressed, and unmistakably familiar. "Trinn? You stabilize a deep-phase signal from a voidstream corridor and this is what you request? Historical data? I assumed you were calling to say you were coming home."

Trinn's mandibles clicked together in rapid succession. She didn't respond immediately.

"Don't tell me you've taken the most advanced cruiser in our arsenal and parked it to play archaeologist."

"This world is worse than I reported. Something has gone wrong here, worse than Soundbloom. The Precursor signatures are active, but the lineage is muddled. I will not act without context."

A growl of static from the other end. "Then you've failed your original directive. Retrieve your data, Trinn, but don't mistake research for relevance. The Council is... not patient."

The link severed with a snap of collapsing harmonics.

The transmission reformed. A lattice of pulsating neuroglyphs shaped into the faceted form of Drowa Tzaryx Nohl. His projection loomed, thought-whiskers flickering warning red. "Trinn. Still alive I see. I expected a retrieval signal. Instead I receive archival access requests?"

"You will comply." Trinn's mandibles spread wide, then snapped shut with finality.

"You vanished in our most dangerous asset. We've all had to answer for that. Twenty solar arcs of silence and now you're asking for history lessons?"

"This world is anomalous. Precursor influence has resurfaced active, perhaps even sentient.. I require the full historical interface. Their data may offer return pathways that current phase-locks can't."

Tzaryx's tendrils coiled like smoke. "The council expected an update. Some expected your surrender. Others, myself included, suspected something worse."

Trinn did a partial whip of a tentacle, mandibles parting in what might have been amusement. "Now you see why I don't call home much. Every time I dial in, it's like you forgot how to say hello."

Tzaryx's bio mass flared brighter. "You think this is amusing? You vanished with classified assets."

Trinn's own bio mass flared the same glow. "You think I fled."

"Prove me wrong. Because if you're not a defector, you're a failure. And only one of those gets extracted intact."

She cut the transmission herself this time, not with aggression but dismissive finality.

Tzaryx's irate voice crackled back through the intercom. "Leave the channel open. We'll search the vaults for the Precursor data you requested. It'll be sent through the secure thread once compiled."

"Understood."

The voice channel went dark, but the data channel pulsed behind the scenes, quietly alive.

She leaned back in her command cradle. "Selective compliance," she muttered. "Always more polite when they can't talk back."

A chime broke the quiet. Glyphs surged across the console, pulsing with Precursor code. First wave confirmed.

"OLLO. Begin analysis on the Precursor archives. Cross-reference Precursor traversal methods with the genetic anomaly we pulled through the collider. See if they align."

The synthetic assistant replied after a beat. "Specify parameters of correlation."

"Look for patterns. Did the Precursors move through dimensions the same way? Is what came through our collider echoing their method?"

"Analysis initiated. Estimated time: fourteen minutes, twenty-two seconds."

The glyphs pulsed brighter now, ancient code rolling across the black glass display. OLLO's synthesized voice remained steady, but Trinn could hear the subtle modulation that signaled its routines were being stretched. "Preliminary correlation established. Energy patterns align."

Trinn leaned forward. "So it wasn't random."

"Confirmed. Harmonic alignment detected. Data suggests intentional traversal is feasible with correct amplification."

She sat back again, tendrils flexing. "It followed something an echo." Her voice dropped. "That changes things. Continue analysis. Prioritize viable path modeling. If there's enough here to replicate Precursor traversal protocols, I want to know."

"Modeling initiated. Results pending."

She didn't need to speak again. She let the light of the console fade slightly, a single tendril brushing the interface. "Let the others chase what fell through. I'll wait for the map."

The bridge went still, and the data stream trickled on in silence. After a few moments of this, Trinn's patience was exhausted. One claw tapped against the armrest in time with the pulsing holograms above.

"VEX. Please tell me you've found somewhere to plant this station where the dirt dobbers won't keep poking their little sticks in."

VEX responded with mechanical precision. "Preliminary scans of the local planetary surface have yielded seventeen viable relocation candidates. Filtering for geothermal stability, tectonic silence, low atmospheric contaminants, electromagnetic shielding potential, and minimal detection vectors from indigenous civilizations.

"I have narrowed the list to a single optimal region: a volcanic island situated within the Driftward tropics. The island contains an active caldera with a lava lake measuring 1.2 kilometers in diameter, which will provide excellent geothermal masking. Across the bay lies a smaller uninhabited landmass, encircled by dense jungle and buffered by ocean currents. No known civilizations inhabit the zone, and orbital scans show no consistent overflight patterns or satellite activity."

Trinn exhaled slowly through her vents, mandibles clicking with satisfaction. "So what I'm hearing is... perfect. No one's there. No one cares. The lava makes it spicy, and the jungle's got good coverage."

"Precisely. And the tectonic shelf is stable, barring catastrophic celestial interference or orbital bombardment, which I assume are currently low-priority threats."

Trinn chuckled malevolently. "See, that's why I keep you around, VEX. You don't whine when you find paradise on top of hell."

As Trinn turned from the navigation console, OLLO returned to the room.

"Primary data stream has arrived. I am compiling the full archive to a travel disk for your private review."

The Drowa made an approving noise. "That quick? What's in it?"

"Preliminary analysis reveals Precursor genetics are rudimentary yet oddly resilient. Dormant in most, but waiting. Certain patterns have emerged. Shall I summarize?"

Trinn's tendrils flicked with impatience. "You always ask like I'll say no."

"Observed commonalities include an external visual marker, frequently along the upper spinal column. These dermal spirals appear consistent among test subjects known to carry Precursor code." OLLO paused. "More critically, advanced neuro-genetic instructions are embedded in the cerebral cortex of most hosts. These patterns are biologically present but typically locked. Only a subset of hosts those with exceptional neurological pathways or trained cognitive access appear capable of initiating unlock sequences. Once unlocked, the embedded code allows for controlled interaction with dimensional thresholds. This trait was not accidental. It appears the Precursors encoded a failsafe ensuring only individuals of precise genetic and psychological alignment could access dimensional manipulation."

Trinn exhaled, slow and deliberate. "Well, that explains the mess. And why we don't see these freaks hopping through portals on every street corner."

"Correct. The ability appears rare by design."

"And the human? Does she show signs of this cerebral lock?"

"Cortical mapping is incomplete, but signs point to an embedded structure consistent with the pattern. It would require deeper sampling, preferably invasive, to confirm and extract."

Trinn tapped the edge of the glowing disk, the weight of implication settling. "I think we can work it out." Her head turned toward the observation feed. The screen showed the human, still curled up and shivering. "We will see what's on her mind."

Chapter Fifty-Four

The Adhesive Truth

Lanell stepped out into the hall, Earl's words still echoing in her mind.

Where would you go?

She didn't know. But she knew where she was going now. A few turns later, she knocked on the side of the open lab door. Dr. Crusher looked up from a workbench, goggles pushed high on his forehead, a small metal spatula in one hand, something mildly steaming in the other.

"Well, well. If it isn't the intrepid explorer of secrets and sticky situations," he said. "To what do I owe the pleasure? Looking for another adhesive bath?"

She gave a tired smirk. "Just wanted to thank you for earlier. For listening, and for showing me that... goo thing. Helped me think clearer than I expected."

"Hot glue therapy. Highly underrated," he said, setting his tools down. Then his expression shifted. It became more casual but curious. "By the way, I was called out earlier. Near the elevator to the old lower labs."

Lanell raised a brow. "Yeah?"

"Yeah. Someone left the pressure relief spigot on one of the backup tanks cracked open. Released a lot of synthetic rubber." He gestured with two fingers, as if to approximate a foot-deep pile. "Jarvis caught the worst of it. Practically laminated the poor guy."

"Is he okay?"

"I had solvent to break him out, but not before Trace showed up," Crusher said, tone dipping into dry bemusement. "She was not in a good mood. Started cutting his uniform off, took some of his fur with it. Then she turns to me and demands I bring something some high-grade melt agent like I'm a walking vending machine."

Lanell blinked. "Trace was there?"

"Oh yeah. Steaming mad and smelling like burnt rubber." Crusher leaned forward slightly, voice quieter now. "But here's the part that stuck with me. Before I checked the valve, I thought to myself, is this a coincidence? Because someone turned that knob deliberately." He let it hang a second, then added with a sly grin, "And guess whose fingerprints were on the dial?"

Lanell straightened. "Wait. Did she dust for prints?"

"Sure did. After I already handled it." He gave an exaggerated shrug. "Had to check the seal integrity, of course. I'd hate for it to depressurize again." He winked.

Lanell's lips parted, then curved into a slow smile. "You knew."

"Just a hunch." He leaned back. "Can't say I blame whoever did it. Poor Jarvis, though. He's going to need therapy. Or at least a new pair of pants."

She shook her head, still smiling and now blushing. "Thank you."

"Anytime. So, did you find what you were looking for?"

Lanell opened her mouth, then paused. Her eyes dropped for half a second before she looked up again. "I found something, yeah. But... I think maybe it's better if I don't tell you what."

Crusher's eyebrows lifted. "Oh. One of those discoveries. The 'I could tell you but then you'd have to spend the rest of your life dodging black-suited goons and invisible drones' kind?"

She blinked at him, then chuckled. "Something like that."

He gave a slow nod. "Got it. No questions asked. Except one."

She raised a questioning brow.

"Now that you've got answers, what are you going to do about it?"

Lanell's shoulders slumped. "I don't know. I'm in no position to do anything, not really. But I've got this gut feeling that I have to do something."

Crusher's expression shifted again. This time, there was no sarcasm in it, just quiet honesty. "On a serious note? I don't know what I'd do in your shoes," he said. "I love my lab. I love my environment. And I love what I do. I don't want special projects. I don't want entanglements. This is comfortable. And it's mine." He glanced around the lab, eyes lingering on the beakers, the shelves, the snails in their tanks. "If something like that ever happened to me, whatever I found in the lower labs, it would just have to stay. Because it's not worth it."

Lanell looked at him, her brows knitted. "Seriously?"

He nodded. "Hell yes. I know my lab. I know my chemicals. I have freedom. To be a glue god. To create. To study. To bond atoms and molecules. That's what I was built for. So yeah."

Lanell gave him a grateful nod and turned to leave.

Crusher watched her go with. At one point, he made as if to call after her, then appeared to change his mind. He looked down at the vat bubbling beside him.

"Stay in your lane," he muttered. But it didn't sound like a conviction this time. More like a reminder. One that wasn't sticking.

Chapter Fifty-Five

Hidden Corridors

Earl waited until the elevator doors closed behind Lanell and the lobby fell quiet. He shut his office door, slid the bolt, and pulled the Habitat 4 duct schematics across his desk. He traced lines with a fingertip, then stopped. That tug in the back of his mind again. Not ducts. Older.

He rolled the sheet tight and crossed to the file cabinet that never moved. Steel drawers, one dent from a careless dolly. He dug through tubes and folders until his fingers found dust and the title he wanted.

Phase One: Facility Revamp Project.

He unrolled the vellum and the building's bones looked up at him. The old blueprints. The ones the new ones had erased. Edges crisp, notes handwritten in pencil, corridors that no longer existed. Along the robotics footprint, a thin line ran behind the Flowward wall. Not a vent. A corridor, labeled in tiny letters.

Access E-12. Service Spine.

"There you are," he said triumphantly.

The blueprint went under his arm. The door closed behind him. He set an easy pace, the kind you use when you belong.

Robotics smelled like hot metal and optimism. Servo chatter. A printer arguing with itself. Kit Fox bent over a half-built gait rig, magnifier tilted, tongue out in concentration. When he noticed Earl, his ears perked, and a grin climbed his muzzle. "Earl. You got a second? The new stride model is poetry that learned to walk."

"Raincheck, friend." Earl lifted the rolled plan. "I'm in the middle of something."

Kit leaned back. "Before you disappear, what brings you into my kingdom?"

Earl paused. "If I don't take care of this, you may meet some very large spiders."

Kit grimaced. "Spiders? How large are we talking?"

"Uncomfortable."

"Then have at it. I will be over there, bravely supervising from a distance."

Earl slipped past benches and bins to the back wall. The paint line changed shade where the light did not quite reach. He set a shoulder against a storage cabinet and eased it aside. Behind it waited a steel door with a dead status puck and a key lock that belonged to another decade.

He took out his key ring. Facility issue. He tried three, then a fourth that had a scratch on the bow. The lock turned. Air sighed from the other side. The smell of closed places and machine dust.

He looked back once. Kit was pretending not to watch. Earl gave him a nod and stepped through. The door closed with a solid sound that felt like privacy.

Concrete walls painted the color of old paste. Emergency strips along the baseboard that still glowed on tired batteries. Storage containers lined up along one side in obedient rows. Manifolds, fiber spools, obsolete housings with their labels foxed by time. A coil of caution tape drooped over a nail like a tired snake.

He clicked on a small torch and kept the beam low. Camera stanchions jutted from the ceiling at intervals. Their lenses were gone or capped. Old crew stencils still ghosted the paint. The directory pointed to wings that didn't exist.

Earl counted doors and junctions, matching them to the map in his head. Phase markers were still stenciled above the lintels. PH1-S2, PH1-S3. He ran his fingers across the letters as he passed. Dust recorded his touch, then forgot it.

At the first cross passage, he stopped and knelt. Two cart tracks. One fresh enough to cut through dust, the other softened at the edges. He listened. No fans. No voices. Only a far drip counting the seconds.

He went left, behind the robotics Flowward wall and down the original service line toward the sublevels. He passed a rusted fire door with a lever chained shut. The chain was slack. He left it as he found it.

A gate appeared ahead, waist high, the kind used to keep honest technicians from wandering into a construction zone. A faded sign hung on it.

Service Spine Decommissioned. Use Primary Corridor.

Someone had scrawled an arrow and written No. Earl eased the gate open and slipped through.

The floor sloped. The air cooled and picked up the tang of solvent and cold metal. He killed the torch and waited. Slowly, his eyes adjusted. A thin line of light leaked from beneath a door farther on. The light had that sickly green cast of emergency lumens. He clicked the torch back on and hooded the beam with his palm.

Spider thread brushed his cheek. He wiped it away and glanced to the corner where the builder waited under an old junction box. A glossy black knee with opinions. He gave it room. Kit would sleep better for it.

Two more doors. One marked Electrical Aux. One unmarked. The unmarked door wore a circular handle with a mechanical latch. Facility bronze. Old but not broken. He tried it. It stuck. He leaned in and turned. Metal complained, then yielded with a tired cough.

Beyond, the service spine widened. The ceiling rose, and the walls showed scars where conduits had been cut and capped. Here, the corridor ran in a straight shot. On the right, a run of narrow windows looked into nothing. The far side had been walled off during some later expansion. Someone had painted the glass black and never came back to finish the job.

He walked, counting steps. At one hundred twenty, he should meet the first branch to the sublevel service yard. The phase one plan put a stairwell there that dropped to Sublevel 1 without touching the main shafts. No camera mounts appeared here. No motion sensors blinked awake. The only sound was the soft thud of his hooves and the whisper of fabric.

At one hundred eighteen he saw the sign. Faded white on a field of blue.

E-12 Descent. Authorized Personnel Only.

The paint had flaked around the screw heads. The handle was a simple bar with a push plate that no longer lit.

He listened again. Nothing below. He tried the bar. It stuck, then gave. Cold air breathed up past his face. A stairwell spiraled down in squared turns. Emergency strips ran along the wall like tired stars.

He drew the door close and started down. One landing. Two. On the third, a metal grate blocked the way. A padlock hung from it. Not facility issue. Cheap. He took out the key ring, thought about it, and put it away. The padlock opened to a twist of his multi-tool and a firm hand. The grate swung with a whisper.

Below that, the final run ended at a door with a small wired glass window set at eye-level. He thumbed the torch off and leaned to the glass. The hall beyond glowed with that same green emergency wash. Clean floor. Fresh scuff marks. A placard on the far wall read Service Access. Sublevel 1. The font was newer than the paint. The camera in the corner had a black cap snapped over its eye.

Earl let out a low whistle. They had covered this route. They had not killed it.

He eased the latch. The door opened into the hush. He stepped through into the hush. The corridor ahead bent out of sight, lined with old storage containers. A placard he had not seen in years faced him: SUBLEVEL 1.

One problem solved, he thought. Now, the holding area.

A yellowed directory listed Observation 1A–1D, Containment A, Med Support, Mechanical. He wiped the arrows clean with his thumb and followed them through the linen room and the hidden service corridor that ran behind the observation rooms. Frosted squares showed only light and fixture tops. Voices drifted past, one brisk, one tired. He waited, then moved.

At 1A's service door, the electronic strike sat dead. He tried a quarter turn. The core held. Through the wired glass he caught a sliver of monitor glow, a restraint post, tubing, the soft beep of a sedative pump. He traced the route on his palm. Three turns from linen. Blind camera at Junction 2.

The Service Hub at the elbow gave him the view he needed. He slipped in dark and woke the monitors.

OBS 1A. Occupied.

Arrival: PDE-001. 03:17.

Notes: Spiral mark. Right posterior thorax.

Access: L. Hare, M. Moleman.

The big pane showed a plain room. Clean floor. Restraint post and a folded blanket. Against the far wall, the creature lay curled on her side, bare feet toward the baseboard, hair washed gold in the weak light. A line ran from the pump to her arm. She breathed slow and chose the wall over the bed. Not a lab model. Not a mannequin. Someone.

He let the screens go dark and left the hub to the hush. Covered over, not gone. He had the route. He knew where it ended.

Chapter Fifty-Six

Echoes at Home

Lanell let herself in and shut the door with her hip. The lock clicked. The quiet felt like a soft blanket. She toed off her boots by the mat and flexed her toes on the cool floor. That helped. Not much but enough.

Bag on the dining chair, access keys in the little bowl. The house smelled like sweetrise and grogba. In the kitchen, a cold pot sat on the burner. Amber freckles dotted the wall where the sweetrise bottle had hit. A sticky crescent hugged the baseboard, and glittering crumbs of glass winked along the molding.

"Okay," she said to the room. "We fix that."

She tied her hair up, cracked the window, and fetched the broom and dustpan. The big pieces first, careful hands and slow steps. Glass chimed into the pan like tiny bells. Her father's voice echoed as she worked.

You're wasting your life in that place, Lanell. Playing with toys while the world moves on without you.

Her hand remembered the arc of the throw. From the drawer, she took the torch. She knelt and swept the beam along the floor to catch the sly shards that wait for bare feet. Two more glints into the pan, then into the trash.

Bucket, warm water, a little vinegar, a splash of dish soap. She wrung a sponge till it stopped dripping and pressed it to the amber specks. The sweetrise lifted in tired circles. The wall gave up its stain a shade at a time. She wrung the sponge harder than she needed to. Baseboard next, the tacky crescent turning slick, then clean. She wiped the counter edge where the spray had reached, then the cabinet face. The house's breath changed from sugar to soap.

One last pass with the mop took up the pink residue from the floor. She pressed a palm flat to her sternum until her breath evened. Better.

Lanell looked where the mess used to be, and she said, "Next time, before I do that, I just need to remind myself who has to clean it up."

She rubbed the heel of her neck and headed to the bedroom.

Work tomorrow. Replace the spare clothes she stole from her locker this morning. One simple task before she could chill out. She looked at the timepiece on the wall. Earl would be getting off soon, and he was supposed to come over so they could chat. Hopefully there'd be time for a little nap before that.

The closet light hung on a chain that buzzed before it committed. Yellow, old, honest. The spare clothes lived in a cloth cube on the shelf.

She ran her fingers along the hanging row and stopped at the pleated skirt. Black, with a nice swing and a waistband that didn't dig in after a long shift. She tugged it once to feel the give, then held it to her waist. Comfortable, reliable. She kept this cut for the spare because it slid past lab carts and bench corners without catching. The pleats swallowed small smudges other skirts would advertise. Once a solvent splash dried into a whisper, no one noticed.

The red-and-black knit had stretch and no loose threads. The red tights were bright and cheerful. She stacked them on the bed. A neat pile. Locker-ready.

She fetched a small tote from the hook by the door and lined it with a towel so the clothes wouldn't gather dust. Skirt in. Top in. Tights on top so they won't crease. She hesitated, then added a simple hair tie from the dish on the dresser. The last one at work had snapped. No sense repeating that dance.

Something white peeped from the closet floor. She crouched and lifted a costume headband with rabbit ears. White and soft. Beside it sat a fluffy white tail with a safety pin still clipped through the loop. She had forgotten she even owned them.

A late night in Habitat 4. Twelve minutes of silliness between bad news and worse coffee. Kit's laugh. Her own laugh. The way the ears eased a room that had been grinding its teeth all day. Sometimes small absurdities did more work than they were built for.

She turned the headband in her hands. Ridiculous. Cheerful. Unnecessary. That sounded nice right now. After the words. After the bottle. After a day like today, maybe what she needed was twelve minutes of silliness.

"Why not," she said to herself.

She set the ears on the stack. The tail tried to roll away, so she pinned it through its loop and tucked it in the corner of the tote with the pin facing up. Not because she needed it, but because it made her smile.

She looked over the closet again to see if she had forgotten anything. Socks, maybe. She pulled a pair from the drawer and added them. A small bottle of hand lotion followed. The skin at her knuckles looked chalky. The first dab vanished before she finished rubbing it in. She closed the drawer with a hip and stood for a second while her body remembered gravity.

Back in the kitchen, she poured the last inch of tea from an earlier pot into a mug and took a sip. Lukewarm. Still better than nothing. She set the mug in the sink. The house now smelled like soap and night air. The tote on the chair looked like a grocery errand. Perfect. Nothing to explain. Just a swap for the empty spot in her locker.

She went through her mental list. Badge. Wallet. Phone on the charger by the bed. She plugged it in and watched the little charge icon blink itself awake. Ten minutes would help.

On the way back to the closet, she flicked the light off. The chain clicked against the housing, and the buzzing gave up. The room dimmed to a soft gray. She folded the tote closed and slid the zipper partway so the ears wouldn't catch. Finally, she set the bag by the door with her shoes, toes pointed toward morning.

For a moment, she stood still and let her head empty out. The house hummed. Pipes knocked somewhere in the walls and then fell quiet. Earl would be by soon; they would make a plan. Until then, she would shower, then lie down. Kitchen clean. Spare packed. The silly ears tucked in her bag. She felt the day crawl back up her shoulders, gave it half a breath, then set it down again.

Chapter Fifty-Seven

The Map and the Mark

She woke to three soft knocks and the quiet blink of the timepiece. The late afternoon had not yet finished becoming evening. Her mouth tasted like tea and sleep.

The patient knocks came again. She pushed up, smoothed her hair with one hand, and padded to the door.

Earl stood in the porch. He looked her over and smiled. "You look like you just got up."

"I just got up." She stepped back to let him in. "Shoes off if you want. The floor is having a good day."

He toed his boots clean on the mat and came inside.

"Did Hare come back in?" she asked.

Earl shook his head. "No. I didn't see him coming back tonight, but I bet he'll be in early tomorrow. Hell, it looked like they didn't even leave last night."

He set a long cardboard tube on the dining table and tapped it once. By the door, her tote sat where she'd dropped it earlier, zipper half closed, rabbit ears peeking out. He pretended not to notice them and focused back on the tube.

"After you left earlier, I did some research," he said. "Found something that will help us."

Lanell pulled up a chair. "Show me."

He slid the vellum free. Old paper sighed as it unrolled, edges foxed, pencil notes like faded hieroglyphs. He anchored two corners with the salt and pepper.

"Here," Earl said, fingertip landing on the robotics footprint. "Phase one. Before the refurb. This is the Flowward wall, and this thin line behind it isn't ducting. It is a service corridor. Access E-12."

She leaned in. "An old door in Robotics."

"Old and sealed, or it was sealed." He traced the route down with his nail. "This corridor runs behind the wing, then drops to Sublevel 1. Doesn't touch the main shafts. Cameras were disabled too. Someone remembered to blind them, not remove them."

She folded her arms and huffed. "If you were going to find me an access door, why find it in the domain of Kit Fox?"

"Look, I can't control where the access points are," Earl said. "Kit's got what we need, whether we like it or not. Consider it luck they had another way to those areas and just sealed them off and forgot about them."

She scowled. "I just hope he's over crushing on me and has moved on to someone else at this point."

Earl grinned. "Word is he's crushing on Tabitha now."

Lanell rolled her eyes. "Typical."

Earl's pursed his lips. "Tabitha, I can see. She's cute."

"Dad."

"I may be old, but I'm not blind."

Lanell shook her head. "I'm not sure how we veered here, but I think we need to get our minds back to current events." She let herself grin, then sobered and tapped the vellum. "How clean is this?"

"I walked it," he said. "Keyed the old latch. There's a grate on the stairs with a cheap padlock the kind you open by looking at it. The stair lands here." He tapped another square. "Service access, Sublevel 1. It's pretty simple."

"And past that?"

"Observation rooms run along this hall." Another tap. "Back corridor behind them. Linen room opens to the service spine. The holding room is marked 1A." He paused. "When I walked this route, I was able to go into the observation area and see her. She was asleep on the floor, against the wall."

"She was awake when I met her," Lanell said.

He gave a short nod. "I checked her stats. Vitals steady. There were notes again. Mentions of PDE. I still have no idea what that even means."

Lanell leaned forward a little, her voice dropping. "Those notes weren't just vitals. Hare had his own scribbles mixed in. Something odd. I didn't know how to bring it up before, but remember last night when you showed me your mark? When you explained mine?"

He dipped his head in assent.

"There was a sketch of that same mark in with her medical records," Lanell said. "Right alongside her stats. Like Hare thought it mattered."

Earl blinked, then frowned. "Say again?"

"There was a sketch of the shaman's mark. Right there in her file, next to her vitals."

"Why would Hare have that in her records unless..." He let the thought hang a moment before finishing. "Unless she carries the mark too."

Lanell gave him a worried look. "If she carries the mark, that could change things. A lot."

Earl's eyes slid to the access map spread between them. He tapped one finger against the routes marked in red. "Yes. It would. And it would explain why Artemis was so insistent we get her out of there."

Lanell fingered the edge of the map. "If Artemis sensed the mark on her, then she isn't just some anomaly pulled through the collider. She matters. More than we realized." Her jaw set. "But if Artemis wants her out so bad, she can poof in and do it herself. I'm not running errands for visions. If I do this, it'll be my way. My call. Not because someone up in the clouds whispered in your ear."

Earl held her gaze, unflinching. "She asked me to trust you."

Lanell gave a thin smile, more edge than warmth. "Then she can start by earning mine. Hare's notes weren't just tests. He was circling something else. Something that doesn't belong in his hands." Her gaze lingered on the vellum, the thin red lines running like veins into places she had never dared walk. Her voice came quiet, almost to herself. "What do I even do once I get her out?"

Earl didn't hesitate. "You'd have to leave the facility. Take her and go to ground. Then we'd get you both out of here and into Arcadia."

Her head lifted sharply. "Arcadia? That's... beyond the walls."

"Yeah," Earl said simply. "Of course."

Lanell glanced back at the map, at the lines that ended not in safety but in wilderness. Concern tugged at her features. "There are a lot of things out beyond the wall, Dad. We both know there's a reason the walls are there. They keep us in, but they also keep everything else out."

Earl's ears tilted. "I know. And if you're right, if she carries the mark, then hiding her inside these walls won't be an option. Hare will never stop looking. Out there might be dangerous, but staying here is a death sentence. "Lanell ran a hand over her face, suddenly feeling exhausted despite her nap. "So the choice is between predators in the wild or predators in lab coats." Her thumb hovered just over that blank space, as if she could sketch in a road where none existed. The silence stretched until she whispered, "Maybe the blank is the only honest part of the map."

Chapter Fifty-Eight

The Key

Early morning settled heavy in Sublevel 1. Hare and Myles stood shoulder to shoulder at the console, their voices low and absorbed, eyes fixed on the shifting sequences spiraling across the glass.

"Splicing similarities hold consistent," Myles muttered, gesturing with a claw. "But see here? These aren't analogs; they're echoes. Dimensional symmetry, not common descent."

Hare's ears swiveled forward. "Echoes, yes, but stable ones. Look how they've nested. Not mutation. Pattern." He scrawled a note across the margin of a printout, pencil biting hard into the paper. "This isn't drift; it's design."

Diane pressed her palm against the cold transparency, breath fogging a ghost-circle on the glass. She didn't speak. She only watched.

"PDE again," Myles said, almost to himself.

The letters meant nothing, but the reverent dip in his voice made her stomach clench, bracing against something she couldn't name.

"Because she isn't just that," Hare penciled letters across the printout: *PDE* underlined twice.

Whatever those three letters meant, they weren't talking about data anymore. They were talking about her.

A sudden trill cut through the lab, and the console flashed amber. Hare snapped upright, annoyance spasming across his face as he touched the comm switch.

The voice that came through was calm and clipped, edged with something that sent ice through her veins.

"You will bring me down," the voice said without preamble. "I will see her for myself."

Hare's expression froze in a mask of obedience, though a muscle twitched in his cheek. "The lower levels are restricted for a reason, Chancellor."

Silence a heartbeat too long, then: "You'll make them unrestricted. Send someone you trust to escort me or I come alone."

Myles shifted at Hare's side, glancing between the rabbit and the glowing console. Hare exhaled slow through his nose, then jabbed a finger toward the door.

"Go meet her," he said. "Bring her down here. No detours."

The door clicked behind Myles. Hare was already turning back to the data when the comm chimed again another channel, lower band.

"Dr. Crusher to Hare. I've got the new adhesive gun prepped and ready. I'd like to meet and get your sign-off before we proceed with testing."

Hare pressed the mic button without looking away from the screen. "Busy now. Let's aim for tomorrow or the morning after."

He clicked off the comm before Crusher could reply, then he turned back to the console.

Diane didn't move. Her fingers stayed pressed against the pane, her breath still fogging that single spot in the glass. The surrounding silence returned, but it had changed. Now it was charged.

A few moments later, Myles pushed through the door, posture stiff. Gliding in his wake came Trinn. The shark's eyes swept the room in a single slow pass before settling on the glass.

"Hello, Lupus," she said, voice smooth as a blade across ice. "Are you learning much from this new asset?"

Hare straightened from the console, whiskers twitching, a sheet of charts still in his hand. "The data sets are extraordinary. Baseline vitals are steady. Cellular regeneration curves are sharper than expected. Splicing resilience in the nucleotide sequence exceeds our "

"Yes, yes." Trinn flicked her hand, cutting through his speech. Her gaze had landed firmly on the figure behind the glass. "But have you noticed anything... interesting?"

Hare's ears bobbed as he nodded. "Indeed. The subject bears features we have never cataloged before. Most notably" he turned a page, tapping his finger against a sketched diagram "a spiral marking at the base of the spine. Not a scar or a pigmentation variance. It reads like a genetic signature carried from birth."

Trinn's demeanor sharpened. She stepped closer to Hare, eyes dropping to the paperwork spread across the counter. Her head tilted as she lingered on one sketch in particular, the faint spiral drawn at the base of a figure's spine.

"A mark," she said softly. "Show me the genetic workup."

Hare slid the datapad toward her without hesitation. Columns of code and spectral graphs flared to life, scrolling in steady rhythm. Trinn leaned in, studying the curling patterns on the display.

"This shape," she murmured. "Consistent. Recurring. It does not belong in her genome."

Hare moved to stand beside her. "And yet it does. Not an accident. Something deliberate. It threads through her sequences as though placed there from birth."

From her position behind the window, Diane caught none of the meaning, but the way they leaned together over those pages and screens, the hush of their voices as they circled closer to some revelation chilled her to the bone. Whatever it was, it was about her.

"Tell me, Lupus," Trinn said after a moment, "do you believe in a god?"

Chapter Fifty-Nine

The Wanderers War

Trinn's voice carried that strange weight of someone who spoke not from faith but from memories etched in the marrow of her people.

"You ask about the Precursors. Your texts call them myths, shadows of gods. But I will tell you what the stories claim and what remains of the truth.

"They are said to have come first as wanderers, slipping between the veils of creation as easily as you and I step through a door. Some accounts insist they needed no machines, no engines, no contraptions to aid them. Dimensional passage was their birthright, woven into their blood. Where they willed to go, they went. They crossed oceans of worlds, tracing their paths with stone, with spiral, with song. They were not gods, Lupus, they were a people. Brilliant, restless, terrible in their hunger.

"In the beginning, they were welcomed. Many who saw them descend believed deliverance had come. Civilizations bent their knees, hoping the wanderers could end famine, war, and pestilence. And for a time, they gave gifts. They shaped matter, stitched flesh, raised towers that touched both earth and sky. But gifts carry weight. Not all Precursors agreed on how their power should be given.

"That is how the war began.

"One faction, the Dreamers as the oldest songs name them, believed all worlds should remain untouched. That their gift was not for rule but for observation. The other faction, the Shapers, declared that to hold such power and not wield it was weakness. To them, dominion was destiny. And so brother is said to have risen against brother, sister against sister. Their war not waged with armies of steel but with the very fabric of reality.

"The Dreamers sealed rifts. The Shapers tore them wider. Whole continents fractured beneath their conflict. Dimensions collided, folding upon themselves like shattered glass.

They did not fight for land, Lupus. The stories say they fought for the right to determine the order of existence itself.

"The Great War is said to have raged for centuries, though even time itself frayed under their struggle. Entire species vanished as collateral, swept into rifts that never closed. Worlds bled into one another. What was real one moment became myth the next. They fought until their numbers dwindled to ghosts.

"In the end, there was no victor. Only ash. Some say the Shapers scattered, consumed by the very storms they had unleashed. The Dreamers fled, carrying fragments of knowledge, hoping some world might remember them kindly. What remained were ruins. Stone monoliths. Spirals carved in the earth, and marks written in bloodlines. Silent testaments in the flesh of descendants who never knew their inheritance.

"That, Lupus, is the war your kind remembers as the reign of gods. It was no divine age. It was a civil war among wanderers, and it ended with their disappearance. Whether they perished, ascended, or scattered beyond the maps of creation, none can say. But their legacy may remain. You see it in the Torkas that still hum with their resonance. You see it in the blood itself, in marks that echo their passage. And now, perhaps, you see it here."

Her words tapered into silence. Slowly, Trinn turned her head. Her gaze left Hare and fixed on the human behind the glass. "The stories claim the wanderers needed no collider. No rails. No machinery. Their gift lay in the mind itself. Thought that could breach the veil." She touched the datapad once more, gray finger hovering over the spiral display. "The Drowa archives hold fragments, damaged maps of neural flares regions of the brain said to surge when a carrier bent the veil. If those records are true, the gift was not in bone or blood, but in thought. A code written in the folds of the mind."

Her unblinking stare bored into Diane. "And if this one bears even an echo of it, then she may be more than a specimen." Her pupils thinned, mouth curving faintly. "How pitiful they are, these creatures. Frail bodies. Short lives. So much noise, and so little wisdom." Her tone dripped with contempt, each word sharpened to a barb. "It was their kind who first misused what was given. It is always their kind."

She stepped closer, letting her shadow stretch across the pane. "I do not like humans, Lupus. Never have. They are dangerous, not because of strength but because of their ignorance. Given power, they stumble with it. Given knowledge, they twist it. They burn through every gift they are handed."

Diane's throat tightened. Every word struck clean, sharp as a lash.

For a long moment, Trinn studied the girl, weighing her like a thing to be traded. Then her voice shifted, softer but no less cruel. "But if she truly bears the code, then even the most pitiful vermin may serve a purpose."

Hare's whiskers twitched, his breath thin with anticipation.

On the other side of the glass, Diane backed into a corner, breath hot in her chest. She had been reduced to numbers, diagrams, whispers. But this, this was worse. To be seen. To be understood. To be despised.

Trinn let the silence linger, watching Hare drown in the possibilities. Then she added, almost as an afterthought, "Do not think of her as a specimen. Think of her as a key."

Chapter Sixty

The Living Key

Hare had not moved from the console. He clutched the datapad in his hands as if it were the only thing keeping him upright. Trinn's words clung to the air like frost.

When at last he found his voice, it was rough and caught in his throat. "You said it's written into her mind. Explain."

Trinn regarded the human a moment longer before turning back to him. She leaned across and touched Hare's datapad, pulling another sequence into view. Looping patterns poured over the screen, spirals layered over neural diagrams.

"The wanderers needed no engines because their engines were within. Dimensional passage was not invention, Lupus, it was instinct. A genetic inheritance mapped into the highest folds of the brain."

Hare's ears tilted forward, straining to catch every word. "The cortex."

"Precisely." Trinn's claw traced one coil of the graph, tapping where peaks flared like signal beacons. "This region, when active, flares beyond natural frequency. The Drowa archives recovered ancient data, records from the war itself. Neural maps fragmented but clear. The carriers lit their minds like stars before they stepped across the veil."

Hare's twitching nose nearly brushed the glass of the screen. "And these patterns, they match her?"

"They echo," Trinn said. "Dim echoes but real, nonetheless. You see it here and here." She pointed at the spectral peaks. "The human brain carries pathways long dormant in your kind. Most are broken, silent, but some... some still hum with the old code."

"If this is true," Hare said. "If it can be amplified, trained, manipulated... "

"Then the collider becomes irrelevant," Trinn finished.

"Transcendence." Hare whispered the word like it might crumble if spoken too loud.

Trinn eyes narrowed. "Power." She lowered her voice until it was almost conspiratorial. "With the archives and with her, you may prove what no world has managed since the fall: that the code still lives. And if it lives, it can be awakened."

Hare's trembling hand hovered above the data Datapad. Trinn turned from him and crossed toward the glass. The overhead glow caught on the ridges of her brow, the faint shimmer of her skin. She stopped just short of the pane, studying Diane. Diane shrank away until her back hit the wall.

"The cortex," Trinn said, "is right here in front of us. The archives only gave us fragments, but here" her claw hovered near the outline of the girl's skull "here we have a living carrier."

Diane pressed herself back against the wall as though trying to melt through it.

Trinn continued to watch her hungrily. "All we must do to access it is gather what lies dormant. Samples, sequences, imprints of the old code. Unlock it and the doors the Precursors once walked through so freely may open again.

"You can run your tests, Lupus. Draw your samples. Record your strings of data. But when you are ready to move past observation, when you are ready to access what truly lies dormant within this one, call me and, together, we will transcend."

Diane's nails bit into her palms. Every word had been clear. Cortex. Samples. Dormant. Transcend. They spoke of her as if she weren't a person at all, only a vault to be pried open. Her stomach lurched, breath catching high in her chest. For a moment, she thought she might retch.

Her throat burned with a scream she couldn't let out. Part of her longed to smack her palms flat against the glass, as if force alone might make them see her. But Hare didn't even glance her way, and Trinn's eyes regarded her with the same detached interest one gave a dissected organ.

She had endured being studied, reduced to charts and mutters, but to be carved open while she could still understand every word... Her body flinched before her mind could even finish the thought.

Chapter Sixty-One

Purple Armor

The morning started wrong.

Lanell woke two hours earlier than usual and lay staring at the ceiling, refusing to move. It was still dark. The pre-dawn stillness offered no comfort, only silence. All the same, she didn't want to leave it. Didn't want to face the day.

Her thoughts circled restlessly. Hare. Myles. There would be the usual discussion first thing. There would be questions about yesterday. She could already hear them.

If either of them mentions it, I'll just say I had a bad day, that's all. We'll move forward, and they'll leave it alone.

That was safer. Keep her thoughts to herself. Keep the truth buried where they couldn't touch it.

She turned on her side and shut her eyes against the glow of the clock. She told herself she'd get up in five minutes. Five minutes to breathe.

But five stretched into fifteen, then thirty. She listened to the building shift around her the pipes groaning as the heat came on, the muted footsteps of someone starting their day above her. All reminders that time moved whether she wanted it to or not.

And still she stayed.

Lying still was easier than rising. Easier to let the blankets press her down than to stand up and face the questions waiting.

Her mind knew the routine: boots, jacket, tote. Step into the light, into the role, into the mask. But her body wouldn't move.

Just a little longer.

Her hands worried the seam of the blanket until the threads began to fray.

Just a little longer before I have to pretend again.

She lay still until she couldn't anymore. The clock blinked its second warning as the hour ticked over, and the walls felt like they were pressing closer. Growling low in her throat, she shoved the blanket aside and sat up. The cold bit her bare arms, but at least that was real. The discomfort was something she could push against.

The bandana lay folded in its usual place on the bedside table. She tied the soft cloth around her tail with practiced hands. A reminder. A tether to reality.

Her scuffed boots waited by the door. She pulled them close, then dug through the drawer until her hand caught denim. The shorts came out wrinkled, but she shook them flat. Purple tights followed. The rich color stood out against her brown fur. A streak of stubborn brightness.

One leg, then the other. She tugged them smooth and laced the boots tight. Each knot bit firm against her ankles. She tucked her t-shirt into the outfit and drew a breath through her teeth.

Finally, she stood and crossed to the closet. The hoodie waited on the hanger, black and worn soft at the cuffs. She pulled it over her head. There was a comforting rightness to the weight of the hood as it settled against her shoulders.

She stepped in front of the mirror and tugged the hood forward until her face was half-swallowed in the dark. The reflection showed a figure she barely recognized. Purple tights under denim, boots knotted hard, hoodie framing her face. Not Hare's obedient, polished assistant. Not today.

"Go ahead," she muttered. "Mess with me today, you bastards."

Her mouth twitched into a sharp, wicked smile. She held it for a breath, letting it burn into the reflection, then she pushed the hood back. The smile lingered as she turned from the mirror and headed for the door.

She was about to exit the bedroom when something on a high shelf caught her eye. A pair of fingerless gloves, shoved back months ago and almost forgotten. She hesitated, then slid them on, flexing her hands through the cut edges. They weren't for warmth or utility. She just... liked the way they looked.

Outside, her boots crunched on the gritted walk. The air was cool. The warmth of the day had not yet touched the gray edge of morning. She made it halfway across the yard before stopping short.

The bag.

She'd packed it last night spare clothes shoved down deep, just in case. It was still sitting by the chair where she'd left it. If today went wrong, she might need it.

Lanell turned back, slipped inside, and grabbed it. The weight felt reassuring in her hand as she picked it up by its straps. When she opened the flap to check, she couldn't help but grin. Nestled on top of the folded clothes were the old costume ears and the clipped-on tail, white fur gone a little matted with age. She hadn't meant to pack those. Not really. But why not?

She zipped the bag closed and swung it over her shoulder. This time, when she stepped into the morning, she didn't look back.

The city was already in motion, but she ignored the chatter at the corners and the sweet smell of roasted beans drifting from Starducks. No time to stop today.

Inside the facility, the halls buzzed with morning activity. She turned a corner and nearly ran into Tabitha Snickers. The Felinari had an armful of datapads and an energy drink clenched between her teeth.

"Whoa, easy," Tabitha mumbled around the can before shifting it to her hand. Her eyes flicked down and then widened. "Are those... purple tights?"

Lanell lifted a brow. "Observant as ever."

"Bold choice. Planning to blind Hare into submission?"

"Maybe."

Tabitha leaned in, eyes glinting wickedly. "If you want to blind me into submission, I'd let you."

Lanell smirked but kept moving. She pulled the access card from her hoodie and held it out. "Thanks for the use."

Tabitha slid it into her stack of datapads. "Did you get Wait. I don't really want to know, do I?"

"No. But you'll want to watch that access hallway near the elevator that goes down to the basement."

"I'll make a note to avoid that area," Tabitha said breezily.

Lanell adjusted the strap on her bag. "Much as I'd love to stay and give you fashion tips, I gotta run."

Tabitha's grin turned sly. "Yeah. I'll take a raincheck, and we can discuss this further when we both have time, amongst other things."

Despite herself, Lanell was beginning to feel cheerful, but her grin slipped away as her office door came into view. Inside, she set the bag down and pulled out the old costume ears and tail. White, fluffy, a little ridiculous. She laid them on the small table by the wall. They looked almost like they belonged.

Next, she shoved her spare clothes into a drawer. The ankle boots she'd worn the other day sat in the corner under her desk. She nudged them aside and pushed the tote in next to them.

The chirp of the radio shattered the quiet.

"Lanell, you in yet?"

She froze, eyes flicking to the ears and tail still on the table. Her mouth tightened before she pressed the button.

"Yes. I'm in my office."

"Excellent," Hare's voice purred back. "I'd like you to come up. There's a special project waiting. We can discuss it as soon as you arrive."

"I'm on the way. Out."

She clipped the radio back on her belt and grabbed the tote strap. The ears and tail still sat on the table, but she left them where they were. Hare didn't need to know she had a sense of humor.

She passed the lab and heard the sounds they made as they stirred to life low voices, machines ticking and beeping as systems came online. Familiar, ordinary, but it all felt sharper after Hare's summons.

Eventually, she reached the administrative side of the facility. Hare's office door stood ahead, neat plaque gleaming under the overhead lights.

Stacie sat at her desk outside, papers stacked with surgical precision, a datapad poised in hand.

"I'm here to see my boss," Lanell said, stopping at the desk.

Stacie's eyes lifted. Her gaze was cool and professional, though her lips curved with dry amusement. "Another casual day, Miss Lanell?"

"Don't know. Don't care."

For once, Stacie didn't have a ready line. Instead, she gave Lanell a long look that was part surprise, part appraisal. It was as though she were trying to catalog this version of Lanell against the one she thought she knew.

Before the silence could settle deeper, Hare's voice floated out from the office. "Send her in."

Hare didn't look up from his datapad when she entered. "Ah, Lanell. Good. I've got something for you." He tapped the screen, then finally glanced at her over the rims of his glasses. "Yesterday, there was an incident in Wing C. A very big mess. Liquid rubber all over the floor, half the drains clogged. Maintenance is still complaining about it."

Lanell crossed her arms. "And you want me to mop it up?"

Hare's ears twitched, but his thin smile remained fixed. "Not literally. I want you to pull an audit of the liquid rubber supply line between Wing C and Dr. Crusher's lab. Trace the manifests, check the valves, logs whatever's necessary. I need to know whether this was mechanical failure, user error, or deliberate negligence."

He slid the datapad across the desk toward her. "Start with Earl. He's responsible for the environmental systems on that wing. Then speak with Crusher, see what he's been piping through lately. Compile your findings into a full report for me by end of day."

Lanell took the datapad but didn't move. "So, root cause analysis of a spill."

"Exactly," Hare said, already looking back at his console. "Dull work, perhaps, but necessary. We can't afford leaks, literal or otherwise."

Lanell gave a short nod. "Okay."

"Good." Hare said as if that settled it. "The incident left quite a mark, you know. Trace was furious. One of her top troops got caught in the middle of it."

He leaned back and steepled his fingers. "So let's make sure the cause is pinned down before she decides to... assign blame in her own way."

Lanell kept her expression neutral. "Understood."

"Excellent." His eyes flicked up over the edge of his device and lingered on her. "By the way. Yesterday's look. Today's as well." His smile thinned. "Perhaps you should consider other attire. Something more in keeping with a professional environment."

Lanell bit her tongue, tucked the datapad under her arm, and left the office without a word.

The rest of the day blurred into routine. She walked the halls, checked the manifests, spoke with Earl, then Crusher. Logs balanced, valves aligned. Nothing unusual. Busy work dressed up as duty.

Earl had his numbers, neat as ever. Crusher presented his usual mix of muttered formulas and bubbling vats. Nothing out of line, nothing worth more than a shrug. By late afternoon, the datapad was full, the report as dull as Hare had intended.

Lanell sat at her desk, stylus tapping against the margin of the last page. This 'busy work' had bought Hare the time he wanted, and it had shown her just how careful she would need to be.

She detached the radio from her belt, thumbed the button, and kept her tone even.

"Dr. Hare, when you're about to leave this evening, let me know. I'd like a word before you go."

Static crackled, then his smooth reply came back. "Very well, Lanell. I'll call you when I'm heading out."

She let go of the button, slouched back in her chair, and stared at the ceiling. One more line to feed him.

Reports filed, datapads stacked neat on the corner of the desk, nothing left to do but wait.

The radio sputtered to life. "Lanell," Hare said. "Myles and I are headed back to my office. If you'd like that word before I leave, now would be the time."

"Understood. I'll be there shortly."

The channel clicked silent. She set the radio down and pushed herself to her feet. Time to face them.

She made her way back across the facility, shadows stretching long through the corridors as the day wound down. The administrative wing was quieter now, only a few lights burning, most desks already cleared.

Stacie was straightening her own workspace when Lanell approached. The assistant smoothed the edge of a folder, slid it into place, and glanced up with her usual polite smile. "Your usual," she said, nodding toward the inner door.

Lanell dipped her head in acknowledgment and pushed inside.

Hare and Myles stood near the desk. They both looked calm and collected, as though winding down another routine day. But Lanell had seen this before that faint gleam in their eyes when something had gone right for them. They were excited and trying too hard to hide it.

She let the silence hang just long enough to become uncomfortable before cutting it off herself. "Look, I need to tell you both something."

Two sets of eyes turned to her. She kept her posture steady and tried to adopt the contrite tone of someone confessing a weakness. "Yesterday wasn't my best. My head wasn't where it needed to be. That's on me, not you. Next time we work together, I'll have it straight. You'll have my full focus."

The gleam in Hare's eyes sharpened. Myles glanced at her, then back at him, silent but attentive.

"Good," Hare said at last. "That's what I like to hear. Self-awareness. Accountability. It speaks well of you, Lanell. If only more around here had the same clarity. See that you keep your head aligned with your duties, and there won't be any question of your value here."

Myles cleared his throat softly and adjusted his glasses. "Yes, quite right. Best we keep things precise, on track. A level head makes all the difference." He gave a small nod, more to Hare than to her.

Lanell nodded too, feeding the mask one last time. "Understood."

Inside, she felt the lie settle into place. They'd bought it. She excused herself and walked out with calm steps, past Stacie's empty desk and into the dimmer corridors beyond. But she wasn't headed home. Not yet. Instead, she cut into an adjacent break room empty at this hour dropped into a chair by the window, and pulled out her datapad.

From here, she could see the flow of the administrative wing, hear the muffled echoes of doors, footsteps, and voices thinning as the last employees left the building. She bent over the pad, tapping at a blank document, the picture of diligence. But her eyes darted to the hall each time the door opened, watching for the moment when Hare and Myles finally left.

When they did, she'd know she was in the clear. And then, at last, she could make her way to the robotics sector. Toward the old access door.

Chapter Sixty-Two

The Same Mark

Lanell cut left at the vending alcove, past the half-lit poster that still bragged about the robotics expo from three years ago. The farther she went, the thinner the foot traffic.

Light bled from under the door of the robotics bay a tired strip of fluorescence across the floor. She pushed in.

Kit Fox stood on a rolling stool, reaching into an open rack of parts, tail swishing as he counted under his breath. Capacitors in neat rows. Spools, boards, a tangle of labeled harnesses. He glanced over his shoulder when the door clicked.

"Well, hey there, Violet," he said, grin already loaded. "You know, I always loved it when you wore the violet tights."

Lanell didn't slow. "Yeah. Sadly, I just remembered that too."

He winced in mock pain, hand to his chest. "Ouch. Right to the capacitor."

She brushed past him toward the worktables. "Kit, we've done this dance before. It's not worth either of our efforts."

He put a palm to his chest, staggered theatrically off the stool, then straightened. "Right. Right. Efficiency. You wound me, but I respect the time savings."

"Good." She slid past a worktable. Her eyes scanned the back wall where a maintenance door sat half in shadow. "I'm on a special project for Hare."

Kit's ears perked up. "Fun."

"He's been told that you're hoarding capacitors in the old access halls. I have to check it out."

Kit blinked once. "Yeah. Uh-huh. That tracks with the level of fun." He swept a hand toward the rear corridor. "By all means. Just be sure to lock up."

Lanell glanced at the small red cam light above the maintenance door. Still dead. Good. "I will."

Kit rolled his stool back to the rack. "If you find my mythical stash of capacitors, tell it I miss it."

"If I find anything, it's going in my report."

"Tragic." He lifted a palm in a lazy salute. "Stay pretty, Violet."

She didn't bother with an answer. The maintenance door gave under her hand with a tired click, and cool air spilled out from the old access hall. Concrete, dust, the faint metallic tang of machines sleeping. Somewhere deeper, a soft whirr like an electric fan.

She eased the door shut behind her, keying the manual bolt. One step, then another.

Old signage flaked on the walls.

ROBOTICS SUB ACCESS. AUTHORIZED PERSONNEL ONLY.

Ahead, the corridor doglegged left toward the door. A door that used to mean nothing and now meant Diane.

Behind her, in the bay, Kit hummed a few bars of static-pop as if to prove his point. The sound echoed softly in the empty corridor.

She pressed on, boots scuffing faint trails through the dust. After a few minutes, she came across the storage alcove her father once mentioned, the one he'd sworn held scrap worth more than the paperwork ever claimed. A row of cabinets slumped against the wall, doors hanging crooked. She pried one open and found the relics still waiting cracked gauges, outmoded coils, even a set of battered spanners with their handles worn smooth.

She set a few aside, just enough to pass as discovery if anyone asked, then pushed deeper into the corridor.

Cameras sat in their mounts along the ceiling, their red lenses blind. She glanced up each time, waiting for the faintest flicker. Nothing. Hare had pulled power from this section long ago, or so he claimed. Either way, they weren't watching.

Concrete walls closed in around her as the dogleg tightened to a narrow corridor. At the far end, the reinforced panel of the observation room waited, paint scabbed, handle stiff with disuse.

Lanell's breath hitched. This was the place. The one door she'd sworn to ignore. Earl had warned her they sometimes moved assets into the old observation labs out of sight, off the main systems, where fewer eyes lingered. The door's hinges groaned when she pushed, and dust spilled from the frame. The observation lab smelled stale. It was obvious the air hadn't been circulated in years, but it still carried the faint smell of chemical cleansers.

She slipped inside, closing the door with care. Two benches stretched along the walls, clipboards scattered across them, pages curled at the edges. A cracked observation pane loomed at the far end. Everything beyond that point was cloaked in shadow.

Lanell crossed to the nearer bench. Notes lay in stacks, Hare's sharp script carving across the margins. She laid her hand on one and smoothed it open.

Gene charts. Symbols. Complicated diagrams and cramped columns of text. She turned a page and her pulse kicked up a notch not in surprise, but in grim confirmation. There it was again. Her spiral. The same shape burned into the skin at her back..

Her fingers hovered above the page, not touching. That mark had always been hers alone. A shaman's tether, Earl called it. But here it was, sketched by Hare's hand, filed with the same obsession he devoted to any fragment tied to the Precursors.

Another sheet slipped loose beneath her touch. The heading caught her eye: Comparative Record: Drowa Archive. The rest of the page was diagrams looping code-strings and layered genetic structures paired against symbols she didn't recognize.

Lanell narrowed her eyes. "Drowa?" she whispered. The word was unknown to her. It felt alien and awkward on her tongue. She set the page back exactly where it had been and lifted her gaze to the cracked observation pane.

Beyond the glass, the chamber was dim, save for a single light haloing the figure inside. Diane sat curled on the edge of the cot, her head tipped down, one arm wrapped tight around herself.

Lanell pressed closer, fingers brushing the cold surface of the observation glass. For a moment she just watched. Her chest rose and fell in sync with Diane's breathing, then she gave the glass two gentle taps.

Lanell's hand stayed on the glass. That little twitch from Diane, just enough to show she was fighting, hit her like a warm echo in her chest. It wasn't enough. Not this time.

She glanced at the door to the chamber. Heavy, reinforced, designed to seal and lock once it closed.

A cage.

She pulled the latch and eased the door open just far enough to slip inside. The hinges groaned too loudly in the stillness. As soon as her foot crossed the threshold, the weight of the mechanism tried to pull the door shut.

"No," she hissed under her breath, jamming her boot against the frame. Metal bit into leather and ground against her ankle. She shoved her shoulder into the door, wedging it back until the lock couldn't seat. The pressure held, just enough to keep them from being trapped together if alarms tripped. Only then did she step fully into the room.

Diane had risen from the cot. Her eyes were wide and her hands knotted at her chest. She looked smaller up close. The pallor of her skin was stark, even under the low light, and her eyes conveyed both fear and relief.

Lanell drew a long breath, fighting to keep the tremor from her voice. "It's me." She crossed the short distance, crouched to meet Diane's gaze, and gave a slow, deliberate nod. "No tests. No wires. Just me."

Diane's hand shot out and closed around Lanell's wrist. Her grip was tremulous but urgent. She pulled Lanell down until their eyes locked.

"I need to tell you," Diane whispered, voice raw from disuse. "I heard things. When that... thing was here."

Lanell frowned. "What thing?"

"The odd-looking thing," Diane breathed.

"Odd-looking thing? What do you mean?"

Diane's gaze darted toward the corners of the room, as if Trinn might be lurking even here. Her voice dropped to a thin thread. "Tall. Cold. Walks like she owns every room, jaws look sharp, eyes too empty. She talked to Hare, to that mole. Said she needed the collider, that she'd been stuck here for years. That if they didn't give her what she wanted, she'd burn this place out from the inside."

Lanell's stomach tightened. Images pressed in Trinn's elegant posture, her uncanny stillness, her smiles that never reached the eyes. Could the chancellor really be connected with all this?

Diane's grip tightened, her eyes locking hard into Lanell's. "I heard her," she said, voice dropping to a near hiss. "She told Hare they don't even need the collider to break through the barrier, not when they can transcend."

Lanell blinked. "Transcend? What does that even mean?"

Diane shook her head, strands of hair falling wild across her face. "Something about genetics. Symbols. She kept pointing at my mark, talking about how it tied to the brain. The... the cerebral cortex." She gave a hysterical half-laugh. "You know, my brain. The one thing I really need to live."

Lanell gasped. Her father's words about her own spiral mark pressed at the edges of memory, colliding with Hare's scrawled diagrams on the bench outside. The spiral, the genes, the word Drowa.

Diane's voice cracked. "She said the mark wasn't decoration. That it was a map. Some kind of code buried in us. And that with the right push, we don't need machines to open doors. We are the doors."

Lanell froze, every word etching itself into her bones. We are the doors.

She laid her free hand over Diane's to steady her trembling fingers. "Alright. Breathe. I'm here. You're not alone in this, remember?"

Diane's eyes darted toward the door, then back to Lanell. "I-I have to leave. As soon as he's done with me as his pet project, whenever that is. Because it's coming. Any time now, they're going to dig into my skull." She gave another hollow laugh. "And I've got big issues with that. Not exactly a fan."

Lanell squeezed Diane's hand harder, forcing steadiness into her voice. "That's not going to happen. Not while I'm here."

Diane shook her head. "You don't understand. They were talking like it was already decided. My brain's just another lab sample to them."

Lanell leaned closer, her whisper so low it was almost a breath. "Then we make sure they never get the chance. I'll get you out tonight. I just... I need a little time to set things up. Let me get a few things ready, then we'll leave."

Panic flickered in Diane's eyes. "Do you know where we'll even go?"

Lanell swallowed hard. For once, there was no mask, no bluff. "I'm not sure how we're going to get out of here, but we will. We'll make it happen."

She started to stand, but Diane surged up, clutching at her sleeve. "No. I need out now."

Lanell caught her arm firmly. "No. Listen to me. If I take you out right this second, they'll know something's wrong. This facility's too big, too controlled. We'd be caught before we even found the door. Give me a little time. Let me line this up. I'll be back before you know it."

Diane's lip trembled. "You promise?"

Lanell's voice went low, almost fierce. "I promise." She squeezed Diane's arm once more, then pulled herself free and backed toward the open door. "Stay quiet. Stay ready. I'll be back."

She slipped through the heavy door, bracing it with her boot. The lock pulled against her shoulder as she let it close, but she caught it just shy of sealing. One last look at Diane's pale face through the glass, and then she was gone.

She re-entered the corridor with her pulse hammering in her ears.

Spare clothes. Get them from my office. Then we'll get out. That's it. That's the plan.

But her trembling legs stayed planted.

I can't drag her through those halls blind. Not with Trace prowling and Hare watching. Not with every corridor monitored and alarmed. One wrong turn and it's over.

Her hands dug into her palms.

Everything inside me says I have to get her out tonight, but I'm scared. Scared enough that I don't trust myself.

She looked up and down the corridor. Her frenzied thoughts jumped straight to Earl's office. The comforting glow of the lamp. She clutched at her twitching tail and fingered the fabric of the bandana.

I have no plan and no confidence, but I do have Dad. I can start there.

When she reached Earl's door, she didn't bother to knock. She pushed it open and stepped inside, her chest heaving like she'd run a mile.

Earl looked up from the lamp-lit desk, stylus stilling over a half-finished note. He scratched at the base of one horn, and concern creased his face. "Lanell?"

She crossed the room fast and leaned against the desk, panting. "I have to tell you something. You need to hear this."

His brows drew tight. "Alright. Start."

"Diane has a mark but not just any mark. It matches mine."

Earl set the stylus down. "Lanell... no. Of those who carry the marks, they're all unique. Because we're all unique. Each one is different. That's what makes them ours."

Lanell shook her head rapidly. "No, listen to me. They had sketches in the observation lab. They've been studying it. The symbol, they drew it. And it's the same. The exact same as mine."

Earl frowned. "That can't be."

"I know what you taught me," Lanell said. "Marks don't repeat. But this one isn't just similar. It follows the same structure."

"I saw it with my own eyes." Her voice cracked, then hardened again. "It's hers too. Whatever this means, we don't have time to figure it out. They're going to do things to her, Dad. Bad things. The kind she won't survive." A shadow crossed Earl's face.

Lanell's knuckles whitened on the desk. "I have to get her out. Tonight. Before they kill her in the name of their science."

Earl sat back and folded his arms, eyes narrowing the way they always did when he was weighing every angle. "Lanell," he said finally, "if you try this, you'll both be caught. Hare has eyes everywhere. Guards, cameras, Trace. You put one foot wrong and they'll lock you away with her. Maybe worse."

Lanell slammed her palm against the desk. "Don't you get it? We don't have time for caution. As soon as Hare is finished poking and measuring, they're going to put her under, and then they're going to open her skull."

"Lanell "

"They're going to dig into her cerebral cortex." Her voice trembled with fury. "They'll take whatever they think they need from her brain the thing she can't live without. And she won't come back from that."

Earl's mouth pressed tight, but he didn't interrupt.

Lanell shook her head hard, words tumbling fast now. "We can't, I can't let that happen. We have to get her out, now."

Earl's eyes searched hers. He saw the fear, the fire, the line she'd already crossed.

Lanell held his gaze, fists tight at her sides. "We have to get her out, tonight."

Earl's eyes softened, but the worry didn't leave them. He saw the resolve in his daughter's face solid, unmovable, already set like stone. There was no talking her down. No slowing her. Only deciding whether he would stand with her or watch her walk into danger alone. He stepped closer to the desk and lowered his voice. "Alright," he said quietly. "Come here."

Lanell moved in beside him. Together, they bent over the lamp-lit surface and began to shape a plan.

Chapter Sixty-Three

Going Dark

Arriving back at her office, she closed the door behind her and locked it with a quiet click. The room was dark and still, the faint trace of the calming fragrance she burned during breaks lingering in the air. Normally it eased her nerves. Tonight it only reminded her of how little calm she had left.

She crossed to the corner where she kept her spare outfit. It had been meant as a backup, nothing more. Little did she know it would be pressed into service for... whatever this was about to become.

Dropping to one knee, she pulled the storage bag open and inventoried its contents with quick, efficient motions. The red-and-black striped sweater good. She rolled it tight and shoved it into her tote. Next came the black pleated skirt. Then the red tights. Then the short ankle boots with the reinforced soles.

Each piece disappeared into the bag, her breath steadying with each addition. She reached to zip the bag closed, then paused. Her fingertips brushed soft faux fur. She looked down.

The rabbit ears. One ear bent, the other flopped over. The matching tail sat beside them, a ridiculous puff of synthetic fluff. Lanell stared at them for a beat. Then she smirked to herself.

"We're going to get weird tonight," she muttered.

The monitors bathed Trace Finn in icy blue light, sharpening her features. She stood behind the surveillance station deep in the security wing the shark cage, they called it. She never corrected them. Every camera in the building fed into the grid here.

Dozens of them, arranged in a wall of boxed windows: stairwells, labs, maintenance corridors, even thermal reads on exterior gates. Nothing moved without Trace seeing it.

One of the feeds blinked. Sublevel diagnostics, Hallway 7-A.

"Offline," she said softly.

The technician nearby didn't look up. "Probably a maintenance reroute. No alert came through."

"There wasn't a reroute scheduled." Trace's voice didn't rise, but the temperature around her dropped. She stepped closer to the monitors, eyes scanning the secondary feeds. One square pulsed to life. The robotics wing. Sensors detected motion. A figure moving at speed. She zoomed in.

Lanell.

Trace's nostrils flared. "What are you doing, ferret?" She tapped her comm. "Hey, Grent. You're on the access hall for Sublevel 1, right?"

The reply fizzed back. "Ten-four. Holding position."

"Keep your eyes sharp. Something's twitching. I don't know what yet, but if it gets weird, I want you weirding faster. Got me?"

"Yes, ma'am."

She cut the line, still watching Lanell as she vanished out of frame. One finned hand rested on the back of the chair. "Come on," she whispered. "Show me your tail."

Lanell moved swiftly and silently. Back through the facility. Down the admin wing. Past the vending alcove and the dusty robotics expo poster, into the Robotics Bay.

Kit was gone. Good. One less obstacle. One less witness. She hurried through the rear maintenance door without hesitation and continued down into Sublevel 1.

She passed the broken signage and turned at the dogleg. Cold air clung to the walls. Her fingers tightened on the tote. No matter how many times she'd imagined this moment, it had never looked like this.

The observation room waited.

Diane was sitting up when Lanell entered, red light from the ceiling flickering behind her. When she saw Lanell, she stood up eagerly. "Is it time?"

Lanell nodded, lifting the tote. "Quick. Change. Be fast."

She set the bag down and pulled out the clothes. Diane held up the skirt and tights, then stared at Lanell. "A... skirt? Seriously?"

"It's a look. Try not to trip in the boots."

When she pulled out the ears, Diane's jaw dropped.

"What the hell?"

Lanell gave her a flat look. "I'm not sure if you're up on current events, but you don't exactly blend in around here. So just humor me and be a bunny."

Diane sighed. "Fine. Do I at least get a "

Before she finished the word, Lanell tossed the white fluffy tail and it smacked Diane in the face.

"Go. We're on the clock."

As Diane changed, Lanell crossed to the lower access door and pulled the power fuser from her side pouch. The mechanism buzzed in her grip, warm and alive. She slid it against the seam of the door, thumbed the trigger, and watched the weld arc to life.

The sharp scent of scorched steel filled the air. Heat shimmered against her face. Molten metal sealed the frame in a series of tight lines. The lock fused, and the hinges groaned under the heat.

"One way only," she muttered.

When she turned back, Diane stood in full disguise.The sweater hung slightly off one shoulder, the ears were crooked, and the tail bounced when she shifted.

Something about seeing her like that tightened Lanell's throat. It was... an attempt. She smiled. "You look absurd. Perfect. Let's go."

A junction box buzzed quietly as Earl leaned in. The light from his headlamp cast sharp shadows across the wall. One hand held the panel open while the other worked the insulated snips with practiced care.

Snip. Sizzle. Another wire down.

The diagnostics relay flickered once. Two red indicators on the camera control grid went dark. He exhaled slowly through his nose. No alarms. Just silence.

Earl reached for the bypass switch and pressed it twice. A quiet pulse ran through the floor feedback disguised as routine interference. Should buy them five minutes, maybe six if Trace was having one of her brooding fits.

He tapped his comm once. Static. Excellent. No traceable transmissions.

"Alright, kid," he said quietly. "Your turn."

Lanell and Diane were halfway to the freight lift when they turned a corner and nearly ran into Jarvis Pellick.

He jumped, then squinted. "Lanell? Who's the bald rabbit?"

Before Lanell could say a word, Diane straightened her posture and fired back, "Exchange student. Vellmoor campus."

Jarvis blinked. "What happened to all your fur?"

Without missing a beat, Diane said, "Mange."

Jarvis recoiled. "Mange?!"

"Very advanced. Lost all my fur, and my sense of smell. It's extremely contagious."

Jarvis backed up fast. "Wait, seriously?"

Lanell finally caught on. She pulled a surgical mask from her pocket and slapped it over her muzzle. "Highly airborne. You don't want this."

Diane leaned closer. "There's no known cure. Last intern that caught it shed like a long hair cat in August."

Jarvis clutched his whiskers like they might jump ship. "Oh no. No no no."

Lanell stepped in, deadly serious. "Don't even look at her. We've lost three guards that way."

She grabbed Jarvis's hand and clapped it over his eyes. "Too late. You already made eye contact."

"Eeeeep!"

Jarvis turned and bolted down the hall like his tail was on fire.

Lanell and Diane stood in the silence that followed.

"I can't believe that worked," Diane muttered.

Lanell gave a slow nod. "You're terrifying."

Trace Finn stared at the darkened feeds on her board. Four dead zones now. No alerts. No flagged reroutes. They had simply gone dark. The system was failing around her, and she didn't like it.

She spun toward the technician. "Tell me that's not a cascade."

He pushed his glasses up his nose wiped sweat from his forehead. "They all just dropped offline."

Trace shoved off the desk. "Get eyes on the Sublevel 1 access door. Cross-check robotics wing, ventilation shafts, everything between. I want a full sweep initiated now." She tapped her comm. "All security units, this is the shark cage. We have a possible breach in Diagnostics and lower-level corridors. Sweep protocols authorized. Full lockdown pending. Report in."

The tech flinched as another feed blinked out. Trace's dorsal ridge twitched.

"Oh, hell no."

She opened a private channel. "Earl, this is Trace. I've got cameras going down like dominoes down here. Are you seeing anything? Anyone running patches? Diagnostics? Anything?"

Static. Then his voice came through. "Yeah, I'm on it now. Should have the issue isolated and resolved soon. I'll get you feedback as fast as I can. I think the fault is above

Habitat 4 could be a line arc. I'll need a couple troops to guard me while I access the panel. I don't need to be spider food while fixing an emergency."

Trace clenched her jaw. "Yeah. Sure you do."

She killed the channel and slammed her palm down on the console.

"All units, lock everything from Sublevel 2 up through Admin Driftward. Nobody in or out until I have visual confirmation. Move. Now."

Her gaze snapped back to the dark monitors. "Let's see what you're hiding, you ferret ."

Somewhere below her, the facility shifted.

And within it, someone was already moving. They kept walking. Fast but not too fast. Mainline corridor. Lights overhead flickering in and out of sync. Boots quiet on the tile.

A group of security troops came around the far corner. Four of them armed, alert, and walking fast.

Lanell and Diane both slowed. The soldiers saw them. Every instinct screamed that it was over. But the guards didn't break stride. They passed right by with neither a glance nor a nod. It was as if Lanell and Diane didn't exist. Not invisible. Just... unimportant.

The second the troops were out of sight, Diane exhaled hard and looked at Lanell. "Did that really just happen?"

Lanell didn't look back. "Yes. Don't press it."

They picked up speed, cutting toward the next junction. Toward Earl's office.

Earl stepped past them and cracked the office door, peeking into the hallway. "Go. Now. Stay out of the center corridors. You've got a window, but it's shrinking." He turned back, eyes steady on both of them. "This place is not safe for either of you. Not anymore." His voice dropped to an urgent whisper. "Leave and be safe."

Lanell froze, unable to put her emotions into words. Then Earl stepped forward and pulled her into a firm hug, one arm around her shoulders the other cupping the back of her head, the way he used to when she was small.

"I love you, little root. When you get to the plant, look for Cecil."

Lanell held him for half a breath longer, then stepped back with a nod. No more words. She turned, and Diane followed.

The door clicked shut behind them.

Chapter Sixty-Four

The Escape

The door opened with a muted hiss as the servos gave way. Lanell let out a loud exclamation of disgust as her boots sank into the loose earth just outside the side maintenance corridor. Diane followed close, head down, her breath catching slightly in the cold.

Sharp, frigid wind slapped them in the face. It carried the scent of dead circuits and distant grass. A hint of metal. A warning on the breeze. Behind them, the dome loomed quiet. Lanell had expected wailing sirens and pounding feet. Whatever Earl had done, it was working. The cameras were still blind.

They moved fast, no chatter. Every step mattered now. The path curved around a loading dock, then cut between two cooling towers. Their high metal sides sweated faintly in the cold.

Lanell yanked the hoodie's drawstrings tight over her ears. "This way," she said. "Stay low when the fence cuts."

Diane kept pace. "I didn't realize it got this cold here."

"Wait till midnight."

A shape flickered in one of the tower windows maybe a reflection, maybe not. Lanell didn't break stride, but her hand brushed the pouch at her side, fingers grazing the emergency fuser.

Still no alarms.

They skirted the edge of the reactor outflow before Diane broke the silence again. "This a rubber factory?" she asked. "As in tires and goo?"

Lanell nodded. "Synth materials. Lots of tanks, heat. It's a blind spot. That's why."

They moved quickly through the bramble at the fence line. Lanell ducked low and pressed through the gap left from an old storm. Diane followed close behind.

They crept down a slight hill, the hum of the industrial sector growing louder with every step.. Ahead, the rubber factory stretched like a sleeping beast, smokestacks yawning skyward, rusted vents curled like claws. A faded sign read GLAVIN SYNTHMATERIALS, the red paint flaking from years of neglect.

"Who's Cecil?" Diane asked as they crouched near a half-buried pallet.

Lanell hesitated. "I'm not sure I've ever met him."

Diane blinked. "Wait. Seriously?"

"But my dad trusts him. That's enough for me."

Diane gave a wary nod. "If he tries to dissect me, I'm biting someone."

"No one's dissecting anyone." Lanell smirked. "Unless we find a real mad scientist hiding in there."

They slipped along the slope behind the main outflow. A low mechanical hum throbbed underfoot.

Diane pulled her sleeves tighter. She glanced up at the shimmer above them, the faint, glimmering wall that curved across the sky. "Okay," she said. "I need to ask. That dome, are we on a spaceship? Was I abducted? Are you aliens?"

Lanell slowed, startled. "No. Just.. what? No. We're not aliens."

"Well, you've got ears. Your dad's a goat. I got zapped by lightning and now I'm here. Inside a dome. With chemical plants and this whole thing screams sci-fi abduction."

Lanell almost laughed. "We're not on a spaceship. This is a domed city. Rith. One of seven."

"Seven domes?" Diane looked up again. "Like floating space biodomes?"

"No. Just cities on a planet. Earth.

Diane did a double take. "Are you saying this is Earth?"

"I don't know what I'm saying," Lanell admitted. "But it's not outer space, and it's not a dream."

"That's exactly what someone in a dream would say."

Lanell shrugged. "Maybe. But if you were dead or dreaming, could you feel this?"

She kicked up some mulch at Diane's boots. It hit with a wet splat.

Diane groaned. "You're the worst alien tour guide ever."

Lanell pointed ahead. "That short brick building, that's where Cecil should be."

They ran across a narrow open patch, gravel sliding underfoot. Lanell knocked twice, then tapped again in rhythm. A pause.

A slit opened in the door.

"You the ferret and the human?" came a gravelly voice.

Lanell gave a short nod. "You must be Cecil."

"That's me." The door opened a little way. "Get in before someone with stripes spots you."

They slipped inside.

The office smelled like old coffee and dust. Wall maps cluttered the space, pins jammed in ancient junctions. A radio crackled softly with static-laced weather reports.

"I've got a spot to hide you," Cecil said, already closing the door. "We'll talk about moving you out come morning."

Lanell nodded. "Thank you."

Cecil handed her a cloth-wrapped bundle. "From your dad."

She opened it. Inside was a handwritten note and a small piece of white stone etched with a faint spiral.

Diane leaned in. "What's that?"

Lanell traced the spiral. Her face betrayed just a flicker of a smile. "Hope."

Chapter Sixty-Five

Already Gone

The camera bank snapped back to life with a scatter of beeps and flickers. One after another, the feeds returned. Corridors blinked into view, labs stabilized, exterior angles sharpened into crisp clarity.

Trace stood at the center of the room, arms crossed, eyes glued to the main console. "Finally."

She scrolled through the feeds with a flick of her hand. Sector 6. Habitat 3. Sublevel 1. All clear. She tapped again. Slowed. Watched the monitor as one hallway blinked, stuttered, then steadied.

"Tell me what happened," she said, not looking up.

Earl's voice emerged from beneath the console. "Looks like your spider friend from Habitat 4 developed a craving for wires."

"What?"

Earl scooted out from the access hatch, tool belt rattling. "The crawler chewed through primary insulation near Junction 18. Melted three contactors before the short took out the feed loop." He stood, brushing his palms against his pants. "Looks like it picked a nest right by the main run. Probably gnawed on it for a day or two, then poof." He thumped the wall lightly. "I've rerouted power, rebalanced the feeds. Should hold."

Trace's gaze returned to the screen bank. "And this took how long to notice?"

"You were getting scrambled feeds, not dead ones. Didn't flag until the whole loop collapsed."

She tapped the console again, initiating a live scan on the routing matrix. The diagnostics flowed across the screen in pale green. "Redundancy held better than I expected."

Earl nodded. "I'll include that in the report, along with a list of cables we probably ought to upgrade before something else chews through them."

He pulled off one glove and tucked it in his belt. "You'll have full documentation tomorrow. Logs, photos, and a list of suggested countermeasures."

Trace eyed him. "Which is tech speak for spider-proofing?"

He half-smiled. "You said it, not me."

Earl started for the exit, pausing just long enough to nod toward the flickering image of the sublevel access panel on Screen 19. "If anyone's trying to sneak around down there, you'll see them now." He gave a short wave. "Evening, Chief."

Trace grunted, then scrolled the feed back three minutes, running it in double time. Hallways scrolled past. Lights flicked on, then off. The facility moved like a beast shifting in its sleep.

One of the night crew let out a low whistle. "Hey, Chief, pretty sure I saw Lanell earlier."

"Where?"

"Down by Habitat 4, near the auxiliary stairs."

Trace's eyes flashed. "Alone?"

"Nah," said Jarvis, sidling into view with a grin. "She was with that new rabbit, the weird one with the patchy fur. Looked like they were sneaking off somewhere."

Trace blinked. "New rabbit?"

"Yeah, you know. Mange-bunny. Creepy eyes. She brushed past me earlier, and I had to sanitize my entire soul." He held up a hand. "Would've been cute, honestly, but the lack of fur was just off. I never knew mange could be that... ugh."

Trace raised an eyebrow.

Jarvis kept going, undeterred. "You ever seen mange so bad it looks back at you? But yeah, I passed by them. I think Lanell was showing her around or something like that. Not totally sure, I was a little distracted." He gave a worried glance toward the ceiling. "I've heard mange can take off a mustache. Like, quick. And I've been working on this one for weeks. What do you think? Clean, right? Bit of old-school charm?"

Trace sighed heavily. "Jarvis... just put it in a report."

He threw a sharp salute. "On it, Chief."

The chief turned back to the screens, one hand rubbing her temple. Too many ghosts tonight. Too many places to look. She gave the console a final sweep, then reached for her radio.

"You all have it handled," she said. "I'm finishing my report and walking the campus perimeter. Then I'm off for the night."

She pointed to the screen that displayed the lower access door. "Stay on task. That feed stays hot. Anything moves anything I want it on my desk."

"Copy that," the tech said.

Trace had walked the campus a thousand times. She knew its rhythms, its moods, the way the wind sounded through the exhaust towers when nothing was wrong.

But tonight, the wind carried an unfamiliar note. Tonight, shadows fell at wrong angles. Tonight, her keycard took two swipes instead of one.

Access was restricted below. Only Hare and Myles had that clearance from this end. She'd seen the logs herself. She adjusted her belt and kept walking, checking each door handle as she passed.

Her night wasn't over. Not yet.

Chapter Sixty-Six

Rage

The morning lights buzzed to life in the corridor outside Sublevel 1. Professor Hare strode in, datapad tucked under one arm.

A security trooper stood at the access checkpoint. When he saw the professor, he immediately stood to attention.

"Report," Hare said.

"Quiet, sir. Been quiet all night."

Hare scrutinized him. "Quiet," he repeated.

"Yes, sir. Since I came on shift. Nothing to note."

Professor Hare said nothing more, just turned and keyed in the override. The doors slid open. Lights inside the lab flickered, then brightened.

He crossed the room, glancing at a few loose papers on the counter. "Final cycle of bloodwork looked clean," he muttered. "Muscle response baseline was within tolerance. Should be ready for invasive study this afternoon."

Hare walked to the window and tapped the glass. No response. He peered in. His eyes widened. The gurney sat empty. What he had taken for a hunched figure was nothing more than a crumpled pile of discarded robes.

His hands trembled. No. No. Not possible. He was in control. He had protocols. He had safeguards. He had Myles. He had surveillance, locks, schedules, failsafe's. He had...

He had her. Didn't he?

He smashed the nearest panel with his palm. Lights flared red.

"Trace! Get to Sublevel 1 access, now!"

Another button. "Myles, emergency protocol. We've lost the subject!"

Hare pushed his sweaty fur out of his eyes and hit a final button. "Lock down the lab. Full sector containment. Block every exit. I want boots in every hall and eyes on every camera."

He was already moving, storming out of the lab, up the ramp. The checkpoint guard looked up in confusion.

"What the hell do you mean quiet night?!" Hare bellowed, storming toward him. "My asset was right here. I left one instruction. One! Watch this corridor. Watch this room."

The trooper stiffened. "Sir, I swear I haven't seen anyone. No alarms. No access breaches. Nothing."

Hare's voice became soft and lethal. "You want to see what 'nothing' looks like? I can take you down there and show you the empty bed and the empty gown."

The stunned guard blinked.

Trace's voice rang out behind them. "Sir! That's one of my best "

Hare turned on her. "Then your best is worthless." He pointed at both of them, ears quivering with fury. "I asked for one thing. One! Secure the lab. Don't let anything in. Don't let anything out. And now the specimen from Sublevel 1 is gone."

Trace's breath hitched. "What do you mean, gone?"

Her eyes darted to the nearest camera feed, and she staggered back half a step.

Hare threw the datapad across the room. It cracked against the wall, screen flickering. And then he roared a full-throated, primal howl of rage that slammed against the corridor walls, shook the fixtures, and curled toes in boots two levels up.

"SHE WAS RIGHT HERE!"

In the sterile, humming quiet of the lab, Professor Hare's control shattered.

And war began.

Chapter Sixty-Seven

Demonstration

Hare's office door slammed open so hard the left hinge cracked. He stormed inside, coat half-off one shoulder, eyes blazing.

Inside, Myles sat nervously on the edge of the couch. Dr. George Crusher stood nearby, adjusting the regulator on his custom glue gun. He barely seemed to notice Hare's entrance and continued with the speech he'd been delivering.

"I've been recalibrating the PSI," he said, gesturing with one clawed finger. "If I tweak the output in real-time, I can shift both range and volume mid-shot. Turn a pinpoint tether into a field lock."

Hare didn't even look at them. He stomped to his desk, flung the broken datapad down with a crack, and barked, "She's gone."

Myles stood. "Sir "

"No," Hare snapped, pointing. "You sit. You “he turned that cold, hard stare on Crusher "you stay."

Crusher's ears lowered slightly. "Alright then."

The door opened again. Trace Finn entered at a jog, pulling her gloves tight. "Sir, I just got word. Patrol's assembling now."

"Oh, good," Hare said. "Just in time to congratulate our employee of the month." He gestured broadly. "Everyone, a round of applause."

Myles looked at his boots. Crusher raised a brow.

Trace crossed her arms. "It wasn't my team."

"No?" Hare demanded.

"It was Lanell." Trace's voice was tight. "She manipulated the logs, overrode schedules, dropped external sensors during the outage. She must've slipped in and out without using the main corridor."

Crusher's expression shifted minutely.

Hare's voice went quiet again. "So you're telling me a lab assistant, a ferret, outsmarted your entire security system, snuck into the most classified section of this facility, took our primary specimen, and walked out?"

"She had help," Trace said.

"Oh, I have no doubt," Hare drawled. Then raising his voice, he said, "I want every inch of every sublevel searched. If there's so much as a boot scuff, I want it presented to me before sunset."

He rounded on Trace again, raising his fingers and wiggling them in the air with theatrical venom. "And then I want you to activate your 'operations teams.' You know, the ones that work off the books. Find that ferret. Find the human." He walked closer, voice dropping to a cruel purr. "You can leave the ferret dead in a ditch for all I care, but I want that girl back."

His words lingered in the air. Crusher flinched. He looked from Hare to Trace, then back.

A long silence.

"I don't think that's necessary, sir."

Hare turned slowly. "What was that?"

Crusher took a breath. His gut told him to stay quiet, but something deeper rebelled. "I think," he said, "you're going about this all wrong."

"George..." Myles tried to whisper a warning, but it was too late.

Hare stepped forward, face dark. "Well then, Doctor Bondo, enlighten us."

Crusher took two steps toward the center of the room, then stopped, turned,

and fired.

The glue gun didn't even whine. It merely emitted a soft hiss. A wide spiral of reactive gel arced from the nozzle and splattered in a perfect spread at Trace's feet. It hissed again as it made contact with the floor and seeped outward, curling around the soles of her boots like living amber.

"What the hell " Trace shifted her weight, but the adhesive kept her rooted to the spot.

Crusher turned slowly and locked eyes with Hare. He didn't even glance at Trace he didn't need to. He knew.

She lifted one heel. The glue flexed, stretched, then pulled it back down. She jerked her other leg with no more success. Her mouth twisted. "I... seem to be anchored."

"I know," Crusher said. He stepped closer to Hare and regarded him with calm, clear eyes. "You've lost Lanell. You've lost the human. But they're not gone, they're scared. They're moving. And what you're planning? Dead ferret, full lockdown, panic, and fire? That'll drive them deeper. Make it worse." He gestured toward a still squirming Trace. "That's 8147S. Pressure-reactive. The more she fights, the more it holds. I trust it. I built it. I believe in it." The glue made a wet slurp sound as Trace tried once again to lift her boots. Crusher turned back to Hare and squared his shoulders. "Give me what I need. Unrestricted access. Full clearance. Flight codes." He tapped his temple. "I don't need a team. I am the team. I'll bring them back. Both of them. Alive."

Hare gave him an appraising look. Crusher held the gaze, unfazed. The professor's throat bobbed as he swallowed convulsively. He stepped in close. His cheeks were flushed with rage, but his voice was low and deliberate. "I know what you are, Crusher. You're a lab rat. A freak with a pressure gauge and a glue fetish." He paused with a cold smile. "But I also know you're the best damn bond chemist in all seven cities."

Crusher held his ground. He didn't so much as blink.

Hare nodded once, appearing to have made up his mind. "You'll have it. Full access. All tools. All clearance. Every ounce of this facility bends to your task until they're back in containment."

He turned first to Trace, then to Myles, and finally, back to Crusher. The glare cut like a razor. "But hear me." His voice dropped further until they had to lean in to hear him. "You fail me and what I had intended for the ferret becomes your fate."

After a moment's pause, Crusher gave a small shrug and turned toward the door. "You've got nothing to worry about," he said over his shoulder. "Let me go get my stuff together." He paused and looked back at Trace with a smirk. "I bet you'd like to move again."

Trace shot him a scowl. "That would be nice."

Without missing a beat, Crusher reached inside his coat and pulled out a small spray can. He gave it a shake. The rattle echoed in the tense silence. Hope you like citrus," he said casually, leaning down and misting the floor around Trace's boots. The glue fizzed and sizzled, melting away in bubbly streaks that left a glossy clean circle beneath her. He turned to Hare with a grin. "Fun fact, I've noticed the solvent leaves the floor cleaner where it dissolves. I think we've got a side hustle as a commercial cleaner. Patent pending." He winked at Trace on his way out of the door. "If you'll excuse me, I've got some ferret hunting to do."

Then he was gone.

Chapter Sixty-Eight

Rubber and Reckonings

The stink of rubber coated the air thick, humid, and stubborn. Dim light filtered through smeared windows in the breakroom above the main warehouse. The floor creaked. Somewhere below, a vent fan groaned in its sleep.

Lanell and Diane lay curled on a threadbare couch, wrapped in a shared blanket that smelled faintly of chemical soot. Sometime near dawn, sleep had finally claimed them. Now they stirred in the foggy warmth, limbs tangled, breaths slow and quiet.

Then there was a soft tap at the breakroom door.

Lanell woke first. Her ears twitched at the sound, and she eased herself upright, rubbing her face. Diane groaned behind her.

The door opened. Earl Kidd stepped in like a ghost with a mission. His coat was damp at the edges. Mud stained his boots. Deep lines framed his eyes, and his mouth pressed into a tight line.

"Dad," Lanell breathed.

He didn't speak. Just crossed the room and wrapped his arms around her. Her taller frame bent easily into the hug.

For several heartbeats, neither moved, then he stepped back, keeping one hand on her shoulder. "How are you doing?"

Lanell gave a soft huff, part laugh, part sigh. "I'm still standing."

He nodded. "You're my daughter. You'll be fine."

He sat beside her and glanced toward Diane, who was in the process of standing up and sliding on her boots, with a quiet nod. "Did you get the stone?"

Lanell reached into her coat and pulled out the white oval. "Yes."

Earl exhaled like he'd been holding his breath for hours. "Good, that's what we need. Just hold on to it and think of me and I'll be there."

Lanell furrowed her brow. "What does that mean?"

He stared at the floor for a moment before answering her. "There's so much I should've told you. Secrets buried so deep they nearly buried me too. I'm sorry, Lanell." His gaze drifted toward the window. "We've been here, watching Hare. Watching all of this. And now you've forced his hand. That's dangerous but necessary." His eyes returned to Diane, and his shoulders slumped slightly. "I know you're scared. And I know you feel lost. But we're going to get you home. I promise." He looked down and squeezed Lanell's hand. "Not before you take on a great journey, though," he added.

Lanell searched his face. "Where will we go? What do we do now?"

Earl met her eyes. "You already know." He stood with effort. His joints cracked louder than he'd admit. "I can't stay long," he said. "Not safe."

Lanell rose beside him, her height casting a longer shadow in the growing light. "Where will you go?"

"Back where shadows collect." His mouth curved upward, but the smile didn't reach his eyes. "I have a few strings left to pull, and a few people to warn."

He turned to Diane and offered a hand. She shook it, uncertain but genuine. "Thank you," she said.

"No need," Earl replied. "You've already changed everything."

They walked him to the warehouse stairs. At the top landing, Earl paused, looking back at Lanell with a steady gaze. "Remember what I said. The Torka knows more than it shows. So do you."

Then he descended boots ringing on metal grating until the warehouse door groaned shut behind him. Lanell and Diane stood there a moment, staring at the space he'd left behind.

Diane finally exhaled. "Your dad's intense."

Lanell rubbed the back of her neck. "You should see him when he's trying to cook."

Diane stretched, her joints protesting. "So, we're fugitives in a rubber plant, with one blanket, no toothbrushes, and a stolen artifact that might be magic?"

Lanell tapped the Torka stone in her pocket. "Pretty much."

Diane nodded slowly. "Okay, that's fine. "I've always wanted to die of swamp mold on an alien planet," she said, eyeing the damp, rubber-stinking walls.

Lanell smirked. "We'll find a toothbrush."

They turned and walked back to the couch. From outside, pale light spilled through the filthy windows, painting the rubber-coated floor in fractured gold.

Epilogue Spoken in Silence

Ilurion, Chronicle-Keeper of the Lost Threads:

They do not yet see the whole of the thread,nor feel the tension drawn tight from ages past.

They do not yet know the teeth that turn in shadow,or the oath that carved stars from stone.

But they have begun to move.

The ferret. The girl. The glue-born alchemist.Each touched by echoes.Each carrying a shard of the first secret.

The journey opens now,
across forest, across fracture,
across the lies that once held the world still.
Arcadia remembers.
And the truth,
has already begun to wake.

Acknowledgments

This story exists because of the people who stood nearby while it took shape, sometimes knowingly, sometimes without realizing how much they mattered.

These characters lived in my imagination for years, fully formed but unseen. Without the artistic talent of David, I would never have truly seen Lanell or Bizlok come to life. Thank you, David. This is only the beginning for both of us.

To Diane, the original Purple Footed Ferret, thank you for the inspiration, patience, and encouragement that finally gave this story a voice. I love you.

To the members of The Ink Tank — Chrissy, Jeff, Andrea, Vee, Trish, Bob, Jen, and Diane — thank you for nearly four years of weekly meetings, shared lessons, and honest conversations. I have learned because of you, and I have grown because of you.

To Shana Thornton, thank you for planting the seeds that became this group. Your influence created something that helped shape me into the writer I am today.

And to my sons, Nick and Alex. You were both beginning your own journeys when I started writing this book. Along the way, I discovered a skill I never knew I had. I hope you remember that it is never too late to discover new parts of yourself, and you are never too old to stay young at heart. There will always be a world filled with evil bunnies and heroic honey badgers, as long as imagination is allowed to run free.

Thank you for helping bring Arcadia to life.

About the Author

G. Scott Freeman is a science-fantasy author whose work explores identity, displacement, and the consequences of progress without conscience. His stories are driven by character, moral tension, and the quiet moments when people are forced to decide who they are when the systems around them begin to fail.

A U.S. Army veteran and cancer survivor, Freeman brings a hard-earned perspective on authority, survival, and resilience to his writing. His voice is shaped by a skepticism of unchecked power and a deep interest in how individuals endure within structures not built for their well-being. Raised on the science fiction and fantasy of the 1980s, from *Star Trek* to *Transformers*, he learned early that imagination could be both refuge and rebellion.

Encouraged by his wife Diane, the inspiration behind his heroine Victoria Lanell, Freeman began building the world of *Ferret Run*. His debut novel, *Ferret Run: Secrets of Arcadia*, is the culmination of a story he carried for years before finding the confidence to tell it. Blending speculative science with mythic undertones and expansive worldbuilding, the novel reflects his belief that imagination is not escapism, but a way of understanding the world and surviving it.

Freeman lives in Tennessee with his wife. He believes it is never too late to discover new parts of yourself, and that staying young at heart means refusing to let curiosity die.

Connect with the Author

Website

authorgsfreeman.com

YouTube

youtube.com/BizloksRetroHour

Facebook

facebook.com/authorgsfreeman

Instagram

instagram.com/authorgsfreeman

X / Twitter

x.com/authorgsfreeman

Follow along for updates, artwork, behind-the-scenes worldbuilding, and future stories from the *Ferret Run* universe.

Thank you for reading and helping the world of Arcadia continue to grow.

www.ingramcontent.com/pod-product-compliance
Lightning Source LLC
LaVergne TN
LVHW100518110826
845146LV00002B/685

* 9 7 9 8 3 5 0 7 6 2 6 0 0 *